The Serpent's Gift

Benjamin Oneal

First published by Dog Ear Publishing 4010 W. 86th Street, Ste H Indianapolis, IN 46268 www.dogearpublishing.net

This book is printed on acid-free paper.

First Published in 2011

Published by Benjamin Oneal, Anderson, IN

Second Printing, 2020

ISBN: 978-1-7346368-0-2

I want to thank my wife Huong, for putting up with my long hours at the computer, my children, Lucas, Kimberly, Stacy, and Justin for being often reluctant sounding boards to help me work out problems with my stories, and my three wonderful grandchildren, Aria, Merrick, and Hannah who are responsible for keeping me young.

Special thanks to Autumn J. Conley, who worked her magic, and made me realize how important a good editor can be in bringing a story to life.

Other books by Benjamin Oneal

The Benjamin Kroh Series:

Die Laughing

Die by Proxy

PART ONE

In the Beginning

Chapter 1

On their way back from a scouting mission in the Purgatorian sector, the three ships of the Alliance suddenly found that they were targets of the Empire's attack, a sudden and vicious onslaught. The five battle cruisers of the Empire dropped out of deviant space, their forward guns ripping white-hot lines of destructive force through the star-studded blanket of cosmos before them. Although the trio of Alliance scout ships were capable of much faster speeds, they found the element of surprise working against them, and they were sadly caught off guard. All three suffered damage before they were able to defend themselves.

Unable to inflict any measurable harm on their attackers, their only chance for survival was to avoid critical damage before they moved into deviant space. Suddenly, one of the small Alliance ships was sliced in half, and the resulting explosion ensured that no survivors were left to tell the tale.

Mere seconds before the courier could find solace in deviant space, an Empire battle cruiser locked on and activated a brutal firing sequence. Death was certain if the impact came, so all the courier could do was brace for the inevitability of his fate. Just as the Empire ship fired, though, the one remaining Alliance vessel sent to protect the courier flew into the path of the oncoming, ion-charged particle beam. With no time to mourn the loss of his comrades, and unwilling to allow such a sacrifice to be made in vain, the courier activated his jump into deviant space.

The Empire fleet had all but destroyed the special courier's chance to reunite with the family he dearly missed. The ship was damaged beyond all hope of traveling to the star system he called home. In fact, his instruments indicated that he would soon have to desert his vessel altogether if he wished to survive. While deviant space did offer some relief, that would be short-lived; the sustained damage would not allow for a long flight. The courier just hoped his vessel would have enough oomph left to let him escape the Empire ships. Within minutes of entering, however, he was forced to drop back to normal space, where they could quickly locate him. For that reason, and because his ship was so crippled, his only recourse was to play dead.

The power of his craft was draining as quickly as his faltering hope, he realized as he tapped the indicator before him. *They must've hit my power cell.* He thought. He cut all power to his ship, rigged a small explosion, and rode the explosive shockwave. He climbed into a shielded area of the small ship, did his best to slow his body functions, then floated aimlessly, a prisoner of zero-gravity, hoping to fool his attackers into believing he was dead. They must have fallen for his ruse, because about a half-hour later, the predators abandoned their prey, dismissing him as useless space debris.

Broken and desperate, the courier hurried to find a safe place to land, before he lost every ounce of power at his disposal. His sensors located a nearby system, and the third planet from its star was a distinct possibility. There, he thought he might find the technology required to repair his ship. Regardless, it was vitally important for him to complete his mission. That, above all, was his primary concern.

The planet was just outside Empire boundaries. It was orbited by one satellite, and the courier thought that would offer an umbrella of protection, a safe place to hide his ship while he attempted repairs.

"Earth," he muttered to himself, reading from his instruments. Those on that world had just recently begun to explore beyond the safety of their own atmosphere. By most standards, the third planet from the sun was still a primitive world. It was common opinion that the inhabitants there had a real chance to someday reach for the stars, but they were in serious jeopardy of taking a giant step backward. Their juvenile bickering was a familiar tale known throughout the galaxy, a tragedy of sorts. The world had gained the ability to destroy their entire civilization, but were blinded by something that came to be known as the Trinity of Evil, a nasty conglomerate of ignorance, arrogance, and apathy. The Earthlings were ignorant of the consequences of their own greed and quest for power, arrogant enough to believe they were in control of the environmental devastation they had caused through waste and inaction and the destructive forces they had created, and too apathetic to act on the glaring signs that were so readily evident to their adolescent eyes. Some worlds survived that dangerous glitch in their societal evolution to become islands of light in the vastness of the galaxy, but Earth would not be the first or the last to be consumed by the darkness of the cosmos.

Sandel, the courier, knew that the information he was tasked with delivering could change the balance in the continuing battle with the Empire, but first things first. At the moment, it was crucial for him to survive. Once he was sure the Empire ships were out of range, he limped to the one satellite that orbited Earth. Due to a phenomenon called tidal locking, only one side of the moon was ever visible to those on the planet. Sandel thought it best to hide his vessel a few hundred miles past the horizon, beyond the terminus to the dark side of the moon. He opted for the deepest crater he could find in the region Earthlings knew as the North Pole. There, the sun never shined, and he hoped that would help keep him out of the Empire spotlight as well. He was fairly certain the forces of the galactic lord believed they'd destroyed his ship and him in their attack, but he could not take a chance and underestimate their need for proof. At the very least, the space rubbish would certainly remain invisible to the people of Earth, since the inhabitants lacked the means to travel there routinely and had yet to discover the technology to detect it.

4

The Serpent's Gift

He was happy to find that the damage was not to the power cells after all; rather, the junction that relayed power to the thrusters had taken a hit. Nevertheless, Sandel had to move quickly. First and foremost, he had to shut down all nonessentials, to ensure that the ship would maintain power during his search for the materials to repair her and to make a safe return to Alliance territory. Unfortunately, the shuttle was also damaged in the attack, so he had to use the body shield for his journey to Earth. Time was even more important because the body shield was not designed for that purpose, and that would force him to hibernate for part of the trip.

While Sandel calculated his course, he tied his shoulder-length, brown hair in the back and donned the gear that would provide food and air. After a few last-minute adjustments to the ship and his gear, he was off. All it took was a push against the gravity of their moon. After just a few moments, he rounded the dark side of the moon and spotted Planet Earth. Sandel beheld the blue-green planet rotating before him, drinking in the beauty and feeling a little homesick. If it weren't for his star maps to tell him otherwise, he could have sworn he actually was home. Sandel's speed increased, heading toward optimal acceleration. If all went well, he would intercept Earth in just under three galactic days. Till then, all he could do was hibernate and hope he'd reach his destination alive.

As his hibernation began, his body functions slowed to preserve the precious oxygen to sustain him during the journey. He dreamt of his home world as he traveled silently toward Earth. His computer recorded every second and alerted him constantly to any changes or dangers along the way. As he neared the planet, he was gently lifted out of his deep sleep. The courier's pulse quickened, his lungs gasped in more air, and his mind cleared.

As Sandel awakened, Earth loomed large in front of him. He slowed, for it would have been nothing short of disaster to enter that atmosphere at his present speed. Just a little push against the planet slowed his progress, but it wasn't long before he realized something was wrong. His breathing was

5

labored, and the air felt thin. Sandel could not afford to lose consciousness, and it became imperative for him to make subtle adjustments to secure a safe landing. Another push slowed him yet again. His body shield would protect him from the atmosphere, but he had to remain conscious as he made his descent. The friction caused by entering the atmosphere would result in heat and flames that certainly had the capability of incinerating the shield and his body along with it. With concentration and a few minor adjustments to the shield, he found the temperature inside to be tolerable. The flames rendered him momentarily blind, but the more disturbing issue was that he felt a bit lightheaded.

Finally, he reached the lower atmosphere and looked down upon the beautiful world. He extended his arms to slow his descent. Careful pushing would allow him to float safely to the ground, but his concentration was waning, due to the dizziness behind his eyes.

With just a short distance to go, Sandel blacked out completely. He plummeted the last 100 feet in a freefall and hit the ground violently. His body shield protected him from most of the effect of impact, but because he'd lost conscious control of it, the protection it offered was limited. Sandel's body was broken, his breathing still labored, but he was alive. Among the rubble of his damaged body shield, he lay hurt and unconscious, not to mention defenseless against so many unknowns.

Chapter 2

A short distance away, Justin Grant, Professor of Religious Studies at Purdue University, was getting ready for his morning hike. He was currently on bereavement leave, grieving the loss of his beloved wife and child, who were killed by a drunk driver as they were returning home from lunch at McDonald's. For the past two weeks, he'd been nursing his emotional wounds at a friend's Kentucky cabin, just outside of Louisville. No one knew where he was, not even his family.

He looked in the mirror and studied his stubble. His scraggly facial hair, the result of not shaving for several days, was a little darker than his ash-brown hair. He had never grown a beard before, but he really didn't mind it much and decided it might be a style worth keeping for a while.

At 7 o'clock on the nose, it was time to head out. Professor Grant had found that sticking to a routine helped him cope, and the daily hike proved to be quite cathartic and therapeutic, for mind as well as body. He thought he'd made some progress, because at least the reflection looking back at him didn't have rivers of tears streaming into that unkempt forest on his chin.

Justin had walked for about twenty minutes before he noticed something strange in the sky through a clearing in the canopy above. He watched as the unknown object seemed to float down to Earth, then suddenly plummet to the ground. At first, he thought it could be some sort of skydiver, but there was no parachute above the shadowy figure, and they descended from too short a distance to be safe. Justin was aware that it was a silly notion, but he truly thought he might be witnessing the arrival of an angel, some heavenly being, with his arms outstretched, halo and all. When the stranger ceased to float, his arms dropped to his side, and he fell rapidly. At that point, Justin's angelic thoughts left him, and he instinctively ran in the direction of whomever or whatever had surely collided very painfully with the terrain.

Justin ran through the woods toward the closest clearing. There, about twenty feet to his left, lay a body, unconscious and bleeding. He quickly dashed to the strangely dressed, injured man and checked his vitals. The stranger's pulse was strong, his eyes were not dilated, and his breathing seemed normal. His left forearm and leg were definitely broken, but all in all, he seemed fairly okay, considering that he'd just fallen nearly 100 feet.

It was only about a quarter-mile to Justin's friend's cabin and his Jeep, so he decided it would be best to carry the incapacitated fellow the short distance. Of course, it was at that moment when Justin first noticed the size of the unconscious stranger. He was in excellent shape, but he had to weigh around 220 pounds and was about six-five in height. Justin was in good shape himself, but hauling the man would not be an easy feat.

In fact, Justin had to rest twice during their commute. A couple times during the trip, the man groaned, but he did not fully regain consciousness. Only when they reached the cabin about a half-hour later and Justin tried to put the man into his Jeep did the broken stranger wake.

"N-no... No!" he said, refusing to enter the vehicle.

"Buddy, you need a doctor," Justin retorted.

"No! Please just take me inside. I'll be okay," the unknown one argued, doing his best in his groggy state to keep Justin from forcing him into the vehicle.

"I'm not a doctor. I can't help you," Justin pleaded.

After Justin realized just how adamant his would-be patient was, he reluctantly took him into the cabin and laid him down on the couch. "Listen, dude, you need a doctor," Justin said, trying one more time to convince him.

"No," the man said flatly. "They must not find me here." Then, he closed his eyes and passed out once more.

What's that supposed to mean? Who mustn't find him here? Justin asked himself. *Is he a criminal or something? What the hell is he wearing anyway? It's not Halloween!*

He had so many questions, but the most pressing problem was that the man still needed medical help. Justin had no idea know why, but he had a strong feeling that he should honor the strange broken man's wishes, even if he was a criminal. Nevertheless, he wasn't about to let him die on his couch, so he covered him with a blanket, then drove into town to pay Doc Simon a visit.

Doc was retired, and rumor had it that he was originally from Chicago, where he'd done some undocumented favors for certain organized crime figures there. He was a white-haired man with piercing hazel eyes, and he had the air of someone who'd experienced life to the fullest, albeit not always on the right side of the law.

A short time later, Justin returned to the cabin with Doc Simon in tow. The doctor quickly examined the unexpected visitor and offered him the best medical attention he could without access to a proper hospital. He administered something for pain, but that didn't stop the man from reacting as the doctor worked on him.

Justin marveled at the skill with which Doc set the bones in the destroyed arm and leg and applied the casts. As he watched with great wonderment, the doctor looked up at him curiously.

"What the hell is he wearing anyway?" Doc asked.

Justin shrugged and smiled at the medicine man. "Not sure. I asked myself the same question. Quite a getup, huh?"

"Yeah, quite. Tell me how you found this guy."

Justin went on to fill Doc in on some select details; he only told him he'd found the man in the woods while he was hiking and completely omitted the part about the floating and plummeting. He definitely left out his inclination to believe it was an angel, halo and all. The last thing he needed was for Doc Simon to prescribe him something for insanity.

Forty minutes later, Doc had finished patching up the stranger. He gave Justin some medicine from the small supply he carried in his bag, along with after-care instructions to help him care for his patient.

As Justin drove Doc back to town, the doctor noticed a worried look on his face. "Don't fret," he said. "He's doing fine and should be up and around in about two weeks, as good as new in six."

Two weeks? Six weeks? Justin thought, cringing a bit. *I don't even know the guy, and I have to play nursemaid to him and let him stay in my cabin for two weeks, maybe a whole month and a half? What if I'm harboring a criminal?*

As if he could read Justin's disgruntled thoughts, Doc explained, "Just give him the regular medicine twice a day and the pain meds as required, and he'll soon be fit enough for you to take him to wherever he wants to go."

"Two weeks though?" Justin asked, a little unnerved.

Doc smiled. "You'll do fine."

As Justin dropped him off, he asked, "What do I owe you, Doc?"

"How does $150 sound?" Doc said without much thought.

"Sounds pretty good to me, especially for a house call," Justin confessed. "You sure that's all you'll take?"

"Sure as shootin'," Doc said, "on one condition."

"What's that?"

"Please be kind enough to, uh, keep this to ourselves. It never happened, right? Uncle Sam doesn't need any more of my money," Doc said with a laugh.

Justin chuckled, shook his hand, and handed $200 to him. "Thanks again, Doc," he said, then waved and took off to head back to the borrowed cabin and an uncertain couple of weeks.

Chapter 3

A few days later, as Justin cooked some eggs and bacon for breakfast, he received an unexpected compliment from behind him: "That smells truly wonderful."

"Whoa! You scared the stuff out of me," Justin said, almost dropping the skillet in the process. "S-So, uh, how you feeling?" he asked after he recovered safely, and rescued a nearly escaping slice of bacon with his spatula.

The stranger winced as he propped himself up on his good arm. He took a moment to inspect himself, smiled, and said, "I probably feel a little better than I look."

Justin scrutinized his patient. The man was ruggedly handsome patient, more so than most male models he'd seen, even after being passed out on the couch for two days. Whoever he was, he reminded him of Sean Connery in the James Bond film *Dr. No*. He'd never been self-conscious or insecure, but he suddenly found himself wondering how a guy with a broken arm, a broken leg, and crap load of bruises could look no worse than a bodybuilder finishing up his day at the gym. *Oh well*, he thought before he asked, "Hungry?"

"If whatever you are cooking tastes as good as it smells, sure," the stranger said.

Having enjoyed the unmistakable aroma of bacon and eggs for most of his thirty-six years, Justin thought the stranger's statement a little weird, but he was quick to dismiss it. *The guy did take a pretty good bump on the head, I guess,* he surmised, *not to mention all those drugs Doc put him on.*

Over the next couple days, the stranger's recovery was nothing short of remarkable. While he was on the mend, he watched television constantly and thoroughly enjoyed Justin's DVD collection. Much like his guest's unfamiliarity with the ever-popular bacon and eggs, it struck Justin as odd that he acted as if he'd never seen a movie in his life, not even that old standby *The Godfather.* Another thing that was strange was that he didn't seem to find comedy movies or sitcoms funny at all, as if he didn't understand the witty, subtle humor, but he was highly amused by and laughed hard at the slapstick antics of *The Three Stooges.*

What most captured his interest, though, were the news and history channels; he couldn't seem to get enough of those. When he turned to a religious channel, however, he only watched for a little while before throwing his hands up in disgust and choosing something else to watch.

Is this guy some kind of atheist? Justin pondered. It didn't raise too much of a red flag, because it certainly wasn't the first nonbeliever Justin had encountered. *Hey, maybe I can bring the stranger to the glory of the Lord.* He smiled at the thought.

Justin and Sandel, whom he now knew by name, spent many hours talking about the world and its customs. The visitor was tremendously curious and wanted to know about everything. It was almost as if Sandel had amnesia or had just arrived on Earth.

One day, as they were talking, Justin recalled thinking Sandel looked like an angel coming to Earth, and he laughed audibly at the ridiculous thought.

"Did I say something that amused you?" Sandel asked.

"No. I mean, uh, well... It's really silly, but... No, never mind. Just forget about it," Justin stammered, suddenly embarrassed.

"Come on, Justin. I need to know if I am speaking correctly and sensibly, if I sound all right. It's very important to me," Sandel prodded.

Against his better judgment, Justin continued, "This is

going to sound stupid, but the other day, when you fell from the sky, you kind of floated down slowly at first. With your arms outstretched like they were controlling your descent, and the light bending around you like it was... Well, at that moment, Sandel, you kinda looked like an angel, halo and all." Justin chuckled nervously. "I warned you that it was really silly."

With a look of concerned interest in his eyes, Sandel leaned closer and asked, "And what do you know of angels?"

At that point, Justin couldn't help but beam a smile back at him. He was more than happy to have the opportunity to regale Sandel with stories about his lifelong religious training, his career at the university, and how he'd spent almost his entire life seeking religious truth. Although he knew it was wrong, he felt a surge of pride as he told Sandel about his lifetime studies and the book he'd penned, *Angels: The Good, The Bad, and The Fallen.*

"A book?" Sandel asked.

"Yes. It is still selling well, even though it's been out for over three years, so I guess you could say I know a lot about angels," Justin said, with more of a braggish tone in his voice than he intended. He wondered if the look Sandel gave him was a sign of being impressed or amused, but he decided not to ask before continuing with his verbal autobiography.

When Justin revealed to Sandel his faith crisis over losing his wife Leah and son Joey to a tragic automobile accident involving a drunk driver, the pain boiled up again. There were so many questions his tortured mind simply could not answer, which was part of the reason he was out in the woods in the first place. Those questions haunted him day and night, tearing his heart in two and making him question his deeply held beliefs: *How could God let such a thing happen? It's not fair that the driver walked away with barely a scratch, even if he will be in prison for the rest of his pathetic life, without the possibility of parole. He's still alive, and my family's not! Is that justice?*

"I am very sorry about your wife and child, Justin."

"I am too," Justin sadly said. "My Leah was the very essence of good, and my son was perfect. They both prayed

13

every night to a God who allowed them to die!" he spat bitterly as tears ran down his face.

Sandel listened intently to Justin's story, and tears of his own began to burn in his eyes. He had also lost loved ones recently. In fact, he'd lost one of his brothers in the attack just days before. Much of Earth felt foreign to him, but the pain of loss was something that spanned all worlds and generations. Nonetheless, when Justin finished his story, Sandel spoke softly, "Do not be too quick to blame God for things that happen on Earth."

Justin felt a little better about Sandel when he heard him come to God's defense. *Maybe he's closer to the Lord than I originally thought,* he considered hopefully. *Maybe he can help me get through this, straighten out my thoughts somehow.*

They talked long into the night and shared a beer or two, which Sandel found he enjoyed quite a bit.

"So, Sandel, tell me... What's your story?"

Feeling the buzz, Sandel was tempted to reveal everything, but then he thought better of it. "No, I'm afraid you are not ready for that. I do not wish to lose this friendship that's just begun."

"Come on! I told you about me. It's only fair," Justin pushed.

Sandel shifted and winced from pain, then said, "Let us sleep tonight, Then, if you still want to know, I will tell you...everything. Of course, it may require help from a few of these... What do you call them? Beers?"

Justin laughed. "Yes, beer."

"With a few of these bottles, perhaps I can share my tale," he said, "although I daresay you will never believe me."

Like a doomed cat, Justin's curiosity was piqued, and he hoped it wouldn't kill him off before he had a chance to learn about his bizarre new buddy. He desperately wanted to know where Sandel had come from and what he was up to, and he would have pressed him to continue talking into the night if he could have. As it was, though, he reluctantly relented only because Sandel was still on the mend and needed his rest.

Chapter 4

Justin felt like he used to on Christmas Eves as a child, giddy and unable to sleep, wondering about what the next day would bring. Santa had nothing to do with it, and there would be no presents other than the story of the life of Sandel. New questions popped into his mind, a refreshing change from the depressing ones that tormented him: *Why would Sandel worry about losing me as a friend? Is he a thief? He could be a modern-day D.B. Cooper, considering that dive he took out of the cosmos. Worse yet, what if he's some murderer or a terrorist? And by the way, who doesn't already know about beer?* As all of these thoughts raced and rattled through his mind, preventing him from his slumber, he became convinced that no matter what the story was, he would not be disappointed. It wasn't until about 5 a.m. that exhaustion finally won out and forced him to sleep, but his subconscious took over, and he dreamt of the possibilities. It was the first time since the accident that he did experience fitful nightmares about the tragedy of his beloved wife and child.

After breakfast, Justin took his daily hike. He wouldn't forego it, not even for Sandel's story, because that was his time to commune with nature and be with his family again. As the sunlight sneaked past the leaves above, breaking the shadows on the woodland floor, Justin remembered walking hand in hand on that very path with his precious Leah while Joey found adventure in every step. His vision blurred slightly with the salty tears of his loss, but there was still a smile on his face as he felt the warmth of cherished memories of the family who'd walked with him each and every day.

He made it back to the cabin a little before 1:00 in the afternoon and went about his daily chores. Around 5:00, he prepared a couple steaks, some red potatoes baked with olive oil and seasoned as Leah had taught him, and a tossed with Italian dressing. It seemed only fitting: a special meal for a special story.

As they ate, they talked of Justin's hike and of world events Sandel had read about on the internet. It suddenly struck Justin then that it might not have been a good idea to give Sandel free access to his computer; it was no secret that serious damage could be done with a computer and a little Wi-Fi. For some reason, though, he couldn't fathom that the man sitting across from him at the coffee table would ever do him harm.

After dinner, Justin cleaned up the dishes and the mess he made in the kitchen, growing ever more excited to hear the story of his new cabin roommate. Unfortunately, when he dried the last spoon and threw the dish towel down, then rushed into the living room, his heart fell.

There was Sandel, fast asleep once more.

"Damn!" Justin uttered with an exhale, thoroughly disappointed.

Sandel opened his eyes and grinned. "Just kidding!" he said.

"That was a good one," Justin remarked with great relief. "Just for that, you get nothing to drink."

Sandel's smile disappeared momentarily, but he found it again when Justin returned.

Instead of beer, Justin brought out a bottle of wine and filled a glass for each of them. "Now, let's hear it, Sandel. Tell me your story," he said.

Sandel took a long drink of wine, looked Justin straight in the eye, and blurted, "I am not of this world."

I knew it! Justin thought, wearing a smug smirk as he stared at Sandel.

"I come from a star system much closer to the galactic core." At that point, Sandel paused and took in a deep breath, as if he regretted what he was about to say next.

"Go on," Justin coaxed. "You promised."

"I am, in fact, an angel, Justin," Sandel announced.

Justin spat a mouthful of red all over his lap, then laughed so hard that a bit came out his nose.

Sandel just sat there, without a hint of irritation, patiently waiting for the laughter to subside.

Justin wiped the tears from his eyes and said, "Please don't tell me I need to build an ark." Then, he laughed even harder than before.

Sandel gave a gentle push against the couch, then slowly rose into the air above it.

Instantly, Justin's laughter stopped, his eyes grew wide, and his wine glass hit the floor as he stood in awe. He shook his head, struggling to make sense of the sight before him. "How the... Huh? What the hell?" he stuttered. He looked around to see how Sandel was pulling off the magic trick, but there was no logical explanation. If he'd had a hula hoop at his disposal, he would have swiped it around Sandel to be sure there were no ropes, strings, or fishing line holding him up. "What the...?" he repeated, stunned.

"Do I have your attention now?" Sandel asked as he gently lowered himself back onto the couch.

Justin unconsciously dropped back into his chair, seemingly unable to close his gaping mouth. He stared at Sandel with a look of utter disbelief, and he tried to form words, but they would not come.

"Would you like me to continue now?" Sandel asked with a smile.

As no words were forthcoming, Justin could only raise his hands and sheepishly nod, relinquishing control to Sandel.

Chapter 5

"Like I told you, I am an angel." He paused to give Justin time to process the reality of that for a moment, then went on, "Justin, it is time for you to know the real truth about our galaxy. Please sit back and try to take in what I am about to tell you."

Justin shook his head, surrendering what little control he might have held. After watching his new friend hover above his furniture, he couldn't possibly will his legs to carry him anywhere. It was sure to be a great story, and he wouldn't miss it for the world

"Our galaxy is in the middle of what you would call a holy war. Almost 9,000 years ago, on Planet Heaven, the capital of the Galactic Empire, before the God that you know, took the throne as the ruler of the galaxy, he and my father were great friends. God was the eldest son of the royal family, and my father was on Heaven, training to become an angel. They were inseparable. Whenever my father wasn't training, he was with God. No brothers could have been closer. When God took the throne, my father, now one of the greatest angels, was ever at his side. They fought many pivotal battles together, with God as the leader and my father as his chief counsel and head of his armies. They were responsible for bringing peace to the galaxy." Sandel beamed with pride when he said, "That peace lasted for thousands of years.

"As they say, no good thing lasts forever," he sadly said.

"God's downfall began at a celebration party on Heaven, after a particularly successful mission where God and my father brought fifty-seven new worlds into the Empire. The downfall came in the form of a woman. Dilyla was of noble birth and unequaled beauty. Unlike Mary, Jesus' biblical mother, her virginity was never an issue. As you would put it, Dilyla was a...party girl. In fact, she was quite the embarrassment to her very prominent heavenly family, until the night she happened to party with God. God fell for her beauty and succumbed to her many charms. Dilyla's family, who dreamt of regaining the galactic power they believed God's father had wrongfully taken from them so many years before, now saw her not as an embarrassment but as a sliver of hope to finally claim what they believed was their rightful place in galactic history.

"On the day of the God's wedding to Dilyla, my father was his best man. Dilyla was the jealous sort, and she quickly grew to envy the brotherly, unbreakable closeness between God and my father. She could not understand why she was not her husband's chief counsel, and she blamed my father for that. In fact, it was God who kept her ignorant, because in his great wisdom, he knew that anything she learned from him would be quickly shared with her power-hungry family. For that reason, she was excluded from all but the most mundane matters of state. Although she made her feelings well known throughout the upper echelons of Heaven, she dared not publically voice her underlying disdain for the will of God.

"In spite of the trouble between them, God and Dilyla were soon blessed with a son."

"Jesus?" Justin cut in.

"Yes, Jesus," Sandel said. "God loved him dearly. Soon after, I was born, and the two of us were like brothers, constantly together with each other and our fathers. During our childhood, if you saw one of us, the other was always close by. As much as I adored Jesus, however, I felt strangely about his mother. I always felt that Dilyla resented me, and she kept us apart as much as God would allow. Jesus rebelled against this, saying, 'Sandel is my best friend, and nothing in the universe will break our bond.'

19

"Unbeknownst to both of us, when we were about 18 years old, our seemingly unbreakable bond would shatter. A girl had captured our attention, and we both wanted to be with her. Nevertheless, being the brothers we were, we decided that no matter whom she chose, the loser would happily concede. Jesus, using his position and wealth as God's son, showered her with expensive gifts and dinners to impress her. Meanwhile, I followed the advice of my own father, who had always told me, to just be myself. As it turned out, the girl was flattered by my humility and the realness I exhibited. In the end, I proved victorious in that love battle, but that did not set well with Jesus. To this day, I do not know if it was losing the girl or losing my undivided attention that bothered him more.

"As time went by, Jesus began to spend less and less time with me, until we hardly ever saw each other at all. When our paths did cross, he seemed to act arrogant and superior, as if he no longer believed me worthy of his friendship. I was sure Dilyla used our shared desire for the girl to turn her son against me, but it was not my place to speak against the queen or to voice my objections. Regardless as to why, it was a long time before we spoke again.

"When Jesus came of age, he was included in the council meetings, where affairs of state were discussed. My father confided in me that Jesus always offered childish, short-sighted solutions to problems when he was asked to contribute. He quickly realized that he was there to learn, not to participate. He hated that his father, God, disregarded his counsel and instead put all his trust in my father's words. That did not sit well with Jesus or his mother, and his envy and hatred of my father grew.

"With the help of Dilyla and her family, Jesus was taught the skills he needed to be taken seriously in council chambers. They stroked his ego, made him feel important. Of course, they had an agenda of their own, an ulterior motive, as their teachings were meant to bring them to power when the time was right. Still, it wasn't long before Jesus was seen by the other council members with a reluctant respect.

"With constant pushing from Dilyla and Jesus, day after

day, year after year, God reluctantly gave Jesus more say in galactic affairs. As time progressed, my father watched help-lessly as God seemed to shrink from power while Jesus took control. Not only that, but God began to avoid public ap-pearances, becoming something of a recluse. In time, Jesus blatantly rejected my father's counsel and soon excluded him from all meetings. Just like that, Dilyla's family gained the power they sought, through their grandson, Jesus.

"Wow," Justin said, shaking his head. "That's nothing like what I've been taught."

"I know, and that is not the only contradiction, my friend," Sandel said. "Jesus also had a wife."

"A wife?"

"Yes," the angel said, nodding. "In fact, he was married twice. His first wife was also a very beautiful woman of noble birth. It was well known throughout Heaven that Dilyla did not approve of Sarah. Now, that could have been because Sarah was my father's niece, my cousin, but Sarah was an intelligent woman with a mind of her own. Whatever the rea-son for the animosity between Sarah and Dilyla, Jesus began to cling to her and distance himself from his mother. That even allowed Jesus and I to rekindle our relationship a bit, and we began resolving the problems between us.

"Sadly, on their first anniversary, Sarah was found dead in her chambers, the result of an apparent suicide. Believe me, Justin, I knew Sarah very well. She was a strong, hap-py woman, full of life and ready to face her future. I knew there is no way she took her own life. The false tears of Dilyla fooled no one but Jesus.

"His second wife, Magdalene, was the daughter of a family who had strong political ties to Dilyla's parents. She became the mother of his two children, Kadosh and Sophia. Although Magdalene had a strong will and a mind of her own, she never let it surface, for obvious reasons. She, along with Dilyla, continued to push their agendas with Jesus. They yearned to push me out of his life completely, for one thing. That has little to do with my story, really, but it's probably helpful background information."

"It's interesting, that's for sure," Justin said, eating it all up.

"My father grew increasingly dissatisfied with Jesus' leadership. A great many angels felt the same way my father did. They hated the changes they believed God had sanctioned, and they sought my father's advice. These were honorable angels, and they were sickened by the direction the Empire was headed. They met clandestinely to avoid suspicion among Jesus' loyal followers, but meeting in secret was not easy to do, thanks to the Holy Ghosts."

"Ghosts? As in...plural?"

Sandel snickered, then went on, "As I said, there are many contradictions you are not yet aware of." He then continued, "The Holy Ghosts, also a once honorable organization of spies, intelligence gatherers, and messengers who worked for the good of the galactic government, degenerated into a dark, unseen cache of spies, blackmailers, and assassins who answered only to Jesus. They can go almost anywhere, at any time, without anyone detecting their presence. That is why they are called Ghosts, though I can't vouch much for the Holy part anymore. It was common knowledge on Heaven and in the Empire that crossing the father or the son or underestimating the reach of the Holy Ghosts could be fatal.

"This became most evident when 174 people, including Dilyla's parents and 36 other members of her family and 23 of Magdalene's family, died under mysterious circumstances one bloody day. It was rumored that they were plotting against Jesus and that he had them killed by the Holy Ghosts to strike fear into anyone who dared to rise up in opposition against him. It was also rumored that Dilyla was part of the murderous conspiracy, so she was never again allowed in Jesus' presence unless she was heavily guarded. The story is that Jesus had her tongue cut out so he would never have to hear her lies again.

"The moral of this story is that no one was or is safe from the wrath of Jesus, not even family. In the name of God, Jesus changed the very nature of power in the galaxy. Instead of democracy, he ruled with fear and intimidation. It reached a point where one could not even speak out against the word of God. Many were imprisoned or even killed for their beliefs.

Jesus sought blind devotion from his followers, demanding the removal of free will from all of his subjects. The word of God—or, rather, the word of Jesus—was to be absolute.

"When my father felt there was no other option, he formed an army of angels to fight the injustices of the Galactic Empire. Their rebellion had to be based on the truth that all beings are equal and entitled to certain rights, until they prove themselves unworthy of that through action or inaction. Incidentally, their ideals were pretty much the same as those of your founding fathers. My father was voted in as leader of the rebellion, and he reluctantly accepted the role. It meant going against his oldest friend, but he knew that it was Jesus, not God, who was pushing the Empire from a democracy to a dictatorship.

"At first, they secretly did whatever they could to disrupt Jesus' self-serving plans. At the same time, they visited their home worlds to prepare them for the impending battle, and they organized means to allow the beings on those worlds to take their families to safety.

"Back on Heaven, my father felt the weight of his responsibility, and it was a heavy burden on him. Most of all, he felt alone. He longed to speak with God, the old friend he'd not seen for many years, except on the rare occasions when he sat in his throne behind Jesus as his son spoke to the masses throughout the galaxy. During those times, my father could see that God was not the same as he was in days of old. Still, he was determined to see God again. So, using a secret entrance they'd discovered in their youth, one known only to God and my father, he sneaked into the palace and found God in his private room. What my father saw that day brought tears to his eyes. God was feeble, a mere fraction of the man he used to know, a prisoner in his own palace.

"The first words God uttered, in a matter-of-fact and emotionless way, spoke volumes. 'Are you here to kill me, old friend?' he asked. This tore at my father's heart. He assured God that he could never hurt the best friend he'd ever known. He spent hours with his once-mighty friend, talking of old times and the present. In those conversations, he learned about the lies Jesus and his mother Dilyla had told God over

23

the years, and he discovered just how much God despised all the cruel, selfish things that had been done in his name. My father suspected that God had also been drugged. That, along with the lies, had poisoned his mind with thoughts of deception and assassination plots and had made God paranoid of all but his family.

"Before my father left, he gave God a pentagon-shaped stone they had found while exploring the royal grounds many years earlier. As God took the stone from my father, a tear fell for the times past, for the long-lost memories of two young men who hadn't any cares in the world, two naïve souls out fishing and discussing their unknown futures. God held that stone close to his heart. When my father left that day, he assured God he would return as soon as he could. Sadly, a few days later, as my father watched another of Jesus' 'I AM that I AM' speeches on the video screen, he noticed in horror that Jesus was holding the very stone he had given God. Then, more than ever before, he feared he would never be able to fulfill his promise to see his old friend again. My father has always believed that if he could have taken God from the palace and helped him regain his health, God would have stood beside him in the rebellion against the evil Jesus created. According to my father, God was a noble, deeply honorable man, a believer in democracy and the inherent right for all beings to be free.

"Along with the clandestine disruption of Jesus' plans, captains of Heaven warships began to disobey orders to kill innocent beings whose only crime was to choose free will above heavenly domination. In each case, the captains were executed in front of their crews to illustrate the high penalty for disobedience. Loyalty and respect had been earned by God, but Jesus, who was nothing like his father, forced it on the citizens of the galaxy through fear and intimidation.

"It was at that point that my father decided to take his battle off Heaven. Without his friend, there was nothing left there for him anyway. Vicious attacks had been ordered on worlds that were sympathetic to the rebellion, and those assaults were getting dangerously close to my father's home world. Except for the angels left behind to gather informa-

tion and further disrupt the enemy, all who were loyal to the
rebellion left Heaven. The angels of the rebellion escaped with
only 40 percent of the warships from Heaven's fleet. Some
traveled to strategic locations throughout the galaxy, but
most fled to my father's home world, where they could start
the rebellion in earnest. War was coming, and the fate of the
galaxy was at stake. That war, Justin, continues to this very
day, and it is the reason I happened upon your beautiful
world." Sandel paused, looked over at Justin, and said, "I'm
sure by now, you have guessed the name of my father."

Justin blinked, suddenly aware that Sandel was speaking
to him. At first, he just mouthed the name. Then, when he
found his voice again, he stammered, "Lu-Lucifer?"

"Lucifer Satanis, in its complete form."

"So, you're Sandel Satanis?"

"I am. Now, I imagine you have some questions. I will answer them the best I can," Sandel finished.

With a little sudden anger in his voice, Justin said, "If
you are who you say you are, then all the training I've received my entire life tells me you are a liar. Why was I chosen
to be tested by the beast? Why me? Why now? First, my family, was snatch away from me, and now this! Damn it all!"

Sandel sighed. "First of all, I am sorry for your loss, but
you were not *chosen*, as you say. It was pure luck on my part
that you found me and that you were kind enough to care for
me as you have. The only reason I am here at all is because
the forces of Jesus damaged my ship. We were outmatched
five to three. Though we fought with honor, our scout ships
could not overcome the power of their battle cruisers. I lost
many good friends up there. In fact, I wouldn't be here at all
if my brother Saleos had not sacrificed his life to save mine."
With that revelation, a tear coursed down his cheek.

When Sandel reached up and wiped it from his eye, Justin noticed, for the first time, the tattoo on the back of Sandel's hand, three markings that looked very much like three
sixes. Considering what he'd just learned, the symbolism was
unmistakable: It was the sign of the beast. He wasn't sure he
wanted to know the answer, but he had to ask, "Uh, Sandel,
feel free not to tell me if you don't want to, but the body art

on the back of your hand... Does that, uh, symbolize anything?"

Sandel looked at the ink on his hand and said, "Yes. It is
a mark proudly worn by many who have joined the rebellion."
He held his hand up and pointed at the tattoo. "These are
three sixes, with good reason."

Justin's mind reeled with the implications. The Bible
warned of such a mark, and now it was right before him, sitting on his couch and sharing a bottle of wine with him. For
the moment, he was at a loss for words.

Sandel, noticing Justin's quick change of mood, smiled.
"Again, contrary to what you have been taught, 666 is simply
the number of worlds that first formed what we now know as
the Free Will Alliance. It started with a few soldiers but has
grown exponentially. It is completely voluntary, but many in
the Alliance wear these tattoos on the backs of their hands,
so they are clearly visible when their fists are held up. I've
also seen them on arms, chests, and the foreheads of some of
the more passionate soldiers."

"Say I believe you, at least the bit about you being the
son of Lucifer. Why should I let you stay? I mean, I feel like
I've been preparing for this moment my whole life, the moment when I'd confront the beast, and now I'm at a loss
about what I'm supposed to do," Justin said matter-of-factly.

Sandel winced as he pushed himself up from the couch.
"I feel much better, nearly healed, and I am thankful for all
you and your doctor have done for me. If I can prevail upon
your good will once more to bring me my clothes, I will leave
immediately."

Justin shook his head. "No," he said, somewhat hesitantly. "We're both tired and full of wine, and Doc said you'll still
need a few days of recuperation. Let's sleep tonight, then see
what tomorrow brings." He smiled and continued, "Besides,
you haven't taken my soul so far, so..."

Sandel laughed, thanked Justin once more for his kindness, then gulped down the rest of his wine.

Chapter 6

Just as he'd done the night before and on so many nights, Justin tossed and turned in his bed. No matter how physically exhausted he was, sleep, for him, was always a distant hope. This time, however, it was different. Instead of anticipation for an adventure story, he now found himself struggling with great internal conflict. He was torn between his duty as a lifelong Christian and the possibility that the man who was staying with him, a possible angel, had spoken the truth. If what Sandel told him was the truth, then all Justin had ever known was a lie. Not sure what else to do, he prayed hard, then listened for an answer.

His fatigue finally proved victorious and carried him off to sleep, but chaotic dreams made his slumber fitful. A while later, he vaguely realized that he left his bed, and silently moving through the kitchen. Then, he suddenly found himself standing over Sandel. He looked down at his hand and noticed that he had a firm grip on a butcher knife. *What the...? Am I really about to kill this angel?* he thought, shocked by his own semi-conscious behavior. *I guess it is my duty as a Christian, isn't it?* he reasoned. *I mean, the mark of the beast and all that...*

Suddenly, at what seemed the oddest of moments to have a flashback to Casey Kasem's Top 40, a verse from the Eagles' "Hotel California" ran through his mind:

"And in the master's chambers,
they gathered for the feast.
They stab it with their steely knives,
but they just can't kill the beast..."

Justin stood over the son of Lucifer with blade in hand, but he just couldn't bring himself to hurt him. With those lyrics still rolling through his mind, he placed the knife back in the wooden block on the kitchen counter then walked back to his bed, and fell into a deep sleep.

Justin awoke feeling rested and ready for a day of questions. *I had damn better get some answers, too,* he fumed, and he intended to take his Bible along for backup or just moral support. Before the inevitable inquisition, he decided it was best to follow his normal routine; he needed normal to calm him down, and it was an amazing day for a hike.

As he walked, he first thought of his family, per usual. It wasn't long, though, before thoughts of the story Sandel had told him the day before intruded on his psyche. He wanted to doubt what the man said, but he wasn't sure if he could. Had Justin been granted one superpower in life, he would have desired the ability to discern when people were telling what they thought was the truth. Sandel certainly believed what he had told him; that much was evident.

Justin had counseled countless people during his lifetime. As a professor, he listened to many excuses, stories students wove and hurled at him to explain their classroom shortcomings. During those years, he'd become rather adept at telling truth from fiction. As a member in good standing in his church, he had counseled his fellow congregants, and he'd been a confidant for inmates at a nearby prison. The truth, in those cases, wasn't so much his primary concern, but it certainly made it easier for him to help those who came to him.

After the evening meal, Justin and Sandel sat down together. Before the interrogation began, Justin placed his Bible in front of him on the coffee table, hoping it would serve as a quick access to information, if not a shield against the evil Sandel represented. He even wore a cross on a chain under his shirt, just in case.

"Ah, the book," Sandel said with a knowing smile.

Justin arched a brow, a little surprised. "You know about the Bible?"

"Yes. I read that particular version yesterday, while you were hiking," his evil friend answered.

"You read it?" Justin asked, taken aback. "I was only gone two hours, and... Well, never mind that. You said you read this version yesterday. Should I take that to mean you've also read other versions, like the American Standard or the New Living Translation?"

Sandel, a little amused but sympathetic to his friend's shortsightedness, continued, "No, my friend. This book, in many forms, exists on thousands of worlds. Although the language varies, the general message is the same. Simply put, God is good and Lucifer is evil. God is all-powerful, all-knowing, and everywhere at once. This is taken on faith alone, as is the premise that Lucifer is evil."

Justin grinned, ready to make a solid point. "Okay, so if the Bible, or some version of it, exists in all these worlds, isn't that a strong argument for its truth? I mean, it is very improbable, if not impossible, that the same story would simply pop up in thousands of completely different worlds that have no communication or connection. How do you explain that?"

"Oh, but there is a connection," Sandel said, a bit snarkily.

"So, enlighten me," Justin pressed.

"It started about the time my father took his rebellion off Heaven," Sandel said. "Jesus, fearful of the growing rebellion, sent emissaries into the galaxy. Their sole mission was to find inhabited worlds and ready them to enter the battle against Lucifer and all he represented. They visited these worlds before their people had any technology, so the inhabitants naturally thought they were performing miracles. That effectively created belief in an unseen God, a blind following Jesus could use to his advantage when the time came. Those angels spent many years cultivating their tales, revisiting those deceived worlds again and again. When the worlds advanced to the point of space exploration, one or more representatives were permanently stationed there to watch over their progress."

Justin frowned. "Are you saying there is an angel of God here on Earth right now?"

"Of that, I am sure," Sandel answered with confidence.

"Where? Who is it?" Justin asked.

"I have no idea, but it must be someone of power and position, someone who is able to reach the ear of top government officials," Sandel answered thoughtfully. "If that angel ever discovers that I am here, everything in their power will be done to capture me and return me to Heaven."

"Why would they do that?" Justin asked, only to immediately feel naïve.

"An imprisoned son of Lucifer would be quite a prize for Jesus, don't you think?" Sandel asked. "I imagine God's army would surround this planet to block any chance of my escape. Earth would be thrust into the war without any way to protect herself. Life, as you know it, would be forever gone.

"There was a planet much like this one about a quarter of the way around the galactic rim. A cousin of mine was sent there on a reconnaissance mission to attain information about the strength of God's forces in that sector. The local representative learned of his presence, and, knowing Jesus would be thrilled with his capture, ordered a complete sweep of that world to locate him. Since the people of that world had been forced into the war earlier than planned, drastic measures were taken. As they were not of any real importance to the Empire, they became the lowest level of servants for the warlord of Heaven.

"Over the next fifty years, their planet was decimated. Any and all resources that could prove valuable to the Empire were extracted and depleted, and the people became slaves. Their free will was taken from them, and all collected knowledge was destroyed. Since no care was taken to ensure the health of the people, the elderly among them died quickly, taking their knowledge and experience to their graves. Once the Empire deemed the world entirely unusable, after they sucked it dry, they departed, leaving the people to try to survive on their gutted, dying planet.

"As if that wasn't bad enough, without the collected knowledge of their once prosperous world, their societal evolution was set back thousands of years. Billions died that first year. Billions! They were unsettled from a society much like your own and reduced to scattered groups of scavengers, living off what little rubbish was left to them. Today, their population measures only in the thousands, and they are still struggling. I have great fear this could happen to your Earth, if great care is not taken," Sandel concluded. "For that reason, I must leave as soon as possible. I am putting you in danger just by being here."

Justin sat quietly for a moment, pondering Sandel's story. Everything his otherworldly friend made sense, but that was the trouble. *Isn't that precisely what the Bible and my years of religious training warned me about?* he thought, recalling one particular passage: *"Ye are of your father the devil, and the lusts of your father ye will do. He was a murderer from the beginning, and abode not in the truth, because there is no truth in him. When he speaketh a lie, he speaketh of his own: for he is a liar, and the father of it."* (John 8:44) As the scripture poured into his mind, he looked at Sandel with an icy glare and demanded, "How in the world do you expect me to believe you when the teachings of my entire life tell me you cannot be trusted, that you will lie about anything and everything?"

In the voice of a patient father explaining a difficult life lesson to his son, Sandel said, "I do not *expect* you to do anything, Justin. I know you are predisposed to see me as a liar, and I cannot blame you for that. I only hope you will learn to trust me before it is too late. At the very least, please keep all I have told you to yourself. Although I am concerned about my own wellbeing and have a family I wish to see again, I am far more worried about you and your world."

"I want to believe you, Sandel. I really do," Justin said. "It's just..." He paused for a moment, then confessed, "Despite our opposing philosophies, I still consider you a friend for some reason. Please don't ask why, as I'm not sure of that myself."

"Thank you. That means more to me than you know,"

Sandel said, extending his hand and smiling broadly. "I feel much stronger now, thanks to you, and I think it's time I prepare to leave your Earth, before it is too late. I will require a few things to accomplish this task, so I've taken an inventory of the objects I will need. My research on your computer validated that I should be able to collect all these items rather easily. You have done so much for me, but may I ask you for one last favor?" Sandel asked.

Justin nodded. "I will do what you ask, if only to err on the side of caution."

"I need your assistance attaining these things, but please be very discreet. It would be best to spread your purchases around, so we do not leave a trail that would cause suspicion. I do not wish to cause you any undue grief. You may not believe all I say, but please take it to heart when I tell you that your world is at stake."

Justin looked at the list and scrunched up his brow. It was certainly a weird combination of items, but he decided it was best not to ask what all of it was for. "I'll start shopping tomorrow," he said. "The last couple days have worn me out, and I need to sleep. Let's hit the hay."

Once Justin was finished explaining that hitting the hay had nothing to do with actually striking a pile of dried grass, he left Sandel, and marched off to bed.

Some undetermined number of hours later, Justin staggered out of his room, and headed for the restroom. He lumbered along like a zombie, with his eyes closed, but he was jolted completely out of his near sleepwalking when he heard a voice. He moved down the hallway toward the sound, and discovered that Sandel was wide awake, and wearing a strange contraption on his head, talking as if he was dictating a journal into some sort of recording device. Justin listened for a while but soon felt guilty for eavesdropping, and decided it was prudent to go back to his room. Sleep came quickly when he did, but his last thoughts were on Sandel and the audio diary he was voicing.

Chapter 7

Justin awoke early but very rested, and ready for his busy day. He quickly made and ate breakfast, and headed out the door. Since he had business to take care of in Indianapolis anyway, he decided to shop there for added discretion. He shopped at five different electronics stores in Indy, and he was glad he managed to find everything on the list. He was also wary enough to use only cash, knowing credit or debit cards would leave a paper trail. He did his best to avoid showing his face too much; he tried not to be too paranoid about it, but it was the day and age of Big Brother, with cameras everywhere, and the last thing he needed was to show up in a random news clip or on YouTube or to inadvertently photobomb someone's post to social media.

Around 6:30 that evening, Justin returned to the cabin. He proudly spread his purchases out on the coffee table in front of Sandel, then went about preparing dinner.

Later, after Justin returned from his daily hike just before the sunset, he found the front room empty, but he heard the shower running in the bathroom. The futuristic headgear Sandel had donned the night before was lying on the coffee table. He walked over to the device and stared at it, then looked toward the bathroom. In the end, his curiosity got the better of him. He picked up the device and, with some trepidation, placed it on his head. Immediately, his mind filled with an information rush into his head. Then, like a computer bombarded by too many downloads at once, Justin crashed and fell into the chair behind him, in a semi-conscious state.

A multitude of dreams seemed to be occurring in three dimensions simultaneously. He witnessed the wicked battle that had ensued only days ago, along with every other event, the very incident Sandel had told him about. He experienced lucid visions of God, Lucifer, Jesus, Sandel, Heaven, and Hell, and these now inhabited his mind as if they were his own memories. He saw Jesus standing in front of countless followers in Heaven, preaching blind devotion, while God sat behind him, unmoving and almost catatonic. There it was, the pentagon-shaped stone that Sandel had told him about, the night before.

It dawned on Justin, even in his near-catatonic state, that if what he was seeing was true, Jesus was a major pain, and the real bad guy in the book behind his beliefs. He watched as the son of God ordered the pointless deaths of millions, simply because they refused to relinquish their free will. He smiled sadistically when his angels told him of their victorious mayhem. Jesus was nothing like the biblical hero Justin had been taught about, other than some parts of his physical appearance, like his long hair and beard. Of course, even that was skewed by the evil in his eyes.

There had been a great role reversal somewhere in history and definitely in Justin's mind and heart. What he once knew as the perfect good was now the purest evil, and vice versa. The blood of Christ, which he once thought of as holy, was really just the heinous evidence of what Jesus had done, the bloodshed of billions of innocent lives taken in the name of an evil tyrant. Then, as suddenly as that presumed history of the galaxy unfolded in his mind, it was over.

Justin opened his eyes and sat, dumbfounded, as he lifted his gaze to find Sandel sitting right across from him.

"Welcome back, my friend," the angel said, smiling.

Justin slowly reached up to remove the gadget. "I-I'm sorry," he said sheepishly, looking down at the floor. "I shouldn't have... Oh, Sandel, I'm so sorry."

At that, Sandel laughed. "It is quite all right, my friend.

You are free to use the Illuminator as you please, but I should show you how it works. As you might have noticed, it can be quite overwhelming if you do not know how to control the flow. The next time you try it, clear your mind and, as you say, show it who's boss."

"Are the events I witnessed real or fiction?" Justin asked, still in awe.

"Everything that entered your mind is part of galactic history, and all that I've experienced in your world will be added upon my return home," Sandel explained with conviction. "See, my friend, memories are fluid. We can recall some emotions and facts about our past experiences, but details sometimes seep through the cracks and are not always accurately recounted. The Illuminator eliminates that problem, allows us to accurately relive events as they actually happened, good or bad. With this technology, time can no longer alter memories to sugarcoat past indiscretions or exaggerate accomplishments. The Illuminator ensures reality.

"That's pretty amazing," Justin said, imagining the possibilities of such a device.

"Yes, I know. The Illuminator has been used to discover diseased minds, and help them when possible. Because with it, no lie can be hidden. It is of great benefit if used properly, and it has allowed people to evolve in thought."

"But in the wrong hands, it could be...bad," Justin surmised.

"Definitely. There are still evil ones among us whose intentions are not honorable, and they hope to get away with their wrongdoing. The good thing about the Illuminator is that it has given us the ability to find the truth and punish them."

Over the next few days, Sandel continued preparing for his flight while Justin delved further into galactic history, both in conversations with Sandel during their hikes and with the help of the Illuminator. The two talked about everything: galactic history, family, philosophy, movies, and even Hell.

"As it turns out, Hell is much like your Earth," Sandel said, "with oceans, forests, deserts, and even icecaps. Quite like here, life finds a way to survive in each of those environments."

On one of their treks, a pressing question entered Justin's mind. "While I was using the Illuminator, I saw your father and God meeting with the Holy Ghosts. The Ghosts seemed open and friendly, not invisible or evil. Are they really that bad, Sandel?"

Instantly, some underlying anger stirred in Sandel, and his expression and tone changed to match it. After a frustrated sigh, he said, "At one time, the Holy Ghosts were much like your Federal Bureau of Investigation or Central Intelligence Agency. Their mission was to protect the Empire, and they were answerable to the citizens. However, when Jesus became the leader of Heaven, their mission grew darker, more secretive, more subversive. They are now dedicated to the purpose of protecting Jesus and his hold on the galaxy. They hold fear in one hand and death in the other. They are free to go anywhere and kill anyone who poses the slightest threat to the word of Jesus."

Justin didn't want to piss his angelic friend off, but he was compelled to retort, "It is hard to believe that they all just suddenly...turned evil."

"You are right, but they did not all succumb to the will of Jesus. Many died in the first few days of the change, but some escaped and found a place in the rebellion. Those loyal to my father's cause remained as Holy Ghosts and gather information vital to the fight against the evil that threatens us all."

"Sorry I brought it up, Sandel," Justin apologized when he noticed the tension in his friend's voice and the slowing of his gait.

Sandel shook his head, suddenly realizing that his mood had soured. "No, it is I who should be sorry," he said. "It's just that I have lost too many friends and family to those bastards, and my emotions tend to get in the way. Again, I am sorry."

Justin gave him a pat on the back, and they made the rest of the hike in silence.

Days later, on what was to be their last walk before Sandel had to head home, Justin mentioned something else that had been troubling him: "Sandel, I've spent much time with the Illuminator and have seen many weird and wonderful things, but one thing still bothers me. If you are an angel, where is your halo? Jesus was never without one, nor were the angels who guarded him. Did you lose your divinity when you left Heaven? Was your halo taken from you over your, uh...dishonorable discharge?" Justin asked.

"A halo?" Sandel asked, genuinely puzzled. "What do you mean?"

"You know, your halo, that ring of holy light that circles the heads of all divine beings."

Sandel thought about that for a moment, then burst out laughing. His chuckle was deep, but when he saw how serious Justin was and how taken aback and insulted he appeared to be, he calmed down and placed a hand on Justin's shoulder. "I am sorry if I offended you, my friend. First of all, I am not divine, and neither is Jesus. The ring of light you've seen in the historical documents on the Illuminator and those in earthly paintings such as *The Last Supper* are merely an effect caused by the body shield. Let me show you." With that, Sandel took one step back, and an aura immediately circled his head.

Now he's a proper angel, thought Justin before he said, "That was what I saw as you floated in midair, just before you plummeted to Earth the day this all started. If it's some kind of shield, why didn't it protect you when you hit the ground?"

"Well, just like the Illuminator, it works best when controlled. I passed out during the descent, so I had no control over my landing," Sandel explained.

"Why didn't you just continue to float? Why'd you drop so fast, like a ton of bricks?" the inquisitive earthling asked.

"As I demonstrated the other day, we have the ability to use gravity to our advantage." He levitated as he continued, "When I lost consciousness, I was no longer able to defy gravity, to fly, so to speak."

As Sandel lowered himself to the ground, Justin asked another question: "What about your wings? All angels have wings, don't you?"

"On a few worlds, the inhabitants have wings, and they are also represented in the angelic ranks. It appears that many angels who've visited Earth were of the winged variety. I guess it was an effective tool in their preparation of your planet," Sandel surmised.

A slight scowl twisted Justin's face before he asked, "Just what do you mean by preparation? What were they preparing us for?"

Back on the ground again, Sandel took a moment to marvel at the beauty of the world around them. He then turned to Justin and said, "They were preparing you to enter the war on the side of the Galactic Empire. There are probably very few places on Earth where God-versus-Satan stories are unheard of. As the war progresses, Jesus will need more soldiers. Once Earth is pulled into the fold, you will be stripped of your free will. Praising Jesus will no longer be a choice. Rather, it will be the law, and disobedience to it will be punishable by death. Dissenters will not be imprisoned. They will be eradicated. A few fortunate people will be allowed to become angels, gaining all the power that entails, and they will quickly dominate their fellow earthlings. They will take positions of power over every nation, and your world will be stripped of anything the Empire deems important."

The last few words carried Sandel to a serious bout of introspection. When he regained his composure a few moments later, he continued, "I must go, Justin. It is too dangerous for your world, for me to be here. I am a danger to you, and, besides, there are things I must do. Also, there is one more thing I think you should know."

"And what is that?" Justin asked as they entered the clearing where the cabin stood.

"God is a title, just as king or president is on Earth. He has a name, a given name."

"I've been wondering about that," Justin said, turning his full attention to Sandel. "So, come out with it then. What's God's real name?"

"Hmm. Maybe I've said too much. Perhaps that is something that should be left unsaid," Sandel said, suppressing his urge to smile.

Justin's curiosity was way beyond piqued, and his patience was quickly waning. "What!?" he squealed in an octave higher than normal. "Oh, hell no! You can't just throw that out there then pull it back. No way, Jose! Come on, Sandel. Have a heart."

"Oh, all right, if you insist. God's actual name is..." He paused for effect, then finally blurted, "Shemp."

"Wait," Justin said. "Shemp? Really?"

Sandel stopped walking, braced himself on a nearby tree, and almost fell to the ground laughing.

Finally, Justin realized the reference to *The Three Stooges*. "Okay, okay. Very funny. You're a real shit, Sandel. You know that?" he said as the joke hit his funny bone hard, and they both laughed all the way back to the cabin door.

Just before they entered the cabin, Sandel stopped and turned to Justin, with a serious look on his face. "God's real name is Elohim. I feel it is important for you to know that. He was my father's dearest friend and a truly great leader. You would have liked him."

Chapter 8

Back at the cabin, Sandel got to work. First, he gathered the supplies Justin had purchased for him. "I have a very good feeling about my chances," he said. "These items you helped me obtain will go a long way in repairing my vessel."

"Do you have enough?" Justin asked, truly concerned and rather unskilled in the area of spaceship repair.

"If not, I suppose I'll end up stuck on your moon," Sandel said with a coy smile. Inwardly, however, he felt more than a bit uncertain of his fate, but he did not want Justin to know that.

The two unlikely friends sat down to enjoy a last meal together, their literal last supper. For a fond farewell, Justin made all the foods he knew Sandel liked best: medium-well ribeye, baked potato oozing with butter, macaroni and cheese, and bacon-laced green beans. They even discussed the sound the macaroni and cheese made while stirring it when it was prepared correctly.

In spite of their laughter over slurping, sloshing pasta, the feeling of impending loss was thick in the air. Sandel, who had first thought of Justin as means to an end, now saw him as a true friend. Justin, on the other hand, had gone through an even more major change. Even he couldn't believe he now saw Sandel, the son of Lucifer, as his best friend, the one who'd opened his eyes to the truth and changed his entire philosophical outlook. To say that Sandel's visit had spiraled Justin into an emotional and spiritual 180 would have been putting it lightly. Nevertheless, as much as he believed Sandel and all he'd seen courtesy of the Illuminator, it was difficult to think of God and Jesus as actual living, breathing, mortal beings, rather than the unseen, faith-based omnipresent deities he'd depended upon to guide him throughout his life.

As the earthling pondered this, something of an identity crisis seemed to overcome him, as if he didn't know who he was anymore. He looked at Sandel sincerely and asked, "So what do I do now? I can't go back to work, and church is out of the question. I've spent my entire life living a lie, but for the most part, I felt pretty damn good. The truth didn't set me free after all, Sandel. Rather, now that I'm closer to it than I've ever been, I feel lost and miserable. To top that off, you're leaving. I'll be left all alone here to contend with all this difficult truth, without a job, without a purpose, without...a friend," he finished, frowning.

Sandel looked at Justin and felt a tear burn a path down his face. "I will miss you, too, my friend, but I have a sense that you will be quite all right. I would encourage you to carry the real truth to your people. I realize it will be a hard road to travel, but now that you are part of the galactic society, it is your responsibility to do what you can to save your people and your beautiful planet."

"Yeah? That go-and-tell bit sounds just like what I've been taught all my life," Justin said, a bit sarcastically.

"Yes, but now you know the real story to tell," Sandel said with a consoling grin. "Another thing you can do is search for the insidious angels who strive to keep your world on course for heavenly domination. To this end, I am going to leave a device with you. In the event you discover their identity, you can send a message that will reach my world. Of course, all of this is by your choice, because I am a firm believer in free will, and many have fought and died to preserve that right. I can only trust that you will make the right decision, but at this time, I must take my leave." With that, Sandel headed for the restroom.

Justin smiled, almost laugh. "An angel has to make a

pit stop?" he quietly mused. "What's he going to do, pee his space pants?"

Outside a few moments later, the two shook hands, and Sandel pulled Justin into a close hug. "I will always treasure our time together, Justin. You are a true friend, and I will miss you greatly. I have left something for you in the cabin. Use it wisely, for it will be of great help to you as you embark on your new life."

They both had tears in their eyes as Sandel pushed against the Earth and rose into the air. He waved as he disappeared into the night sky.

Justin stood there in the cool night air, staring skyward for many minutes, till he could no longer catch a glimpse of his friend. After a moment to grieve the sad goodbye, his curiosity got the better of him, and he hurried inside to see what Sandel had left behind.

He smiled as he spotted the gift on the coffee table. There, in all its glory, was the amazing Illuminator, sitting on top of an envelope with his name written on it. He picked up the Illuminator and examined it for a long moment, then tore the envelope open, pulled the letter out, and read it aloud: "Use the Illuminator wisely, my friend, and take great care to never let anyone know of its existence. As we discussed, if this device falls into the wrong hands, it could bring disaster to your world. I hope one day to be in your presence again. Perhaps you can even visit my world, for I would be proud to introduce you to my family. Contrary to what you have heard, my father is, as you would put it, a pretty cool guy, not all fire and brimstone as you've been led to believe. For now, farewell, dear friend. Sandel."

Chapter 9

It had been almost three years since Sandel's ascent into that starry sky. Justin often wondered how he was doing or if he'd made it back at all. *I miss him dearly,* he thought every time he looked up to the moon and imagined Sandel there, stuck and lonely. There was no evidence that Sandel had made it, and Justin had little hope of ever reuniting with his friend again. Since Sandel's departure, though, Justin's life had turned into an adventure all its own.

When Sandel left, Justin found himself without the job and the religion he'd always relied upon. He did, however, discover that he still had a purpose, perhaps a greater one than ever before. Justin took every opportunity to use the Illuminator, knowing he needed to collect as much information from those archives as he could if he would have any chance to fight the unseen enemy that threatened his world. He faced two grueling questions that rang into his head night and day: *How can I reverse thousands of years of religious conditioning?* and *Who are the resident angels, these chess masters who aim to turn our powers-that-be into unwitting pawns, and how am I to find them?*

To attempt to answer the first question, he tackled it straight on. It didn't take him too long to create a website, *TheSerpentsGift.com.* It extolled the virtues of free will and liberty in all forms. It was a shrine to choice, and it provided a few alternative interpretations of biblical events pertaining to just that. He made sure to sprinkle in some facts he'd gleaned from his time with the Illuminator, as well as some things Sandel had told him. His hope was that it would garner the attention of the powers-that-were. As Justin saw it, it was somewhat of a tribute to the God, that Sandel's father knew and loved, the God who believed in choice and democracy.

Justin quit his job at the university not long after his return home. He simply could no longer stand in front of classrooms full of hungry minds and lie. Although it would have been a good cover for his current activity, he just didn't have the heart for the deception. While he now knew his book about angels was complete and utter crap, about as truthful as the gossip rags in the local grocery aisle, it was still selling well, and the royalties were enough to sustain him for a while.

Along with delving into the wisdom of the Illuminator, Justin also dug deeper into the Bible. Stories that had once brought him great comfort now reached out to slap him with the reality of their purpose. The nativity story, the tale of Jesus' birth on Earth, was particularly hurtful. What he once knew as the Immaculate Conception, the beautiful narrative of a virgin birth that resulted in bringing forth the son of God, he now knew as the Immaculate Deception. That would forever spoil his December holiday season. *Talk about a blue Christmas! Sing it, Elvis*, he thought with a pained smirk. In an instant, Santa Claus regained the top position as king of Christmas, the rank the oversized elf had held for Justin when he was reasoning things out with an innocent 5-year-old mind.

Let the so-called miracles begin, he thought sardonically as he read on. With an angel's ability to control gravity, walking on water must have been a breeze for Jesus. Healing the sick was simply the result of thousands of years of medical advancements far beyond what was even known in Justin's time. Then, there was the incredible miracle of Easter, the very crux of Christianity. *How easy it would have been to fake the death and the alleged resurrection that followed,* Justin realized, a truth that pierced his heart like an arrow. *We, our-*

selves, have deluded others this way in our own recent past, those poor, naïve tribes who existed for hundreds of years without change brought on by the outside world. Our more advanced civilized society performed what seemed like miracles for the unsuspecting people, then destroyed their way of life to save their souls. Halleluiah! Praise the Lord! If only Jesus were a myth, an urban legend who could be pushed into the realm of other fantasy creatures like Santa Claus or the Easter Bunny. If only he were as foolish a notion as the Tooth Fairy! Life would be so much easier then, Justin reasoned, but now he knew Jesus was a real, living, breathing, flesh-and-blood being with malevolent delusions of galactic domination, and that was far worse than any fairytale villains anyone could dream up.

Jesus' attempt to control the people of Earth and prepare them for the eventuality of their role in the galactic war was scattered throughout the Bible. Even the Ten Commandments failed to escape that obvious pattern. In fact, three out of the ten dealt with humans relating to God. Justin realized as he read Exodus 20:3-6 that it was all pretty straightforward: "Thou shalt have no other gods before me... Thou shalt not make unto thee any graven image, or any likeness of anything that is in Heaven above, or that is in the earth beneath, or that is in the water under the earth..." As he read on, he saw a glimpse of Jesus' true nature and a reference to God's jealousy. Finally, the third commandment stated, "Thou shalt not take the name of the Lord thy God in vain; for the Lord will not hold him guiltless that taketh his name in vain." *Those first three are basically the message found in all of Jesus' speeches to the Galactic Empire,* Justin surmised, with great angst, shaking his head.

It came to Justin's attention that the Bible preached one main theme: fear. That was especially evident in the stories of the sinful cities Sodom and Gomorrah and in the well-known Sunday School telling of Noah and the Great Flood. In both instances, God wielded his mighty power in a seemingly unmerciful rage, to uphold his fierce commitment to punish unbelievers. Sodom and Gomorrah were decimated by fire and brimstone simply because the people there refused to keep the commandments God had so graciously heaped upon the sinful humans. If that wasn't enough to scare people into becoming blind followers of an unseen God, the horror story of a watery grave would knock people to their knees, begging for forgiveness. In the Great Flood, God shamelessly killed every man, woman, child, and animal upon the Earth, save Noah and his family and two of every kind of creature. The moral (or rather, immoral) of both stories was clearer to Justin than ever before: Do what God says or die. Justin could only imagine the terror his ancestors must have felt when they heard that, along with the sleight-of-hand, faux miracles they saw that seemed to emphasize God's power. He was no stranger to that fear; he'd felt it while growing up as a Christian, even without the magic tricks to persuade him.

He read on for a while longer, exploring the Old Testament with new, wider eyes and shocked by what his new perspective seemed to be revealing to him. It was a lot to bear, to realize he'd been living under a fallacy his whole life, so he soon slammed the so-called Good Book closed and stared at the Illuminator. *Enough for now,* he thought, feeling a bit apologetic for the psychological, soapbox rant that had been going on in his head for the past hour. "Who the hell am I ranting to anyway?" he had to ask himself.

Chapter 10

Justin's search for the power behind the power was proving fruitful, as difficult as it was. Little by little, he was getting closer to revealing the resident angel. Three names in particular kept showing up in his research. The first was Michael Abraham Smith, a reclusive billionaire whose fortune was the product of mass media. Ironically, the media that had made him so wealthy was also a bit of a thorn in his side; Smith despised the paparazzi and made a concerted effort to be rarely seen. He was presumed to be a very fit, attractive blond, a middle-aged man with or light-brown haired, middle-aged man with piercing blue eyes. The story was that he'd started out at a small-town newspaper in Montana but had climbed the ranks to become the founder and CEO of the largest media conglomerate in the world. He now owned a number of major newspapers, radio stations, television companies, publishers, movie production firms, and even the newest information portal, the internet.

Michael Abraham Smith was also reported to be a devout Christian and had boasted that he had "the largest collection of religious artifacts in the world." Besides allocating unbelievably large sums of money to conservative politics, he donated heaps of cash to the church. Although he spread his wealth around to various religious organizations worldwide, the majority of his benevolence fell into the offering plates of the Church of God's Promise. It was that bit of information

Benjamin Oneal

that brought Justin to the next name on his list.

Reverend Gabe Brown, the founder of the Church of God's Promise was in uncommonly good shape for a person his age who preached the word of God for a living. His coal-black hair was always combed straight back, with nary a strand out of place. He had strikingly handsome features, and his remarkable talent for moving people with his words made him the best in his chosen field.

His humble beginnings were in a small church in southern Indiana. When the former pastor died from a mysterious illness, a relatively new associate pastor, Gabriel Brown, stepped up to fill the position. He was a charismatic, engrossing, powerful speaker with a strong and unapologetic message and all the prowess of a sleazy but successful used car salesman. Not only that, he was believed to be able to heal the sick, with a little help from the power of God. His popularity grew rapidly, as did his number of followers. Since physical buildings had limited capacity to hold a certain number of souls, Brown decided it would behoove his ministry to take to the airwaves. He turned to radio, then television, to spread the word of God. His alleged healings found an even broader audience through the wonder of television, and the church that had started with a measly congregation of only fifty-six now numbered in the millions.

Some well-known conspiracy theorists purported that Brown's early broadcasts on radio and television contained subliminal messages, which was the source of his astounding popularity. Of course, this became a moot point when a fire broke out at the studio where the tapes were stored, destroying any would-be evidence. Whatever the case and however he managed it, be brought in very large sums of money, much of it untraceable. Those tithes and offerings funded his church, his ministry, and his political and charitable donations.

The third and probably the least likely suspect was the ultra-liberal Joanna Ariel Williams, the richest female in the United States. She got her start fighting for women's rights in Atlanta in the seventies and eventually made her way to California and television in the eighties. Along with her

48

growing fame as an entertainer, her aptitude in business was legendary. Her ability to choose successful stocks and up-and-coming companies was phenomenal. She was often accused of having some psychic ability to read the future. When cornered and asked about this, Williams simply smiled and said with a shrug, "Maybe I do, or maybe I don't." That same sound bite was oft recorded when she was asked why she did not appear to age at all over the years. Though Justin couldn't dig up anything about her religious affiliations, her political activities were well known. Most interesting of all, he discovered that she was a leading personality in the fight for the betterment of the environment. While he was quite uneasy with the idea that she could be some sort of evil angel, he couldn't help but find her global concerns most admirable.

One thing that tied all three together was their membership in a powerful, religiously based environmental group known as The Temple. That group wholeheartedly believed the premise that human bodies were the temples of the Holy Spirit and, therefore, God's. They also took it as truth that Earth was the temple of mankind, so it should be treated as such. They openly fought for the protection of all of God's creatures, aimed to stop pollution in all of its dirty and damaging forms, took steps to reverse global warming, ensured protection of rainforests, and generally stood up for a clean and healthy planet. Justin did not want to align with the forces of evil, but in this case, he couldn't help being in total agreement with him.

Whether or not they were directly involved, they were persons of interest. They were all powerful and politically connected, seemingly untouchable. Nevertheless, Justin hesitated to contact Sandel with his report, as he had no solid evidence to back up his gut feelings. He felt he was on the right track, and since his eyes had been opened three years earlier, he'd begun to see things far more clearly, but he wanted to be sure before he involved his old friend. The last thing he wanted to do was waste Sandel's time or Earth's, because time was one precious resource, they were all quickly running out of.

Chapter 11

After a while, Justin began to fear that his odd actions were raising some red flags. He knew inquisitive people with dark agendas were watching his home in Indiana, probably keeping track of his every movement. In times like that, he was glad the cabin belonged to a friend of his; there was no real way to connect him to it, and even his parents knew nothing about his secret hideaway in the woods. That place was his private haven, the one place he could go without anyone knowing his whereabouts, when it was time to get lost. It worked out well, because the owner would be in Europe for at least another month, entirely unaware of the great epiphany Justin was experiencing among those wooden walls.

***

In an abandoned military installation in a secret location, near Los Angeles, the City of Angels, the angels of God met for an update on the subjects of interest to their mission. The human agents who served under the angels were keeping their eyes on over 700 subversives who were working, some of them unknowingly, against Jesus' interests. One who was rapidly moving up the list was Justin Grant. His website, *TheSerpentsGift.com*, was of particular interest. The subjects explored there fell amazingly close to the truth, and this disturbed the host of angels.

As such, the agent in charge reported his findings to his unseen superiors. He related the information about Justin's life, all the intel they'd collected since their last meeting. When they discovered a cash purchase Justin had made three years prior, recorded by a security camera at an electronics store, the three looked at each other and suddenly dismissed the agent.

"This is...most disturbing," one of the hidden figures said after the agent dutifully left the room.

"Yes, and we must report it to Michael immediately!" exclaimed another, with a bit of panic and anger in his voice.

When Michael received the information, his reaction was one of concern. "It is time we had a talk with this Mr. Grant. The topics exposed on his website are too close to this world's indoctrination, and actual galactic events to be a coincidence. That, in conjunction with his odd conglomeration of purchased items, indicate that we may have a problem."

The others remained silent but nodded in agreement.

Michael continued, "Before we report this upsetting news to Jesus, we must learn what this earthling knows, as well as where he is obtaining his information. It should not be common knowledge on Earth. This world is too important to Jesus and the Empire to let this go. Do you know where he is right now?"

"Yes, sir."

"Bring him in," he ordered, pounding a fist on the table. "Now!"

Chapter 12

Sandel years since his departure from Earth had also been quite eventful. As soon as he rose into the night, he felt the sting of missing his friend. He was sure his trip back to the dark side of the moon would be less traumatic and that the repairs he had made to his body shield and life support would assure a successful return to his vessel. The equipment Justin helped him obtain on that blue planet was just what he needed to repair his ship. When he escaped Earth's atmosphere, he pushed harder to increase his velocity and thereby shorten his journey to one of less than two days.

He arrived at his ship without incident, quickly made the necessary repairs and adjustments, then set off at top speed through deviant space to the closest outpost, which was only four days away. Two days later, he was gladly back on his home world.

The first thing Sandel did was call his father to let him know he was home. "I'll meet you soon, after I see my family," he said. The need to hold each of them was overwhelming, and he relished the chance to spend an afternoon with the loved ones he'd so missed. His children filled him in on everything that had happened while he was away. They wrestled, played, laughed, and talked for a while, and after a delicious evening meal, Sandel kissed his wife and headed for his father's estate.

As soon as he arrived, he was met with a tight embrace

from his father, a hug that lasted for several moments. It was a bittersweet reunion for both of them though, and rivers of tears stung their cheeks from the loss of a brother and son.

When they finally broke apart, Lucifer looked sincerely at Sandel and said, "My son, we feared the worst, my son. We thought we lost you both."

"I am sorry, Father. It was an ambush. His ship was hit first as he maneuvered to protect me. He died to save me. I am so, so sorry," he cried, leaning again into Lucifer's broad shoulder, letting his bottled emotions finally flow uncontrollably free.

Lucifer patted his back and pulled his son closer. "You would have done the same, given the chance. You know that in your heart. His sacrifice will not be in vain. The data you brought will greatly advance our cause."

After they sat down, others began to file in, smiling at Sandel.

"We must know all about your mission, son. That planet you were stranded on... Earth, wasn't it?"

Sandel nodded. "Yes, Earth," he said.

"That world is not unknown to me," Lucifer continued, "but I feel we must learn more about that isolated planet as it is today."

Sandel handed an Illuminator to his father, and they watched and listened to all that had taken place, from the battle in space, to the trip and his landing on Earth, to his miraculous recovery, thanks to a Good Samaritan. A tear ran down Sandel's face when he re-watched his brother's valiant death, and he winced when he saw himself hit the ground in his clumsy, unconscious landing. He felt a ping of pain and longing when he saw his earthly friend's face and witnessed himself laughing riotously at *The Three Stooges* on Justin's television.

All of the nostalgia and emotion aside, because of Sandel's successful mission, the Free Will Alliance had gained much-needed information regarding the strength of Empire forces along the borders of Purgatory, an area of the galaxy that was still controlled by the Empire, albeit untouched by it. That would be the central point of attack for the Alliance.

If the battle proved successful, it would deal an enormous blow to the Empire and its unchecked expansion.

Valuable time had been lost, however, due to Sandel's extended stay on Earth to recover. The intel about Purgatory was time sensitive; waiting to strike was not an option. Therefore, just one week after Sandel's return, *Operation Purgatory* was set in motion.

The Purgatorian War was a success right from the start. With the information provided by Sandel's mission, the rebellion was able to make a hard, fast, unexpected strike, hitting weak points and pushing forward to enemy strongholds. It was the first major victory for the Free Alliance since the war began. Although they had successfully thwarted the Empire in many minor skirmishes, *Operation Purgatory* showed the Empire that the Alliance was a true force to be reckoned with in the galaxy, a worthy opponent. Over the next three years, the Alliance held its grasp on the area of the galaxy known as Purgatory, despite repeated attempts by the Empire to regain its losses.

During all that time, Sandel often engaged with the Illuminator, studying the history carefully and in vivid detail. He yearned to know everything about Earth, but there was little information to be found there. The oddest part was that it was not as if Earth was just not a target for study; more so, it was as if the blue planet had never existed. Every known planet was mentioned in the galactic archives, save Earth, as if it had been purposely deleted, erased from the archives of history. Troubled by this, Sandel approached his father and told him about his findings—or, rather, his lack of findings.

"Strange indeed," Lucifer agreed. "I do know a way we might discover the truth about that secluded, little world though," he suggested.

He went on to explain that through their agents still on Heaven, they could gain access to the full galactic library and search the archives. Sadly, it appeared that even those records had been altered. Luckily for Sandel, a librarian who was sympathetic to the Alliance remembered an all-but-forgotten book simply entitled *Life*. The volume was promptly smuggled out of the library and off of Heaven and soon found

The Serpent's Gift

its way to Hell. What Sandel and Lucifer read from those pages changed the whole focus of the war against the Empire and its power-crazed leader, Jesus.

Chapter 13

It was fortunate for Justin that his instincts to flee were right on the mark. The car parked along his street, occupied by two unknown men, had unsettled him, and they'd been there since the wee hours of the morning. Justin had a strong suspicion that they were agents of the angels, and that was his cue that he couldn't wait a moment longer to take his leave.

All along, he'd known this moment would come, and he was prepared. He had been withdrawing money from his bank accounts over the last three months, sporadically and in varying amounts, hoping it would not raise any flags. Now, he removed all but the bare minimum. The royalties from his nonsensical book would continue to direct deposit, but he felt that he had enough cash to hold him over for a pretty long while. Getting out of the house without being noticed was relatively easy. The people who'd lived there prior to him were members of his former church, and the husband had swayed a little toward the side of paranoia. That worked in Justin's favor, because the previous owner had constructed an underground passage that led to a wooded area at the back of the property, perfect for an undetected escape. Although that man's enemies might have been imaginary, Justin's were very real. So, he made quick work of gathering all the information he'd obtained over the last three years, mostly stored in the Illuminator Sandel had left for him, and grabbed the important amenities, like his toothbrush and plenty of underwear.

At 6 o'clock in the evening, he was nearly ready; it would be dark in a couple hours, soon time to go. At 8 p.m., Justin called 911 from a disposable phone. "I'm, uh, Larry Bishop," he said, as calmly as he could, the gave them his address. "I just heard two gunshots. I think it came from across the street. I just saw two guys coming out of the house, carrying guns!" He went on to explain to the emergency dispatcher that Emmett Johnson, his neighbor, had been growing marijuana in his basement.

"Do you know where the intruders are now, sir?" the dispatcher asked while pecking away on her keyboard.

"Yeah. They're still sitting in a car in front of Emmett's home."

Just a few minutes later, sirens were blaring and lights were flashing as the Cavalry whooshed in from both directions.

Perfect, Justin thought with a satisfied grin and took the opportunity to leave while his diversion played out.

As he climbed out of the tunnel and into the woods, Justin sneaked a look back in time. He saw the two men sprawled out over the trunk of a police cruiser, handcuffed and pissed. A very puzzled Emmett Johnson, also cuffed, was talking anxiously to officers at his front door. Justin knew he should have felt some remorse for throwing Emmett under the bus like that, but then he reasoned, *Oh, well. I've never liked that asshole anyway.*

Justin closed the hatch to the passage and hid it from view with some foliage and debris, making a mental note of where it was, in case he needed to return at some point in the future. He then turned and ran through the woods; toward the bike he'd hidden at the other end of a copse of trees. He mounted the bicycle, pulled up his hood, and pedaled hard toward the car he had parked in a garage he'd rented with cash, under a false name. The vehicle was already paid for, also with cash, and registered in a bogus name. With two suitcases full of clothes and his trusty Illuminator, he was ready for the long haul. In less than an hour, he was on his way to the cabin.

Benjamin Oneal

He traveled down I-65 toward Louisville and stopped only briefly in Scottsburg to make another cash purchase: a new laptop and a spare generator. He'd always had a natural aversion to using credit cards anyway, so it felt good to pay for his items with paper Benjamins instead. It would prevent a paper trail and, hopefully, make it all the harder for the angels' agents to track him down. He was as careful as possible, knowing he had to do his best to keep his whereabouts unknown. Of course, that would also require some bit of luck.

A little under three hours later, he finally reached his friend's cabin, his secret hideaway in the forest. Knowing it was always prudent to be safe as opposed to being sorry, he was careful not to naïvely walk into a trap. To avoid that, he depended on the other gift Sandel had left for him, a strange device that he called an electronic device detector (EDD). He wasn't sure of the official name of it, but it served well to alert him of any electronic surveillance devices watching the cabin.

Justin parked the car about a quarter-mile away and moved toward the cabin on foot. The closer he got, the more relieved he felt; the EDD remained quiet, sounding no alarms. Nevertheless, when he reached the log domicile, he watched it for an hour for any hint of anyone being there. His scans did not indicate any signs of life, other than the indigenous wildlife of the Kentucky woods.

Feeling confident that no one was around except a few curious critters, Justin ventured closer. He quickly recovered the key stored under the third rock by the water pump, then cautiously twisted it in the door lock to enter the cabin. From what he could tell, no one had been here since he and Sandel had departed. A coating of fine, undisturbed dust covered everything, and that gave him a good reason to believe nothing had been touched. Justin checked the fireplace and found ashy remnants of the papers he had burned, just in case angels found this place, and those were also undisturbed.

Once he was convinced of his safety, he quickly ran back to where he had left the car and drove it to the cabin. He maneuvered it into the barn to keep it out of sight. Inside, he unpacked quickly. After storing his gear and devouring a quick snack, he went straight to bed. It had been a long, eventful day, and he was exhausted.

Huh? It's, uh...11 already? Justin thought when he woke up midmorning the next day. *God, I must have been tired,* he surmised, but he knew the real reason he'd lingered in bed: He just couldn't face the harsh reality that he was alone and on the run.

He longed to see Sandel again and wondered if he had enough information about the angels on Earth to justify sending a message. He held the device in his hand and looked at it, debating about what to do. After a few moments of soul-searching and deliberation, Justin placed the relay back in his safe, alongside the Illuminator, and headed out for his daily hike.

As Justin walked, serenaded by birds and the skittering of creatures in the vegetation that flanked the trail, he thought about his plan. He looked up at the blue sky above the canopy of trees and inhaled the fresh, earthy scent of nature. *Why didn't I move to the cabin earlier?* he thought. *If there is a heaven, this must be it.* Then, he caught himself and said aloud, "No! This is even better. This is my beautiful Earth!"

Chapter 14

The hike did much to lift his spirits and clear his head, as well as rejuvenate his tired body. By the time he returned to the cabin, Justin felt great and fully relaxed, for the first time in weeks. He was confident that he was safely away from the prying eyes of the angels.

Justin walked to the refrigerator and grabbed a bottle of water, then began to gulp it down, only to nearly choke when a voice shocked him from behind: "Going to the mattresses, huh?"

The plastic bottle fell to the floor, and Justin turned around frantically, certain that the agents he'd screwed over the day before had somehow escaped police interrogations and put a tail on him. Instead of foes, however, to his great surprise, he saw a friend standing there.

"What the...? You're here! Man, you scared the shit out of me," he said. Instantly, he blurted the question that came to his mind. "Wait. What did you just say?"

Sandel smiled. "I said, are you going to the mattresses, my friend?"

Justin couldn't help but smile at *The Godfather* reference and shake his head. "Yes, I guess you can say I am. It is so good to see you, my friend." Justin pulled him into a tight hug as a tear escaped his eye. He felt the happiest he'd been since Sandel left. "I was just debating whether or not to contact you. See, I believe I've finally found the resident angels on Earth. Unfortunately, they've found me, too, I think. I fear they're after me, Sandel." He paused to pick the dropped water bottle off the floor. "I have so many questions and so much to tell you, but I don't know where to begin," he said as he placed it back on the counter.

Sandel pulled Justin in for another hug. "Let us eat and enjoy a couple beers while we catch up. You do have beer, don't you?"

"I don't leave home without it," Justin teased with a wink.

During dinner, they kept the conversation light and refrained from discussing the business at hand. Afterward, they sat down to relax on the couch, and Sandel twisted the cap off his bottle, then proceeded to give an account of all that had happened in the three years since he left.

"Once I reached the moon—which is not made of cheese, by the way—I quickly repaired my ship with the supplies you obtained for me. I returned to Hell, raced home, and spent some much-needed time with my family. Thanks to you, I was able to hold my wife and children once again."

"What about your mission? The intel you collected?" Justin asked.

"The information my brother gave his life for proved most valuable to the Alliance. Within a month of my return, we attacked strategic points along the Purgatorian border. The element of surprise was our ally, and within three months, we had cleared every Empire ship out of that vast region of space. Naburus, an Empire prison planet, was also infiltrated, and we were able to free thousands of those loyal to the Free Will Alliance."

Sandel stopped there, rose from the couch, walked to the refrigerator, and brought back two more beers. "Now, tell me your adventures. What have you done since my departure? Anything at all?" Sandel asked with a smirk.

After they shared a laugh, Justin took a drink of beer, then walked over to his hiding place and reached in to grab the Illuminator. He reached out to hand it to Sandel, but the angel just shook his head.

"No. I'd rather hear your version first, straight from you, Justin," Sandel said.

"Okay, but first, one thing. Why didn't you warn me of the painful memory side of the Illuminator?"

"Oops," Sandel said, which was kind of redundant, since his face and shoulders conveyed that very thought.

Justin grimaced, then continued, "Well, the first month and a half after you left, I started thinking of my family while wearing the device. It felt like I was actually there, reliving those moments in real time. There was no memory I couldn't bring to life. I wore the device almost all the time. I only slept when I was too exhausted to do anything else, and I only ate sporadically. I lost ten pounds in a couple weeks, man! I began to realize that taking too many strolls down Memory Lane was killing me. I had to stop dwelling on the past."

"So, did you?" Sandel questioned.

"Well, the only thing that snapped me out of it was a memory of my wife and a promise I made to her. I told her long ago that if anything ever happened to her, I would carry on with my life. Sandel, I never broke a promise to her while she was alive, and I can't and will not in her death either. She is still with me in my heart, but it's my duty to her to go on and live. It took the Illuminator to...well, illuminate that for me." Justin wiped the tears from his face and smiled. Once he regained his composure after several loud sniffles, he went on, "Now, back to the productive side of my three years without you.

"After you left, I felt a desperate calling to do something, anything, to help the people of Earth. I am not as powerful as you, of course, but I am pretty tech-savvy. I created a website, *TheSerpentsGift.com*, and I used it to post information and write a blog, endeavoring to educate mankind."

"What information did you post...and what is a blog?" Sandel asked.

Justin laughed. "A blog is sort of a series of articles, a log of thoughts. I think it's short for weblog. It's written in a sort of casual, conversational way but conveys a lot of information. Of course, I got that information from the Illuminator. I used the power of the internet to reveal the unabashed truth about Heaven and Hell and the galactic war that threatens our very existence. Over time, the website has gained many followers.

"Along with the popularity, though, came the red flags. I believe the angels of the Empire began to take notice. It wasn't long before they were able to determine the source of the website and blog. Over the last few months, I have felt the eyes of the angels watching me. That is why I'm here, hiding out in the cabin. I believe they were ready to grab me, literally right at my doorstep, so I got the hell out of there."

Sandel had a good laugh when Justin told him about calling the police on his stalkers. "Brilliant, my friend," he said, giving Justin a pat on the back.

"Well, I still feel a little bad about setting up Emmett Johnson but not too bad," Justin admitted, blushing a bit. "I swear, whenever he opened his basement windows, it looked like that van from Cheech and Chong."

"Cheech and Chong? I don't believe I know them," Sandel said. "Are they angels?"

"Hardly," Justin said, shaking his head. "Never mind, Sandel."

With tears of joy in his eyes from their happy reunion, Sandel said, "My friend, you are good. No regrets, and I don't feel you did anything wrong. I am only sorry I was not there to see the look on those agents' faces when your police arrested them."

"Well, about my research into the possible resident angels here..." Justin began.

"Yes, about that," Sandel coaxed. "What have you discovered?"

"As far as I can tell, there are three who fit the profile you gave me before you left." Justin handed Sandel three manila file folders that he'd well stocked with all the intel he had, including photographs, detailed biographies, and current activities for each candidate.

Sandel studied the documents for several moments, then said, "You have done well, my friend. They are indeed angels, very powerful ones at that. I notice there are no pictures of Michael Abraham Smith."

"No, he's not exactly into selfies and freeze-frames," Justin said.

"If you mean pictures, it is possibly with good reason," Sandel replied, with a look of concern on his face that made Justin more than a little uneasy. "If the other two are here, he is very likely Michael himself."

"Michael? As in...the archangel?" Justin inquired, recalling his religious studies for the book he'd authored.

"The one and only," Sandel said. "Michael is an angel of the highest level and answers only to Jesus. If he is here, that can only mean Earth is of the highest importance to Jesus, and I think I know why."

"Tell me, oh great one," Justin joked, his interest piqued.

Sandel stretched and yawned. "Later. I am exhausted. Let us sleep, and we will continue this tomorrow."

"You, Sandel, are a dog, a big, dirty dog," Justin said, trying to guilt his confidante to continue.

Sandel feigned hurt feelings. "I traveled millions of miles through space to see you again, and you insult me? That hurts, my friend. It truly hurts."

Finally, Justin relented. "Okay, okay. Tomorrow is another day, I guess."

Sandel wrinkled up his brow in confusion. "You Earthlings seem to have a penchant for stating the obvious," he said. "Goodnight, dear friend."

Chapter 15

Much to his surprise and relief, Justin's rapid, three-year growth of awareness had the effect of calming him while he waited for new revelations from Sandel. Somewhere along the way, he'd learned patience. Although he was beyond eager to know what he had to say, he slept like a baby. Mostly, he was just grateful to have his old friend back in his life. He awoke feeling refreshed, and that was certainly a change after so many restless nights of fearing he was being watched.

The two of them spent the day watching DVDs, starting with the 1951 science fiction classic, *The Day the Earth Stood Still,* one of Justin's favorites.

"Hmm. Some very good commentary in there on the situation in the galaxy today, don't you think?" Sandel critiqued. Then, of course, he insisted on watching more of *The Three Stooges*. He was still laughing at the antics of Larry, Moe, and Curly when they embarked on their daily hike.

After their trek, when they returned to the cabin, Justin said, "Hey, Sandel, pop a couple six-packs in the fridge. I'll be back with dinner in about forty-five minutes."

A short while later, as Sandel walked out of the bathroom, a delicious aroma penetrated his nostrils. "Oh, that smells really wonderful," he said, reminiscent of his compliments to the chef so many years ago, when they'd first met. "What new delights have you prepared for us now, my friend?"

Justin held up the steamy box that contained a new treat for his hellish companion. "Sandel, allow me to introduce you to a Mama De Luca pizza, one of the ten culinary wonders of the world. Fetch the beers, then sit and get ready to visit food paradise," Justin said with pride.

"Wow! Dis is dareecious!" Sandel said with his mouthful of pizza.

"I told you so," Justin said.

The two ate, drank, laughed, and just plain enjoyed each other's company. After they finished the whole cheesy pie, they scraped the crumbs into the trash, wiped the table off, and carried their beers into the living room.

As they took their normal seats on the sofa, Justin crossed his arms, still holding his beer. "Okay, so I gave you a place to sleep, fed you, and hopefully loosened your tongue with some cold ones. Get on with the rest of the story like you promised."

Sandel smiled and licked a glob of pepperoni from the corner of his mouth. "First, I must thank you for introducing me to the pleasure of pizza. You must thank Mama De Luca for me the next time you see her," Sandel said as he clanked his bottle against Justin's.

Justin just smiled and shook his head, deciding it was best not to tell Sandel that Mama De Luca was a brand, not a person. Besides, he had other things on his mind, deeper things than any deep-dish crust. "Sure," he said. "Next time I see her."

"Okay," Sandel said. "Before we go on, I have a question." A serious expression flashed across his face when he asked, "While using the Illuminator, did you ever delve into the story of the Garden of Eden?"

"Huh?" Justin asked, puzzled. "Not really. Why?"

Sandel continued, "Many of your historians on this planet have mistakenly pinpointed Eden as a real place on your African continent, but this couldn't be further from the truth. Eden is real, but it is more than a garden. It is a whole planet, Justin, one God and my father discovered over 9,000 years ago. It was something of a paradise, a utopia, of sorts. The inhabitants there happily enjoyed their simple lives, residing in tune with the nature around them. It closely resembled your Gaia theory. They soon discovered that the inhabitants were extremely elderly, and the source of their remarkable, unique longevity was a tree, one indigenous to only that planet.

"Heavenly scientists studied the tree for years and confirmed their suspicions. In the DNA of that tree, they discovered a longevity strand. At first, it was used only by the prominent members of society, but the aim was to mass produce it to protect everyone. There was a flaw though."

"Yes, most things that are too good to be true aren't," Justin wisely acknowledged. "What was the flaw?"

"The aging would not stop until a man reached 27 years or a woman reached 21 years, give or take a year either way. That still puzzles the scientists today. Although the scientist knew about the longevity strand in the DNA, they could not reproduce its effects. The only source seemed to be the fruit of the tree itself. As you might imagine, that made the tree a most valuable commodity, and Planet Eden a most valuable world among all those in the galaxy. Although the inhabitants of Eden were a sheltered bunch, somewhat wary of dealing with outsiders, they saw the truth in God's words and agreed to an arrangement. They would supply the Empire with the fruit, as long as they were left alone otherwise. To this day, Eden is one of the most well-guarded planets in the galaxy."

"The Tree of Life!" Justin said with amazement and a snap of his fingers as the coincidence dawned on him.

"Yes, just like in the so-called Garden of Eden you learned about in the Bible," Sandel said.

"Sorry," Justin said, embarrassed by the interruption. "Please continue."

"It was a great time in galactic history, especially for the Empire, which grew exponentially. Each new, inhabited world they discovered was offered the opportunity to join them. Most were quick to sign up, enticed by all the fringe benefits the wealthy, powerful Empire could offer. Those who rejected, which was their choice, were left to their own devices, as long as they agreed that they would never attempt to harm or overthrow any worlds under Empire protection. Even then, free will was still a commonly accepted, basic pillar in the foundation of the galactic government. For the next 4,000 years, the galaxy enjoyed wonderful peace, but as someone on your planet once so wisely said, all good things must come to an end. As Jesus rose to power, free will was soon abandoned, and democracy was no more. Suddenly, there was a new choice to be made, join Jesus or be destroyed."

"That's not really much of a choice at all," Justin muttered.

"Exactly," Sandel agreed with a nod and another swig of beer.

Chapter 16

"At about that same time, some of the first who were well past their twenties when they first started using what came to be known as the Longevity Factor started to grow old and die, whereas the inhabitants of Eden continued to remain ageless. Scientists came to the conclusion that the Longevity Factor had a limited effect on those not indigenous to Eden. That terrified Jesus, and the realization that he could die after all sent him into a rage. The first thing he did was position more warships around Eden. Your Bible talks about this in Genesis 3, '...he placed at the east of the Garden of Eden, cherubims, and a flaming sword which turned every way, to keep the way of the Tree of Life.'"

"Yes, I've read that," Justin chimed in. "I've just never thought of cherubims as warships before."

"Symbolism, my friend," Sandel said. "Anyway, Jesus then ordered his scientists to find a solution or die. His scientific advisers' first recommendation was to forcibly evacuate the people of Eden to many different worlds. Without blinking an eye and without any consideration for their feelings, the selfish son of God ordered the relocation of as many inhabitants of Eden as the scientists deemed necessary. His scientific experts warned him that removing all of the residents of Eden could result in an imbalance in the planet's eco-structure, and that could adversely affect the Tree of Life's ability to produce the Longevity Factor. Thus, the elders of humanity still reside on Eden, but they are very controlled, only able to reproduce with the Empire's consent. Although they retain their immortality, some documented at over 25,000 years, they have no free will. They are prisoners on their own world.

"With the same uncaring disregard your own slave traders and owners had for black people during that very dark period in your recent history, the Empire tore the Edenites away from their serene home world. On every planet where life had not yet reached the level of cave dwellers, Eden's population was seeded. They were left there with nothing but their minds and their own bodies, but they somehow prospered. That had the effect of killing off the existing dominant life forms. With gentle prodding from resident angels, the exiled Edenites were indoctrinated into Jesus' plan, just as your people have been over the last 6,000 years.

"On each planet where the Edenites were seeded, the effect of the Longevity Factor began to erode. The lifespan of each generation fell, until it leveled off at far fewer years than was their rightful legacy. In almost every case, however, life continued, and populations grew. Along with the Edenites, seeds from the Tree of Life were also planted on each planet, in an effort to reproduce the Longevity Factor. Trees sprouted and grew from those seeds, but the hybrid fruit did not carry the longevity strand in the DNA. The Tree of Life seems to be a phenomenon that only occurs on Eden. Sadly, there is an even darker side to this story."

"I'm not sure it could get much darker," Justin said.

"Trust me, it does," Sandel stated matter-of-factly. "When all the worlds that met the prerequisites and requirements were populated, Jesus felt there were still too many people left on Eden to be managed effectively. Contrary to the advice of his scientific advisers, he ordered his angels to continue uprooting Edenites until the optimal number was achieved. As there was nowhere for these souls to be placed, he ordered his underlings, 'Use whatever means necessary to dispose of them.' As it turned out, there is a barren planet not far from Eden where millions of displaced Edenites were left to die."

Sandel paused and looked into Justin's eyes; he saw Justin wince and knew his friend was keenly aware of the brevity. He waited for a moment, allowing Justin time to ask the inevitable question.

"I am sorry to interrupt again, Sandel, but I need to know. Is Earth one of the planets Edenites were exiled to?"

"Yes," Sandel answered solemnly.

"Whoa! So, you're telling me that on top of us being prepared to be indoctrinated into galactic society on the side of the Empire, we are also...an experiment? We're galactic guinea pigs?" Justin asked, though he already knew in his gut that it was true.

"Yes, my friend. Earthlings, for the most part, are direct descendants of the Edenites. The story of Adam and Eve being cast out of the Garden of Eden is basically true. Your ancestors were taken from your home world and scattered throughout the galaxy, and you are the result of the Edenites who were left here on Earth. The Bible, although a blatant attempt to lead you into the arms of Jesus' rule, has many truths hidden within its pages. Your early earthly ancestors were castaways from Eden. Their lifespans, from Adam to Noah, were close to 1,000 years, yet over the generations, that lifespan has continued to decrease. I suppose the story of Noah and his ark is some sort of symbolic nod to the people of Eden being forced onto the great spaceships to be hauled off to new worlds.

"One other thing I must reveal to you is that Michael and Gabriel have been tasked with checking on the progress many of the worlds populated by Edenites who were left to live or die. On every world they visit, they spend 50 to 100 years, reviewing the results of their experiment. They then go about pulling those worlds into the claws of the Empire and squeeze every last valuable resource from them, without any care for the inhabitants. Thanks to your diligent research on the history of the resident angels, I now have a timeline. I can tell you, Justin, that we are now within the range of a possible decision for the fate of Earth."

Chapter 17

"If Michael is truly here, then the Holy Ghosts are also present on your world. That, above all else, is a most disturbing development. As I you told before, they are a very insidious, dangerous group. They are super spies with the ability to go anywhere and everywhere, entirely unnoticed. They are untouchable and can easily gather detailed intelligence on anyone they choose. You are not safe here, Justin. We have to go."

"Where?" Justin said, looking around. "The cabin is the best hideout I know. No one knows where I am. I have been very careful to keep this place a secret."

Sandel spoke in a voice that underscored Justin's fear when he said, "I know you have, and you were wise to do so, but we cannot take any chances. You are too important to me and to the future of your planet to risk your wellbeing at this time. We must go to a place where they cannot reach you. You must come with me to my home world, and we must leave tonight."

"What!? Look, I've been told to go to Hell a few times in life, but no one's ever meant it literally...I don't think," Justin said, then tried to smile at his joke but failed. "How, Sandel?" he asked, trying to wrap his mind around what Sandel had suggested. "I mean, not to be cliché here, but I'm only human."

"You'll be fine," Sandel assured him. "We must go now.

Take only what is absolutely necessary and hide the rest. There is a chance that your location is unknown to them, but it will only be a matter of time before they find you. They have every resource on Earth at their disposal. This includes the FBI, CIA, satellite imaging, and your Earth technology, along with any advanced technology and devices they brought with them. We must not tarry here."

Still in a daze, Justin prepared for the unexpected journey. He gathered all his research and proof of his existence and locked it away in an old, metal U.S. Army foot locker. He and Sandel carried the locker about an eighth of a mile north of the cabin and stored it under a tarp, buried in a cave he'd found on one of his hikes. Even though the entrance was obstructed from view by some shrubs, they did their best to further disguise it. Once they finished hiding what remained of Justin's life, they hurried back to embark on their voyage.

"Try this on," Sandel advised, handing Justin the body shield he'd brought for him. Then, after his earthly friend squeezed into it, he offered a quick demonstration of how to operate the very user-friendly controls. "As these are really the only way to travel to and from Earth, they've been enhanced for a safer journey," he said. "You'll have an easier landing in Hell than I had on Earth first time I stopped by."

It was decided that they would leave close to midnight, but Justin thought it would behoove him to plead his case once more. "Sandel, I'm sure I left no possible connection between me and this cabin. There is no way they'll ever, ever find me here. Do we really have to go?"

Sandel took on his fatherly tone again and said, "Justin, I know you are reluctant to leave your home world, but they will talk to anyone and everyone who knows you. They will sneakily question friends, family, co-workers, and students to find any possible lead. Have you ever told anyone about this cabin, even in passing?"

Justin thought about that for a moment and suddenly recalled, much to his chagrin, that he had mentioned it to some of his co-workers, but he still wasn't ready to give in so easily. "Maybe a couple people, just casually, but... Hey, even if they capture me, what can they do to me? I won't talk, no matter what they do."

"You will not have to," Sandel grimly countered. "The Illuminator will do the talking for you. Think back to what you told me about that first month after I left. The Illuminator is the perfect interrogator. It harbors the truth in three dimensions. The Illuminator knows all, good and bad, and it will share with anyone who asks it."

Once Justin was finally convinced that leaving was the only option, there was one more thing he had to do. He quickly gathered hard copies of his research of the identities of the resident angels, albeit carefully excluding any and all information about himself, Sandel, and the Illuminator. He shredded some documents, certainly making sure they were micro-crosscut so they couldn't be reassembled, and he burned others, along with the laptop he'd purchased on his trip from Indianapolis, ensuring that nothing could possibly be retrieved from the hard drive.

The icing on the cake was what kept a smile on his face and what had Sandel snickering. In the shredded documents, as a gift to the resident angels, he left references to informants within the organizations of the angels and government officials, the sources of his information. Probably the best thing was burning corners of pages of documents, not leaving enough to reveal the identities. That, he hoped, would keep the angels busy for a while, a messy jigsaw of document shrapnel that would need to be pieced together and would lead to endless interrogations of their staff.

"Brilliant," Sandel complimented, "but don't you feel a bit evil causing suck a ruckus?"

Justin grinned. "No! To Heaven, with all of them!"

At ten minutes to midnight, under the silvery light of a full moon, Sandel, with his human in tow, pushed against Earth, and they were on their way. They fit a covering over the shields near each of their heads to hide the light of the body shield, what Justin first mistook as Sandel's halo.

For his part, Justin didn't mind the trip so much; it reminded him of the sensation he'd experienced before on a ride at an amusement park called Kings Island near Cincinnati, Ohio. Unlike the most frightening part of the Drop Tower, however, the quick descent didn't seem to be forthcoming anytime soon; rather, they just kept going more and more upward. He simply could not nail down the feelings that raced through him, a heart-pounding casserole of excitement, fear, and joy, all fighting for attention.

Once they were outside the atmosphere, Sandel pushed harder, and their speed increased greatly. Earth, once the only thing in their view, now looked spherical, as it did in all the space movies and science books back home. Like all the little boys and girls who'd dreamt of rocketing up with NASA, Justin was living his number-one, most impractical dream, seeing the Earth from space. A tear coursed down his face, and he choked up a little at the thought.

"It is time for you to sleep now," Sandel suddenly announced through a microphone in his ear.

"But I want to—" Justin started to argue, but Sandel had already activated hibernation sequence. In an instant, he just drifted away into the deepest slumber of his life, dreaming of planets and stars and angels and magic trees.

Sandel woke Justin as they neared the far side of the moon, as he knew the glowing orb was a sight his friend would likely want to see. He turned Justin around to look at Earth. From that vantage point, the planet was clearly larger than how the moon looked when Justin had gazed up at it from his front yard, but the swirling whites, blues, and greens were so majestic and spectacular a sight that Justin's breath caught in his throat with a gasp.

"Whoa. H-How long was I out?" the Earthling stuttered, looking at Sandel with wide eyes.

"About forty-six hours, my friend," answered Sandel

The next wonder Justin saw was one only twenty-four humans had ever witnessed with their own eyes, the far side of the moon. Within a half-hour, they were dipping below the edge of a crater. The contrast between light and dark was absolute there, and it was in that black space where Sandel's ship awaited them, ready to carry them to Hell.

After stowing their gear, Sandel led Justin to the bridge of the ship. Two men were there, busy working the controls. Within a few minutes, they were underway. Justin felt no sensation of motion and wouldn't have realized they were even in motion at all, if not for Earth and her moon shrinking in the view screen. When they moved into deviant space, everyone seemed to relax a little.

"Justin, meet Agares and Sorath," Sandel said, by way of introduction. "Agares is an expert navigator, the best in the fleet. Sorath is my trusty copilot. Now, of course he is not nearly as good as I am, but you know it is hard to find good help these days."

Sorath stared at Sandel then presented a gesture that was likely similar to the middle-finger salute on Earth. Justin found it comforting to know that banter between friends was a universal trend.

Sorath had close-cropped, brown hair and piercing, green eyes. One distinguishing feature was the long, angry scar that ran down the left side of his face, a wound that had blinded him eons before.

Agares was also a brunette, but his hair fell to his shoulders. He was missing a finger, as well as a piece of his ear. As Justin would soon learn, one constant among the freedom fighters from Hell was that they all seemed to carry battle scars.

After both men turned to Justin and shook his hand by grasping his wrist, Sorath smirked. "We are glad to finally meet you," he said. "We have heard so much about you. In fact, Sandel has not shut up about you for the last three years. I think he just might leave his wife for you. Good for her though. We all know she could have done better."

Justin, no stranger to trash talk, countered, "Meh, Sandel is not my type, but I could really go for you, Sorath."

For a millisecond of awkward silence, Justin worried that he had gone too far, especially when he noticed the enraged look on Sorath's face.

Suddenly, Sorath burst out laughing, and the others joined him. "Justin, I do believe you will fit right in aboard our ship," he said. Then, once the chuckling died down, Sorath had only one thing to say: "I like this Earthling, but if he touches me, I will space him."

They laughed hard again, then got down to the business

of flying home.

As they hurtled through space, one of a million questions crossed the threshold of Justin's lips: "Will we stop anywhere along the way?"

"Why, Earthling? Do you need a potty break?" Sorath teased.

"No. I was just curious."

"We will not have to deal with any layovers on this journey, Justin," Sandel clarified.

To that, Justin had only one thing to say: "I can't believe it. I've been good all my life, done good deeds, and helped my fellow man, and I'm still going straight to Hell!"

Everyone smiled in full appreciation of the joke. In quick order, however, the three hellions resumed their tasks, and Justin just sat back to enjoy the ride.

"How about a little music?" Sandel said with a little smirk as he turned a knob to blast AC/DC's "Highway to Hell" from the speakers.

While Sorath and Agares danced in their seats, Justin just looked at Sandel and sighed. "Great. I think I've created a monster."

Chapter 18

Upon their approach to Hell, Justin marveled at Sandel's home world. Especially interesting and surprising was that it looked very much like Earth, just as Sandel had told him. It was a beautiful, blue and green ball, surrounded by a blanket of fluffy, white clouds. Justin still couldn't believe he was about to set foot on an alien world, Hell, no less. As far as he knew, he was the only person from Earth who'd ever traveled that far in the galaxy. *Wow. My frequent flier miles balance must have just gone through the roof!* he thought to himself with a giggle. *Take that, Neil Armstrong!*

When they landed, Justin was separated from the rest of the crew, quarantined, and given a complete physical. Disease and sickness were rare on Hell, and they couldn't risk any strange Earth bacteria or viruses seeping into their population. It was also decided that his origin would remain a secret. From that point on, everyone knew Justin as simply a man Sandel had befriended during the Purgatorian War, and he was reassured that as long as he kept a low profile, no one would even think to question the story.

Of course, to go undercover fully, he had to use a codename, and Sandel thought of the perfect one. "Don Vito," he said, a callback to his love of *The Godfather*, "because you're going to the mattresses!"

After the quarantine period, Justin was reunited with Sandel, and they went directly to Lucifer's estate. As they walked into the hellish equivalent of the Oval Office, Sandel's father rose to greet them. He was slightly taller than Justin, with long, brown hair, tied in the back, and a bit of gray around his temples. A resemblance to Sean Connery ran in the Satanis family, Justin noticed. In fact, Lucifer looked a lot like Connery in his role in the 1986 *Highlander*, complete with a mustache and goatee. *Not bad for a man of 10,000 or so,* Justin thought. In fact, to Justin, the two of them looked more like brothers than father and son. He also noted that there was no sign of horns, a pitchfork, or a speared tail like that creature on the label of those Underwood Deviled Ham cans.

"Welcome to Hell!" Lucifer boomed, words Justin used to hope he would never hear, especially from the beast himself. "My son has only good things to say about you. While you are here, please consider this your home and make yourself comfortable. Now, sit. We have much to talk about."

"Thank you," Justin politely said, resisting the urge to tremble and/or beg to not be thrown in a fiery pit. "Sandel has told me many great things about you as well. Please forgive me for saying this, but you look nothing like I imagined you," Justin said.

Lucifer and Sandel both laughed, and Lucifer continued, "I am sure you will find that many things about me and Hell are contrary to what you've been taught. That is part of the reason I wanted to meet you myself before you interact with my advisers. Oh, and just in case you're wondering, I keep my horns and trident in the cabinet over there."

The unexpected humor from the king of Hell instantly calmed Justin. Suddenly, he felt welcomed and like an equal, standing there in the underworld with the devil himself.

For a long while, over an hour, they discussed Earth and the angels residing there. Sandel helped Justin explain all that he had learned, and Lucifer listened intently, hanging on every word his son and the Earthling had to say.

"I am very impressed with the amount and quality of your research," Lucifer complimented. "I am very interested in what you intend to do with your future, Earth friend, as it will be greatly extended now. "

Justin wasn't sure what Lucifer was getting at, and he dared not make any uneducated guesses about eternity or immortality, so he answered, "I-I don't know. I guess I will continue to fight against the brainwashing the Empire has imposed on Earth."

"Good. I was hoping you would say that. We would be honored for you to join us in the fight for free will and democracy for Earth, Hell, and the entire galaxy."

"I am a stranger to your world and your customs, but if you will permit me the time to learn, I will gladly stand alongside you and Sandel in the battle," Justin promised. Suddenly, he felt his cheeks flush with embarrassment as another pertinent question came to him, but he asked it anyway: "Uh, sir, I... You mentioned an extended future, and... Well, um... Will I be given the Longevity Factor?" He wasn't sure what the apprehension was all about, whether he more feared being told no or being told yes.

Lucifer looked at Justin sincerely and said, "I am afraid we must hold off on that for now. Our plans prevent us from giving it to you at this time, but rest assured that we will not deny you long life, a much longer lifespan than you would have lived had you stayed on Earth, particularly if those vicious angels or Holy Ghosts had caught up with you."

Justin instantly felt deflated and disappointed, but he trusted Lucifer and was sure he had his reasons. "Sir, I have been studying with the Illuminator," he said. "I would very much like to sit down and talk about the Dumah War."

This time, Lucifer frowned. "First of all, please call me Lucifer. Secondly, whenever you are free, I will gladly share with you anything you want to know. That is the least we can do for all you've already done for us."

After the meeting, Sandel escorted Justin home to meet his family. His wife, Lilith, was the most incredibly beautiful 5,000-year-old woman Justin had ever met. Sandel's children, Naberius and Deumos, were a delight. The little ones asked a thousand questions, just like children on any world. It was obvious to Justin right away that the home was filled with warmth and love, not the "furnace of fire" with "weeping and gnashing of teeth" he'd read about in Matthew so many times. Together, they ate a delicious dinner, then sat and talked for hours, sharing stories of Earth and Hell, family, and anything else that came to mind.

The next day, Justin met with Lucifer, Sandel, and the advisers, to discuss the intel Justin had gathered on Earth. They had all been briefed on his research and had watched all the historical content stored on the Illuminator. All were enraged by the brainwashing Earth inhabitants had unknowingly endured, including Justin. They also determined that there were still many questions that screamed for answers. Most of all, they needed to know how strong Heaven's forces were on and around Earth and if the angels were close to a decision about the fate of the planet.

As they spoke and shared ideas and concerns, the meeting took on a sense of urgency. Since Earth was already within the 50- to 100-year timeframe, they knew they had to act quickly. "Once the decision is made to pull the Earth into the Empire, it will be much more difficult to save that world," one of the advisers said. In the end, it was decided that Justin should return to his home world to discover more, but before they sent him, he would be fully trained in the ways of the angels.

Chapter 19

Justin was a bit nervous, but deep down, he couldn't wait to start his training. That all changed, though an hour before the sun rose on Hell. His trainers woke him crazy early on his first day, and Justin was surprised and more than a little put off to see that his fellow trainees were no more than 10 years old. He was told that most Hell fighters were experts by the ripe, old age of 16. That embarrassed him, but it was at no fault of his own, and he was serious about learning. Now that Justin was training to be an angel of the Alliance, he threw himself into it, 100 percent.

Considering that all of his classmates were children or adolescents, he felt a bit humiliated and dejected when he wasn't the top of the class. Two students, a male and a female, easily left him in the dust. For the first six weeks, along with his introduction into gravity manipulation and body shield control, the focus of his training was physical. He assumed it was quite like the strenuous basic training military troops underwent on Earth, except that the drill sergeants were a bit nicer. Although he was not in bad shape, the intense physical training pushed his body to the brink of exhaustion, but as the days went by, he found his fitness and stamina improving significantly.

Jarod Marbas, Justin's personal trainer and teacher, had flowing, dark hair and emerald-colored eyes. Although Justin knew he was well over 5,000 years old, he looked like a man in his forties. He was strict and pushed Justin hard, teaching him many forms of combat. It was uncanny for Justin to enjoy the training, considering that he'd always considered himself a pacifist. Now, he was becoming a warrior, and he wasn't the least bit ashamed about that.

Some days, he fell into bed bleeding and bruised, but he was always happy when he met new challenges head-on, and he never gave in to defeat. By the end, the visitor from Earth managed to surpass even Omael, the male student who'd once blown past him. Only Dabriel, the female that had Justin coughing up dust in the beginning of training, continued to best him.

After basic training ended, Justin began delving into the angelic mindset, a valuable part of their overall success. He was also trained on more thorough use of the Illuminator, so he could utilize all the benefits of it. His teacher for this part of his training was Jarod's daughter, Salome, an attractive woman. She had something of an Asian look about her, complete with black hair and brown eyes. She pushed him even harder than her father had, and Justin found himself working harder to impress her.

Soon, he realized what an amazing teaching tool the Illuminator really was. With it, he studied galactic history, mathematics, physics, astrophysics, and more. Shockingly, he understood it all, even subjects he'd never touched on in high school or college. Just halfway through his training, he was far smarter than the most intelligent human on Earth. He would have loved to sit and talk with the late Stephen Hawking, as there were now a few things he could teach him. It saddened him to ask himself, *If Hawking had been given the Longevity Factor and could have learned from the Illuminator, how much further could that great thinker have advanced the understanding of the universe?*

Another beautiful mind among humans was that of Albert Einstein. During his training with the Illuminator, Justin was reminded of a quote from him: "The more I learn, the more I realize how much I don't know." That turned out to be very true, because the more Justin learned, the more he discovered how very unaware he had been and still was. The revelation of his ignorance only fueled his thirst for more knowledge, to the point where he sometimes willingly traded sleep for learning; that was a far cry different from his schooling on Earth, when he was often caught sleeping during his early classes.

Justin was also taught how to resist the probing properties of the Illuminator, a crucial skill. Because they could not afford any vulnerabilities in their fighters, Salome stressed that part of his training more than any other. "This will be most important for you to know if you are ever captured by the Empire," she explained, in no uncertain terms. He even learned how to manipulate the probe to give false readings. It only worked if interrogators were unaware that he knew about the Illuminator before the procedure. His captures would have to assume that Justin's was a fresh mind. So, just as he had in every area of his training, he gave it his all and learned everything quickly. He wanted to be safe and valuable in the battle, but it was also because he had a strong desire to live up to the faith Sandel and Lucifer had placed in him. Not only that, but truth be told, some of his success was owed to trying to impress a certain brown-eyed trainer, though all of his teachers were pleased by his progress in every area.

Nine months later, his training was complete, though he vowed that he would never stop learning. He was proficient in manipulating gravity, so much so that he often pushed himself outside the atmosphere of Hell to test his control of the body shield. He had never been in such good physical shape on Earth, even in his prime, his lean, muscular physique even surprised him. "Once the Longevity Factor is administered," Jarod explained, "you will witness even greater changes."

During his training, he came to know Jarod and Salome as friends. When he was not with Sandel, he was with one or both of them. Sandel and Jarod were childhood friends, which placed him at somewhere around 5,000 years older than Justin, but he knew, sure as he was alive, that either of the ancient ones could have kicked his butt on a whim, without even breaking a sweat. Nevertheless, that didn't stop

Justin from letting them know, every once in a while, "Y'all are a couple of really old bastards," to which they called him something akin to Hell's version of a whippersnapper and went about their business.

Chapter 20

One night as Sandel, Lilith, Jarod, Salome, and Justin sat around the living room, celebrating Jarod's birthday, Sandel said, "Jarod, I think now is as good time as any to tell him."

Justin, suddenly realizing that he was the only other him there, said, "Who me? Tell me what?"

"I guess you are right, old friend," Jarod said, rubbing his chin. "Justin, Earth is not new to us. We have known about your planet for thousands of years. Besides that, group of angels who resided on Earth for a while, those who were forced to leave, I have been there myself."

"Wait. Another group of angels lived on Earth?" Justin asked. "You mean other than the troublemakers there now?"

"Yes, but that is a story for another day," Jarod vaguely answered. He then went on to regale Justin with the story of his mission to Earth over 400 years ago, his mission to explore developing planets to catalog them as possible contact worlds. "I first visited your world in the beginning of the sixteenth century," he said. "I traveled throughout Europe, seeking the most intelligent minds Earth had to offer. While in Florence, Italy, I met a man named Leonardo da Vinci, and we became fast friends."

"Whoa! You knew da Vinci?" Justin asked, amazed.

"Of course. Leonardo and I spent many nights together, drinking wine, experiencing the local night life, and discussing the universe. He was a very smart man, truly ahead of his time, but he was not much for the ladies.

"On my second visit to Earth some fifty years later, in France this time, I met someone you may have heard of, Nostradamus. He was very devoted healing his fellow humans. He seemed like a decent fellow, but something about him bothered me. My instincts proved right when I caught him going through my things one night. Can you believe that asshole ran off with my Illuminator? It took me two days to finally track him down and retrieve it. I tried to explain to him that what he saw was fantasy, but he was intent on moving toward the occult at the time, and he was sure he had seen the future. After learning of recent history and the effect of his predictions on some Earthlings of today, I can only say I am truly sorry.

"On my third and final visit to your world, I found myself in England in 1687, at a party at the home of Isaac Newton, who was celebrating the publication of his latest book. There, I met a woman, so beautiful she took my breath away. Anh was the niece one of the Newton's guests, and her parents had passed away when she was a little girl in Vietnam. Her hair was as black as a raven's feathers, and her eyes were brown. Her unforgettable smile captured my heart. We spent much time together over the next few weeks and became the talk of London society.

"Justin, I found I could not lie to that endearing woman. I told her everything, and somehow, she knew it to be true. We married a month later and told everyone we planned to move to the American colonies. Instead, I brought her here, to my home, and we never looked back. She never left my side. Anh gave me many years of true happiness, a beautiful daughter, and a lifetime of wonderful memories." A tear ran down his face as he held Salome close. "She died during the Purgatorian War. She believed in the cause and fought with everything she had to defend freedom for all living beings."

As a tear ran down his own face, Justin slowly came to the realization that Salome was the daughter Jarod had spoken of, and her Vietnamese roots explained her Asian appearance. He remained silent for a moment before offering, "Your

Salome is the child of the best of both worlds."

That remark pulled a smile onto Jarod's face, and the talk became much lighter after that, but Justin's thoughts couldn't seem to stop dancing around Salome.

Chapter 21

As he lunched with Sandel and Salome in his new favorite restaurant, fittingly dubbed Hell's Kitchen, Justin glanced out the window and saw a group of older people wearing uniform attire, all riding vehicles that looked similar to motorcycles. The two-wheeled contraptions didn't appear to have gasoline engines, and whatever the power source was, they were completely quiet. "Who are they?" he asked. "Are they law enforcement or something?"

Sandel explained, "They are basically retired soldiers, angels who once served under my father on Heaven."

Justin pondered that for a moment, then let loose with a small laugh.

Salome looked over at him in puzzlement, arching a brow at him. "What's so funny?"

Justin wouldn't have expected her to see the humor in it, but he answered, "Hell's Angels…literally, bikes and all," he said, then chuckled again. To their blank expressions, he could only say, "I'll explain later, my friends."

"An Earth thing, huh?" Sandel said.

"Yes, Sandel. An Earth thing," Justin said, shaking his head before taking another bite of his tasty hellish fare.

Soon, Salome excused herself to teach an afternoon class, and Justin watched as she walked out of the restaurant. A thought suddenly occurred to him, and he glanced over at Sandel. "Hey, remember the story you told me back at the cabin, about the girl who came between you and Jesus? She must have been quite a woman if two of Heaven's most eligible bachelors were fighting over her. What happened to her? Did you dump her as soon as the next fine piece of tail came along?"

Sandel smiled and answered, "You should know. You've met her."

Justin's mind raced through all the females he'd been introduced to since his arrival on Hell. While there were many attractive, alluring ladies of the underworld, none jumped out as a potential divider of worlds. "Who?" he asked.

Sandel's grin broadened. "She is home with my children now," he said, wearing a smug, pleased-with-himself expression. "I fell in love with her, and I am happy to say that she is the only woman I have ever loved."

Justin's face burned red with embarrassment. "Oh. Sorry about that tail remark then."

"Don't be. As far as that is concerned, there is no finer piece in all the galaxy," Sandel answered with a wink. He then laughed again as Justin squirmed awkwardly in his seat. "It is truly okay, my friend. Luckily for me, Lilith has chosen to give her fine piece of tail only to me."

***

As the time neared for Justin to make his return to Earth, he began meeting daily with Lucifer and his council. They went through every scenario they could think of, and prepared the best they could for anything that might happen. Ultimately, they all knew the success of the mission would rely on Justin's quick thinking. While the Earthling would basically have to rely on himself, it brought him some comfort to know that there would be some angels on Earth to serve as backup if he needed them. In fact, angels from Hell had infiltrated and assimilated themselves into Earth's society some time ago, right after Sandel initially returned to Hell.

Just one month, and I'll be home, Justin thought. He wasn't exactly homesick, because he enjoyed his friends, and Hell was a spectacular place, but he had a mission to accomplish. His objective was set, and he knew what he needed to do. It would be dangerous, but many had worked to ensure that he was as ready as he could be. His fate and the fate of everyone on Earth were in his hands, and the survival of his home world hinged on his success. hinging on the success of his mission.

Before he left, he wanted to spend as much time as he could with his newfound friends. He and Salome went out almost every night to eat, take long strolls together, and, mostly, to talk. It puzzled Justin, that two beings from completely different worlds could have so much in common, but he enjoyed her company, and she seemed to feel the same.

On the day prior to his return to Earth, Sandel hosted at his home, and everyone came to bid Justin a fond farewell. It was a delight to see Lucifer with his grandchildren, rolling around on the floor, wrestling with his grandson, and having a pretend tea party with his granddaughter and three dolls. Justin could only sheepishly smile at the thought that he once believed the man was the father of lies, the most vile creature in the universe.

Later, as Justin walked into the kitchen to help clean up, Lilith walked over to him. "A fine piece of tail, huh?"

Justin's face again burned bright red. He stammered, "Uh, I-I-I'm sorry! I, uh…didn't mean anything. Look, it's really a compliment…sort of, I guess."

Lilith laughed and placed a friendly hand on his shoulder. "Oh, I am not mad. I actually want to thank you."

"For what?"

"For validating my theory that men are the same wherever you go!" With that, she gave him a sweet kiss on the cheek, then headed back to the party.

On the day Justin left, there was an impressive crowd there to see him off, the evidence that he'd made a great number of friends during his time on Hell. Even his young competitors from his angel training were there to wish him well.

After the goodbyes and well-wishes were exchanged with Justin's friends and Sandel's family, Lucifer, Sandel, and Jarod took him aside for some last-minute instructions.

As usual, Lucifer spoke first: "Justin, be very careful. I have known Michael for a very long time, and he is an extremely dangerous individual. Do not underestimate his power."

Then, just before he entered the ship, Salome pulled him aside. "I will miss you, Justin."

"I will miss you too. I—"

Before he could finish his heartfelt sentiment, she pulled him close and gave him a deep, passionate kiss. He put his arms around her, and greedily kissed her back as the last call sounded.

"I have to go," Justin said, looking deeply into her beautiful eyes.

"I know...but I will be here when you return. Be safe," she said, "and remember all we've taught you."

Justin entered the ship wishing he had more time to travel down that unexpected romantic road. Moments later, he found himself moving quickly toward the space over Hell. Soon, he would be back on his beautiful Earth.

Anticipation for the days ahead made him squirm in his seat again, but thoughts of Salome and getting safely back to her took his mind off any fear or trepidation he had. No matter what happened during his mission, whether he would return successful or not, he could not wait to explore that new development with Salome. He had not felt that way about anyone since his wife Leah was still alive. When that thought passed through his mind, Justin suddenly felt a bit of fear and guilt, as if he was cheating on her, but he didn't know if he could help himself.

Chapter 22

The three-man Alliance shuttle carried Justin as close to Earth as possible without attracting the Empire's attention. They decided to park in the same crater where Sandel had almost four years before, just across the border on the far side of the moon.

With just one gentle push against the moon, Justin was on his way. As he crossed the horizon, an emotional rush hit him hard. When the vivid blues, greens, and whites of Planet Earth came into view, uninhibited tears formed in his eyes. Even though he had witnessed the same sight upon his departure from the planet, he knew it would never become mundane. He wanted to stop and just take in the beauty of the Earth in her perfect rotation, but time would not allow it. Knowing he had much work to do, Justin pushed with maximum force against the moon, and he soon reached optimal speed. After one last look at his beautiful mother world, he activated autopilot, followed by the hibernation sequence, just as Sandel had taught him to conserve his life support.

If his calculations were correct, Justin would soon be standing on Earth, about a half-mile from the cave where they'd diligently hidden the supplies he'd need upon his return. About 5,000 miles outside Earth's atmosphere, he awoke and began pushing to slow his fall. Unlike the case during Sandel's descent, Justin was in no danger of losing life support, and he could make a controlled landing with ease.

He marveled at the comfort he felt as the friction of the atmosphere burned hot all around him. That passed quickly, however, as Justin slowed further and landed gently. A smile was the only sign of his pride over the expertise with which he had managed to control the gravity for his perfect landing. He knew he had many to thank for the expert training he'd received, and he thought again of Sandel and the beautiful Salome. As planned, he was only about a half-mile from the cave.

At night, the going was a little slow, but he made it to the cave in about twenty-five minutes. He couldn't chance being caught, and he had to stay under the radar until everything was in place, so trekking to the cabin was out of the question. He dug out the Army foot locker that contained his duffle bag full of money, clothes, and night-vision goggles. He quickly changed and stored anything and everything that could connect him with Hell, then buried the locker again. There were still three hours of darkness left to camouflage him as he made his way to the car he'd stashed just outside of town. Although he knew the way by heart, it was a treacherous hike in the dark, so he whispered some thanks to himself for remembering to pack those night-vision goggles.

As he walked, Justin marveled at the scent of the forest, the woodsy, earthy aroma he'd missed. The chorus of the multitude of insects looking for love on a beautiful night was something to behold. He didn't know if it was because of his training on Hell or because it had been a while since he'd been there, but he seemed to hear every nuance of the symphony erupting around him.

Two hours later, he was motoring north on I-65. "Ah, these Midwest summer mornings," he mumbled to himself. For Justin, there was nothing quite like riding in a car with the windows down as the cool of the night turned to the warmth of a new day.

His first stop was in Fort Wayne, Indiana, about 130 miles north of Indianapolis. He sat in a restaurant and ordered a coffee, then used their public Wi-Fi to check on his website. He logged in as an administrator and purposely created new posts and updates that he knew would attract the attention of those who were looking for him. That would accomplish two things: First, it would put his pursuers on notice that their adversary had returned; and, second, it would help to distract them from realizing where he'd been hiding all along. The last thing they needed to know was that he'd undergone effective training on Hell itself.

After a carb-heavy, yummy, greasy country breakfast, Justin resumed his trip, moving toward Indianapolis. He didn't know if his enemies had the capability to track him, maybe with satellites or something, like they did in the movies, but he wasn't ready to be captured yet. In downtown Indy, he pulled into a busy parking garage and transferred his stuff to another car he'd left there in long-term storage. He waited about twenty minutes before he exited in his new ride. It was one of only many vehicles he'd scattered strategically throughout the Midwest during the three years of Sandel's absence, and that former paranoia was paying off now.

There were also several locations where Justin had stashed money and supplies, so he visited those to stock up for his mission. He then traveled to Chesterfield, about thirty miles northeast, to look in on his parents. It pained him to watch them from a distance, like some kind of spy, and he missed them greatly. He longed to tell them everything, wanted to ease their worries about him, but he knew now was not the time. *If I want to save them, I have to stay away from them for now,* he told himself.

Once he was sure his mother and father were okay, he continued his journey north. He'd secured a little place near Big Otter Lake, in the northeast corner of Indiana, about a mile from where I-69 crossed the Indiana east-west toll road. It was the perfect location because it gave him quick exit routes in all directions, should the need arise for him to flee.

Raum, an agent from Hell who could have been Justin's twin, and with a few minor tweaks, was spot-on doppelganger, had occupied the safe house for the last nine months to create the appearance that Justin was still alive and well on Planet Earth. Justin met his lookalike in a hotel near Fremont and thanked him profusely, and Raum was quick to fill Justin in on all that had transpired while he was gone. Through the Illuminator, Raum gave Justin his memories of his life near Big Otter Lake, including all the comings and goings of his neighbors.

After that, there was nothing left to do but switch cars and get on with his new life. He figured he had about a week before all Heaven would break loose. He settled into his new home, interacted with neighbors, worked around the yard, shopped, fished, and managed to get an overall feel for the new area. He knew all of that would strengthen the memories of his life around Big Otter Lake for the past nine months.

Once Justin felt he had cemented the foundation of the deception Raum had helped him generate, he went to a coffee shop in Fremont, just a few miles east. He logged into *TheSerpentsGift.com* as site administrator and explained that his recent absence had been due to a much-needed vacation, then mentioned that he hoped it had not caused any inconvenience. He answered emails from a few of his favorite followers and updated the site with new information that was sure to attract the attention of Earth's heavenly hosts.

From this point on, he made daily trips to the coffee shop to enjoy the atmosphere and manage his website, purposely skipping a couple days here and there to avoid stirring up any suspicion.

Near the end of the second week, as he sipped from a cup of his favorite brew, he noticed a pretty blonde with a to-die-for smile, a girl he'd seen there for at least the past three days. As he studied her, their eyes met, but she quickly looked away. Thinking that a bit odd, he went about his business and acted as oblivious as he could, but he kept a watchful eye on her.

The next day, before he went to the coffee shop, Justin left the Illuminator memory storage at one of his clandestine pickup locations, where one of the agents would pick it up and send it to Hell. He couldn't help but marvel at the beauty and usefulness of the Illuminator. He quickly finished a little shopping before, then made his way to the coffee shop.

This time, he did not see the blonde when he first scanned the room, but a short while later, he spotted her in the corner, hidden by other patrons. She was talking casually to another customer, looking every bit as normal as the other cappuccino connoisseurs and latte lovers who surrounded him. *Maybe I was wrong about her,* he thought. *After all, humans are nothing if not creatures of habit.*

After dismissing the thought that the pretty girl was up to something, Justin went on about his normal business. However, a little while later, when the waiter brought him a second cup of coffee, he noticed a note on the napkin. It appeared to be written in coffee but was legible, and he read it under his breath:

"They are watching. Do nothing to attract attention. Meet me as soon as possible. Lives depend on it." It was signed, HellsWarrior32, with a time and place for their rendezvous.

HellsWarrior32? Justin considered, for it was a name he recognized as the online handle of one of the followers who frequented his website. He looked up at the blonde, and she looked away once again; this time, however, she first offered a nearly imperceptible nod. He stared at the napkin for a moment more to memorize the time and place, then feigned an accidental coffee spill. He used the napkin to wipe up the beverage splashes, making sure the information it contained was destroyed. When Justin looked up again, the girl was gone.

Chapter 23

At around 8:00 that evening, he drove his car south on I-69. A little over a half-hour later, he pulled into the parking lot at a strip mall in Auburn, Indiana. There, he sat in his car, awaiting a signal.

At 9 o'clock, the woman from the coffee shop came out of one of the stores, and got in her car.

Justin stepped out of his vehicle and headed her way, wondering who she was and what she was going to tell him.

She unlocked her car, and nodded for him to climb in.

"Warrior32?" Justin inquired.

"Yes. We have to hurry," she said nervously, looking around.

"I have a few questions first," Justin countered.

"Sure, but not here," she said as she started the car. She briskly pulled out of the parking lot, taking a turn so fast that her tires screeched in agony against the pavement.

Justin persisted, "Okay, tell me what this is all about."

"Look, the same people who are after you are after me," she said, glancing in her rearview mirror as if she suspected they were being followed. "Just know we're on your side," she said. "Ever since you opened our eyes to the truth, we've been researching, looking for proof of the ideas on your website. We've learned that much of what you say is true. Wow. I can't believe I've actually got you right here with me, in my car."

Justin looked over at her and again wondered what

he'd gotten himself into. Thoughts of Stephen King's *Misery* screamed in his head. *Dear God. Is this some modern-day Annie Wilkes? If she says, 'I'm your number one fan,' I'm jumping out of this damn car!*

After one more look in the rearview mirror, she relaxed a bit. She noticed the petrified look in his eyes and said, "Look, I'm not some crazed fan girl, if that's what you're thinking. I'm not a kook or an axe murderer, so chill."

Justin felt heat rush into his cheeks, and he suddenly felt very silly. On the other hand, though, he felt he had every right to know what was going on. "Tell me more right now, or let me out of this car," he demanded.

She slowed the car a bit, sighed, and calmly said, "Fine. I'm a card-carrying member of Followers of the Truth."

"Okay..." Justin said, urging her on.

"Well, as I said, ever since you opened our eyes, it's been our mission to find out everything we can about you and your cause. In so doing, we have inadvertently drawn the attention of the same people who are on your tail. We know you've been in hiding since your very creative escape from your home nine months ago."

"Oh."

She smiled. "Yeah, we know about that too."

It suddenly occurred to Justin that he had no idea where she was taking him, but before he could ask to be sure she wasn't hauling him off to some snowy cabin somewhere to be hobbled, she pulled into the parking lot of a hotel near the interstate.

The blonde looked over her shoulder once more, then said, "We're here. C'mon."

They got out of the car, and she led him to a room on the ground level. She knocked on the door in some kind of rhythm reminiscent of Morse code, and someone opened it to allow them entrance to the dark room. Once the door was locked and bolted, and after one last look out the window, someone flicked on the lights, revealing six very nervous people sitting on the chairs and beds.

Warrior32 made the introductions, using only their screen names: "Meet BeelzebubsBrother75, HellHathNoFury666, LucifersLady88, TruthBSatan105, SatansLittleGirl82, and Triple6Soldier," she said.

Of the thousands of names, he'd communicated with as administrator, those stuck out as frequent flyers, his most loyal and worthy followers. For this reason, it didn't take him long to warm up to them, because he felt like he knew them a little already, due to interacting with them on his boards and forum posts and comments on his blogs.

LucifersLady88, a brown-haired cutie with a killer smile, gave him a bottle of water, and he listened as each of them told stories of the journeys that brought them to that very room. While they all lived different lives and came from different backgrounds, there was one common theme: a need to warn him of imminent danger.

"If we found you, they can't be far behind," they chorused before they unanimously pledged their full support. "We're here for you if you ever need us."

"That's a good thing, because we might," Justin said. He knew the Alliance needed every soldier they could find to help them fight the forces of Heaven, so he was glad to have that web-savvy militia on his side.

While he instantly liked the majority of them, the one who called himself Triple6Soldier made him a little uneasy. He had the look of an American Indian, with long, dark hair and strong, chiseled features. He was a good-looking kid, not a typical website nerd. Nevertheless, he didn't seem to trust Justin and kept looking at him with a scrutinizing eye. Then, when the time came for Justin to leave, Triple6Soldier said, "I should go with you."

HellsWarrior32 quickly replied, "No! We cannot afford to be seen together. I'll see you when I get back. Then we'll head out."

"Is that Triple6 always wound that tight?" Justin asked when they were back in her car.

"He's not. It's just... Well, he cares about me and wants to keep me safe. Between you and me, I think he might be a little jealous. By the way, my real name is Becky Simms. I'm from Chicago."

"Nice to meet you, Becky Simms from Chicago," Justin

said with a smile. "I'm Justin from... Well, you already know that, I'm sure."

"Yeah, we know a lot," she said with a wink. "You know what those old ads said. Knowing is half the battle!"

"Maybe, but it's the other half I'm worried about," Justin teased.

Soon, they pulled back into the strip mall parking lot. As he climbed out of the car, he told Becky to be careful and encouraged her to keep in touch. He couldn't help but wish he had many more followers like those he'd just met, but he also hoped they wouldn't get in the way of his mission, as he didn't want anyone to get hurt.

At a quarter past midnight, he finally returned to his place. He went straight to bed, and sleep came quickly.

The next few days dragged on like most of his days since embarking on his new life. However, on the third day after the meeting, as he was lying down, a frantic knock came at the door.

"Wh-Who is it?" he yelled sleepily. "Who's there?" he asked with a yawn, startled awake.

"Justin, it's me, Becky. Please let me in!" she cried.

Justin hopped up and quickly ran to open the door, and she nearly fell into his arms from the others side. "What's wrong?" he asked, with worry dripping from his voice.

"They-They got her! They took her!"

"Who? Who, Becky?" Justin asked.

"LucifersLady88...and they almost got me," she said, sobbing hard.

Quickly, he locked the door behind her and guided her to his couch.

For the next few moments, Becky cried and stammered through the traumatic events of her day. She and LucifersLady88, who Justin now knew as Jennifer Lundy, were supposed to meet at fast-food place in Fremont. "She said she discovered something important, and she wanted to show it to me. I-I waited, but she never showed up," Becky said, sniffling. "I called, but she wouldn't answer or return my calls, so I decided to drive by her house. I knocked and called her name, but it seemed no one was home. I knocked harder, and the door slid open. The front room was a wreck. I thought I'd better check the whole house, and... Oh my God! It was horrible!"

"What?" Justin gently coaxed. "What happened, Becky?"

"I-I found J-Jennifer lying on the bathroom floor, with a bloody hole in the middle of her forehead. She just looked up at me with those eyes, staring with those dead eyes!" she cried. "I-I f-found this in her hand." Shaking, she lifted a broken chain that Justin remembered as the one Triple6Soldier had been wearing when they met. With that, she burst into tears, and Justin just let her cry and patted her back.

When Becky finally calmed down enough to fall asleep on his couch, he sat and watched her. She was fitful, obviously having nightmares, and she kept trembling. As he was covering her with a blanket, the door burst open.

"Bitch!" Triple6Soldier yelled, his face a picture of rage.

Justin tried to intercept him, but Triple6Soldier pushed him aside and screamed again, "You bitch!"

BLAM!

What the...? When the gunshot rang out, knocking Triple6 to the floor, Justin struggled to wrap his thoughts around what was happening. He glanced up, only to see Becky standing there with a smoking gun.

The shooter was trembling and breathing rapidly, her eyes wide. She looked at the weapon and quickly opened her hand to let it fall to the floor, then scurried away from it as if it were a poisonous snake. "I-I had to," she stuttered. "He's... He was one of them!"

Justin crawled over to check on the fallen Triple6Soldier. His pulse was weak, his breathing labored, and there was a pool of blood around his head. "What the hell, Becky?" he said, looking up at her. "Why? And where in the hell did you get a gun?"

"He's crazy, Justin. He killed Jennifer and came here to kill me. We gotta get out of here before *they* show up. Let's go! Now!" she said, wide-eyed and sounding a little crazy herself.

"Hold up. He's hurt badly, but he's not dead. We have to call 911 and—" Justin said in a yelling tone, only to be interrupted.

"No way!" she retorted, shaking her head wildly. "If they catch us, we're dead. We have to run!"

Ignoring her, Justin reached for the phone. Just as he began to dial the last digit to call for help, four men rushed through the door. Two grabbed him, and the others crossed the room and cornered the screaming Becky. Justin watched as they sprayed something in her face, some sort of chemical that knocked her out cold. He could do nothing for her as she fell limply into their arms, for he was struggling to free himself from the grasp of the others. A moment later, he felt a mist of moisture in his face, and the world fell away as he was engulfed by a dreamless darkness.

Chapter 24

Consciousness came in waves of confusion as Justin opened his eyes and struggled to focus on his surroundings. Still lying down, he surmised that he was being held in some sort of eight-by-ten-foot cinderblock room. There was a sink and a toilet, but all the walls and the floor were cold and rock hard. He tried to sit up, but dizziness forced him to recline again. He waited for a few more minutes, then tried again, more slowly this time, and managed to maneuver his body into a seated position.

As his mind cleared a bit, he realized he wasn't in a regular jail or prison cell; it was isolated, with no windows. He had no way of knowing how long he'd been out, where he was, or exactly why he was here. One thing he did notice was that his solitary confinement wasn't exactly solitary.

On the other side of the room, Becky was still unconscious from whatever they'd been sprayed with. Justin walked slowly and a bit clumsily over to her, hugging the wall all the way, and tried to revive her, to no avail.

He spent the next half-hour checking every square inch of the cell. Everything that was not cinderblock was bolted securely to the floor or walls, and there were no sharp corners anywhere. Even the mattress was made of a material he couldn't tear, so hanging himself or fashioning any kind of rope was out of the question.

He was just checking the vent covers when Becky made

a sound that scared the crap out of him. Even though Justin had been trained for a captive situation, it was then that he realized just how on edge he was. *I've gotta calm down,* he told himself as he walked back over to her to prepare her for the shock when her mind cleared from that dreamless sleep, only to realize she was caught in a real, waking nightmare.

For the next few hours, Becky was inconsolable. She was a quick study in the five stages of dying. First, she went from denial, "This can't be happening" to anger, "This is all your fault! If you hadn't created that damn website." Next came the bargaining phase: "Please let me out! I'll do anything." Finally, she settled into a nice depression and brooded in the fetal position on her bed. Acceptance would come later.

When she finally calmed down enough to communicate somewhat rationally, Justin decided it would be wise to give her a physical checkup. She seemed okay, other than a few scrapes and bruises. He had already checked himself out but asked her about some pain he felt in his back that he could almost reach but could not see.

"It's just a scratch…and a big, purple and yellow bruise that looks like Africa," she said.

After what Justin assumed was about twenty–four hours, the lock clicked, and the door flung open. This time, there were only three men. Two grabbed Justin, and the other held the screaming, flailing Becky back while he was dragged from the cell.

"Where are you taking me?" Justin demanded. Then, when no response seemed forthcoming, he yelled, "Why am I here? What do you want from me? The girl is innocent. Just let her go."

His silent captors pulled him into a room much like his cell, except that it was furnished with a lone chair to which they promptly and snugly strapped him. Once they were confident Justin's bindings were secure, the men drew some blood from his arm and then left him alone.

An hour or so later, a familiar but undetermined voice filled the room. "Good morning, Mr. Grant," the voice said. "You, sir, are in a lot of trouble."

"What trouble? I've done nothing wrong," Justin respond-

"You don't feel murder is wrong, Mr. Grant?" the voice snidely asked.

"Murder!? Whoa! If you're talking about the man at my house, you are mistaken. He broke in and tried to attack Becky, so she shot him in self-defense. I've never touched a gun in my life," Justin said, with more than a little anger in his voice.

"Then how do you explain your fingerprints on the gun and the ammunition?" the interrogator asked.

"That's impossible! I never..." Justin trailed off, sickened by the sudden realization that it was a setup. "Look, if I am being charged with a crime, then read me my rights and give me my phone call."

"I'm afraid it's not that simple, Mr. Grant. Why not confess and let go the burdens of your heart?"

That was the last thing Justin heard before the voice went silent and the lights dimmed. As he sat there with that stupid question lingering in his mind, dawned on him where he'd heard the voice before: *That's Brown! Reverend Gabe Brown.* It was that last statement that sealed it for him, although the reverend's actual words were usually, "Confess your sins to Jesus, let go of the burdens of your heart, ask for forgiveness, and the promise of Heaven will be yours forever more."

Soon, the only thing he could physically hear was his breathing, but his mind was racing with a cacophony of thought. Now, Justin knew for certain that he was in the hands of Jesus' angels, and that brought him no comfort whatsoever.

Somehow, Justin managed a few hours of uncomfortable sleep. His slumber was broken, however, when the door to his new cell creaked open and a strikingly handsome man in an expensive-looking, gray suit walked in. While Justin was not one to find himself physically attracted to men, he had to admit that this one was probably the most physically perfect individual he had ever seen. His shoulder-length blond locks were tied back, and his features were striking. The only being who could even compare to this man's elegant aesthetic was

Lucifer, as far as Justin was concerned.

"Good morning, Justin. I can call you by your first name, can I not?"

Justin remained silent, resisting the urge to spout a horrid chain of four-letter words as his joints and muscles ached from sleeping while tied to a chair.

"You may call me Michael."

Yeah, I know a few things I'd like to call you, buddy, Justin silently seethed.

"I need a few answers before we can proceed. Your life seems to be a contradiction. For your first twenty-eight years, you followed a very religious path. Then, a few years ago, you suddenly turned your back on all of your beliefs. Why? What in Heaven's name turned you away?"

Justin just stared at him, his eyes flaming with anger.

Unfazed by his prisoner's defiance, Michael continued, "Even the horrific tragedy of the loss of your family did not shake your faith. In fact, I daresay it may have strengthened it."

At that point, at the mention of Leah and his lost child, Justin could no longer hold his tongue. "Leave my family out of this!"

Michael continued, "I'm sorry. I mean no disrespect, but I need to know what happened."

"You need to kiss my ass!" Justin spat, just before intense pain tore through his body. It wasn't until a moment later that he realized he'd been screaming and was sore all over.

During his questioning, all sarcastic comebacks or blatant lies were followed by immediate punishment. This came in the form of intense pain. Every molecule in his body seemed to scream out at once. It was like being kicked in the jewels and feeling it everywhere. Justin wanted nothing more than to rip the bastard's head right off his body, but he was too drained to even hold his own head up by the time the inquisition was over.

Such torture dragged on for what seemed like a couple weeks. Every day, he was dragged to the interrogation room, strapped down, and endured Michael's endless questions about his fall from grace and why had he turned his back on God. Completely ignoring Justin's questions about the murder or Becky, Michael just kept asking, "What happened to you? You were once a man of God."

Bravely or stupidly, or maybe a little of both, Justin looked into his eyes and replied, "I had an epiphany. For the first time in my life, my eyes were open to the truth."

"An epiphany? What caused it, and what truth did you see? Do tell," Michael inquired.

"Hmm. Well, I think it was a candy bar, and the truth I saw is that you are an asshole," Justin said, then waited for the pain to begin.

When it finally ended, he felt as if he'd grabbed hold of a live power line. He was trembling from head to toe, his body racked with pain. Not one muscle or bone in his body was saved from aching, throbbing, burning, and stinging.

Finally, Michael released the bonds that held Justin in the chair. He grabbed Justin and, with one hand, picked him up by the throat and slammed him against the cold, concrete wall. He held him there for what seemed like an eternity and hissed, "Your sarcasm is unwelcome here. Be careful how you speak to me. You may not like me, but you will respect me; you insignificant piece of human dirt." Then, Michael dropped him to the floor as if he weighed no more than a discarded paper wad.

Justin, crumpled and broken, fell silent.

After hours of more questioning, he was taken back to a cell exactly like the one he had been taken from, except that Becky was no longer there. That was when the real torture began. Hymns and songs, he'd learned in Sunday School as a child were played over and over, sometimes softly but sometimes almost too loudly to bear, screaming rhyming dogma at him in surround sound.

The music he once appreciated because he felt it spoke to his heart and brought comfort to his soul, he now despised with a passion. As he lay on his mattress trying to sleep, his training kicked in. He began to pick up on the faint subliminal messages in the music: "Confess your sins... Jesus loves you... Ask the Lord for forgiveness." *Jesus loves me, my ass!*

thought Justin. The music was speaking to him, but there was no comfort in it anymore.

Between hymns, he sometimes heard Becky screaming. He feared she was being tortured, too, but he could do nothing to relieve her pain. *Be strong, Becky, be strong,* Justin thought, with a tear in his eye for the beautiful girl who'd left so many posts on his website.

As it all became quite routine, Justin realized he needed to act as if they were weakening him, so they would not suspect that he'd been through training on Hell. He stopped asking about where he was and when would it stop, and he stopped begging them to free Becky, showing his resignation to the fact that they were not going to answer. He did his best to act the way they would expect a normal human to act, a human who had not interacted so directly with their enemies on Hell.

One day as he was taken to the room of pain and questions, a door in the hallway was left open. As Justin passed that door, he noticed what looked like a photo of Caribbean on the far wall. He tried to read the caption under the map, but the door was quickly closed before he could discern any of the words. That brief few seconds of scenery from the outside world was the only deviation he'd experienced since the day he arrived.

Justin wasn't sure how long he had been there, but he felt it had been at least seven or eight days. Thanks to his training on Hell, he had given them only what the Alliance wanted them to have. Of course, he had to make it seem as if they'd forced even that out of him, and that was the hard part.

Most of all, he worried about Becky. He hadn't seen her for a long time. He thought of her every minute but refused to ask about her any longer. All he could do was hope she was okay. He wondered if she had been arrested for the murder of Triple6Soldier. Worse, he feared she might have been eliminated, since she really knew nothing and also knew too much. For that reason, her screams brought him some twisted relief; *At least she's alive,* he thought when he heard her cries. He figured she was strapped into the chair, being asked questions for which she had no answers. Unlike him, Becky was untrained, so Justin feared for her safety and hoped like hell that she would not give up the names of her fellow Followers of the Truth. Talk about lambs to the slaughter, he grimly pondered. Although Becky nor her group could really do much to spoil his mission, they would likely all face the same torturous agony he and Becky had endured if they were caught. *And that really would be all my fault,* Justin thought, consumed by the pain of such an idea.

Chapter 25

About a week later, in Justin's best estimation, everything changed. They came to his cell to escort him to the
room of questions, but when they reached the hallway that
led there, they took a sharp left rather than turning right.
they led him to a door at the end of the corridor, and his
mind spun with horrific thoughts of what horrors might lie
behind it.

When the door opened, he was surprised to find that
it led outdoors. It was nighttime, but even in the dark, the
smell of fresh air and the warm breeze that teased at the
sweat on his face felt wonderful. He was unsure of the time or
even what day it was, and he strained to find any reference to
his location.

He was taken to a black, windowless van and thrown in
the back. He slammed into something soft, but he couldn't
tell what it was in the dark. Only a moment later, when he
heard soft crying, did he realize he'd been thrown up against
Becky. It took a few moments for his eyes to focus in the
dark.

Before any words came, she put her handcuffed hands
around his neck and hugged him tight. "I-I thought maybe
you were dead," she said with a sniffle.

"I wondered the same thing about you. C'mere," Justin
coaxed, smiling broadly at her.

When she saw the gleaming of his grin in the darkness,

she snuggled into his cuffed arms, and they both shared a good cry.

After about ten minutes of silence, both of them just enjoying the reunion and happy they were still alive, Becky softly said, "Goddamn religious music!"

Despite their circumstances, they laughed hard, and it felt good to be with each other.

As he'd been advised to do in his training, Justin tried to memorize turns and to estimate the speed they were traveling. After a short while, he lost track, so he sat back and did his best to comfort Becky.

POP!

About an hour into the trip, the van started swerving, throwing the cargo against the sides in the back, causing them to moan and groan. The driver did his best to maintain control, but he overcompensated, and the vehicle tipped over on its side and skidded for a distance, throwing sparks off the pavement. It stopped suddenly when it struck something.

Justin and Becky were thrown violently against the front wall of their moving prison cell. Although Justin was sure nothing was broken, he felt bruises and gashes all over his face, and he felt a warm trickle of blood from a deep laceration in his forehead. He heard Becky whimpering, so he rolled over to check on her.

After a moment of self-assessment, she assured Justin that her injuries were nothing serious. "I'll live," she said. "You and I both know I've been through worse."

There was no sound coming from the front, so they slid the little window open to peer into the cab. Justin quickly realized that the driver and passenger were either unconscious or dead. Knowing their window of escape could be small, he lay down on his back and started kicking the rear doors with both feet. Becky joined him, and the stubborn door finally gave a little.

"On three?" Justin asked.

"On three!" Becky answered.

"One...two...three!"

With newfound energy born of impending freedom, they both reared back and kicked together, and the door popped open.

Justin hurried out of the back and ran around to the front. He carefully looked in through the shattered windshield. Both men were still and bleeding badly, so he quickly reached in to grab the handcuff key from the passenger and also pickpocketed his wallet and gun. He then went to the driver and did the same. He also pilfered the GPS unit, and the thought it might be a good idea to relieve the driver of his phone so he couldn't call for help.

Suddenly, the driver regained consciousness and grabbed his wrist, but one firm blow from Justin's elbow sent him to Dreamland again.

Once they had the handcuffs off, the two scavenged the van for anything that might prove helpful for their escape. They found a leather case that contained a computer and other electronic devices, as well as some paperwork Justin thought might be useful. After they determined that both men were alive, they checked the GPS to see where they were. As a final insult, he handcuffed them together, through the steering wheel, so they'd be rather incapacitated when they woke up. He thought about calling 911, then decided against it. "Fuck 'em!" he said before he threw the phones as far as he could.

The GPS told them they were on Norris Peak Road, in South Dakota, just inside Black Hills National Forest; ironically, perhaps, they needed to get to Rapid City as rapidly as possible, and it was about ten miles away. They headed south, toward Johnson Siding, and found an unlocked vehicle outside a bar. While Becky stood guard, Justin quickly hotwired the Chevy pickup. It started a bit roughly, but it was the best they could do for grand theft auto, and as soon as Becky jumped in, they were off, heading east on South Dakota 44.

In Rapid City, they stopped at an out-of-the-way minimart to clean themselves and grab something to eat. While they nibbled on chips and snack cakes, Justin thumbed through a stolen phonebook and quickly located the nearest pawn shop. Since the place didn't open for a couple hours, they took the opportunity to ditch the truck, but not before

113

absconding with the owner's handgun and binoculars.

The pawn shop looked like the kind of sleazy place where no questions would be asked, and Justin was sure he could make a good deal without the required paperwork. The guns he'd taken from the Jesus freaks were Beretta PX4 40 pistols, which sold for over $500 new, and the one from the truck was a Smith & Wesson Model 4506, also valued at over $500.

Ray, the owner of the gritty establishment, seemed very interested in the items Justin brought in but was wary of how they were obtained. "I don't know, man," he said as he examined the guns. "What are you lookin' to get outta these anyway?"

"Well, what I really need is a car. My girlfriend and I need to get out of town quick, if you know what I mean."

Ray looked over Justin's shoulder at Becky, then nodded at Justin. "Yeah, I get it," he said.

"I figure I need at least 1,000 bucks, no questions asked. We're sorta in a hurry," Justin pressed.

Ray frowned and rubbed his chin. "I don't feel real good 'bout givin' you that kind of money on no-questions-asked merchandise, buddy, but I got a little somethin' you might go for instead."

"What is it?" Justin asked, growing impatient.

"Out back, I got a 2000 Chevy. Now, she looks a little rough, but she runs great. For what you got here, I'll give you the car and $400 pocket money. I ain't gonna ask no questions at all and won't answer any if her old man comes askin'," he said with a sly wink.

"If you're sure the car will get me to LA, you've got a deal," said Justin before he sealed it with a handshake.

As Ray led them around back, keys in hand, another question dawned in Justin's head. "Ray, this car can't be traced back to you, can it?"

"No. Why?" the pawn shop owner asked, suddenly sounding more than a little concerned. "I got somethin' to worry about with you two?"

"Nothing bad," Justin said. "It's just... Well, once we get where we're going, we will probably abandon it."

"Oh. Well, that's fine. Besides, even if they did come

knockin', I'd just say it was stolen," he said with a smile.

The car really did run just fine, so they drove it to the nearest shopping center and cruised the parking lot until they found a car that matched the style and color of their new ride. They quickly and cautiously exchanged the license plates. Then, with some of the cash Ray had given them, they gassed their vehicle up and purchased a few more snacks and sodas for the journey.

Instead of traveling west, they headed east on I-90. They took I-29 south at Sioux Falls and I-80 east into Chicago. In the Windy City, they swung into Chinatown and left the car and keys in a place where it would soon disappear. Next, they took the Redline north to Argyle Street in the Vietnamese district. They quickly made it to a safe house Justin had secured for just such an occasion.

After they cleaned up, Justin treated Becky to his favorite Vietnamese restaurant. The chicken fried rice had never tasted so good, and Becky seemed to enjoy her huge bowl of phở, a Vietnamese beef noodle soup.

Justin decided it would be best for them to stay at the safe house for the night. It was not a big place, and it was furnished with only one bed and no couch, so the sleeping arrangements were a bit awkward for him. For her part, Becky seemed quite comfortable with the situation and never complained; she just easily stripped down to her underwear and snuggled up close to Justin. Justin was hyper-aware of her presence, with the feel of her warm body next to his and her small hand on his stomach. He was embarrassed by his arousal, but it had been a long time since he had been with a woman.

A short while later, she moved her face close to his and gently kissed him. Helpless to her advances and his own neglected libido, he kissed her hard and pulled her closer. As her hand slowly descended to unfasten his pants, thoughts of another woman danced into his mind. To his surprise, those lustful thoughts were not of his wife but of Salome. He wasn't sure if it was his residual religious training or his own value system that stopped him, but casual sex didn't seem appropriate at the time, so he reluctantly pushed Becky away, with nothing but a friendly peck on the forehead.

Justin guessed they were feeling the high of surviving a traumatic experience together. It always happened in the movies, but it was a case of art imitating life; there was undeniable, intense attraction that came with the shared relief of enduring mutual suffering. He felt an intense emotional bond with her but knew that it was only the endorphins and his hormones talking. What he really wanted to do was protect her. "This isn't right, Becky, not here and not now," he said, as gently as he could.

"Please don't stop," she begged as a tear coursed down her face. "I have wanted to do this since the moment you first got in my car."

"I'm flattered by that. I really am, but I... I'm sorry, but I just can't right now. I want to more than you know. Maybe later, once we've gotten through some of this stuff and once we get to know each other better, but for now, let's just get some sleep."

He pulled her close and allowed her to lay her head on his chest as he cradled her in his arms. Within thirty minutes, her breathing deepened, and she drifted off to sleep.

Justin, on the other hand, found sleep elusive. He was just fighting too many battles: his grief over his family, his mission and his battle with Heaven, and now, the internal conflict over a strong urge to take a young, willing, very attractive blonde to bed rather than holding out for the daughter of the underworld. *I might ever even see Salome again,* his mind argued, but in the end, it was the beautiful resident of Hell who ruled his thoughts before he finally drifted off.

Chapter 26

Justin awoke early but decided to let Becky sleep a while longer. He retrieved the laptop he'd hidden in a special place in his room, and used it to email the resident angels of Hell, briefing them on all the important details about his capture and incarceration, his interrogation, his eventual escape, his current location, and his plans. Justin also requested to meet up with them to give a full account.

Sometime later, a knock came at the door, and Justin rushed over to answer it. He peered through the peephole first, just to be sure it wasn't unwanted company. When he saw Ronwe, an agent he knew, he opened the door. He introduced him to Becky as merely Ron and quickly added that it was a cousin of his who lived nearby.

A little less cautious than Justin, Ron reached into his bag and produced an Illuminator, which he handed to Justin.

"What's that?" Becky asked, curiously eyeing the device.

It was Justin's assumption that the less Becky knew, the better it would be for her in the long run. Thus, he quickly conjured up another fib: "Oh, it's just, uh...some doohickey my uncle invented to relieve migraines." He winced and rubbed his temples, doing his best to feign a headache.

"A doohickey?" she mocked, then giggled. "Whatever you say."

"Really," Justin lied. "Ron's dad is always inventing things, and I knew Ron would have one of these gadgets at his house. Please excuse me for a moment while I try it." With that, Justin sat on the bed, donned the Illuminator, then rested his head against the headboard. About fifteen minutes later, Justin sat up and said, "Ah, I feel much better now. It's a truly wonderful device. Thanks, Ron, and thank your dad for me. Hey, are you hungry?"

"I could eat," Ron said with a nod.

"All right. I'll be back in a bit," Justin said before he walked out. He knew it was best to leave Ron with Becky, as it wouldn't have been good to be seen with Ron in public. Besides, he didn't want to leave Becky alone after the traumatic experience they'd been through.

He was only gone for about a half-hour. When he returned, he unlocked the door and pushed it open with his foot, since his arms were full of a delicious-smelling feast for three. When his eyes caught the sight before him, all he could do was gasp and let the bags of food hit the floor, along with his jaw. Ron was lying on the floor in a pool of blood, and Becky was tied to a wooden chair. To his horror, what must have been the ghost of Triple6Soldier walked nonchalantly in from the bathroom.

"Please, Justin! Help me!" a crying Becky screamed.

Wasting no time, Justin launched himself at the fiend and collided with him in a violent tackle that would have been the pride and joy of any NFL linebacker. Triple6Soldier fell onto the bed, and Justin eagerly pummeled him.

Just as he was preparing to deal the evil bastard another fist to the face, he heard a voice from behind him: "Justin, stop!"

At that moment, he realized two things: First, Triple-6Soldier was not fighting back, only doing his best to protect himself and, second, the voice was one he'd heard before, one that sounded like music in his ears. When he turned and found Salome standing in the kitchenette, he looked at her in confusion.

"Stolas is a friend. Please let him be," she pleaded.

Suddenly, Justin found himself on an emotional roller-coaster. There, right before his eyes, was the person he wanted to see more than anyone on Hell or Earth. The trouble was, she seemed to be linked somehow to an assassin. When he found his voice, he argued with a growl, "A friend? But he killed Jennifer and Ronwe."

"No, it was Rebecca," Salome corrected. "She is an agent of Heaven. In fact, she is one of the Holy Ghosts. She killed Jennifer when the girl discovered the truth about her, and she almost slew Stolas when he tried to save you from her at the safe house. It is a good thing he has an incredibly hard head. The bullet only grazed him and knocked him unconscious."

"Becky is on Heaven's side?" he asked, stunned. "And what about Ronwe? Was he an agent of Heaven too?" Justin asked suspiciously, in need of fast answers.

"No, he was a friend. We were too late to save him. She killed him as we burst into the room, and she was planning to destroy you next," she explained.

Justin's mouth fell agape once more, and a dumbfounded look flashed across his face. He glanced back at Stolas and felt utterly stupid. "Sorry, man. I thought you were one of the bad guys."

"No problem. Like she said, I have a head like a rock." He smiled and offered Justin his hand. "Nice right cross though," Stolas said, rubbing his jaw.

"No! They're lying!" Becky called out. "I—"

She wasn't able to sputter another word before Salome gave her a backhand that rocked her world.

Becky straightened up after the smack, tried to regain her composure, and said, with blood pouring from a gash on her lower lip, "It doesn't matter. They will be here soon. You're all dead anyway."

For that, Salome offered her another hit, so hard this time that it knocked her out cold. Then, entirely unfazed by the corporal punishment she'd had to inflict, she matter-of-factly said, "She's right though. We must move, with great haste. Turn around," Salome said.

Still struggling to wrap his mind around the current situation but happy to have Salome close again, Justin did as he was told.

Salome quickly brandished her knife and went to work

119

on Justin's back. He winced as she cut a small line where Becky said he was only bruised. After a bit of painful fiddling around back there, causing him to squirm, Salome showed him a small metal thing, which he correctly assumed was a transmitter. She handed it to Stolas, who dropped it to the floor and crushed it with his foot. They removed a similar transmitter from Rebecca and disposed of it.

"Hopefully, that will buy us a little time to get the hell out of here," Stolas said.

They carried the blacked-out Rebecca and the body of their fallen comrade to the car and quickly left the area.

Once they were on their way, Justin had time to think. *It was the Illuminator,* he decided, with a sickening feeling in his stomach. *When Rebecca saw that, she realized Ronwe was an angel of Hell, and her job was done. All she needed to do was to report back to Michael.*

Salome placed an Illuminator on Becky and set it to induce a dreamless sleep. It was an important precaution to take, due to Becky's Holy Ghost training. "She may look like a beautiful, petite young woman, but don't be fooled. This one is extremely dangerous," she warned. "If she wakes up with the device on, it will be easier to bypass the blocks she will attempt to set. Also, we may be able to obtain valuable information from her to better our chances for success on our mission."

"It's all my fault," Justin said sadly as they drove.

"What? What are you talking about?" Salome asked.

"I let her see the Illuminator, so she knew he was from Hell," he confessed tearfully. "It is because of me that Ronwe is dead."

"I think she believed you work for Alliance, regardless of what she thought about Ronwe," Salome assured him. "That is why they let you get away, so she could find out as much information as she could before killing you. Rebecca is a brilliant strategist and an excellent liar, like many from Heaven are. She could have ruined everything we have worked to accomplish here on Earth, but we have her in our grasp now."

"But Ronwe didn't have to die." Justin said, unable to mask his grief or his guilt.

120

"It's more likely that Ronwe realized she is a Holy Ghost and tried to confront her before you returned," Stolas explained.

"Stolas is right," Salome agreed. "Ronwe should have waited, but that was not his style."

In spite of his friends' efforts to console him and ease his remorse, the anger in Justin's heart burned fiercely. From that point forward, he refused to refer to her as Becky. *She is just Rebecca, the killer of Ronwe,* he thought, cringing as he glared at her and remembered his momentary indiscretion at almost bedding her.

On the way to the safe house, Salome revealed more details to Justin. "When Rebecca made contact with you at the coffee shop," she said, "Stolas was already suspicious of her. He received a call from Jennifer, who told him of her suspicions about a possible spy. He went to her house to talk to her about it, but when he arrived, he noticed Rebecca driving away. Stolas and Jennifer were very close, so that was why he burst into your house the way he did. He was there to make Rebecca pay for what she had done to Jennifer, but his first priority was to protect you."

Now, it made sense why Stolas was always watching Justin the way he did, not because he was jealous or wary of him but because he was trying to make sure no one hurt him, and that included the evil bitch Rebecca. Justin felt awful for having suspected him of wrongdoing, but he was glad to be in the company of true friends now, friends who would do their best to save him from the not so holy Holy Ghosts who wanted him dead.

Forty minutes later, they pulled into an abandoned warehouse in Gary, Indiana. A handful of agents took Rebecca away, and others prepared Ronwe's body for the trip home.

Another group went to work on Rebecca's Illuminator, replacing the memory chip with one that would induce a coma-like state. That would prepare her for her trip to Hell, and would also make it easier for them to probe her mind for valuable information. Even with their amazing devices, it would not be easy to extract information from a Holy Ghost, but it was imperative for them to try.

Chapter 27

After they'd checked in and passed the responsibility of Rebecca on to others, Justin pulled Salome aside. "I am so glad you're here," he said, looking deep into her beautiful, dark eyes. "You have been on my mind ever since that day at the space port." He moved closer and continued, "I felt a real connection between us. I-I hope you feel it too."

In reply to his sweet, honest remark, Salome closed the gap between them. Justin pulled her into his arms, and their lips met. When their mouths parted, he chuckled.

"What is so funny?" Salome asked, sounding a bit hurt.

Justin quickly explained, "I just...Well, to be honest, I never thought I could feel this way again. You make me so very happy." A tear of joy welled in his eye. "Do you think a beautiful girl from Hell could ever love a not-so-attractive man from Earth?"

She cocked her head to the side in thought, then smiled. "I already love you, Justin, and I do find you quite...attractive." She reached up and touched his face. "I have known for a long time that my heart is yours, so what took you so long?" she inquired with a smile.

Justin shrugged as he blushed, then answered, "What can I say? Some of us Earthlings are a little slow in expressing our feelings, I guess." He kissed her deeply, emboldened by the bliss of the new, blossoming love between them.

Salome took Justin by the hand, and led him to a room

on the second floor of the warehouse. It was no luxury hotel suite, but it was furnished with a bed. They barely shut the door before they were in each other's arms, kissing and cuddling, all the while backing toward the mattress and tearing at their clothes along the way. He gently laid her down, and they succumbed to their passion.

Justin had not been with anyone since Leah, and he suddenly felt some trepidation, like a silly schoolboy experiencing love for the first time. *Will I even still know what to do?* he questioned. Fortunately for him, nature and passion took over, and as quickly as that terrifying thought entered his mind, it was replaced with a deep desire that only her lips could satisfy.

After a while, Salome moved his hand to her breast. Even through her top, Justin felt the wonderful warmth of what was hidden behind that thin layer of fabric. His hand burned with desire as he caressed her body, and she seemed to quiver at his touch. After a moment, she kissed him deeply, then stopped, rolled onto her knees, and started to finish undressing him.

Justin couldn't help himself; he quickly yet awkwardly returned the favor by disrobing her. He was so nervous, as if it was his first time. His hands were shaking, and his fingers seemed clumsy. Nevertheless, everything about it was magical. When they were both naked, Justin's hands became emissaries of his desire. He pulled her close and thrilled at the feel of her naked body against his. He didn't know if it was his maturity that made their first interlude different than his long-ago first time, but this time, his aim was to make her happy, not just to find pleasure for himself.

Although he desperately longed to ravage her, Justin did all he could to concentrate on foreplay. Salome, however, seemed to have other plans. Every time he tried to prolong the experience, she moved to a more aggressive position that left him few options. Realizing she was in no mood to take her time with him, Justin gave her what they both wanted. He entered her slowly, and she moaned aloud. He tried to move in a slow, deliberate rhythm, but as soon as their bodies connected, she morphed into a wild woman. She pushed

123

hard against him, gyrating and holding him tightly, and it wasn't long before they were both lost in a mind-blowing, body-tensing fit of lust. Their bodies took control, and it was a blur from that point on.

Some indeterminable time later, as they lay in each other's arms, Salome looked up at her lover. "Thank you, Justin," she said, then kissed him softly.

How can such a beautiful creature thank me? I should be thanking her. Justin thought.

They held one another in silence for a while longer, just enjoying the feeling of being close. There was so much he wanted to say to her, but words seemed so trivial and unnecessary. It was at that moment that Justin realized, without a shadow of a doubt, that he could love again, for he truly loved Salome.

Justin looked into her eyes and could not resist pulling her face close. He kissed her softly, and carnal desire dominated them once again. This time, the frenzy of raw, naked want took a backseat; they took their time with their love-making, basking in the pleasure of every touch. They had exorcised their demons the first time, and this time was for love. They went at it till the wee hours of the morning before they finally dozed off in a dreamy, fully sated embrace.

The others let the paramours sleep until about noon, sensing they might need the rest. Once Justin and Salome were up, they quickly showered and grabbed something to eat before their big meeting.

As they entered the conference room, Justin was surprised when Sandel and Jarod, Salome's father, greeted them with a hug. Stunned as he was by Jarod's presence, Justin was truly happy to see him, albeit a bit embarrassed because he was sure the man knew about the tryst the previous evening.

Sandel looked first at Justin, then at Salome. "So, what's been going on here?" he asked.

Justin blushed a little, but held his tongue.

As Sandel gave Salome a friendly hug, he spoke to Justin over her shoulder in an exaggerated whisper that was intended for Salome's ears as well, "Fire and brimstone, my friend.

I'm warning you!"

Salome punched him in the chest and pushed him away with a smile.

"If we find half the happiness you and Lilith know, I will be a very happy man for the rest of my life," Justin said as he reached for Salome's hand. He then bravely approached Jarod, fearing his reaction. "Jarod, I feel the same way about Salome that you must have felt about Anh. She is a part of every breath I take, of every beat of my heart. I cannot imagine life without her by my side. If she will have me, I will truly be the happiest man in the galaxy."

Salome kissed her father. "I love him, Father," she said, smiling over at Justin. "For one thing, he reminds me so much of you."

"What!? Don't you dare compare that puny Earthling to me. If you ever say that again, I'll put you over my knee and spank your ass, young lady," Jarod spat with an angry growl. The faux wrath quickly dissipated, however, and transformed into an ear-to-ear smile. "No, I am truly happy for you both. Justin, I would be proud to welcome you to the family."

Salome hugged her father tight, and, after one final, loving kiss, returned to Justin's side.

"Excuse me, sir," said a technician as he approached Justin. "I hate to break up this happy moment, but I need to give you an injection."

Justin trusted his hellish friends entirely, so he didn't hesitate to dutifully raise his sleeve and take his medicine like a man. He did, however, as, "What's this for?"

"It is the Longevity Factor, sir," the tech answered before he promptly walked away.

Justin paused, waiting for something great to happen, but he felt normal, as if there'd been no change at all. He thought for a moment, then suddenly realized the reason he was not given the Longevity Factor earlier: When his heavenly captors drew his blood, they were not checking on his health but for the Factor. *Genius*, he thought, thankful for his comrades' brilliant foresight.

After everyone arrived, they all sat down to study the results of Justin's time in captivity.

Andras, someone Justin had just met, rose to begin the meeting. "First, I'd like you all to know our attempts to extract information from Rebecca have been slow going. Her blocks are deep and very strong. Our plan is to take her to our home world for more in-depth study." He then paused for a moment and turned to Justin. "There is something you should see," he said. "This memory from Rebecca was one of her last, strong and, therefore, easy to extract."

On the video screen before the attendees appeared Ronwe, in the apartment in Chicago, as seen through Rebecca's eyes. "I know who you are, Rebecca," he said with a growl, "and your treachery ends here!"

He moved toward her, but she was ready for his attack. There was the sound of a silenced gunshot just before Ronwe collapsed to the floor.

Those in the meeting sat quietly for a moment, grieving their loss as they took in the horrific scene of a friend's death.

Andras spoke again, breaking the quiet reflection. "While it was unfortunate to lose Ronwe, it was, in part, because he acted too quickly. He should have waited until he had someone there to help him. Rebecca is a Holy Ghost, and Ronwe was simply no match for her treachery and skill."

"See?" Salome said, wrapping an arm around Justin's shoulders. "The fault was not yours, Justin. Ronwe acted too quickly and forced her hand."

"Yeah, maybe," Justin halfheartedly responded, but he was still not so sure.

"Maybe nothing, boy," Jarod admonished. "Ronwe was there to protect you, because you are crucial to the success of this mission. He served us well and fulfilled his duties, so we must celebrate his life and his loyal service to the Free Will Alliance."

"Second," Andras continued, "Justin's memories we have gleaned from the Illuminator have proven very promising. In this excerpt, pay close attention to the voice you hear."

The video screen played through a terrible reminiscing of Justin's first interrogation in the room of question. It was then that Justin discovered that the voice he knew as Reverend Gabe Brown's was, in fact, the voice of another archangel, also known as Gabriel. *Son of a bitch!* he fumed, clenching his fist on the table in front of him. *No wonder he has such an enormous following. He's the real deal.* With that awful thought on his mind, Justin made a mental note to kick his ass the next time he met the so-called reverend face to face.

As the next memory came into view, Andras announced grimly, "As we suspected, Archangel Michael is alive and well, residing on Planet Earth."

Justin had spent far too many days enduring that heavenly bastard's cruel questioning. This time, he gripped the arm of his chair so tightly that his fingernails left marks in the upholstery. Just the sound of Michael's voice brought vivid memories of the pain and torment.

Salome took his hand in hers when she felt the tension engulf his body. That calmed him a bit, and he gave her a weak smile.

"Now comes the most interesting part," Andras said, pointing at the video screen.

The scene replayed of the day Justin was led to the room of questions and walked past the open door. Much to his surprise, the map and the numbers written under it came into view on the high-definition screen. Now that he was not groggy and in agony, he could better read them.

"Note the aerial photograph of what is known as Caribbean. More importantly, it is specifically a shot of Puerto Rico. What is most interesting about this memory is the revealing caption beneath the photograph, 18°18' 30" N, 65°46' 13" W"

"Planetary coordinates!" Justin blurted loudly.

"That is correct, Justin," Andras said with a nod. "The location is the eastern side of Puerto Rico, twenty-five miles southeast of San Juan, in El Yunque National Forest. Attempts to retrieve satellite images of that area have proven impossible. Our agents working within various governments have learned that the area has been deemed a restricted, no-fly zone since 2001. We are forming a reconnaissance team, and they will be en route tomorrow."

Justin stood and looked directly at Andras. "I want to go," he said.

Andras smiled. "We thought you might, so we have already taken the liberty of preparing the necessary documents and travel arrangements. You will travel at night via low-level, antigravity flight, avoiding restricted areas or those with heightened security radar. We must avoid detection at all cost. Our greatest weapon right now is their belief in our ignorance. Remember, this is only a reconnaissance mission. Our goal is to get in and out, leaving not a trace behind. Please be ready to depart at 10 p.m. tomorrow."

"Thank you," Justin said and reclaimed his seat.

"No, thank *you*," Andras said with a grin. He then turned back to the table and continued, "I'm pleased to announce that we have made some enhancements in our shield technology. We have recalibrated the shield to remove the halo effect. This will make you virtually invisible as you travel to your destination. Also, we have perfected the night-vision glasses," he said, pointing at those on the table in front of everyone. "Please put them on."

Once everyone complied, someone turned out the lights.

"Can you all see clearly?" Andras asked.

Everyone gasped and grunted their approval.

"Whoa. Clear as day," Justin said. He removed the glasses for a second but couldn't make out anything in the room, not even his hand in front of his face. He turned his head toward Sandel and put the glasses back on just in time to see his friend giving him that gesture that meant the same as the middle-finger salute, so he stuck out his tongue at Sandel and smiled.

"We've added another impressive feature," Andras said before he unexpectedly shined a light into their eyes.

Justin marveled as the glasses instantaneously compensated for the new development. "Impressive is right!" he said. The glasses made even the darkest night seem like day and instantly compensated for changes in illumination and visibility, such as headlights or intentional blinding. Even better, they were not clunky, bulky things like the ones on Earth; they were more like a cool pair of shades.

The rest of the afternoon was spent going over flight plans, strategies, countless glitch scenarios, and solutions and actions that would hopefully result in a successful mission. By 6:00 that evening, they decided they'd done all they could to prepare and that it was time to relax and have something to eat.

Sandel, Salome, and Justin enjoyed a dinner the Earthling had introduced to Sandel during their time at the cabin: pizza and beer, peppered with good conversation. Around 9:30, Sandel called it a night, and he suggested they do the same.

While Justin and Salome were not quite ready to visit dreamland, they still headed straight for the bed, where they spent the next hour rediscovering each other. Afterward, they lay in each other's arms, exhausted yet satisfied.

Before sleep took him, Justin's thoughts were pulled in many different directions: his mission, his life on Earth that seemed like it had happened a million years ago, and how much he truly loved Salome. He also felt a tinge of guilt and debated as to whether or not he should tell her about the night he and Rebecca spent together. Although nothing had really happened to speak of, he wanted no secrets between them. Nevertheless, he feared confessing the truth to her; he was no expert on women, but those he'd met on Earth seemed to desire truth and honesty, only to struggle handling it. As he lay next to Salome, he wondered, *Are all women the same, no matter what planet they call home?* With that on his mind, he looked at the warm body next to him and asked, "Salome? Are you awake?" Justin asked.

"Yes. The thought of you leaving in the morning saddens me, and I want to hold on to every moment I can," she answered.

"Good, because there is something I need to tell you." Justin paused for a moment, swallowed the lump in his throat, then continued, "The night before you came to Chicago, Becky...er, Rebecca and I... I, well, uh... We... I mean—"

"I know what she tried to do, but I also know what you did not do," Salome interrupted, putting him out of his misery. "I do not truly know what is in your heart, but I only hope it mirrors my own. Justin Grant, my love and life are yours, if you'll have them."

"And I love you," he said, as sincerely as he could.

They looked into one another's eyes for a moment, two people from two different worlds but sharing a love deeper than either had known. When Justin's lips met with hers in that moment, he was as happy as he had ever been. They snuggled close to one another and strolled into the Land of Dreams, and one of the two had a big smile on his face.

Chapter 28

The next evening, Justin, Stolas, Sorath, and another angel named Buer listened as Andras provided some last-minute instructions. Justin was wound up; the thought of flying to Puerto Rico without the aid of a plane had him vibrating with anticipation. As excited as he was, however, he was also focused on the task at hand. He was keenly aware of the danger and the importance of his mission. He kissed Salome, to the tune of catcalls, whistles, and laughter from all those within sight of the fond farewell, then climbed into an older-model Chevy van, waving like a movie star.

To be as discreet as possible and to use the cover of darkness to their advantage, they were driven about thirty miles south of Gary, to a less populated area. They pulled off I-65 on State Road 10 near Roselawn, a site famous (or infamous) for the nudist colonies that had clustered there since the 1930s.

Their carefully orchestrated flight plan allowed them to avoid all major cities. They traveled through the deep darkness of rural areas until they reached a secluded beach just north of Miami. From there, they rose into the air and headed south. They hovered low, just over the tree line, to avoid detection, but maintaining that altitude entailed dangers all its own. Stolas destroyed an old, wooden windmill that seemed to leap up at him from out of the darkness; Buer put a nice, big hole in a billboard; and Justin clipped a tractor-trailer because he wasn't paying enough attention and was too busy enjoying the starry cosmos above him. *It's a good thing we've got these body shields,* Justin surmised, *or this would have already been a mission impossible!* Wisely, at that point, Sorath, the designated team leader, decided it would be prudent to put on their night-vision glasses, and after those three narrow escapes, no one disagreed.

Undoubtedly, the insects were the biggest nuisance. They collected on the outside of the body shields, forcing the foursome to descend or land frequently, every 200 miles or so, depending on the terrain. On the ground, they had to deactivate their shields to remove the smashed creepy-crawlies. Justin couldn't help but marvel at the sight of all the bug guts momentarily hanging in the air before falling away.

Even at an average speed of 120 miles per hour, it took 2 days to reach the secluded beach. The quartet was limited to traveling during the darkest hours, between 10 p.m. and 4 a.m. They spent the following day in Chattahoochee National Forest, just over the Georgia state line. All things considered, it likely would have been faster to drive, but they couldn't take the chance of being pulled over or caught in an accident. When they finally reached their sandy destination on Elliott Key in Biscayne National Park, about twenty-five miles south of Miami, they sought shelter from the heat of the day in the nearby trees and took turns sleeping and playing lookout until nighttime returned to shield them.

Promptly at 10:00, they took to the air again. Their next stop was seven miles south of the Mars Bay Settlement on the southern tip of the Bahamas. Flying just thirty feet above the water, Justin was taken aback by the extreme quiet. He was also grateful there were no insects to contend with. Another thing that caught his attention was the stunning light show; being away from the light pollution of civilization made the sky come alive, glittering with billions of stars. Since there were no major cities to avoid this time, they increased their average speed and reached their destination in less than two hours. They rested for about thirty minutes, then resumed their journey toward their next stop.

About two hours and fifteen minutes later, they touched

down on the northern tip of Little Inagua Island. They planned to spend the day at the uninhabited land and sea park, where they were sure they were safe and would not be noticed by anyone other than a few wild donkeys and flocks of flamingos.

Justin bit into an energy bar, but he longed for real food, and he knew it would be at least another full day before they reached Puerto Rico. He quickly finished his miniscule feast and took his turn at sleep, lullabied by the sound of his growling belly. His spirit felt brighter and lighter as night fell upon them, for that meant food was only a few hours away.

Next, they made it to a little beach on the northern shore of the Dominican Republic in less than two hours. They spent very little time there before moving on to their next stop. Justin suspected the urgency had something to do with his companions' appetites; they were longing for real food as much as he was. It took almost two and a half more hours to reach San Juan, but they were all glad to have finally arrived.

Chapter 29

Immediately, the travelers headed for La Perla, a brightly colored but rundown slum in Old San Juan. It would serve as perfect cover for their brief stay. *Wow. What a difference a few feet make,* Justin thought, for just across the street from that squalid area, he saw some of the priciest real estate in all of San Juan.

As soon as they walked into La Perla, they felt all eyes on them. The residents were very suspicious of any outsiders. They found the least seedy hotel and settled in for the night. Using the Illuminator, they pushed Carlos, the owner, to believing they were like family and were in need of protection. They also delved into his mind; in case he was harboring any helpful information about the area. It proved beneficial, for it helped them locate a trio of local hoodlums who would be useful as lookouts, to make sure no one entered their room. After that, they quietly revisited their mission plans and pre-pared their gear.

They spent the first part of the day resting and studying the Illuminator. Thanks to Carlos's memories, they knew as much or more about La Perla and San Juan as many of the locals did. Sometime around noon, they ventured out to find food and supplies. At a local restaurant, Justin feasted on the house specialty, *arroz con pollo,* a delicious, savory dish of perfectly browned chicken stewed with rice, onions, gar-lic, tomatoes, and smothered in queso cheese. He was a very happy man, and from the looks on the faces of his overstuffed comrades, he knew they felt the same.

It didn't take long for them to find the three would-be door guards, because Cruz, Alfredo, and Cordero were exactly where Carlos said they would be, hanging out near a little shop that faced the rough, moss-covered, northern historic city wall of Old San Juan. The men loitered often in the little parking area adjacent to the store, beside a wall-sized mural of Che Guevara, listening to what Justin decided was an odd mixture of reggae and hip-hop. The Puerto Ricans eyed them suspiciously as they approached, then quickly moved to confront the strangers who were stupid enough to invade their territory.

Moments later, in what looked like the makings of a drug deal, an exchange of American dollars for services was made. When the three young men were lured away by the cash and alone, they were fitted with Illuminators. They didn't argue about it, because they were promised, "This is the best virtual reality in the world!" It didn't take long to give them their instructions using the devices. Just like that, the hotel room and its contents would be safe. The Illuminators also ensured that the La Perla locals would not speak of the strange visitors to anyone, especially outside the neighborhood.

At 10:00, they walked to the far eastern side of La Perla, near the old fort wall. When they were sure no one was around, they made their ascent. They headed east, toward El Yunque Rainforest, about twenty-five miles southeast of San Juan. They landed about a quarter-mile from their target and opted to go the rest of the way on foot. It would be an arduous trek, even with the help of their souped-up night-vision gear. The dense vegetation made it impossible to see the forest floor, which made for unsure footing.

Eventually, they made it to their preferred position. There, they spread out in a circular pattern, approximately equal distance apart, about 100 yards from the target coordinates. They were quick to get to work. Shields were a no-no, since the energy signals could be noticed. For that reason, their protective skins were a good bet; they would safeguard them against almost anything, even bullets, though anyone who was hit would still suffer major bruising. As their name suggested, they fit snugly, like a second skin and virtually unnoticeable. Another interesting thing was their chameleon-like properties, which kept the wearers camouflaged at all times.

Justin rose into the higher branches of the nearest tree and started building his blind. He tried to make it as comfortable as possible, since he would be there for at least eighteen hours. He collected as much foliage from his host tree as he could without creating a noticeable spot, then filled in the cracks with stuff he found on the forest floor. Once he was sure his hiding place was sturdy and practically invisible, he lowered himself to the ground for a quick potty break and a stretch. *It's gonna be a long day,* he thought as he yawned.

Seated comfortably in his blind, and with nothing else to do but wait, Justin began to really take notice of the melody around him. The rainforest was alive with the sounds of thousands of frogs looking for love, millions of insects hoping to find mates, and the occasional screech owl to round out the symphony. It was simultaneously deafening and tremendously peaceful, but every once in a while, the chorus of life would give way to silence, usually after an unexpected noise. Justin smiled at the thought that the silence seemed louder than the music, but it was always short lived. As soon as the forest dwellers realized they were in no immediate danger, they resumed their choir rehearsal, slowly at first, then building to its previous glory.

Justin sat back and listened as the orchestra changed composers. The opus of the night slowly transitioned to the concerto of the day as he settled in. His suspicion that it would be a long day turned out to be right, especially when he saw and heard no signs of human life.

A large, windowless, cinderblock building stood directly on the coordinates that were captioned below the aerial shot captured in Justin's Illuminator memories, but there was nothing else there, save trees and exotic plants, birds, insects, lizards, frogs, and the occasional mongoose. Justin and his three comrades studied the building but found nothing of importance there. Their night-vision glasses also served as excellent binoculars. With them, he could even count the legs of the insects crawling on the walls of the building, but regardless of their powerful technology, they discovered no sign of any bipedal life forms.

At their meeting later that night, it was decided that they would remain in their blinds to keep watch one more day. Barring any activity that would prevent them from making any brash moves, they would move in on the following day. Once that decision was made, it was time to sleep.

Justin was thankful he'd had the foresight to fashion a blind with enough legroom for him to stretch out. It was relatively easy to hang his makeshift hammock in complete cover. He climbed in and thought about the day: his extreme hunger, the caked-on bugs, the seedy hotel and all the people they'd encountered, and, finally, about Salome. A smile curled his lips as he envisioned her, and the choristers of El Yunque Rainforest serenaded him into his sweet dreams of the woman he loved.

The next day played out exactly like the previous one had. On the third day, though, late in the afternoon, Justin and Buer ventured again toward the building. For all intents and purposes, the looked like a couple of lost hikers. They approached the structure with great caution, attempting to keep up the act that they were tired, dirty, and hungry; it wasn't all that difficult of a role to play, not much of a stretch after two and half days in the trees. The premises around the building had been cleared, so some sunlight reached the ground there. They walked around, calling out and looking for anyone who could hear them. They even pounded on the big, metal door, pleading for help, but no one answered.

Walking away in defeat from the mysterious, seemingly vacant place, Justin was once again tortured by hunger pangs. He'd grown very weary of the energy bars he'd had to rely on for the last two days, so he decided to pick some fruit along the way, something to supplement his meager portions. *All that technology, and the angels can't come up with some sort of meals ready to eat that tastes like a real burger and fries? A milkshake? Some steak and potatoes?* He thought, shaking his head as he jerked a yellowish-orange something from a nearby bush, hoping it wasn't poisonous. *Wouldn't it be just too ironic if he ended up dying after everything he had been through?* he wondered and laughed aloud.

They stayed for one more day to see if their presence at the clearing would stir up any unusual activity. When none was observed, they decided to head back to La Perla. Before they left, at strategic points around the building, they placed very small cameras capable of recording a couple of years' worth of happenings, of course equipped with automatic night vision. Justin sensed that his fellow travelers were as ready to head back as he was, and he was glad for that.

They returned to their room, cleaned all the jungle debris off themselves, then found a late-night eatery within short walking distance from their lodgings. Once their hunger was sated, they packed up their gear, thanked Carlos and the boys and bid farewell to them, then headed home.

Quite purposefully, they took the same route home, moving in the exact opposite pattern and, thankfully, without close calls. They met their ride in the same location near Roselawn and were then driven back to the warehouse.

As soon as Justin piled out of the van, Salome ran into his waiting arms. "Whew! You need a shower," she said before she greeted him with a hard kiss, all the while scrunching up her nose. "Damn! And a toothbrush," she declared with a smile.

"Yes, a shower would do you good, my friend," Sandel said. "I will take Salome's word for it about the toothbrush. He smiled and looked at the others. "You all need rest. We will talk in the morning. It's good to have you back," he said as he shook their hands.

The next morning, after breakfast, everyone gathered for a meeting. Sorath, their team leader, was in charge of presenting the intelligence they'd gathered, as little as it was. Images of all vantage points around the block building and the surrounding area were projected onto the wall in the conference room. Although there wasn't much to share, everyone listened intently, looking for clues as to the importance of that strange structure nestled in the middle of a rainforest.

Three hours or so later, Justin found his stomach gurgling once again, so he reached into his pocket for a snack. He popped it into his mouth and chewed with delight, but before he could take another bite, Sandel suddenly grabbed his arm.

"Where did you get that?" Sandel barked, so loudly that the room fell silent, and everyone looked their way.

"Huh? This?" Justin stammered, wondering why Sandel was looking at him that way.

"Yes, that! Where did you find it?" Sandel said, still glaring at him.

Justin was completely taken aback and confused. "Uh, I found them in the clearing around the block building in Puerto Rico. Why?"

Chapter 30

Sandel set an Illuminator on his own head, and the screen in the front of the room came to life, showing a younger Lucifer and a much younger Sandel in the palace on Hell. Lucifer handed little Sandel a piece of fruit, the exact kind Justin was holding in his hand in the conference room. "Try this, my son," Lucifer said.

"What is it, Father?" Sandel asked.

"Just taste it and tell me what you think," Lucifer instructed.

Sandel took a bite, and a smile crossed his face. "Mmm! It is wonderful! May I have another, Father?" Sandel said.

"Just one more, my son."

Sandel nodded his head vigorously as Lucifer handed him another treat.

"Sandel, this is one of the rarest, most wonderful things in the galaxy, the fruit of the Tree of Life," Lucifer said.

Sandel, having learned of the Tree and its effects, marveled at actually seeing such a thing. The only other time he'd ever seen fruit like that was behind glass, at the museum. It was a remarkable, special delicacy, and the taste was a sweetness he would never forget.

The memory faded as Sandel removed the Illuminator. Everyone stood and gathered around Justin and the precious, tasty jewel in his hand, each of them dying to taste it for themselves. Justin felt like a fool for even entertaining the thought that the fruit could be poisonous. He could hardly believe that he was truly sitting there with the forbidden fruit actually sitting on the table in front of him. He could have sliced through the awe and reverence with a knife. Only a few Hell residents had ever laid eyes on such a thing, other than the one piece carefully preserved in the Galactic Museum in the capital city of Hades. Certainly, none of those in attendance, other than Sandel and Justin, had ever tasted the most remarkable miracle in all of the galaxies.

As everyone stared longingly at the fruit of life, Justin reached for his bag and poured about thirty pieces out beside the first one. Instantly, all eyes fell on Sandel, and they looked at him pleadingly, as if asking permission.

He smiled and said, "There are enough here for everyone to have one piece, but we must save the rest for analysis." He grabbed one for himself and shut his eyes as he ate it. The memories of Sandel's first precious bite rushed into his mind, the very memories he'd just shared with them all through the Illuminator.

When everyone turned their attention back to the video screen, they realized what had been right in front of their eyes the entire time: hundreds of those trees, bearing forbidden fruit.

"No wonder the angels of Heaven want to keep this place a secret," Justin muttered. "I guess Earth is one of only two places in the entire galaxy where the trees are able to grow."

He sensed the monumental reality as he tried to grasp the concept: *Earth, my Earth, is...the next Eden!* He had always thought highly of his home planet and considered it the work of miracles, but with the fate of Planet Eden in question, his mother world's ability to grow the most coveted thing in the universe made it one of the most important places in the galaxy. Suddenly, the significance of The Temple dawned on him, as did the angels' underlying motives to make Earth an environmental paradise. Justin, as well as everyone else in the room, now knew why Earth was erased from the galactic records and why the Empire ships had attacked Sandel as they flew through this area almost four years earlier.

Sandel rightly concluded. "Now, our mission must proceed with the utmost secrecy. If the Empire suspects that there is even the slightest chance that their secret has been discovered, they will flood this area of space with every ship they can spare. They will spare no expense to decimate us before we can unravel their devious plans."

As everyone sat savoring the fruit, Justin looked toward the future. He saw the enormity of the changes and challenges ahead for Earth, for the galaxy, and for himself. *What now?* he thought as he stared at the wholly remarkable produce in his hand. Then, before he even realized the question was escaping his lips, he asked aloud, "What now?"

PART TWO

New Earth

Chapter 31

Planning the takeover of any planet would have been a monumental task, but it was even more daunting since it was his beloved Earth. Their purpose was clear: force the Empire to release their hold on Earth without causing the deaths of millions and while somehow preserving the planet's integrity as its own, independent, self-governing entity. *Easy-peasy, right?* Justin mused. *Just a walk in the park really!* As if the feat itself was not difficult enough, Jesus would be beyond pissed if the plan succeeded and would throw a temper tantrum of biblical proportions. Then, there would be the naysayers of Earth to contend with, those who naturally resisted change.

The last few months had been a whirlwind for Justin. The only calming solace in his recent stay on Hell was his time spent with Salome. Lately, the two had been discussing making their relationship a permanent one. While Justin had found himself thinking less and less about Leah and Joey and his past life, now that he was growing so close to Salome, he still talked to Leah about things that bothered him. "I think I'm going to ask her to marry me, Leah," he whispered under his breath, and he knew his former wife would wholeheartedly approve. He was sure she would have liked Salome; in fact, he surmised that they would have been great friends if they had ever had the chance to meet. They were so much alike. Salome's favorite movie turned out to be *Fools Rush In,* a chick flick Leah adored. It was a fun film about two people from completely different backgrounds finding each other and falling in love. While Justin didn't want to openly admit it, it was one of his favorites too. It amazed him that he had somehow managed to find the two most perfect women in the galaxy and especially that they both wanted to be with him.

In their next meeting, the discussion moved toward Justin's role in the upcoming battle. It seemed they wanted him to serve as an ambassador, of sorts, a liaison between Earth and the Alliance. While he was willing to help however he could, this bothered him a great deal. He had always shied away from leadership positions and preferred to take safer support roles. Those duties were never quite as rewarding, but they weren't as demanding either. *After all, why would the leaders of Earth even think about taking me seriously?* He wondered, with great doubt about the hellish ones' faith in him. On the other hand, Justin knew he was the best person in the galaxy for the job, if not the only one who had any chance of pulling it off. No one from an outside world could represent the Alliance, and as far as he could tell, he was the only Earthling in that meeting on Hell. It would be his job to convince the people of Earth to completely change everything they had ever believed in, to follow an entirely new path. Most importantly, it had to be the decision of an Earth majority to join the Free Will Alliance. He felt it was his duty to help his home world make the correct decision. *That's it. I guess I'm da man, he* conceded, though he was still uneasy about it.

As fate would have it, the date chosen for the liberation of Earth was a masterpiece of ironic happenstance. When the timetable for the offensive was announced, Justin almost burst out in uncontrollable, gut-busting laughter. "December 21, 2022?" he said. "Really?"

All eyes instantly fell on the hysterical man who should have been the one to take it the most seriously.

Sandel looked at Justin with a half-smile and inquired, "My friend, is there something you would like to share with us?"

Justin, wiping tears from his eyes and still fighting to control his laughter, replied, "Yeah, it's that date. Uh...maybe

145

I should just show you." With that, he donned the Illuminator and let them witness firsthand, courtesy of the video screen, the story of the Mayan calendar.

By the time Justin removed the Illuminator, everyone was grinning from ear to ear, and a few were laughing almost as loudly as he had.

"Oh, the irony!" Lucifer bellowed, holding his middle.

Straining to control chuckling of his own, Sandel asked, "Would it be prudent to change it then?"

"No, just leave it as it is," Justin said, wiping the last of the happy tears from his face. "Other than being ten years late, it's perfect. If nothing else, it'll shake things up a little. It will give them something to talk about for many years. It just makes me wonder just where the Mayans got their info."

The upcoming battle for the liberation of Earth was the most closely held secret in the Free Will Alliance. Only the most trusted generals were aware of all the details; everything was shared only on a carefully guarded, need-to-know basis. Lucifer and Sandel knew all too well, there were those who are loyal to the Empire on Hell, and even within the higher ranks of the Alliance. The Holy Ghosts were, after all, masters of infiltration. For that reason, coordinates for the location of the upcoming offensive would not be revealed until the last possible moment. Top-secret meetings were held for the higher-ups about the further expansion of the territories along the Purgatorian borders, an effort to divert suspicion away from the truth. The future of Earth was at stake, and Lucifer refused to leave anything to chance.

Scout ships had been keeping careful watch on regular and deviant space around Earth for the last six months. Their sole mission was to discover any information about Empire presence in Earth's vicinity. Hell's most skilled covert agents manned the cloaked ships, and all findings were reported directly to Lucifer. He, in turn, told his closest, most trusted colleagues. With that information in hand, they finalized their plans and sweated the details. There was no room for mistakes, or an entire world and its inhabitants would pay a devastating price.

In preparation for the battle, Justin studied the plan

146

carefully, and he admired what they'd come up with. If all went well, there would be minimal bloodshed. He had never been in the military, nor had he ever considered himself a fighter. He had never seen much sense in violence, but now, he was ready to do whatever it took to free his beloved Earth. For most of his life, he'd been fooled, just an unwitting accomplice to Jesus' plan, and that pissed him off beyond all rationale. Not only was he tricked, which was cruel enough, but he had fallen for their lies without ever bothering to question them. "Blind faith my ass!" Justin said, to no one in particular.

Just a few short years earlier, he would have driven right into Hell, fueled by a heavenly lie. He had to thank fate that he was at the right place at the right time to avoid that. Now, he was prepared to face a future he'd chosen, not blindly but with his eyes wide open. He would now gladly fight Heaven's army, not because he was told to do so but because it was the right choice. Even now, the thought of being allied with the real Hell's angels made him smile.

As the day of the mission neared, Justin learned of something that surprised him, in a bad way. "What do you mean, I won't be on the front lines?" he asked. "This mission is of great significance to me and my home planet. It's my right to be there!" he protested.

Sandel put a hand on Justin's shoulder. "And you are of great significance to us, my friend," he said. "You are too important. We cannot risk losing you in combat. The battle to free Earth from Heaven's control will be minor compared to the battles you will face in the coming months and years. I hate to say it, but you may find yourself wishing for an early death after you commence with your duties as liaison for the Alliance."

"Wow. That's positive thinking," Justin murmured.

"It's the truth," Sandel said. "I'd much rather die fighting Jesus than to tackle the foe you must face. What is it your people say? Oh, yeah. It sucks to be you!"

As Justin boarded the *Leviathan*, the ship that would take him home, he still felt cheated. He wanted to fight, but deep down, he knew Sandel was right. He did feel safe in the hands of Captain Agares, whom he'd met on his maiden voyage to Hell. As they left normal space, Justin knew he was taking another step into a future that was so uncertain, even if he had agreed and chosen to face it. What he wanted most of all was for it all to be behind him so he could settle down with Salome. For the time being, however, he could only sit back and enjoy the ride.

Chapter 32

The six Alliance ships dropped into normal space within the orbit of Mars. Their sensors detected seven disciple ships already moving to intercept the Alliance vessels. It was somewhat disconcerting that the disciples knew they were coming, but their intent was clear: Every weapon was locked and loaded, ready to fire on the Alliance invasion. As the enemy neared weapons range, six more Alliance ships dropped into normal space directly behind them, trapping them between a seemingly overwhelming force.

The Alliance hoped the blockade might give the angelic warriors pause to reflect on the futile nature of forcing a battle at that moment. Not desiring to needlessly take lives, and hoping to end the conflict with minimal fighting, the Alliance signaled the disciple ships with a message: "Disciples of the Empire, we order you to surrender! We have no desire to fire upon you, and we will not unless we are forced to defend ourselves."

Sandel's transmitted offer was immediately rejected, as all three enemy ships fired their forward and rear particle cannons at the Alliance, cutting white-hot streaks through the dark blanket of space. Three of the twelve Alliance battle cruisers reported minimal damage as beams pounded their shields.

With their offer of peace declined and the need to defend themselves prevalent, Alliance forces returned fire.

They aimed to strategically disable the seven battle cruisers with precise hits that would take out their engines, weapons, and communications. Their phasonic disruptors tore at the shields of the Empire ships. Next, the Alliance and the disciples released their fighters. Like bees pouring from their hives, the more agile ships swarmed into space, some protecting the much larger cruisers and others attacking the enemy. The Alliance did their best to jam the signals, but the alert to the forces of Heaven went through.

Just as the Alliance seemed to be bringing the disciples to their knees, one Alliance ship moved off course, then another.

"Captain! *Apollyon* and *Legion* are breaking formation," said Pruflas, the com-tech.

"*Apollyon*, *Legion*, stay on course! We will follow the plan. Release your fighters," Sandel barked angrily.

The Alliance ships continued to move away, ignoring Sandel's command.

"Stay on course, damn you!" Sandel shouted.

Suddenly, both the *Apollyon* and the *Legion* began firing on their own Alliance ships.

Sandel's eyes grew wide when he saw it, and he struggled to breathe for a moment. All along, had feared that people sympathetic to the Empire were holding high-ranking positions within the fleet, but the majority of those on those vessels were loyal to the Free Will Alliance. His options were limited, because he was not about to kill his own people. "Do not use deadly force on the *Apollyon* or the *Legion*. I repeat, do not use deadly force! Aim only for their weapons systems and engines," Sandel shouted.

"Sir, we are getting a weak signal from the *Apollyon*," said the com-tech.

"Let's hear it," Sandel said.

"Hellfire, this is Commander Rumel of the *Apollyon*. Captain Orobas has locked himself in the emergency central control room (ECCR) and has taken complete control of the ship. We are attempting to regain control, but the captain is countering our every attempt. Please advise."

A similar grim message was received from the *Legion*. The

only difference on that ship was that the commander had taken control. "He's holing up in the failsafe room, the ECCR, and we can't get him out of there!"

The rogue warships continued to fire on the remaining Alliance attack force. That, along with the barrage from the disciple ships, stole the advantage away from the Alliance and gave the Empire an edge.

"Continue to target those disciples," Sandel ordered, doing his best to keep the fear and anger out of his voice, "but take only a defensive posture toward our ships."

Although most of the other Alliance ship captains wondered about the reasoning behind his decision, they followed Sandel's orders to the letter. With a focused attack, they quickly rendered the disciple ships powerless, but the vicious firing from the rogue ships continued to tear away at their shields. Then, just when it looked like the tables would be turned on the Alliance, the engines and weapons systems of the two renegade Alliance ships went dead.

"Yes!" Sandel hissed.

The command crew was equally bewildered by the new development. "Why did the traitors give up so soon?" one of them asked.

Sorath, whose mind and body were still abuzz with the heat of battle, said to Sandel, "What in Hell's name happened?"

Sandel replied simply, "We will talk later, my friend. For now, we must regain control of our ships." He smiled to himself as the words tumbled out. He was among a very select group who knew precisely what was going on: Each Alliance ship was equipped with a kill switch that would render rogues helpless if they chose to betray the Alliance. It was a most useful tool, since the depth and severity of the Holy Ghost's cancer in the Alliance was yet unclear.

First, a message was received from Captain Turel of the *Legion*: "We have breached the ECCR. Commander Lotoss is dead, by his own hand, sir. We have detained his co-conspirators and will await further orders."

Next, came a communication from Commander Rumel of the *Apollyon*, which paralleled the previous one.

151

"Transport the prisoners to a disciple ship. They should be well received by their own side," Sandel ordered. He paused for a moment, then continued, "Captain Rumel, the *Apollyon* is now yours. Command with honor and always remember that we fight for the free will of all. Sandel out." After he ended the communication, he looked over at Sorath. "My friend, you are in charge of the disciple ships. Study them, inside and out. Perhaps we can find weaknesses we can use against them in the future.

Sorath left promptly, with a smile on his face. *This is going to be fun,* he thought, picking up his pace.

"Captain, the *Eligos*, the *Pithius*, and the *Valefar* have reported heavy damage and are commencing with repairs," Pruflas reported.

"Very good! Let us know if they need assistance. Also, please signal the rest of the fleet to enter normal space. We need to remove the enemy ships and secure this system before more of those blasted disciples arrive," Sandel said. At that moment, one thought occurred to him, and it was not a pleasant one: *Now comes the hard part.*

Since the seven disciple ships were without weapons, communications, or engines, they were suitable for safe transport. As prisoners of war, they would be towed to Planet Naberus, in the Purgatorian sector. Unlike the captives of the Empire, who were mercilessly tortured, killed, or left to die on barren planets, prisoners on Naberus were treated with dignity and respect; it was assumed that they were, for the most part, just good but misguided people. The prisoners of war were even supplied with all the technology and conveniences required to live comfortable, decent lives. They only lacked any means of escape, and they were not able to communicate beyond the boundaries of the planet. They were left to govern themselves as free citizens of their new home, but they were planet bound, and space was off limits. They didn't have to settle for bread and water or meager prison food, because they were free to farm the land so their planet could provide for them.

Some did find it to be cruel and unusual punishment that the prisoners of Naberus were denied the Longevity Factor. As the effects of the Factor wore off in time, they would live lifespans in the hundreds of years, not in the thousands. There were plans in place for their new home to be visited and explored in the distant future, to see if a new society would arise, one that could grow past their hatred of the truth.

Everyone sentenced to the prison planet was shown the undistorted truth about the Empire and the leader for whom they had so valiantly fought. They witnessed what the Empire had done to the planets they came from. They saw the reality of all the terrible things they had brought forth in the name of Jesus. Many who were shown the truth believed it and opted to join the Alliance. After years of careful screening, several of those would be accepted into Alliance ranks.

As Sandel and his attack force dealt with the bulk of the Empire forces, more Alliance ships attacked key locations throughout the solar system around Earth. The scouts had accurately pinpointed where every disciple ship would be at any given time. That knowledge made it possible to minimize casualties during the takeover, but winning the battle would mean nothing if they were not able to hold on to their prize.

Within 24 hours, 250 Free Will Alliance battle cruisers had positioned themselves at strategic locations in normal and deviant space. The bulk of the force was concentrated around Planet Earth. It would be their first real test of power since the Purgatorian War, and it was a battle they could not afford to lose. With that in mind, another 350 Alliance ships traveled through space on their way toward Earth, ready for a fight.

Earthlings who bore the responsibility of keeping an eye on the atmosphere had no doubt that something strange was happening in outer space. Their gadgets and technology registered the Alliance ships around their planet, but no one knew what to make of their findings. As curious and uneasy as they were, they would not encounter first contact until the system was secure.

For the Alliance's part, they knew that even after the space around Earth was secure, the hardest part of the transition was ahead of them. Not only were they poised to fight off a potential heavenly attack, but they also had to convince a majority of Earthlings that they had good intentions. That, in and of itself, would be a tremendously trying task. To be sure, indoctrinating the world leaders would be daunting enough, but pleading their case to the entirety of the human race, to all those heads already filled with dogma and beliefs and philosophies pounded into them since childhood: That seemed like an impossible undertaking in its own right.

Chapter 33

Jesus was beside himself after he heard the news. Rage tore through his mind, and his body vibrated with intense fits of anger. Unable to control his wrath and in need of an outlet, he reached under his robes, pulled out a knife, killed the servant who brought him wine, then stepped over the bleeding corpse as if it did not even exist. "First Purgatory, and now my precious Earth! Kill them! Kill them all!" the son of God screamed, with a teeth-clenching growl. "I want every ship in Heaven's fleet to attack the Alliance. I will not lose that planet!"

Furious, he grabbed a large handful of hair of a female who'd just pleasured him, a poor creature cowering by his throne, and he savagely cut her throat. His rage seemed to abate somewhat as his hands and robes were stained with crimson, but he screamed for the seraphim, cherubims, and thrones who made up his council. The seraphim were at the highest level, with the cherubim ranking right behind them. The thrones were the lowest and the most expendable. Their goal was to influence Jesus' decisions, to move him toward the mature and rational and to dissuade him from following his tendency to rant and rave and behave like a power-hungry, paranoid, spoiled adolescent. The most difficult part for all of them, however, was making Jesus believe their better ideas were his own.

As his council entered the room, they barely registered

the bodies that now adorned the throne room. It was not un-usual for them to see servants cleaning up one of their own, an unfortunate soul whose only misfortune was to have been close to Jesus at a time of extreme stress. Even in good times such as Jesus' carnal gatherings, it was common for slave girls to be carried out to be disposed of like common trash. The only apprehension the council felt was their fear that they would be unable to calm him down before he turned on one of them. Every word had to be chosen carefully, so as to not anger Jesus further, and they had to somehow bring rea-son into the decisions that followed.

"I want my planet back!" he shouted like a petulant child who'd lost one of his prized toys. "What are you doing to make it so? How could this happen?" Jesus screamed, clearly still unable to control his rage.

No one in the room dared to remind him that it was his order to place minimum presence on Earth, hoping to avoid raising Alliance suspicion. All they had to do was glance at the bloody bodies on the floor to put the fatal thought of fin-ger-pointing out of their minds.

Seraphim One, the leader of the lord's council, spoke first. "Most Exulted One, 200 of Heaven's finest battle cruis-ers are Earthward bound. Their mission is to regain control of Earth at all costs, and they are under strict orders not to fire on that world."

"Only 200?" Jesus snapped. "Not good enough! Send 500. No, send 1,000! They must give me back what is mine!" Jesus screamed.

Seraphim One continued cautiously, "Lord Jesus, this is but the first wave. Their mission is to weaken the Alliance's hold on Earth's system so the second wave can defeat our en-emies. Sire, as you know, we dare not weaken our defenses in the regions of the galaxy we hold or around Heaven, lest the real Alliance objective is to attack our precious Heaven itself."

The last statement seemed to bring a rational but reluc-tant calm to Jesus. When they saw his gaze soften a bit, the entire council let out a collective breath they'd been holding since they walked into the room. Although there was still a chance that someone there would die before the meeting was over, everyone's chance of survival seemed to have increased ten-fold.

Higher ranking in the council did not automatically ensure that one would be shielded from the wrath of the Lord Jesus. Seraphiel, the previous Seraphim One, was beaten to death by Jesus after he made the mistake of inferring that a decision Jesus had announced had bordered on insanity. That, as it turned out, was a major mistake. Zabkiel, current Seraphim One, rose to that rank after serving as a throne. He had saved Jesus' life in an assassination attempt, so, in addition to his promotion, he'd been the closest thing Jesus had had to a friend for the last 200 years. Even though Jesus confided in him and told him many secrets, he was always mindful of his place. He, too, wisely chose his words, lest he suffer a similar fate to that of his predecessor. His appointment did not set well with Jahoel, who would have naturally ascended to the position had it not been denied him because of Zabkiel, being in the right place at the right time.

Magdalene was another whom Jesus sought for council. Since the birth of their two children, their relationship had completely surpassed the physical. Although she was ever-present at the palace, she and her husband rarely spent time together, save for when she had to perform ceremonial duties as queen or on the rare occasions when Jesus sought her counsel. Truth be told, most people at the palace feared her more than they feared Jesus. All knew she thirsted for pleasure and harbored deep bloodlust. This was not out of misplaced anger; it was simply her favorite game to make love to someone, then kill them, as slowly and painfully as possible.

As attributes went, Magdalene was as smart as she was beautiful, and she knew her place. She was aware that the status quo of that fate was very precarious indeed. She had only to look at Dilyla to find reason to be true to Jesus. It was well known that Jesus had the Holy Ghosts systematically seek out and exterminate every living member of Dilyla's family. They followed the branches on the family trees of both of her grandparents, working their way from the most distant to the closest, and cruelly saved her immediate family for last. An entire bloodline was wiped out within a matter of months. Once one of the most powerful people in the galaxy, she was now a broken woman. Dilyla was a laughingstock, with no power, no standing, and no family except for a son who had taken everything she had ever loved away. Magdalene reflected on this often and made sure not to make the same mistakes to incur Jesus' wrath.

It was uncertain if God had died of old age or by the hand of his only begotten son, but the announcement sent a shockwave through the Empire. Jesus was now the one and only omniscient, all-powerful god. All those who had been holding out for the slightest possibility that their beloved God would return and free them from Jesus, died a little inside, but the tears they shed were for themselves. Everyone on Heaven knew that God was finally free, but his followers who were left behind, would somehow have to endure the cruelty of his offspring.

Chapter 34

As the disciple ships neared Earth's system, the Alliance maneuvered strategically in an effort to block their way. At the same time, a stern message was sent to the Heaven fleet: "Withdraw, and no harm will befall you. If you choose to advance, we will be forced to open fire."

No sooner was that communique sent than the disciple battle cruisers opened fire.

Seeing the blatant rejection of their message gave the Alliance, the just cause it needed to return fire, as promised. Smaller, faster, and more easily navigable fighters exited the battle cruisers and surged like a swarm of locusts in and around the larger ships, all of them fighting fiercely and dying bravely.

The next few hours passed quickly, at least in the minds of the soldiers on both sides; in the heat of battle, no one felt time passing. Particle weapons burned through the vacuum of space, tearing away at shields and ultimately ripping large gashes in the unprotected metal of the ships of both sides. As the war raged on, there was no clear winner. Both sides sustained significant, painful losses.

As new waves of Alliance cruisers joined the battle and attacked from all sides, the disciple fleet began to realize the futility of their mission. Feeling helpless and defeated, they began to fall back, albeit not so much retreating as regrouping, as if to ponder their next move. The Alliance took advantage of the opportunity and continued their onslaught. As soon as the Heaven fleet signaled for an official retreat, the Alliance attack ended. It was simply not their style, or their desire, to unnecessarily spill blood.

It wouldn't be long, however, before the vengeful, heartless Empire mounted an all-out offensive to reclaim a planet Jesus had deemed most valuable. In response, Sandel sent a simple, direct message to the retreating enemy: "Earth is now under the protection of the Free Will Alliance. Any act of aggression against the planet or the ships protecting it, will be met with extreme force. Your noncompliance with this warning will result in the destruction of every living thing at the following Earthly coordinates:

18° 18' 30" N, 65° 46' 13" W
14° 26' 24" S, 62° 51' 37" W
00° 46' 53" S, 57° 40' 26" W
01° 13' 48" N, 26° 30' 42" E
01° 33' 35" S, 22° 56' 05" E
03° 44' 06" S, 104° 36' 54" E
11° 25' 28" N, 108° 08' 27" E
15° 51' 36" N, 121° 25' 50" E
05° 43' 18" S, 141° 17' 16" E

"If you wisely withdraw your ships now and refrain from any further aggression, we will petition the people of Earth to supply the Empire with the Longevity Factor at a fair and equitable price. The Longevity Factor is meant to be shared, but only if it is the will of the Earthlings. You will not take it from the planet by force, for the Alliance will boldly protect Earth's right to choose their future, whatever it may be."

***

"Earth is under the protection of the Free Will Alliance? Why? How?" Jesus fumed. "Free Will Alliance," he muttered with a growl. "I want them all dead! Dead now! Do you hear me? Kill them! Kill them all!" the lord screamed, sending the fear and panic in the throne room to an all-time high.

At that point, all Heaven broke loose, and the holy shit hit the fan. For a few moments, Jesus was uncontrollable, in a mad rage of epic proportions. Seraphim One labored for almost an hour—of course at a safe distance—to try to calm the paroxysm of screaming and fist-pounding that the Alliance message had provoked. In the skirmish, three seraphim were badly wounded, and two cherubim and six thrones met their deaths before their lord's rage settled. The smell of blood and fear permeated the great hall.

As a deflated Jesus brooded on his throne while the bodies of the unfortunate council members were carried from the room, Seraphim One approached him cautiously. "Your Holiness, what has transpired is a most unfortunate event, but as you have already surmised in your infinite wisdom, sire, we dare not attack Earth for fear that the heathen Alliance will, in their ignorance, carry out their promise to destroy our only hope of obtaining the Longevity Factor. Eden is a dying planet, and even we may not be able to change that. Earth is the only other place in the universe that has successfully produced the Tree of Life. As you are no doubt aware, Most Omniscient One, there is still hope. Not all is lost."

Jesus looked up, puzzled and still struggling to calm down. His eyes begged Seraphim One to continue; this was often the case when Jesus wanted the seraphim to state aloud what he, in his infinite wisdom, had known all along.

Seraphim One continued, "Only our Lord Jesus, who sees and knows all, could have foreseen this tragedy. In your great and mighty wisdom, you placed Michael and his team on Earth to fight our battle from within. How brilliant you are, Lord! Our seeds have been planted, and the people of Earth, with Michael's help, will soon harvest the fruit of the Bible's teachings. They will clearly see the evil within the words of the ambassadors from Hell, and they will rise up against the Alliance. The Alliance boasts about their free will, but the very thing they fight for will turn out to be the thorn in their side. The Earthlings will see that it is the Alliance that is evil, and by their own free will, they will ask the fiends of Hell to leave. By their own creed, the Alliance will have to comply. I still marvel at the miracle of your wisdom, my Lord. What you saw thousands of years before, we, in our finite thinking, are just now bearing witness to."

Blinded by his own arrogance, Jesus proudly smiled as Seraphim One stroked his ego and commended his genius.

161

Not for the first time, he contemplated the greatness of his plan that was finally coming to fruition. He barely noticed the servants cleaning the mess under his feet and replacing the bloody clothes on his body, for he was utterly consumed by the fact that he truly was the most powerful being in the universe. "I am...God!" he declared, and no one in the throne room dared to offer a retort.

Chapter 35

"Leaders of Planet Earth, you have no doubt discerned our presence already. Therefore, we respectfully request your permission to approach, so that we may discuss the reason for our entry into your planetary system," Sandel's soothing, confident voice echoed simultaneously from almost every audio device on Earth.

Since the message was instantly translated into all the major languages worldwide, the entire globe was soon abuzz with excitement over the new development. Suddenly, the tweets and posts and DMs and IMs about the adolescent acts of celebrities and the sex scandals of politicians were a moot point. Old news, fake or not, no longer deserved to be in print, for it was easily upstaged by something truly important. Even, reports of human wars breaking out around the world were replaced by information about a possible threat from without, an otherworldly presence with something to say.

Ufologists were the experts, spouting their theories that quickly became hot topics on every news station and every talk show and podcast. On local news channels, those little-known know-it-alls who'd obsessed over spaceships and conspiracy theories for years puffed their chests out and testified about the future, with subtle I-told-you-so tones dripping from their every word. Along with them, however, another group had become very vocal, occupying the airwaves and the internet.

Just as it had always been, theirs was a message of fear and doom, which they intended to exploit by any and all means possible. Reverend Gabe Brown was one of many who seized the opportunity to spread viral soundbites of terror, in the aim that he could benefit from the global hopelessness. Benefit he did, for the pews and offering collection plates overflowed at each service. That put a smile on his face, even as the founder of the Church of God's Promise preached horrifying sermons about the unavoidable Armageddon, making it very clear that the Antichrist was alive and well on Planet Earth, on the prowl for human souls.

"It is time for all religions of the world to join together and rise up against the forces of evil," the irreverent Reverend screeched from his pulpit. "It is time for Christians to sit down with nations of Islam, for the Jewish to seek partnership with Buddhists, for all of us to form an army of mankind who will fight for our religious freedom. We must also welcome those who have turned their backs on the word of God, for they will soon ask forgiveness when they see the error of their ways. We cannot be drawn into the arms of Satan, or we will suffer eternal damnation."

Michael was also busy in the background, speaking with the religious leaders around the world. In Vatican City, he had ready access to the Pope. He was also welcomed by the leaders of Jewish community. The leaders of Islam were a bit reluctant but did grant him an audience. Although he was greeted with open arms by the Jewish hierarchy and the Pope, he had to reveal himself and prove that he was, in fact, Archangel Michael before the worshippers of Islam could trust him. In each case, he advised, "Rally your followers to be ready for the battle ahead. The time is here, ladies and gentlemen. The future is now!"

Michael had always found the sheep-like religions of Planet Earth and other planets a bit laughable and pathetic. Most could be controlled easily, he knew, but the Islamic extremists were wildcards among the faithful foolish. If anyone could destroy the very thing he was trying to obtain, it was the followers of Islam. The archangel was well aware that the only way God could regain control of Earth was from within, and that he and the seeds he had planted were Heaven's only hope.

Chapter 36

Sandel entered the room where Justin and Salome were watching broadcasts from Earth. "What is going on, my friends?" he inquired.

"We have a major problem, Sandel. It seems many earthly religious organizations are warning their followers of the impending arrival of the beast. This is not good," Justin said, shaking his head.

Sandel offered a half-smile that didn't look very reassuring. "Did I not tell you that you would wish you had died in the first wave, my friend? You have a big job ahead of you, but if you stick to the plan, we will win the hearts of the people of your Earth, even the religious who are blinded by their faith. We will open their eyes, Justin."

"I hope so," Justin said, looking over at Salome with deep concern.

"Let us go. We have a meeting to attend. The leaders of Earth await you," Sandel said.

Justin stood up from his seat with a frown on his face, already hating the leadership role he was about to play. He'd agreed to it, of course, and no one was forcing him, but he certainly wasn't looking forward to it.

As they headed for the ship that would carry them to Earth, Sandel revisited his safety concerns. "Remember, never be without your shield. I do not much like you, but some of the others have grown fond of you. You are like...a beloved family pet," he teased with a grin.

Salome punched him in the arm but also couldn't stifle her own giggle.

After their difficult goodbyes, Justin boarded the ship. He tried to think positively and keep his mind clear of worries, but during the trip to his home planet, his concerns nagged at him: *Convincing the people of Earth that my alien friends have good intentions is going to be a hard sell. Once they know the details of who they are, where they're from, and who they're fighting, it's going to get pretty dicey down there. How do I tell the people of Earth that they need to side with Hell to fight Jesus? God, it even sounds ludicrous to me,* he thought, fearing an uprising of religious and non-religious alike.

Their destination was the United Nations building in New York City. There, they would rendezvous with the many world leaders and representatives who had agreed to attend from various corners of the globe. The one guarantee was that it would be a summit like none other in history.

They landed on the circular drive in front of the tower. With as much security as any head of state and the largest crowd that had ever gathered at the U.N. building, they were escorted into the building. Their plan was to get in and get out as quickly as possible.

After a brief introduction, Justin glanced over at the men in black, the Secret Service-looking security force posted around him. His gait to the podium was a bit nervous and shaky, but he surprised even himself when he began his speech with practiced confidence: "My fellow people of Earth, I am Justin Grant. I was born in a little town in central Indiana. Until just a few short years ago, I was like you, pretty much content. I thought I had life figured out, and I was somewhat oblivious to the universe around us. Also, like many of you, I believed in the possibility of beings from other worlds, but I doubted I would live to see them for myself. I was wrong."

He paused as a hush fell over the crowd, as if everyone was hanging on his every word. Once he knew he had their undivided attention, he continued, "That is why I am here before you today. I am an Earthling, like you, but I represent the Free Will Alliance, and I would like to welcome you all into the galactic community. The Free Will Alliance is a collection of thousands of worlds, founded on the worthy principles of freedom and free will for all."

Justin continued his well-rehearsed speech, revealing more details about the Alliance and all they represented. He offered some tidbits about the what and when of things, but he was careful to omit certain aspects of the who and where, especially the Alliance leadership and the location of their headquarters; he knew that as soon as those hellish facts came to light, his mission would become so much harder.

"Entry into the Alliance is, by no means, a sure thing," he said, adding an important caveat he was advised to share. "We, the people of Earth, will maintain our free will. That means we must *choose* to be part of something greater than we have ever imagined."

For the next half-hour, the prepared speech went on, accompanied by video provided by the Illuminator. He told them of all the Free Will Alliance had to offer, many wonderful things that would make Planet Earth a better place in the present and in the future. He touched on medical advances that would eradicate disease and prolong life, agricultural advances that would eliminate world hunger, technological advances that would benefit many elements of everyday life, and environmental advances that would restore Earth to the paradise it was meant to be.

"Membership in the Free Will Alliance means we can boldly go where our new allies have gone before!" he said excitedly, cleverly countering the famous Captain Kirk's opener. "Space and all those strange, new worlds we've only fantasized about and seen in our movies will be open to you all. If we join the Alliance, we will be able to visit other planets. We will encounter new life and new civilizations. No longer will our commerce be limited by the perimeters of our Earth. We will be free to trade goods and services throughout the galaxy. I have tasted foods so amazing and unique and delicious that I could only eat them with my eyes closed, so as to experience every nuance of their flavor," Justin said, then closed his eyes to emphasize his point. It might have been an odd gesture in any other world gathering, but in this case, it looked genuine because it was genuine.

When he opened his eyes again, Justin's expression became stern. He looked at several audience members directly, moving his eyes from one to another. "We are not here as peacemakers," he stated matter-of-factly. "The Alliance has no interest in Earth squabbles or our differences. These are your concerns, and you will have to deal with them in the coming months. The Free Will Alliance will not accept a divided Earth. You must end your conflicts and overcome your differences to form a government that represents all of Earth with one clear, unified voice."

Justin let that soak in for a moment, taking note of the guilty looks that flashed across the faces of many of the world leaders, then finished, "Other than resolving our pitiful, trivial conflicts, one thing stands between Earth and all that the Alliance has to offer to her. A decision must be made. The Free Will Alliance is precisely that. We do not and will not force any choice upon anyone, for that is at our very foundation. Now, please deliver this message to your peoples in all nations. Over the next few weeks, we will visit the leaders of each to discuss the details of membership in detail and answer questions as necessary. Remember, only a majority vote will be accepted. Free will is our foundation, and it must become yours if you want to join the Alliance. The choice is yours, and I hope, for the sake of all the people of Earth, that you will choose wisely. Thank you."

Blam! Blam! Blam! Blam!

As soon as Justin turned and stepped away from the shelter of the podium, four shots silenced the mumbling crowd. The bullets found their mark in his back and head, but they ricocheted off his shield. One struck the podium and bounced, then spun to a stop on the floor behind him. Jeqon, Justin's head of security and personal guard, was instantly at his side, with far greater reflexes than any security Earth had to offer.

A few screams and a collective gasp erupted as everyone in the room waited to witness Justin's fall to the floor. Their eyes grew wide, and another, louder gasp escaped when he instead turned and looked at them. All watched as his attacker was tackled, forcefully handcuffed, and led from the room. Justin frowned and shook his head, before calmly walking from the room.

Over the next few weeks, the meetings with the individual governments went as planned. National leaders and their advisers were permitted to wear Illuminators, just a small sampling of the technology they'd be privy to if they managed to meet the Alliance's conditions and join them. First, they were guided through memories from their own pasts. That revealed the power of the devices and the truths they held. Then they were shown the wonders of the galaxy and the potential benefits of Alliance membership. Finally, they saw the truth about the galactic conflict and all the players involved. They saw Heaven as it was in its glory, but they also witnessed its downfall under the rule of the power-hungry Jesus and the threat he represented. Finally, they bore witness to Hell, a planet with as much natural beauty as their own. They even caught a glimpse of Lucifer rolling around on the floor with his grandchildren, a snippet added at Justin's request. "Don't worry. He keeps his pitchfork safely stored away most of the time," Justin joked, only to be met with fewer laughs than he expected.

At the end of each meeting, the participants were asked, "Do you understand?"

Their responses were gauged by the Illuminators they wore. In most every case, the message was understood and accepted. The common desire among them seemed to be the chance to explore their personal pasts in vivid detail. "Illuminators are just part of the amazing technology you'll have access to with membership in the Alliance," Justin told them. He wasn't surprised by their stunned reaction to the gadgets; he, himself, knew how addicting the Illuminator was, but he also knew how potentially dangerous it could be if uncontrolled. Nevertheless, the benefits far outweighed the pitfalls.

China was extremely hesitant to participate, as they were never ones to rock the boat or upset the status quo. They were at least willing to carefully consider what was on offer and weigh the pros and cons of it. Many nations controlled by purely religious doctrines refused to participate, due to fear so callously implanted in them by Michael. Due to their numbers, they represented a very powerful, potentially dangerous group, but they were still a minority that could hopefully be dealt with after Earth's acceptance into the Alliance.

As a gesture of good will, the Alliance gave Earth two very important gifts. The first was a formula for food production that would put an end to the rampant world hunger. Third-world countries would never again lack the ability to provide for their people. Second was an environmentally clean power source that would eliminate the need for burning fossil fuels anywhere on Earth. That, in and of itself, was impressive to even the most doubtful doubters, as the sustainability of the environment had been in question and weighing heavily on everyone's minds for quite some time.

Chapter 37

Earth was a focal point of excitement as everyone pondered all the positive changes the Alliance represented. As news of the gifts filtered out to the general population, many felt better about the so-called invaders, but others seemed even more skeptical than they were before. A worldwide broadcast was just hours away. While Justin understood the importance of clear, transparent communication of the truth, he was not very comfortable with his face being shown around the world; any hope of anonymity would be lost after that evening. Some would perceive him as a hero, but a large portion of the people on his very own planet would assume him a puppet, a talking head for the voices of evil. The one thing he could be sure of was that there would be very few places he could go on Earth where he would not be instantly recognized, whether it was because they deemed him famous or infamous.

All of his and Leah's surviving relatives were secretly spirited off the planet to enjoy a vacation on Hell. Not only would that ensure their safety until they could make a proper homecoming, but it would also guarantee that there would be no one or nothing that could be used to manipulate or coerce Justin.

At 9 o'clock eastern time, Justin was introduced to the people of Earth. He stood before a huge collection of microphones in the United Nations assembly hall and began, "My fellow people of Earth, I am Justin Grant. I was born in a little town in central Indiana..." The speech continued much like the one he had given a few days earlier, but this one was directed at the masses. The major difference was the Q&A session offered upon his finishing remarks.

As Justin ended his speech, he looked at the crowd gathered before him. Reporters and well-known news personalities from throughout the world were on hand to verbalize the concerns of the people of Earth. It was bound to be a difficult few minutes, but the questions started out surprisingly simple: "What is the main objective of this Alliance? Why are they contacting Earth now, at this time? Does it have anything to do with the Mayan calendar?"

After those concerns were addressed, the more prying interrogations came. A journalist stood, someone Justin recognized from somewhere, but couldn't specifically place. "I am Zach Lassiter, of WORD-TV," he announced.

Ah, that's where I've seen him, Justin thought as he suddenly realized he was staring at the pre-eminent news anchor from the world's leading faith-based television station. WORD-TV was the station that often hosted Reverend Gabriel Brown, and was owned by the devious Michael Abraham Smith. *Great. Here we go,* Justin thought with a groan he hoped the many microphones didn't capture. "Go ahead, Mr. Lassiter," he said, unable to hide the reluctance in his voice.

Lassiter continued, "I have two questions for you, Mr. Grant. First, what is the name of the planet that is home to the Free Will Alliance? Second, who is the leader of the Free Will Alliance?"

Justin braced himself for the expected negative reaction, and cautiously delivered the agreed upon response: "The Alliance is headquartered on Planet Hell."

A murmur washed over the crowd like a tidal wave of shock. those that were in no way religious, responded with nervous laughter.

Matter-of-factly and as calmly as he could, Justin continued, "And the elected leader of the Alliance is Lucifer Satanis."

"What!? Lucifer?" someone screamed.

"Did you say...*Satan*?" another bellowed.

"This is no time to joke around with the people of Earth!" a third admonished.

Justin waited for the commotion to die down a little, then did his best to make sense of it. "I know what these names represent to some of you, and I understand the reason behind your apprehension," he said. "My friends, for thousands of years, the people of Planet Earth have been the victims of thought manipulation. What many of you hold to be true, what many of you have been led to believe is not really—"

"Mr. Grant!" Zach broke in. "Are you standing before us as a self-confessed emissary of Lucifer, the beast master of Hell, and talking to us about thought manipulation? Isn't Lucifer himself the father of lies, seeking to devour us all?"

The reporter shook his head. "Okay. Let me play devil's advocate for a moment...and pardon the pun," he said, looking around at his colleagues with a smirk on his face. "Let's say human beings have been fooled and manipulated for centuries. If that's true, and if Lucifer is not behind it, just who would be so devious as to brainwash us? Who are they, and what do they stand to gain or profit from it?"

Justin knew Zach was pushing him to reveal the name of their enemy, if only to cause an uproar that would quickly put an end to their civil assembly, but there was no turning back now. He squared his shoulders, gathered his courage and confidence, and answered, "The architect of this plan is a flesh-and-blood being, not an immortal. He is from a planet near the center of the galaxy, not a holy realm. The one who has manipulated you for these many years is the son of God, Jesus. He resides on Planet Heaven, the headquarters of the Galactic Empire." Justin recited the calculated response to the question. He had purposely used Jesus' name. He could not bring himself to call him God, out of respect to Elohim, his benevolent father. Knowing all he had learned about Lucifer's old friend, he refused to give his depraved son any sort of title of respect.

At that moment, the people who attended the live broadcast, made such an uproar, that there was no chance of a calm, informative, civilized press conference continuing. The audience simply could not be quieted. In homes all over the world, viewers and listeners were reacting to the information that Justin had just delivered.

As Justin left the stage, an advertisement scrolled across the large screen behind him, along with images of all the worlds known to the Alliance: "*The Truth: A Brief History of the Galaxy* will be shown in theaters around the world and can also be viewed on the internet at *TheSerpentsGift.com*. We invite you to join us in discovering all you have yet to know about your world and the worlds of others..."

The underground movement wasted no time playing on the fears that had been instilled into Earth society under Heaven's cruel plan. Every religious leader in the world spoke out vehemently against the Alliance, whipping their confused followers into a fever. A call rang out to align all the world religions in an All-Faith Coalition, and the name was instantly popular worldwide. Even Vatican City called for unity and openly offered their full support to the Coalition.

Reverend Gabe Brown was quick to take to the airwaves and appeared on every station Michael, always in front of a huge All-Faith Coalition banner. He was at his best, preaching Hell and damnation to all who supported the Alliance but a place in Heaven for the believers in God and the new Coalition. "Whatever you do," he urged, pounding his fists on his pulpit and inhaling huge gasps of air between his words the way the wind-sucking preachers always did, "do not subject your eyes or your soul to that blasphemous video the Alliance has asked you to watch. It is a fiction born of evil, authored by the devil himself. Do not be tempted by its title, its false claim that it is *The Truth*. Do not believe its lies, for God has reserved a place in Heaven for the faithful and pure of heart." In spite of the seriousness of his warning, the reverend's soothing Southern drawl made him sound inviting and his words convincing.

Nevertheless, despite the cautioning of the All-Faith Coalition, the website was bombarded with visitors who watched the video. In nations where communication restrictions banned such sites, hackers stepped in to make it possible for the message to be received by anyone in the world who could access the internet via computer or smartphone. Those living under oppressive, strict government rule were quite open to the truth of the message. They held out hope when the video promised, "Anyone who desire to learn a more complete history of the galaxy may make an appointment with an Alliance representative and experience that history in 3D."

As theaters and cinemas around the world began to show *The Truth* on the big screen, people packed into the seats for the life-changing, eye-opening experience. No blockbuster in history had caused such long lines, and no one even bothered to stop for popcorn. Of course, the naysayers were there as well, the All-Faith Coalition protestors who gathered outside the theaters, warning moviegoers of the dangers of Satan and his lying ways. Power outages and bomb threats were not uncommon, and violent fights broke out between truth-seekers and the objectors. Not so mysteriously, several movie houses burned to the ground.

The 3D glasses provided to watchers of the film were specially adapted to receive signals from an Illuminator. Not only did the audience witness the archives of real history seemingly firsthand, but they also felt every nuance of the experience. They saw God and Lucifer as young men, fighting for freedom throughout the galaxy. They felt they were actually there during Lucifer's last meeting with his old friend. They saw Jesus rise to power and the atrocities acted out in his quest for the illusion of ultimate power. They even had a peek into his throne room, and saw him butcher innocent servants during one of his royal tantrums. They bore witness to the rise of the Free Will Alliance and the 666 worlds that joined in its formation. The Purgatorian War unfolded before their very eyes in the world's best surround sound and better than any high-definition Earth technology. They saw planets and peoples who gained their freedom as a result of that hard-fought battle. Best of all, they knew that none of them had been brainwashed; rather, they all left knowing and feeling that they had finally seen the whole truth and nothing but the truth.

As the weeks passed and more people experienced *The Truth*, some began to call for a one-world government. Always at the forefront of trying to beat everyone to the punch, American politicians took notice of the new development, and many began to campaign for a change. Of course, most were hoping selfishly for some sort of position of prevalence in the new world order, but either way, a government that could represent Earth as one, unified voice was beginning to seem possible.

Chapter 38

Nearly every leader who was willing to view *The Truth*
found reality in its message, and they were keenly aware of
the changes that had to occur to make it all possible. In the
United States, legislation was drafted to move closer to the
one-voice scenario that was necessary for membership in the
Alliance. The few leaders loyal to Michael and the All-Faith
Coalition had neither the power nor the numbers to stop the
forward momentum of the formation of the dreaded unified,
one-world government. A worldwide cry demanded, "Make it
happen! Make it happen soon!" as the people as a whole were
eager to join the galactic community.

Michael, feeling a bit cornered, decided it was time to
take his message to the people, and his worldwide campaign
against the Alliance was unleashed. The archangel used every
resource at his disposal to paint a picture of the Alliance as
evil, the beginning of the end for humanity. He did a nice job
of spoiling their reputation, but it was too little, too late.

After some thought of what else could be done, Michael
happened upon an unlikely source that he hoped would solve
his dilemma. Although he was 10,000 years old, with the full
knowledge of the galaxy at his disposal, he still had plenty
to learn from the Earthlings, specifically the devious, win-at-
all-cost, bait-and-switch, sneaky-car-salesmen-type humans
who worked at advertising agencies.

Michael had come to admire advertising executives

during his years of infiltration on the planet. Most he knew of had made a profitable art of misdirection. They had an uncanny ability to warp the memories of their prey, the rest of humanity, through the use of emotional stimuli. *They truly could sell ice to Eskimos!* he thought with a smile. He also surmised that the most effective advertising campaigns took subtle jabs at the competition and played on people's fears and desires. Depicting the Free Will Alliance as evil, along with brutal images of wars, baby killings, Satan and his demonic partners, and the inevitable Armageddon with the resulting scorched landscape would serve him well, exploiting the humans' deepest, darkest fears. The icing on the cake would be images of the beauty of God's love, with pictures of happy families, laughing children, cute puppies and kittens, beautiful nature scenes. He would send a powerful message of goodness and peace that all would find appealing.

While it was a good tactic to add to his arsenal, Michael knew negative advertising would not be enough to stop the change on its own, even as gullible as Earthlings were. He needed to gather his army together. He did not naïvely expect them all to fight side by side, but at least they would have a common cause and a mutual enemy. Two main groups stood to lose the most if the proposed one-world government came to fruition: organized religion with theology based on Christ and organized crime. As Michael saw it, they were one in the same. Both had unspoken power that crept into every nook and cranny of the planet. As far as religion was concerned, with general acceptance of galactic history provided by the Alliance, religion based on Christ, a yet-unseen deity, would see their attendance dwindle and their coffers run dry. The worldwide, jurisdictional power of the global government would balk at the idea of any unlawful activity that preyed on weakness, and that would put an end to organized crime and terrorism. For those reasons, crime and religion were both in danger of falling apart, and Michael could not afford that.

Thus, the resident angels already in hiding led the plot against the formation of the new Earth government. They had to rely on the conditioning they'd so meticulously set into place over the last few thousand years. They used human fear of the devil as a tool to incite the religious peoples of the world to rebel against the Alliance.

For his part, Michael made it known that peaceful resistance was a thing of the past, and through the voice of Reverend Gabe Brown, elected head of the All-Faith Coalition, it was announced that a holy war was at hand: "We must do everything possible to stop the formation of this unholy government. Armageddon is here! Armageddon is now! As promised in the word of God, all who fight for the lord shall have a place in Heaven, and those who believe in the words vomited from the mouth of Satan shall spend an eternity burning in the fiery pits of Hell," he loudly propagated to his sheep. "Heaven is real, God is real, and his promise of everlasting life is absolutely real."

Soon, church attendance was up worldwide. In fact, many services had to be moved outside or to sports arenas to accommodate all the new warriors of God. The people riding the fence were at the precipice: They had to make a choice.

Religious leaders who saw their way of life being cast aside decided it was time to use their influence, power, and fortunes to fight, both openly and covertly. A new group of religious leaders arose, actively opposing the new order by whatever means necessary. Secret funding of violent groups sympathetic to the All-Faith Coalition became an unspoken portion of each church collection. Attacks against theaters that dared to show *The Truth* increased, and assaults on Free Will Alliance embassies began in earnest.

Michael, pleased to see the All-Faith Coalition finally coming together, turned his attention to another group he'd been working with for centuries. The archangel called a meeting with the upper echelons of crime syndicates across the globe. Scoundrels from every continent gathered in one place and managed to set their own bitter disagreements. The very powerful Russian mafia sat in a truce with the Yakuza; the Mexican cartels worked alongside European crime bosses; and mob bosses from the U.S and Italy avoided killing each other while they were in the same room with their enemies. It made a very diverse collection of the criminal elite. In that den of vipers, there was neither socializing nor laughter, since there existed an inherent distrust of anyone outside their own organizations, but they all had a single goal in mind: to preserve their power and their profits.

"Welcome, ladies and gentlemen," Michael started. "I believe we all know why we are here today. Our very way of life is being threatened by the Alliance and their nonsensical push to bring about a single government that will have no borders or boundaries on Earth. If the Alliance succeeds, my friends, they will stop at nothing to destroy everything we have worked so hard to build."

The two main concerns to everyone in attendance were, of course, power and money. Bearing that in mind, Michael continued his calculated rant, jarring the who's-who of the crime world to a boiling point. By the end of the meeting, a unanimous agreement was in place. They would all fight the Alliance, and they had comprised a general outline of a plan to crush the alien takeover.

Michael was ecstatic but cautious. Now, he had his All-Faith Coalition to spread fear of the Alliance, his criminal organizations to exert intimidation to resist the Alliance, and terrorist groups to carry out violent acts against the Alliance. Still, he feared it would not be enough. The package the Alliance had put on offer was an attractive one; he would have chosen them himself if things were different. Underlying his hopeful confidence, the archangel knew that even with all the power at his disposal, his fight would probably prove futile. What he really needed was something to tip the scales in his favor, but he was at a loss as to what that could be.

For the next few months, Justin and the angels of Hell worked tirelessly to counter the negative advertising Michael had thrown at them. Although Justin was bone tired, he was also excited. *Tonight, will be wonderful,* he was sure, for he was finally going to see his beloved Salome for the first time in six months.

He quickly gathered his things and prepared for his trip to the ship where awaited him, just outside the atmosphere. He activated his shield as he left his secure compound. Then, as he and Jeqon rose into the air, he switched the shield off.

"What are you doing?" Jeqon scolded. "It is unwise to be

without your shield."

"I just want to feel the wind against my skin," Justin countered, more of a plea than an argument. "I've been here for six months, and not once have I been outside without this damn shield. I miss the walks I used to take through the woods."

Jeqon gave Justin a look that let him know it was a battle he was not going to win.

Justin sighed and conceded, but just as he was about to activate his shield, they were both blindsided. Jeqon, still shielded, was only stunned, but the Earthling was down for the count.

Chapter 39

Justin awoke to a voice he remembered all too well.

"Mr. Grant, I am glad you decided to join us again," Michael said, smiling, barely able to control the anger broiling to a wrathful froth inside him.

Justin tried to move, to no avail, for sturdy restraints pulled against his every effort.

"The last time, you were fortunate enough to escape from us. Luck will not be on your side this time," the archangel firmly stated. "In fact, the only reason you still have a pulse is because Jesus wishes it so. Without his command to the contrary, I would have killed you at my first opportunity." Then, without any provocation or warning, Michaels' fist collided viciously with Justin's mouth.

Not wanting the angelic asshole to see him sweat, Justin smiled, causing an even larger trickle of blood to run from his lip. "Hmm. Then I suppose you won't try such a lame stunt again, using a beautiful blonde. What was her name? Rebecca? Holy Ghost my ass. She was more like a holy bitch!"

For that insulting observation, Michael backhanded Justin hard across the face. "She is my daughter, you human scum!" the archangel screamed as he mercilessly struck Justin again, this time knocking him unconscious.

Justin was surprised by two things when he came to: First, he was alive, and second, he could not find it within himself to feel any pity for Rebecca and Michael. He had always considered himself a person of compassion, even when it came to those who chose to do him harm, but the thought of his friends Ronwe, LucifersLady88, and Jennifer Lundy being savagely murdered by the heavenly prick's offspring banished any sympathy from his mind.

He looked around and wondered about his whereabouts. He was unaware that they'd left Earth and were now coursing through deviant space, more than halfway to their destination. What he was aware of was that he was lying on the cold, metal floor of an uncomfortable six-by-ten-foot cell.

As he slowly regained his senses, he felt sore all over. *I'm in deep, deep shit now*, he sullenly realized. He was actually angrier than he was scared, furious at himself and his current situation. After all, *it's purely my fault*, he reasoned. *What happened to Jeqon though?* he thought, hoping his friend was all right. Justin would never forgive himself if he had stupidly caused Jeqon any harm just because he wanted to feel the wind on his face and had stubbornly refused to comply with shielding protocols. As he thought about his companion's possible demise at the hands of the would-be tyrants who now held him captive, regret consumed him, and a bitter tear ran down his cheek. Not only was he worried that Jeqon was gone, but the grief of a missed reunion also stung. He was just about to see his beautiful Salome, and now he might never see her again. *Stupid, stupid, stupid!* he silently berated himself.

While Justin sat pondering his fate and that of his friend, the heavenly cruiser *Rapture* whizzed out of deviant space, on approach to the space around Heaven. Moments later, guards arrived to retrieve Justin.

One looked at the other and said, "We have orders to clean this space trash up before it has audience before the lord."

As the so-called space trash was led away, he dared to ask, "Where are we going? Are you taking me to your leader, like good little aliens?"

Neither guard answered; they just pushed him along without even attempting to be gentle or polite about it.

Soon, Justin was shoved into a room, handed a wad of

unflattering garments, and ordered to, "Clean yourself up, you swine, and put these on. Michael will send for you when the time comes."

It was at that point that Justin foolishly and rebelliously decided to test the limits of his confinement. Without a word, he started for the door and tried to push his way through.

The apparent head guard answered that move with a hard punch to the gut, one that would have sent a heavyweight prizefighter to his knees.

"Argh," Justin groaned as he went down, struggling to breathe. It didn't feel pleasant, but he figured it was a small price to pay to see where he stood. Once he had his answer to that question, he opted to sit down and wait for whatever was to come.

An hour later, the door opened, and the guards returned to roughly remove Justin from his cell. As they walked down the hallway, one put a cloth over his head.

What the...? he thought, in a panic and already trying to prepare himself for the pain he knew he would encounter. *Am I back at the bunker?*

***

Jesus practically vibrated with excitement, very eager but even a little anxious to meet the one who had the audacity to snatch his precious Earth away. At first, he wanted the human insect dead immediately, but his council wisely convinced him that the human might prove more useful as an ally.

When the man with a cloth over his head was led into the throne room and seated before him, the whole room fell silent. The son of God watched with great interest as the shrouded Earthling was seated before him. "Let us see this pitiful insect who has caused me so much misery," Jesus said with a snarl.

The blindfold was removed, revealing to Justin's eyes evil incarnate. He was somewhat surprised by Jesus' stature, as their lord was smaller than he had imagined, maybe four inches shorter than Justin himself. Daringly, Justin darted his eyes around the room, making a show of ignoring Jesus altogether.

Although there were no physical walls or partitions, it was clear that there were three distinct divisions in the room. Justin knew from his research that the three semicircular rings represented the three levels of the council: the seraphim, cherubim, and thrones. He also knew the two seraphim closest to Jesus were Zabkiel and Jahoel, the heads of his unholy council. Justin couldn't be sure, but he thought Jahoel winked at him as he surveyed his surroundings.

"What is your name, human?" Jesus demanded, again drawing Justin's attention back to his evil captor.

Justin was not about to give him the courtesy of a response, and the smug look on his face was a crystal-clear indication that he had no intention of even acknowledging the robed monster before him.

The brutish guard from earlier stepped in front of Justin and issued a backhanded smack across the face, reddening his cheek and bursting stars into his vision.

As a crimson river flowed out of the reopened cut on Justin's mouth, Jesus repeated his question: "What is your name, human?"

"Sorry. You talkin' to me?" Justin said in his best Travis Bickle voice, wearing his best Robert De Niro smirk.

This time, the guard touched him with a rod-shaped device, much like the one used by Michael back on Earth. Every cell in Justin's body cried out with intense pain, but Justin remained adamant in his resolve to withhold from Jesus the pleasure of a proper response.

With a dismissive wave of his hand, Jesus said, "Take this creature away and teach him the meaning of real pain. Perhaps that will loosen his mongrel tongue." Then, when someone suggested using an Illuminator to dig the details out of Justin's mind, Jesus barked, "No! This human garbage will speak to me or die. Take him away!"

Over the next few days, Justin was subjected to various forms of torture and pain like he'd never felt before. As time slowly passed, he wondered how long he would be able to resist before breaking. If not for the preparation and conditioning he'd received on Hell, he would have broken down the first time they even threatened him with such agony. At day's end, he lay in a fetal position, trembling, bruised, and bloody. Deep hunger bit at his neglected, churning stomach, and he had only the moisture of his own warm, salty blood to wet his parched throat.

On the third day, as Justin waited for his next round of attempted speech inducement, the guard who had touched him with the shock stick for his indiscretion in the presence of their lord barked at the guard at the door, "Clean the filthy thing up again. Jesus wishes to see him."

Justin was taken to a small room equipped with a shower. This time, he complied, but that was only because he knew he could drink the droplets that rained down on him as he unsteadily stood beneath the showerhead. He winced as he felt the sting of open wounds all over his body. After a moment, the pain subsided somewhat, and he actually enjoyed the feel of the cleansing, hot water as it danced across his torn skin, soothing his aching joints and muscles. All too soon, the water stopped, and he found himself standing there, dripping and shivering, desperately hoping they'd turn it back on.

Once he was clothed in more ill-fitting garb that irritated his lacerations and abrasions, he was again dragged to the throne room.

"What is your name, human?" Jesus recited once more.

Once more, Justin remained silent, staring at Jesus.

"I said, what is your name?" Jesus asked, impatience blaring into every syllable.

For an answer, Justin began singing an old Sunday school hymn to himself: "Jesus loves me, this I know, for the Bible tells me so..." After the first stanza, he broke out in hilarious laughter, but no one else in the room dared to even smile in the presence of their cruel master. Their wide-eyed, awestruck silence and confusion caused Justin to laugh even harder.

The chuckling eventually proved infectious, because soon, Jesus was laughing from his throne. As his enjoyment grew, cautious giggles erupted from members of his council. With an uncharacteristic smile on his face, Jesus said, "Now, tell me your name."

Justin made a point of looking away and spoke to the guard on his right. "This is Jesus? I always thought he'd be much...taller."

Irate at the tone of Justin's obvious disregard for his status and power, Jesus stepped forward and stabbed the guard Justin had spoken too. Then, for good measure, he sliced the throat of a council member whose laughter had carried on for a bit too long. Finally, ignoring the two dying men, Jesus moved his face close to Justin's. "Take him away," he ordered. "We will try again tomorrow."

As Justin was hauled out of the throne room, he noticed the fear in the eyes of the council; they all lived knowing they were not promised tomorrow or even their next moment. He asked himself, *Did I really just cause the deaths of two people? If I keep refusing to talk, will he kill even more?* It was a question he already knew the answer to, and he decided, right then and there, that the next time he was brought before the throne, he had to answer Jesus. The most irritating thing about it was that he reckoned, *that little bastard surely knows my name already. He's supposed to be omniscient, right?*

To prepare Justin for his final day in the presence of Jesus, the guards made him scream more than ever before. Between those shrieks, though, Justin managed to mock his jailers with laughter. Their irritation was evident in the zeal with which they went about their subsequent rounds of torture. For all they knew, failure to straighten out this human meant a personal date with the wrath of their lord, and none of them wanted that.

After what seemed like an eternity, Justin's reserves of laughter were finally depleted. Just when he thought he couldn't take another round of fun, however, a most curious thing happened.

His eyes stung as blood and sweat seeped into them, but through the red haze, he saw Jahoel, Jesus' number two. When the guards noticed who had entered the room, they quickly stood at attention. Jahoel nodded, then suddenly sprayed something in the guards' faces, something that caused both to collapse to the cold, hard floor as lifeless heaps. Jahoel quickly and calmly stepped over to the fallen guards and neared Justin.

Justin blinked to clear the debris from his eyes. He struggled to understand what was happening as Jahoel unfastened the straps that held him to the chair. Justin tried to say something but found he couldn't speak. After the beating he'd experienced, he just didn't have it in him.

Jahoel helped him to his feet and rushed him through the door. They quickly moved down the hallway, at least as quickly as they could with one man practically carrying the other.

When they slipped through the door at the end of the hall, more hands grabbed Justin. He could not see their faces with his blurred vision, but whoever they were, they carried him through a labyrinth of corridors, only to stop in a dark room where unseen others immediately went to work cleaning the blood and sweat from his tortured body.

"Here. Drink this. It will make you feel a bit better," Jahoel said, handing some sort of beverage to him.

Once Justin's wounds were tended to, they all worked together to fit him into an ensemble of clean clothes. If he hadn't been so out of it, he would've complained that they were treating him like a baby.

Next, he was led through another maze of hallways, till he eventually stepped out into the open air. Straightaway, they pushed him into a vehicle that sped away from the nightmarish palace where he'd been held. Sometime later, they stopped and exited the first vehicle to climb into a second.

Silently, they moved through the night sky toward a third location.

As Justin had a bit of time to think during their journey, he mustered what little strength he had and asked, "Okay, so what the hell is going on?"

His new best friend and savior smiled. "What in the Heaven, you mean?"

"Yeah, whatever," Justin spat, in no mood for puns.

"We are with the Alliance, Mr. Grant. We must move quickly. Once they find out you are missing, it will be next to impossible to get you off Heaven."

"But where are we—"

Before Justin could even finish the sentence, the shot they gave him sent him spinning into blackness once more.

They moved the unconscious Earthling into the trading ship that would snuggle him off Heaven. It was actually piloted by an Alliance spy who knew he'd soon be in need of a new assignment when the Empire discovered the betrayal. With its precious cargo on board, the ship sped out of Heaven's atmosphere and into deviant space, and the pilot set course for a rendezvous with an Alliance cruiser.

As soon as the transfer was made, a skilled medical team began to treat Justin's multiple injuries. Within an hour, he was safe, and on the mend, heading toward friendly territory.

Chapter 40

Jesus took the news of Justin's nighttime escape with his usual amount of calmness and reason. That was evident when the throne room broke out in unparalleled mayhem, a tsunami of a shit storm. Even Seraphim One was injured in his effort to settle his raging master down. Although most of the council backed away from their god, they dared not run, knowing that would mean certain death. As Jesus approached them, they could only helplessly watch their unfortunate peers being struck down by their master's hand. Only after seven council members and several servants littered the throne room floor did Jesus slowly regain his ability to hear the voice of reason.

Seraphim One, bleeding from a deep gash on his forehead, was the first to find his lord's ear. "My Lord, my Lord, a moment, please. There is something you must see." He leaned in close so only Jesus could hear and explained, "I believe it will truly shed some light on the human's escape. It is something only your eyes should witness."

Jesus, with his hands and clothing saturated with the blood of his council and servants, ordered all the living to leave the throne room, save Seraphim One.

Jahoel, the last to exit, cast Seraphim One a suspicious glance over his shoulder before he walked through the door. At that very moment, he was in the process of making his move to remove Zabkiel from the position he believed was justifiably his. Only then would he be able to claim his right-ful place at Jesus' side and carry out his mission. He did not like the idea of Zabkiel holding a private audience with Jesus, and he feared his rival may have discovered his plan. The temporary distraction of the human's escape would benefit him greatly if Zabkiel did not know enough to jeopardize his standing with Jesus. Jahoel smiled to himself, feeling confident once more that, in a very short time, he would become the voice of reason for their lord. There were many individuals on and off Heaven who counted heavily on his success in overtaking that lofty position, and he aimed to see it through.

The next morning, the council was summoned to the throne room. Much to everyone's surprise and relief, there was no gruesome evidence of the carnage from the day before. The chair to Jesus' immediate left, ordinarily vacant, was now occupied by Queen Magdalene. That was a truly unexpected treat for the council, but other than that slight change, the day began like any other. First, there was the ceremonial admiration of their lord, followed by a rehashing of the affairs of state. Then, they discussed updates and news about the battles along Empire borders.

As the day progressed, the council began to feel more comfortable, believe they would not witness their master's wrath for another short while. In fact, Jesus seemed reasonably happy as they broke for their midday meal.

As they dined, Jesus rose and announced, pointing at the curtains that covered the viewing screen, "I think you will all find this quite interesting."

As the curtains parted and the screen came to life, Magdalene suddenly appeared very nervous and visibly squirmed in her seat. She squinted at the screen and immediately recognized her sleeping chambers, a recorded night after one of her special parties. In the video, her scantily clad body was still covered with the blood of her sexual sacrifice. She stared at the screen, desperately hoping it would go dark, as she did not want anyone to see the next scene. She could not run from her past, however, and there was nowhere to go.

The viewers gasped quietly as they watched a panel open on the far wall of Magdalene's chambers. From that secret opening, a figure entered her room and approached her bed silently, hidden in the shadows. The council tensed as the silhouette crept ever closer to their unsuspecting queen. One particular council member seemed tenser than the others and darted his eyes around the throne room, looking for any possible quick exit.

The night visitor, still camouflaged by darkness, began to undress. Fully nude, he neared Magdalene. Everyone in the throne room, other than those few who were privy to the truth, wondered if they were about to witness their queen having sex with one of her concubines. When the man moved into the light, revealing his identity, a louder collective gasp broke out. Before their very eyes, about to commit an indiscretion with their queen, was Jahoel. He pulled the seemingly willing Magdalene into his arms, then coaxed her to lie back on the bed. Sensually, he licked the blood of her unfortunate suitor from her breast, and she arched her body toward his attention.

"Surely we all know what happened next," Jesus said, wearing a sadistic smile. "Let us not subject ourselves to the lewdness of it."

The scene changed to the queen snuggling in Jahoel's arms, both of them still covered in blood but basking in the dreamy afterglow of their treacherous lovemaking.

"Jahoel, we must find a way to remove Zabkiel," the breathless Magdalene said.

"I know, my Queen," Jahoel said, wiping the blood from his mouth. "He stands in the way of me having our lord's ear."

"Mine as well. I hate him, but Jesus is so taken by him. As long as Jahoel is around, you will unable to rise to your rightful position. "

"Yes, my Queen, but please do not fret. I have a plan in place that will ensure that Zabkiel will no longer pose a threat," Jahoel answered, just before the screen faded to black.

The eyes that had been glued to the presentation before them now stared at Jahoel. He was flanked by two of Jesus' personal guards, who had maneuvered their way toward him as he'd watched his plan, his position, and, quite possibly, his very life slip away. Nearby council members distanced themselves from the next target, not wanting to be caught in the crossfire of Jesus' jealousy-fueled rage.

"I'm afraid there is more," Jesus said, gesturing toward the screen with a nod.

The council members followed their master's eyes and saw the room where the human had been taken, the room where he was made to suffer for the blatant disrespect of their lord. They winced as the Earthling was tortured, and some covered their ears to avoid hearing his screams, grateful that they were not in his place. They all wondered what any of that had to do with the previous spectacle, but they were soon rewarded with an answer as Jahoel entered the room, incapacitated the guards, then helped the human escape.

Jahoel screamed, "That is not I, my Lord! I never... I would never—"

One of the guards who held Jahoel drove a fist into his face, putting a stop to his outcry. The other struck him in the stomach, effectively shutting him up.

Jesus raised his hand and ordered, "Let him speak!"

When the guards obediently halted their assault, Jahoel composed himself and said, "Master, I admit that I was weak when I found myself in the arms of your queen. For that, I should be punished, but I would never, ever betray you. I have lived my life in your service, for 1,000 glorious years. I have been loyal to you in all ways, save for my indiscretion, my...weakness of the flesh. For that, I can only beg for your forgiveness, my Lord. Please believe me when I say I am innocent of the treasonous act I'm being accused of. I did not free that wretched human! That was not I! Surely it was an imposter, likely sent by Zabkiel," he said, refusing to call the other by his title. "You are the Alpha and Omega, the all-knowing, all-powerful, all-seeing God of the universe. Surely, my Lord, you have seen the deceit, yet you must truly know my heart. I could never be disloyal to the one, almighty God."

Jesus listened, patiently feigning as much sympathy as he thought appropriate, then rose to approach the accused.

"Let him go," he barked at his guards. Once they let loose of Jahoel, he continued, "Jahoel, I do see the truth in your heart, and I forgive you for your weakness of the flesh." He paused to put his arm around Jahoel's shoulders. "After all, Magdalene is beautiful beyond compare. No one can blame you for falling for her charms."

The queen, meanwhile, sat with her head down, unable to hide her shame.

"There is something you should know though," Jesus went on. "My beautiful queen also tried to seduce Seraphim One. Unlike you, he came to me and immediately made me aware of her potential betrayal. Your envy of Seraphim One is well known, Jahoel. You should have made a friend of him, but your judgment was clouded by jealousy. I have overlooked that all this time, but what I cannot overlook or forgive is your treasonous act against the people of Heaven and the Empire."

As Jesus delivered the last line, the guards again grabbed the protesting, flailing, panicked Jahoel.

Jesus stared at Jahoel for a moment, like a hungry fox torturing a trembling bunny with his gaze, then calmly said, "I will not kill you, Jahoel, but you must be punished for your indiscretions. You will never again defile my queen or any other woman." With that, he pulled a knife from under his robes. With the help of his strong guards, he brutally took Jahoel's manhood and grinned as the seraphim cried out in unspeakable pain. "Here. A gift for my queen," Jesus said, handing the bloody penis to one of his guards. "Please deliver it to her lap, since she has so yearned to be near it."

Magdalene wailed openly, not for Jahoel but for herself. Her tears came from the fear of the fate she knew would be hers. When the organ was flung onto her, she nearly passed out.

A physician quickly stepped up to Seraphim Two and sprayed something on the wound to stop the bleeding, but he offered nothing to obstruct the pain.

Jesus again stepped up to Jahoel and stated, "As I have said, I will not take your life, but I will not allow you to ever again speak your treachery in my presence." Once the guards took their cue to hold the seraphim again, Jesus used the same bloody knife to slice out Jahoel's tongue.

Once again, the physician treated the wound to inhibit the crimson flow, but he administered nothing to put the man out of his misery.

While the freshly emasculated and muted Jahoel whimpered and writhed from the immense pain from two separate places on his body, Jesus sauntered back to his throne. "Let this be a lesson to anyone who dares to try to rise up against me. Jahoel will be on display, for all of Heaven to witness so they will know the consequences of treason. Furthermore, his family line shall be erased from Heaven."

Through his torment, Jahoel struggled to voice his objections. Tears mixed with his blood as agony for the fate of his family tore at his very soul. One thought was present in his mind all the while: *It was not I! It was not I.*

Seraphim One looked on with little interest. He had reluctantly witnessed similar entertainment during his time as a council member. The cruelty of Jesus still made him nauseous, but it saddened him to ponder that he'd grown somewhat numb to the raw depravity of the adolescent madman. He preferred not to watch, but this incident was his own doing. *An imposter indeed,* he silently mused, pleased with himself for having framed Jahoel for the human's escape. His affair with the queen was just icing on the cake.

The top-ranking seraphim had no care whatsoever for the fate of the degenerate who had so often been an eager and willing participant in Magdalene's bloody orgies, but he did feel some pity for his family. *They deserve better, he* thought. *They cannot help it that they were born into the bloodline of sorry Jahoel's. Why should they be held accountable for his actions?* Zabkiel planned to save as many as he could, just as he had done for Dilyla's family and for thousands of others over the years. Jesus' newest batch of scapegoats would escape their unjust death sentence and join the others on Pithom, a rather safe Alliance planet that had no interplanetary communication capability.

As head of the Alliance underground on Heaven, Zabkiel had the means to spirit them away to live under his protection. It proved most useful at times that high-ranking council members and even some of the Holy Ghosts worked for the underground, unbeknownst to their not-so-all-knowing and immature, unstable master.

Many times during Zabkiel's tenure as Seraphim One, he had thought of putting an ultimate end to Jesus' reign of terror. Although Jesus was rarely without his shield, Zabkiel knew it would not be an impossible feat. The seraphim's primary mission, though, was to ensure that he had an effective way to gather information and relay it to the Alliance. He took solace in the fact that Jesus would reap what he had sewn. *We will rid the galaxy of the monster,* he told himself repeatedly. *Jesus will fall, and peace will return to the galaxy... someday.*

Chapter 41

"Mr. Grant?"

Justin slowly awoke, and his pain told him he was still alive.

"Mr. Grant?" the faint, unseen voice called to him again, seemingly from far away.

As the voice came ever closer, he tried to open his eyes. His vision slowly came into focus, and it was then that he realized where he was. "Hell?" he weakly muttered under his breath through his parched lips.

"Yes, Hell, and welcome back, Mr. Grant. How are you feeling?" asked Dr. Corson, the medical professional who'd treated him upon his first arrival so long ago.

When it registered to Justin's hazy mind that he'd been asked a question, he tried to speak again, to no avail.

"Mr. Grant, how are you feeling?" Dr. Corson repeated.

"Like shit," Justin finally managed.

The doctor laughed at his patient's blunt honesty. "Good. That's precisely how you should feel. I know you need to rest, but there is someone here to see you, someone I was sure you wouldn't have wanted me to turn away."

Salome neared Justin's bedside and leaned down to kiss him softly as she sobbed with relief and joy.

Justin wanted to reach up and pull her into his arms, but he was intensely sore all over. Not one place on his body had been spared; everywhere, he felt the remnants of his torturous time on Heaven. Nevertheless, his mind exulted in the joy of being with the one he loved. As he reconnected with his beloved, a question crossed his mind, and he had to know the answer to it. "Jeqon, is he all right?" Justin blurted, desperately hoping his stubbornness had not caused his friend any harm.

"He is right outside. I will ask him to come in," Salome replied.

As soon as Jeqon was invited, he burst through the door and ran over to Justin, blubbering apologies. "I'm so very sorry I let this happen to you, Justin," he said mournfully. "If you can ever forgive me, I promise that I will never let anything happen to you again."

"Stop, my friend. It is I who owes you an apology. What happened to me was my own doing. It was reckless of me to lower my guard."

"But—"

"But nothing," Justin interrupted. "If I had followed protocol and your instructions, I wouldn't be in this mess. So, if *you* will forgive *me*, I can think of no other person I'd rather have to protect my ass." To seal the deal with his new bodyguard, Justin raised his arm to shake hands, only to wince as pain stormed through him.

Jeqon thanked Justin and shook his hand, but he also added a stern warning: "If you ever do such a thing to me again, I will beat your ass myself!"

The three burst out in laughter just as the doctor walked back into the room.

"Mr. Grant needs to rest now, but the worst is over," Dr. Corson assured them.

Jeqon took his leave and walked out behind the doctor, but Justin drifted off to sleep with Salome at his bedside, still holding his hand.

He made a decent enough recovery to leave the hospital within a couple days, so he could recuperate more comfortably at home. When he was ready, he was destined to head back to his mission, so he could continue guiding Earth on its journey into the future. While on the mend, he spent his time catching up on Earth current events. He could feel

Michael's hand in every move against the Alliance, and the thought of getting Michael in a room alone made him smile.

Now that the mission had begun, Justin had become something of a celebrity. Everyone on Hell knew who he really was. Even more surprising, there seemed to be a blossoming worldwide obsession for Earth music. Groups like the Rolling Stones and AC/DC were almost guaranteed sold-out performances for years to come; if Elvis had been alive, he would have been a king once more.

The week before Justin was scheduled to return to his home planet, Sandel hosted a farewell get-together at his place. Justin's mom and dad, Rachel and Thomas, attended, along with his former in-laws, Leah's parents. Many of his friends also made appearances. Everyone had a good time, listening to music and eating their fill. Lilith made a pizza so good that Sandel claimed, "Even Mama De Luca would kill for the recipe!"

It was good to be together with loved ones, and Justin couldn't help but notice the effect the Longevity Factor had on his parents. They looked healthier than they had in years. In fact, they looked so good that it made him smile at the thought that maybe he'd finally be a big brother, if the two of them decided to give him the kid sister or brother he'd always wanted. When Justin and Salome told Leah's parents about their wedding plans, they wholeheartedly gave them their blessing, just as his own parents had.

Looking around at all the people who meant so much to him, Justin hated the fact that he'd soon have to depart for Earth. Time was of the essence, though, and he had much work to do. Except for a few scars and many bruises, he felt fine, and his business on Earth could not wait much longer.

For the next few days, the officials of Hell discussed Justin's agenda. They all agreed that the planet needed a strong push to form the new government. "A unified, one-world government, along with a capable security organization to enforce the necessary laws, boundary free, for all of Earth, must be established as soon as possible," Lucifer declared. "Laws to stop environmental destruction need to be enacted soon if we are to have any hope of reversing the damage to the air, the oceans, and the land. The inhabitants of Earth have carelessly harmed the planet, all in the name of so-called progress."

Everyone in the room was in absolute agreement with that as well. Justin knew, possibly more so than any of the others, that along with the jurisdictional freedom the new government would allow, the environmental steps required to protect the trees were vitally important. "Burning of fossil fuels, widespread deforestation, and reckless pollution of the air and water ae only a few of the things we need to address quickly in order to repair the damage," he said, echoing Lucifer's sentiments.

Knowing he had his work cut out for him upon his return, Justin packed his bags while Salome looked on. It was evident that she had been crying. They both knew the trip could not be postponed or avoided, but the air of impending loss was thick in their room. With only an hour and a half to spend with him before his departure, Justin's would-be bride moved close to him, and he wrapped his arms tightly around her. They fell into bed together and, for the next thirty minutes, forgot about everything and everyone else as they said their sweet goodbyes.

Chapter 42

Upon Justin's return, he was met with a mountain of paperwork, an endless string of meetings, and crucial appearances to push for a united Earth. Considering that he'd been a college professor in his past life, the paperwork and meetings were not so daunting. It was the appearances with his fellow humans and their damned resistance to change that stressed him out the most.

Every time he appeared in front of an audience, large or small, Justin felt the archangel's hand moving to block their progress. Thousands of years of shameless brainwashing had paid off, and it appeared Heaven might have its way after all and retain the planet as one of Jesus' playthings. Religious leaders went into overdrive; churches welcomed record numbers into their flocks, and new, cult-like groups and factions sprung up all over the place. Reverend Gabe Brown was a ubiquitous face on every television, always ready to blast the congregation with his sermons of impending doom. Much like previous campaign seasons in American history, the good reverend bought every other commercial spot, lambasting the Alliance with negative ads like some mudslinging politician. Before long, no one could turn on a television or a radio or peek at the internet without hearing the God damned archangel or his minions.

"Now that Satan has returned to Earth, it is time for church and state to withhold their separation. We have a common enemy, my friends, and we must join together to put an end to him. It is time to render, therefore, unto God the things which are Caesar's and make one law, which is the word of God!" the reverend preached.

Justin often wished for such a powerful evangelical speaker to be on the side of the Alliance. He had always marveled at the power of charismatic revivalist orators, and Brown was the best at what he did. For that reason, it surprised no one when talk broke out about Reverend Gabriel Brown running for president in the next election, on the conservative ticket, of course.

A heated battle raged on, and skirmishes and conflicts continued to break out all over the world, in big metropolises and tiny villages alike. God's warriors fought as if their very way of life was being threatened, rightly so. The extent of their fear was apparent in the determined viciousness of their assaults; for them, the fear of a suffering afterlife was a greater motivator than the fear of dying itself. *Ironic,* Justin thought with a sinking feeling in his gut. *What was that bit about God not giving people a spirit of fear, hmm?*

Not only that, but their determination seemed much stronger than the opposition's desire for change. That was most evident when battles were fought, since most were won by God's warriors. As was often the case in the history of humanity, the resistance to change was only outweighed by a lack of commitment from those who wanted the change. *Let the other guy risk life and limb,* many thought. *Hopefully, our fight will not be in vain, and then we can all reap the benefit of the other guy's struggle.*

Organized crime also continued doing what they were best at: using intimidation to strike fear into politicians and their constituents, thus manipulating and influencing the outcome of crucial votes. Those who stood up against the pressure of the mob lost their lives in attacks reminiscent of killings at the height of the gangster era in New York and Chicago. Police organizations around the world fought hard to bring down those responsible, but the scales of justice had a monumental task ahead of them.

Terrorists upped the ante by targeting their strikes at key

Alliance locations, taking the lives of supporters of free will and igniting even greater fear in those who dreamt of a new galactic future. Attempted bombings of Alliance embassies and the homes of world leaders became commonplace, straining the global military forces tasked to contend with them. The Alliance did what they could to protect everyone involved, but under the current circumstances, they could only do so much. The war on terror, as George W. Bush had dubbed it way back in 2001, was still alive and well, and in many cases, terror was winning.

Although many physical battles were lost to Heaven's warriors, the fight to bring about the one-world government was slowly making some headway. As various governments and the peoples they represented realized that their way of life was not really in danger of being lost, they began to bravely add their voices to the call for change. Even China jumped on the bandwagon, albeit subtly.

Using the power of his trusty Illuminator, Justin treated grieving people the chance to somewhat be with family who had passed on. For those with an interest in history, the Illuminator was beyond amazing and was eye-opening and life-changing for many. For instance, from Hell's past missions on Earth, the device made it possible to see China as it was thousands of years prior. Enticed by that small taste of the power of the device, Chinese leaders hungered for more. With the promise of a place in the new government and full access to Illuminators once their acceptance into the Alliance was granted, China finally became an important ally in the movement. Considering that the Asian nation was home to approximately 20 percent of the world population, the necessary majority was finally in sight.

Once that majority was achieved, the people of Earth would no longer be left to fend for themselves against Heaven. The Alliance would not fight their civil and internal battles for them, but they would be there for support when Heaven and its evil forces were on the prowl. They agreed to provide advanced technology, military training, and valuable lessons and intel learned from thousands of years of experience in fighting Heaven's control.

The Serpent's Gift

When the official vote was just six months away, word spread of an impending, full-on attack against the Alliance and its supporters. Rumors and fake news abounded, exaggerations meant to terrify and dissuade Hell's new followers. One side viewed the other as religious nuts, and the opposition viewed those opponents as hopeless, helpless souls lost forever, Satan worshipers who either knew no better or were just consumed by evil.

The threats ranged from assassinations to all-out global thermonuclear war, dredging up the same fears that prompted the 'Duck and Cover' scenario, that had children hiding under their desks in the 1950s, during the Cold War. Worldwide governments who had joined the Alliance cried out for help, and they were glad to have a powerful ally. Unwilling to take any chances that might put their Earth friends at greater risk, the Alliance shielded what they could, and helped to train and equip local armed forces to handle the rest. Intelligence agencies from many nations used every resource at their disposal to ferret out any and every lead, hoping to minimize the damage of a potential terrorist attack, should any of the terrorists opt to follow through with their maniacal, dastardly threats.

What happened next was shocking: In a bold and wholly unexpected move, Reverend Gabe Brown revealed his true identity, halo, wings, and all. Gabriel was almost as handsome as Michael, though his features were somewhat dainty, even feminine. It was not his celestial appearance that drew people to him though; it was his voice, almost hypnotic as he preached the word of God.

The archangel-controlled stations around the world broadcast the revelation in real time, and all other networks were given permission and full access to replay the event, as long as they aired it unedited. Gabriel's followers now saw the truth and knew him to be the true messenger of God. The most immediate effect was the unification of the many factions within the All-Faith Coalition. A fringe benefit was a final shove of so many who'd been riding the fence, a shove in the heavenly direction. Any who'd been ignorant of the true nature of the disagreement now knew it to be a fight not only

205

their lives but also for their very souls, a Holy War to over-shadow all crusades of the past.

"I am the Archangel Gabriel," the reverend boomed. "I've been sent here to deliver a message from almighty God. Just as I was sent to Daniel to help him see the truth of his visions and to Nazareth to foretell to the Virgin Mary and Joseph of the impending birth of God's only begotten son, Jesus, I am among you once more, to speak on behalf of the one, true, all-seeing, all knowing, ever-present, all-powerful God.

"Make no mistake, my friends. We are in the last days promised to you in God's word. Armageddon is at hand. At no time in the history of mankind has there been a greater threat to the future of your soul. Since God created the heavens and the Earth and placed your ancestors in the garden, he has watched over you, sometimes with delight and other times with concern. Our lord God reluctantly destroyed Earth with a great flood to punish your kind for their sins, but his rainbow was a promise that he will never take such vengeance on your world again, unlike the enemy, the father of lies.

"Satan still prowls about, seeking whom he may devour!" Gabriel shouted. "At this very moment, he is in the process of bringing an end to all mankind. Why? Because he is the purveyor of sin, the destroyer of all that is good. God gave you Jesus, his only begotten, to show you the way to Heaven. These things God has done for you to prepare you for the battle that is to come. Do not be deceived, people of Earth! The so-called Free Will Alliance is merely the hand of Lucifer, enticing God's beautiful creations to stray from the path toward everlasting life in Heaven. He will only lead you and your loved ones, your children and your children's children, to an eternity in the blazing fires of Hell! Do not let the sins of your fathers be visited upon your children! Rise up! Take a stand against Satan and the evil that consumes his being. I say again, Armageddon is at hand..."

As Gabriel continued with his rant, Justin wondered why the angel chose to maintain his Southern drawl. It was definitely an effective tool. In his previous life, Justin would have been glued to Gabriel's every word, awaiting instructions from God. He would have carried out those unholy orders, even if it meant his death. He would have submitted, obeyed, just as he always had before Sandel literally dropped into his life. Back then, the promise of being with God in Heaven was what drove him. Now, it sickened him to see how naïve he'd been. If not for that chance encounter with a falling fallen angel, his life and future would have continued being a lie. He counted himself lucky for the coming-to-Lucifer moment in his life, but at the same time, he couldn't help feeling a deep sorrow for the millions of blinded, brainwashed selfishly indoctrinated followers who would die for a God who cared nothing for them or their lives. He pondered these things until an ominous gut feeling pulled his attention back to the broadcast.

"Hear me, mankind!" Gabriel continued. "I am the messenger of God, here to deliver proof of the lord's power. Once again, as in Sodom and Gomorrah, God finds it necessary to display his displeasure with his creations. Through me, he will perform a cleansing that will serve as a warning, a reminder of his supreme, undeniable power and glory. God has chosen four sinful cities, and you will all bear witness to their fall at the hands of our powerful lord God. Behold!"

As he said the last few words, he raised his arms. Instantly, four names popped up on the screen behind him: Macau, China; Amsterdam, Netherlands; Las Vegas, Nevada; Rio de Janeiro, Brazil. Then, at promptly 7 p.m. eastern time, as a major percentage of Earth's population watched, four simultaneous explosions rocked those cities, striking terror into the hearts of all. Suddenly, those iconic locations were gone, just dusty spots on the terrain, their residents disintegrated into ash and smoking embers.

After the destruction, Gabriel spoke again. "It was with much regret that God was forced to punish his creations," he said, "but know this. God only punished the sinners. Those who were right with the lord God felt no pain. In his mercy, he took them before the great cleansing, and they now rest in the glorious realm of Heaven. Conversely, the sinners and those who would not make a decision will now writhe in eternal pain and damnation. They will experience their agony for all of eternity, for there is no escaping the fiery pit of Hell. Hear me, humans! If you are still alive, listening to this broadcast, it is not too late for you. You must be right with the lord God. Rise up and join your brothers and sisters in the fight against the evil of Satan, who has come to you under the guise of the Alliance. You are all being asked to join his unholy crusade. Do not heed their lies! Say no to Satan and the Alliance and yes to the infinite glory of God and the everlasting life in the kingdom of Heaven." With that, he bowed his head and folded his hands together. As the screen faded to black, three words appeared: "Pray for Earth."

Within a few minutes, regular programming resumed, only to be quickly overtaken by news reports from around the world. Justin watched as reporters offered preliminary death tolls. Early on in the count, it was confirmed that at least nine and half million lives were lost, heinously murdered before a worldwide audience. A nasty stew of all-consuming horror, rage, and fear boiled in the cauldron of his stomach, causing Justin's head to spin and his thoughts to scramble as his heart crumbled. *How? How could anyone kill so many and call themselves loving and just?* he asked himself, feeling like such a fool for ever putting his trust in Jesus and his cohorts.

As the authorities struggled to make sense of the massacre, the rest of the world was compelled to examine and soul-search, to decide where they stood philosophically. The undecided felt an urgency to choose sides, and the so-called sinners felt a sudden calling to behave and give their lives and hearts to God. Among those who'd pledged their loyalty to the Alliance, doubts arose, spawned by the fear of a similar end for them.

Reports from around the world suggested that visions of Gabriel were witnessed in the sky above each blast, his wings spread wide in all their glory. At the time of each attack, Gabriel threw a spear into the city centers. The eyewitness accounts of that only cemented the power of God to the believers, and those who'd been swaying one way or the other jumped down off their fences, onto the side of the Empire, coerced by the power of the one, true God.

The effect of Reverend Gabe Brown's revelation and the destruction of the so-called cities of sin were immediate. Everyone knew that being a believer allowed no wiggle room; it was black or white, with no gray area to wrestle in. Families fell apart when relatives chose opposite teams. For some, the choice was suddenly clear: The Alliance promise of a long life and prosperity meant nothing if eternity would be spent in fire and damnation. Husbands killed wives and wives killed husbands over hostile arguments about the fate of their children. For the next few weeks, murder-suicides of entire families and neighbors ran rampant, and mass suicides of strange cults became part of every newscast. The world was in turmoil, and there seemed to be no end in sight.

"Gabriel was right about one thing," Justin muttered to himself. "Armageddon is here."

Chapter 43

Justin's heart sank as he watched the four cities ex-
plode. He couldn't believe so many people were so callously,
tragically murdered, just so Jesus' cruel angels could make
a point. On a separate screen, he saw the same scene from
a space vantage point. His mind struggled to make sense
of the evil at play, but it finally hit home in his mind: *What
total disregard for humanity, and what lengths those heavenly
bastards are willing to go to in their desperation to hold on to
our Earth.* Tears ran down his face, and it was then that he
realized that Salome's fingernails were digging into his arm.
He looked into her teary eyes and pulled her close, and the
two cried together for a long while, both of them inconsolable.

After the tears ran dry, anger set in. As he watched the
news from Earth, something occurred to Justin, and he
hastily jumped to his feet. "What about the survivors?" he
said, then rushed to call Sandel. "There must be people in or
around the blast areas who are in need of medical attention,"
he told his friend. "We must help anyone who is still alive. We
have to help them!" he cried out to Sandel, sobbing into the
phone.

"Help is already on its way, my friend," Sandel informed
him.

"There will be residual deaths due to the fallout. We must
do everything we can to save as many as we can," Justin
said, with pleading in his voice.

"The Alliance has the ability to treat radiation poisoning. If the victims are not too far gone, we can heal them," Sandel assured Justin.

"Not only that, but we have to make those fucking bastards pay for what they've done!" the Earthling yelled, as furious as he was disgusted.

"Their sins will not go unpunished," Sandel said firmly. "They will reap what they have sewn."

In his heart, Justin knew that it was Michael who had orchestrated the catastrophe, and he made a personal vow to make him pay. "Let no man from Earth or Hell touch Michael. He is mine!"

"You have my word that you will have your chance," Sandel said. "You sound awful, exhausted. Get some rest, dear friend. I mean it!" Sandel ordered. "We have much planning to do, and you need to be at your best."

After Justin hung up, Salome hugged him and pulled him from the viewing room. "Lie down," she said, knowing he'd been up watching continuous news reports for almost twenty-four hours. When sleep wouldn't come for either of them, she led him to the workout room.

This time, Justin tore into his exercises like a madman, and he was grateful that Stolas was there to push him along. After three hours of physical exertion and sparring, Justin felt like he could finally close his eyes and drift off for a while. He showered and lay down next to Salome, who lovingly curled up next to him like a warm, purring kitten, stroking his hair and holding him as he cried himself to sleep.

When Justin awoke from his nap, he could not muster any more tears, but he was just as angry as he had been. He hurried to the strategy and observation room, then headed straight for Sandel's office. "Sandel," he said when he burst through the door, "what are we gonna do about this? We have to make those bastards pay, damn it! Do we know where they're hiding?"

"Well, we—"

"There's no time for all this talk," Justin cut in. "Let's go get them...now!"

After Sandel let him vent a little, he finally broke in.

"Justin, I understand how you feel. I have also lost a great many friends to the evil bastard, but we must do it the right way. We mustn't react with our emotions. Rather, we must learn as much as we can and plan an appropriate, thorough response, then act accordingly."

"But all those people were murdered for no reason other than to strike fear into the masses," Justin countered.

"Yes, I know, and that is all the more reason to reply with a conscious act, a well-thought-out response, not an emotional reaction. If we handle this correctly, those lives will not have been lost in vain. Believe me, you will have your chance to confront Michael. For now, though, let us sit down and consider the best way to deal with this tragedy," Sandel said. He paused to let his suggestion sink in, then continued, "We have already started running open condemnation of the blasts on every station that is not controlled by Michael. Also, as your people seem so addicted to your worldwide web, we have flooded the internet with the truth about Gabriel."

When Sandel said that, something suddenly occurred to Justin. "I hesitate to use the tragedy for personal gain, but shouldn't we provide footage of the Free Will Alliance saving the people of Earth? Those we rescue will be our greatest allies and our heralds. If we save the survivors of the blasts, it will reemphasize the evil of the Empire and highlight the benevolence of the Alliance."

"That is an excellent idea!" Sandel expressed with a smile. "See what you can do when you calm down and act accordingly?"

"Yeah, yeah. I know," Justin said, grinning sheepishly.

"We have some planning to do, my friend."

As they talked, others joined them, and everyone had great ideas to share. No one left anything to chance, knowing that whatever they came up with would make or break all they'd been working toward for so long. The first priority was to figure out where they stood on the world stage, what public opinion thought of them. Although world leaders and governments around the world were still pushing for membership in the Alliance, Gabriel's untimely coming-out party had the opposite effect on the general population, and it was clear that the pendulum had taken a hard swing that was certainly not in the favor of the Free Will Alliance.

As such, it was decided that Justin, an Earthling whom other Earthlings could resonate with, had to take a more active role in moving the cause of the Alliance forward. He countered Gabriel's sermons with appearances of his own. He showed the people of Earth the true Reverend Gabe Brown, mentioning as often as he could, "This sick, twisted individual has slaughtered countless innocent beings across the galaxy, just as we all saw him do on Earth and never with one shred of remorse."

Following his own brilliant, strategic move, Justin also gave a voice to the survivors of the blasts, the ones the Alliance saved and healed. They told stories that struck a chord with families and friends of those who'd lost their lives so needlessly at the hands of the evil Empire. "I was a believer, too, just like you," one said. "I stood idly by as that mass-murdering wolf in sheep's clothing led me astray with false promises, to a mental state in which I was willing to give up my life, my soul, and Earth itself to be with God in Heaven."

"Yes, Heaven exists," Justin chimed in, "and it is inhabited by people much like us. They work, play, raise their families, and fear the same God you do. The only difference is that they know him as an evil dictator who rules like a spoiled child, with no parents to rein him in. They know him as a leader who, on a whim, wipes out entire family lines if one dares to speak out against him. He has ordered the conquering of thousands of planets, only to drain them of every available resource, and he has left the populations of those worlds to die, not once looking back with regret or guilt. He is a monster, the monster who allowed his archangel to turn our cities to rubble and our people to dust," Justin said.

After a brief pause, he continued, "You must decide who you are, what you are, and where your life will take you. As the Free Will Alliance holds at its very foundation, you have the choice. You may choose to walk blindly into the future by following a spoiled, adolescent God who wants all under him to believe he is an all-seeing, all-knowing, ever-present, all-powerful, supreme being, or you can open your eyes to the truth. Look within, my friends, and take heart in the power we humans possess, the power that Jesus and his evil cohorts fear the most, the power of free will! Consider all the wonderful things we have accomplished by putting our minds to it. God wants you to feel helpless and pathetic, like insects under his thumb, but in the last 100 years, we have created things that would make us appear like gods to our distant ancestors. The Alliance offers Earth a chance to move into the future on our terms, without cowering, praying, or blind obedience. The same free will that is the basis of the United States Constitution penned by our founding fathers is the foundation of the Alliance. Your choice is all that is required for you to join. If we side with the Alliance, we will have the free will to speak as a single voice, to govern ourselves as we see fit. With God, there is no choice, but to be with the Alliance, we must make one."

Joanna Ariel Williams, the third archangel, dared to take a stand against the fatal blasts, but she was beaten nearly to death because of it. She approached Justin's people and begged for asylum. In his research, Justin had discovered that Ariel had done much good for the people of Earth. Thus, based on her own actions and his recommendation, she was accepted under one condition: She would supply information about Michael and his group and would have to stand trial for the wrongs she had committed in the name of God.

Ariel agreed to help Justin and the Alliance in every way she could to take down Michael and Gabriel. She also agreed to stand trial for her role in Heaven's plot to control Earth. It was quite evident that she was terribly sorry for the devastation Gabriel had heaped upon Earth and those cities under Jesus' command. Justin even believed her when she claimed she had no part in bringing it about and would have put a stop to it if she could have.

For next couple months, Justin continued going on the defensive every time Gabriel spouted his lies on the air. It was no easy feat, because Gabriel had the gift of persuasion and had years of experience at lying and building on the falsehoods they'd been cultivating for centuries. Meanwhile,

Justin was bound by Alliance laws to tell the truth. He was certainly not an evangelist and didn't aim to be, but in time, he became rather good at tearing away at the lies of Reverend Gabriel. Gabriel took notice of that and decided it was best to stick to his Hell and damnation sermons rather than attempting to badmouth and attack the Alliance.

On the whole, the human beings on Earth seemed to appreciate the idea of choices and maintaining control of their own lives, yet they often did everything in their power to absolve themselves of that, to avoid taking responsibility. The United States political system was a prime example. At the polls, people blindly cast votes in a partisan way, marking their ballots in favor of any party that seemed to represent their personal beliefs. Few took the time to investigate or research the true nature of those parties or their candidates. As long as they were choosing on the liberal or conservative platforms they'd grown to accept, they were glad to exercise their right to election, yet they did not want to take any responsibility for the consequences of what their elected officials did or did not do. It was really no different in the election of Heaven or Hell.

Although many in the general population still clung to the faint hope that God's promise would truly carry them to Heaven, most earthly politicians were quick to replace their religious beliefs with the power and greed of political position. They still professed their faith when their campaign advisers told them they should, when it ensured their continued presence in government seats, but almost every decision they made was based on nothing than their desire for political advancement. Where the Alliance was concerned, most preferred to remain wishy-washy and leave their options open.

As Justin's pro-Alliance speeches improved, more and more people began to see the truth in his words. The All-Faith Coalition saw a dwindling in its numbers as former members found a home in the fight for the Alliance or at least climbed back on their fences to await something that might tip them one way or the other. Justin wisely invited Ariel to participate in some broadcasts, because she had a good reputation. Earthlings who knew her or knew of her considered her to be a good person, so when she spoke out against the All-Faith Coalition, it was a powerful message.

The vote was only one month away, and it was a close race; no one was sure what the outcome would be. As the final days of the campaign rolled on, Gabriel stepped up his trash-talk about the Alliance. His hellfire and damnation rhetoric moved to a fever pitch, and his promise of everlasting life with God in Heaven was mesmerizing in its appeal. Justin countered with historical videos from the Illuminator, revealing Jesus and Gabriel in all their bloody splendor.

Stolas, as Triple6soldier, contacted his underground network and flooded the internet with the truth about the Alliance. Those hackers and brilliant computer minds found new ways to make the internet practically sing the praises of the Alliance. BeelzebubsBrother75, HellHathNoFury666, TruthBSatan105, SatansLittleGirl82 were famous around the world and served as leaders in the fight for the Alliance; of course, their true names—James McKinney, Lucy Beckman, Eric Neal, and Jamie Knox—were only released on a need-to-know basis.

"You know," Justin conveyed to his computer-savvy friends, "a lot of religious zealots have claimed over the years that the internet is the antichrist. I guess, in a way, they were right!"

Chapter 44

The day of the great vote finally arrived. Justin, in view of television cameras broadcasting all around the world, walked into the booth and cast his vote. When he finished and deposited his anonymous ballot in the receptacle, he quickly made his way to the shuttle that would carry him to an orbiting ship. There, he would nervously watch the results of the most important vote in all Earth history.

On the ship, he sat with Salome, Sandel, and Stolas. He couldn't help biting his nails, and he didn't even want to blink for fear that he might miss an update or something on the ticker during the live coverage. More than anyone around him, he was keenly aware that humans had an uncanny gift for disappointing behavior, even when it came to seemingly common sense and purportedly obvious choices. *We will cut off our own feet for the most illogically superficial, mundane reasoning to stymie our own forward progress. Hell, we've been doing it for decades,* Justin thought, trying to replace his nerves with greater hope and more faith in his fellow Earthlings.

A few journalists showed video footage of attempted bombings and violent protests at the polls, blatant attempts to stop people from voting or to intimidate them into voting against the Alliance. All in all, though, the day was relatively quiet.

"All we can do now is wait," Justin said. "They've got

twenty-four full hours to cast the votes, and it'll be a few days before they're all tallied and counted. For the love of everything holy, I hope there are no hanging CHAD scandals!"

"Yes, and you humans always seem to be struggling with a *wait* problem," Sandel teased, pinching a bit of Justin's belly.

"Very punny, you devil," Justin retorted.

"Punny...funny. I see what you did there!" Sandel said, chuckling. "And by the way, who is chad?"

Justin laughed. "Not a who, a what," Justin said, laughing. "Technically, CHAD is an acronym for card hole accumulated debris. Hop on your Illuminator sometime and look up the 2000 U.S. presidential election," he explained, then quickly turned his attention back to the media.

Whichever way the vote ultimately went, he would just be glad it was over. He knew full well that it wouldn't be a win for Jesus, since Earth was now in Alliance territory. Whether the people of Earth realized it or not, the Alliance would continue to protect the planet from that moment forward. Space travel would be limited to their technology and strictly confined to their solar system; intergalactic journeys would be forbidden. That regulation was put into effect to protect neighboring star systems, as well as Earth herself.

Hours seemed like days as they waited for the results of the vote. Finally, at 7 p.m. eastern time on June 13, 2025, the people of Earth were given the results. Almost six billion votes had been cast, and Earth was well on her way to a one-world government, with a billion-vote lead. It seemed the citizens of the blue and green planet saw a brighter future with the Free Will Alliance.

No one could have been prouder of the Earthlings than Justin. He held Salome close as tears ran down his face. "It's just a start, but at least it's that," he whispered in her ear.

"Yes, and all things must begin with a beginning!" she said, smiling up at him.

Justin hurried to his room and brought out a bottle of champagne he'd had been saving for that special occasion. Salome, Stolas, Sandel, and their Earth friend raised their glasses in a toast for the dawn of a new age for mankind.

Three bottles later, Justin decided it was time for he and Salome to embark on some celebrating of their own.

Salome lay comfortably in Justin's arms and asked, "What will we do now?"

Justin thought for a moment, then answered, "Well, I figure there will be a few loose ends to tie up, but the worst is behind us. I guess once things settle down, we can head back to Hell and relax for a while," he said, and the thought brought a smile to his face. He pulled his lover close and kissed her deeply, and they found each other once again before they finally gave in to sleep.

Over the next few months, the world laid a firm foundation for the new government. Earth was divided into eight territories: The Middle East Federation, the European Union, the North American States, the Peoples Republic of Asia, the Australian Conference, the South American Coalition, the Russian Federation, and the African Republic. Each territory would be governed by an elected leader, but those leaders would serve as deputies to their representatives on the newly formed United Earth Council. A representative from the Free Will Alliance was also positioned to as an overseer of the council, to monitor their progress and watch for violations that would potentially breach Earth's agreement with the Free Will Alliance.

Justin took an active role in many of the proceedings in which changes were discussed. He was very proud of New Earth and loved that the people embraced the new beginning as an opportunity to make their world one of enlightened beauty. Not too long ago, they had all taken Earth for granted, but that was no longer the case.

Justin Grant was as changed as his planet, for all intents and purposes. In the past, he'd always avoided being on the frontline, but he was now instrumental in creating the New Earth government. Although he would never admit it, he took some enjoyment in that level of involvement. He was relieved to find that the limelight wasn't as blinding as he'd always thought it would be.

As things wound down, he looked forward to being Hell bound. *I can use a little me time,* he thought, anxious to relax

Benjamin Oneal
with his beautiful beloved, *or, better yet, lots of we time!*

Chapter 45

The next day, Justin slept in till noon, showered, and prepared for his much-needed return to Hell. He planned to spend the next three to six months enjoying time with his bride-to-be. Salome, always the early riser, had already packed and was busy with her duties on the ship. He felt hungry, so he called Stolas to meet him for lunch.

As they shared delicious food and much laughter, Justin received a call from Kimberly Marcus. "Can you join me for an important meeting at the U.N. this afternoon?" she asked.

Justin was sure the agenda would include the announcement of the chosen members of the United Earth Council, the ruling body of New Earth. He tried to contact Salome and Sandel, as he assumed they would want to be there to witness it, but he couldn't reach either of them. Frustrated, he left a message for them both, then boarded a shuttle for Earth.

Jeqon parked the shuttle in its usual spot, and he and Justin entered the United Nations building with ease, since they'd been there so many times before. As they traversed the hallway that led toward the meeting room, Justin had a strange sense that something was different. While it was no secret that he was well liked, Justin couldn't help but notice that everyone was broadly smiling at him. "Hey, Jeqon, is there a kick-me sign on my back or something? Do I have something in my teeth?" Justin asked.

Jeqon, donning a worried expression, stepped back to take a peek. "No. Why do you ask? And who would wish to kick you?"

"Never mind. It's just... Everyone's grinning at me like the damn Cheshire cat, and it's kinda creeping me out," Justin said, doing his best to resist the urge to look down and check his fly.

"I would be creeped out of a cat smiled at me too, my friend," Jeqon said, having never heard of Alice or Wonderland in all his life.

Justin snickered at his friend before entering the meeting room. It was filled to capacity, with the exception of two seats, reserved for him and Jeqon. Nervously, he waited for whatever hammer was about to drop, but he didn't have to wallow in his anxious misery for long.

Kimberly Marcus banged her gavel to call the meeting to order, even though it appeared to have already been going on for quite some time; everyone there looked a big haggard, like college students who'd pulled an all-nighter. "Please, everyone, take your seats!" Kimberly announced.

For the most part, everyone hurried to obey, though a few smiling stragglers took their time.

Once the majority of the crowd was seated and quiet, Kimberly went on, "We are here today to announce representatives of the eight territories, the members of the United Council of New Earth. None of these were easy decisions, as we had to choose from many qualified candidates, all of them excellent choices for these positions. Please hold your applause until all representatives have been named and led to their council seats."

She banged her gavel once more and demanded quiet, then continued, "Your New Earth United Council will be headed by the following. From the Middle East Federation, Ariyasiri Perera of Sri Lanka. From the Peoples Republic of Asia, Wei Cheung of China. From the Australian Conference, Connor Williams of Australia. Representing the South American Coalition, Eduardo Silva of Brazil. From the Russian Federation, Grigori Tereshchenko of Russia. From the European Union, Sancho Díaz of Spain. From the African Republic, Rabah Bendjedid of Algeriaaand."

Although she had warned everyone to be quiet until all names were announced, there was at least one excited outburst as each stood to take his or her place on the council.

Justin counted on his fingers and realized there was one spot left to represent the eight territories. He smiled as he realized who'd been chosen for the job, for he couldn't have been happier about it.

Kimberly Marcus sighed, swallowed the lump in her throat, then humbly stated, "I am proud and humbled to say that I have been chosen to represent the North American States." Then, as applause broke out around the room, she left the main podium and took her seat with the other council members.

When the cheering and whispers and clapping died down, Kimberly said, "As you can see, we have one seat left, right in the middle. That chair will be occupied by the overseer of the New Earth United Council, someone who has, at all times, acted in the best interest of Earth, someone who understands what it truly means to be part of the Free Will Alliance. The person unanimously chosen for this well-deserved position of excellence is..."

Justin ignored the pause and basked in the wonderfulness of that moment. He felt good about the decisions, for he knew that all the chosen members were honorable people, with the skills and moral fiber to lead the new government in the best way. During that moment of silence, Justin noticed Salome, Sandel, and Stolas sitting in the front row, about thirty feet away. His mind wandered, and a running gag from Han Solo popped into his thoughts: *I got a bad feeling about this.* Unfortunately for Justin, he had no Wookie to catch him if he passed out.

"Ladies and gentlemen, allow me to introduce you to our new chief councilman," she said, then paused for effect before proudly spurting, "Justin Grant!"

The roar of applause was ear-splitting this time, and all eyes were on Justin. Many even offered a standing ovation, and Sandel audibly hooted and hollered.

"Mr. Grant, will you please step forward and take your

seat?" Kimberly said, beaming at him.

Feeling like a woman who'd just received a most un-expected proposal, Justin stuttered, "Uh...huh? Who... I mean... What? Who did you say?"

The people closest to him pulled him to his feet and gave him an encouraging push toward the front of the room.

He looked for Salome and shrugged at her wearing a what-the-hell's-going-on-here? expression.

She just clapped and smiled, ignoring the rivers of joyous tears that ran down her pretty face.

Next, Justin darted his gaze to Sandel, who was still cheering, hopping up and down, and clapping more loud-ly than anyone else in the room. "Get up there, my friend!" Sandel screamed, gesturing for Justin to make his way to the prime council seat.

When Justin moved closer to his friends, Salome hugged him, and Sandel clapped him on the back. Still in a daze, Justin walked to his seat at the center of the council. As the room fell silent, he remained speechless for a moment, trying to gather his thoughts.

"Speech!" someone yelled, in a voice that sounded very much like Sandel's. "Speech!"

Justin looked around, then said, "Will everyone please excuse me for a moment? I'd like to have a private word with the council." He then rose and motioned for the council, San-del, and Salome to meet him in the private chambers. While the meeting hall was abuzz with questions as to what was going on, Justin walked toward the back room.

Everyone hurried inside and took their seats, and some-one closed the door.

"Okay. What on Hell's going on?" Justin asked. "Why me? I am not qualified for this, not in any way."

Kimberly was the first to offer an answer: "Justin, you have been the ambassador for the Free Will Alliance since the beginning. You've taken part in every meeting, offered valu-able input as to the changes Earth had to make to become part of our Alliance. Like it or not, you've been right there on the frontlines in our fight against those who opposed what has happened today. You always have your home planet's best interest at heart. The Alliance asked for a united Earth as a requirement to become a galactic partner. You, along with the eight of us, will now serve as that single voice to speak on New Earth's behalf."

Still baffled and overwhelmed, Justin looked to Salome for help, only to hear her say, "Kimberly is right. You are the best and only man for the job, as you so cleverly put it once."

Justin countered, "But what about our wedding? What about spending time together?"

"Do not think for one moment that this will relieve you of your duties as my husband!" she said. "Our wedding will take place as scheduled. Besides, I have never been married to a world leader before."

Justin turned to Sandel, but Sandel just said, in his best Marlon Brando, "It's an offer you can't refuse!"

Justin sighed. "Keep that up, and I'll take *you* to the mattresses, damn it!" he parlayed, but in his heart, he knew his friend and everyone else was right. He could think of no valid argument against him taking that post. Thus, he soon found himself back in the seat of the chief counsel, addressing the people.

Everyone gathered there looked at the council and particularly at Justin as they anxiously awaited the New Earth United Council's final announcement concerning what would possibly be the most important conscious decision that had been made since the dawn of humanity. The brevity of the moment had the room blanketed in utter silence as their new chief counsel began.

"I have been asked to lead the New Earth United Council going forward. I am not sure I am the most qualified," he said with genuine humility, "but rest assured that I will always act in the best interest of Earth, that I will make each and every choice and decision with our planet's future in mind. That said, I'd like to adjourn this meeting at this time, so our new council may discuss mankind's forthcoming journey in depth. We will reconvene on Friday at 1 p.m. Thank you."

The room erupted with a mixture of murmurs, shouted questions, and applause as Justin and the rest of the council stood and left the great hall.

Over the next few days, Justin and the rest of the New Earth United Council met for at least twelve hours a day. With the help of an Illuminator, the eight members were informed about the Tree of Life and its importance to Earth and the galaxy. Everyone saw the need to keep that truth hidden for a while, but they also agreed that sweeping changes needed to made, effective as soon as possible, in many of Earth's policies. They worked hard and put all their brilliant heads together, and by Friday of that week, they'd produced a viable framework to present to the citizens of Earth.

The council entered the great hall and took their appointed seats. Once again, the room was filled to capacity with politicians, dignitaries, citizens, and plenty of press. Kimberly banged the gavel to call the meeting to order, and the crowd silenced. All eyes were on Justin as he began.

"You, my friends, are all part of New Earth, as are we. In the next months and years ahead, we must all make significant changes in the way we live our lives and how we conduct ourselves as human beings. We now know we are not alone in the galaxy, and we have a responsibility to present Earth as a vital part of something greater than ourselves.

"Our planet is truly becoming a unified world, one without borders. Although each territory has the inherent right to govern as they see fit, all will bow to the laws enacted by this council. No place on the globe will be untouchable or beyond the reach of the New Earth government. With that in mind, a New Earth Security force, NES, will be formed to enforce global law. Trivial hostility between nations must end. Terrorism, in any form, will no longer be tolerated."

Justin paused for a moment and ran his eyes over the audience, knowing he was about to bring up a touchy subject for some. Once he knew he still had their full attention, he took a deep breath and moved on to addressing the ongoing battle with the All-Faith Coalition. "Contrary to what some of you might believe," he said, "freedom of religion is an important human right set forth in New Earth law. We saw much hostility during our fight to achieve a one-voice world, but anyone who believes that hostility was a battle against religion is wrong. That fight was against an outside force who has been deliberately deceiving Earthlings for personal gain. Those who choose to continue to follow the teachings of the Bible or any religion are free to do so, provided their beliefs are practiced within the framework of the law and with tolerance of the beliefs of others."

Justin continued with an outline of the new laws and the scope of the NES, both terrestrial and in space. "We have a right to outer space, my friends. When our unified Earth is accepted into the Free Will Alliance, we will be allowed and able to set out into the galaxy to visit other worlds and to colonize new planets. Several stars near our own sun, in Alliance space, provide light and life. These planets are similar enough to our Earth that terraforming will easily make them suitable for colonization. Remember, however, that until we are accepted, space travel will be limited to our Earth technology, strictly confined to our solar system. At this time, travel throughout the galaxy is forbidden."

A few whispers broke out over those remarks, but when the crowd settled once more, Justin elaborated on the changes they hoped to make in the educational system. "We believe education is more than a privilege, that it is a right. Any person on New Earth who seeks learning shall find it, and the knowledge of the galaxy will be available to all mankind. Those who choose careers in education will become the elite in our new society, as long as they continue to prove themselves worthy of those esteemed positions."

For the next hour, Justin detailed more upcoming changes that the people of New Earth would encounter. Then, at the end of his talk, he addressed what he deemed the most important issue of all.

"Over the centuries, humankind has damaged our environment. This is no longer a question but a well-documented fact," he said, trying not to sound too accusatory or scornful. "We have one world, and we must do a better job of caring for it. Thus, new laws dedicated to the preservation and protection of Earth as a whole will be promptly enacted. Those laws will cover three categories. First, land in all parts of the world shall be free from pollution. Oceans, lakes, rivers, and streams shall be cleansed of mankind's deliberate and accidental contamination, in the hope that we can restore it to a robust ecosystem for all sea life, plant and animal alike. The air that surrounds our planet must be free of manmade emissions such as carbon dioxide, as well as any other pollutants that are not byproducts of nature's processes. On New Earth, environmental issues and preservation of nature will be our top priorities. Pollution and litter will be considered criminal acts. Greed and power-seeking will no longer rule the world, no longer be the driving forces behind world policy. The conservation of Earth's natural resources is, from this day forward, fundamental.

"Poaching of animals or plants that are deemed endangered is strictly forbidden. Offenders of this law, along with anyone involved in the buying or selling of these, will face severe prosecution. In addition, rainforests will be preserved, and deforestation will no longer be tolerated. Laws strictly forbidding the burning of fossil fuels will soon be in place."

When Justin saw some eyes widen, he knew exactly what was on their minds. "Unemployment will not be an issue, for those working in the industries that have overtaxed and depleted our environment will be offered job opportunities elsewhere, in the fields of environmental conservation and cleanup. In fact, every person under the age of 25 must spend a minimum of 2 years working in the newly formed Environmental Corps. Our goal is to bring the Earth back to the wonderfully fertile paradise it was meant to be."

As Justin expounded on the Environmental Corps and explained it to his audience in depth, something dawned on him: *Ironic that many of our new environmental laws carry the very same objectives of the Temple.* Although its founders were only concerned with protecting the Trees of Life, the new laws placed the nature of Earth first; the Trees of Life would benefit as a natural side effect of those efforts. That realization helped Justin don a smile as he wrapped up for the day.

"Life, as we know it, will change for the better, fellow Earthlings. For some, the changes will be great, while others will go about their daily lives in much the same way as before. The New Earth United Council will endeavor to do all we can to make the transition as quick and painless as possible. Please believe me when I say that we, your council, will always strive to do what is best for Earth and mankind. In that respect, we welcome any ideas from anyone. What can you do to make New Earth the shining light it was meant to be? This is *our* planet, not just mine or the council's but *ours*. No member of this council, myself included, is immune from the free will of the people. We are here because of you. We are extensions of you, the people of Earth. As was first presented in a speech almost 150 years ago, by Abraham Lincoln, the iconic sixteenth president of the United States, this council represents a government 'of the people, by the people, for the people.' Thank you all."

Chapter 46

Over the next six months, the government of New Earth moved their world closer to membership in the Alliance. Once Earth began operating under a one-world government, tensions around the world decreased tremendously. This was due to most of the population taking the new mindset to heart. It was far from the peace and love movement of the sixties, but there was a greater tolerance toward the deep-seated beliefs of others. People were beginning to accept the differences of their neighbors, and, for the first time in the history of mankind, it seemed that world peace was possible.

The NES quickly grew into a powerful defender of New Earth law. Recruiting from every major law enforcement agency around the world, the NES found strength in its diversity. Every member was rigorously vetted and trained, physically and mentally, to equip them to best represent, defend, and enforce the laws of New Earth. Illuminators proved to be phenomenal tools when it came to training and weeding out those who were merely looking for positions of power. Complaints of abuse were taken seriously, and routine Illuminator scans were mandatory for all members.

Although each territory was entitled to govern in their own regions, territorial and local law enforcement was required to undergo the same training and submit to the same scans as members of NES. That ensured that everyone was working for the good of mankind. Transparency across the board was paramount, so information and communication flowed freely between agencies in every territory, so swift action could be taken as required. World tension all but ended, and while some conflicts continued, the frequency and severity were greatly reduced.

Crime rates also took a nosedive in every territory. While there would always be a criminal element to contend with when human beings were in the mix, the evildoers were forced to go deeper underground and change their methods. Even the biggest bosses in organized crime found it much more difficult to operate profitably, thanks to the growing reach and popularity of law enforcement. In spite of NES efforts, though, crime, like life, would always find a way.

Chief among the evildoers, Michael the archangel, even found that he and his minions were forced to make a bit of a retreat in their fight against the Alliance. They were at the top of the most wanted lists, sought by the authorities for their part in the coldhearted slaughter of millions on the day four explosions rocked the world. Although they remained very powerful from their secret locations, they were confined to do their dirty deeds in the shadows. No longer could they enjoy the freedom of living in open society, and they would forever be forced to conduct their clandestine affairs from places of hiding.

Along with their crime- and terrorism-fighting duties, the NES was also tasked with the enforcement of the new, stringent environmental laws. Pollution had no place in New Earth policy, and consequences were clearly expressed for anyone who took part in it. When the burning of fossil fuels was banned, oil companies protested, until it was made clear that they would be instrumental in creating new, cleaner energy sources to replace oil. The only carbon dioxide that found its way into the atmosphere was that which came from Earth's natural processes. Strict security measures were taken in and around rainforests, and deforestation was a thing of the past. New Earth was quickly on its way to becoming a paradise once again.

Although it would be some time before citizens of New Earth would be made aware of the existence and the true nature of the Trees of Life, countless orchards were planted around the world. When the time came, the fruit of those wholly wonderful arbors would become the number-one export of New Earth, a commodity that would be appreciated by all in the galaxy.

Justin spent many restless nights contemplating what the future had in store for him, just a former college professor from Indiana. The one thing he knew for sure was that a relatively obscure, little-known world orbiting a star located on a spiral arm at the edge of the Milky Way was now destined to become one of the most important planets in the galaxy. The only other thing he was certain of was that if he didn't get his ass out of there soon, he may never get the chance to leave.

PART THREE

No Time Like the Future

Chapter 47

It had been fifty years since New Earth's acceptance into the Free Will Alliance. Justin sat in his chair as chief counsel and enjoyed his daily waking dream about leaving it all behind and spending his days gallivanting around the galaxy with Salome and his children. That daydream always made him a little morose. *It's been half a damn century, and my ass is still here,* he thought, frustrated.

Even after five decades of brilliant service and endless compliments, thanks, and commendations, Justin could not accept the fact that he was actually a world leader. If that weren't bad enough, he had also become a very important person in galactic affairs. New Earth had grown in power and galactic position since the exportation of the Longevity Factor began, and every world now looked toward the previously little-known planet, hoping for a taste of immortality. As countless beings from countless worlds saw it, Justin represented immortality, and Chief Counsel Justin Grant was not only a hero but also the man who was leading New Earth into a successful, brighter future.

His duties as chief counsel kept him earthbound much of the time, but that only made his occasional junkets to Hell more precious. Off-world diplomatic meetings also gave him a break from the day-to-day grind, the often-mundane duties of his office. Still, a leadership position remained a bit out of his comfort zone and made him a little antsy. Although he'd improved somewhat in that regard, he still felt unworthy, to the point where he actually asked Lucifer, "You've been ruling for thousands of years. How do you do it?"

Lucifer wisely answered, "The secret to being a great leader is to listen to your council, your advisers, and the people of Earth, then make the correct decisions."

"Thanks. But wait..." Justin hemmed and hawed, suddenly realizing that Lucifer hadn't really given him a definitive answer.

Justin frowned as Lucifer laughed, clapped him on the back, and said, "You are doing fine, son, and I have every confidence you will continue to do so."

Justin's and Salome's golden anniversary was just a week away, and their love was stronger than ever. They were often accused of acting like lovesick teenagers when they were together. Justin reckoned that was accurate, because Salome was still the only girl who really did it for him, or as he put it, "She makes my man-parts tingle." Before the Longevity Factor, fifty years of marriage was rare, but Justin now couldn't imagine being with anyone else. He only wondered if Salome would still love him after 100 or 1,000 years.

It was a great relief to Justin when Sandel volunteered to take over the day-to-day duties of leadership on Hell, with Lucifer serving as his chief adviser. Now that Sandel seemed to be going through the same angst as Justin was, they often engaged in a two-man pity party.

"I miss the good ol' days, when we were actually out there doing something," one of them would inevitably say during party.

Their misery was so evident that Salome and Lilith noticed it as well. For their wives, it was a bit of pathetic nonsense. Once, their whining was so bad that when Salome and Lilith walked into the room and heard the boys discussing their woes, the women put on an exaggerated performance of mock crying, blowing their noses and generally throwing the despair around until they all broke out in uncontrollable laughter.

Chapter 48

In spite of the happenings on New Earth, on Heaven, life had not changed that much. The heavenly citizens and those connected with the Empire still lived in fear of their lord God. Other than a few minor skirmishes along their borders, life carried on as usual. Much to the council's dismay, with nothing to occupy his mind, Jesus turned to those around him to fill the void. Everyone in the palace, from the council members to the servants, desperately hoped for a distraction. Most knew their lives very much depended on any kind of diversion that that would take the focus off them. Jesus was an overgrown child, many silently believed, and children needed to be entertained.

Since Jesus' favorite toy, Earth, was now lost, he ordered his scientists to step up their efforts to find an alternate planet capable of growing a healthy Tree of Life. He also demanded that all efforts were made to restore Eden to an environmentally sound planet as a sustainable source of the Longevity Factor. While the mandate came at the advice of Seraphim One and his council, all gave full credit to their lord for the idea. It still didn't do much to help the inhabitants of Eden; while their world would be saved, there was no concern for the people who lived there.

In simple terms, the Edenites were slaves on their own world. Many lost hope of ever being free of Heaven's domination. Once, they were peaceful people who shied away from

the allure of technology and chose to live off the grid, as partners with nature. This was not to say they were a backward
people; they did explore space around their star, and they
had encountered many other inhabited planets. Nevertheless,
they just chose the simple life. In the minds of the Edenites,
technology was a necessary evil, and they preferred to live as
faithful caretakers of their beautiful home world.

Before the heavenly invasion, the people of Eden were
known for their highly evolved intellects. They could not stop
the greedy destruction of their gorgeous world, but they could
continue to grow their own minds. They used their intelligence as a weapon, wielding it wherever they could against
their cruel invaders. The found ways to sabotage the angelic
invaders, and that became a diversion from the pain they
endured. This new effort by Heaven to restore Eden at least
made their labor seem worthwhile. The mere act of reviving
their once beautiful world brought hope to their weary hearts
and brilliant minds.

Jesus met daily with his council to plot the expansion of
Empire borders. He wanted Earth back, along with the Purgatorian sector. That came as no surprise to anyone, because
all knew that his ultimate goal had always been to rule the
galaxy. In their meetings, they discussed potential weak spots
in the Alliance, and Jesus' eye gleamed with every mention of
potential victory. He wanted it all, and like the spoiled baby
he was, Jesus was used to getting his way.

Jesus also arranged for several private meetings with
Michael. Those one-on-one rendezvous behind closed doors
worried Seraphim One greatly; such discussions had resulted
in many terrible things over the years. On one particular occasion, Seraphim One, who was near the door right before it
slammed in his face, overheard Michael's question: "What do
you want more than anything else in the galaxy, my Lord?"

What a fool! Seraphim One thought. He knew better than
to ever interrogate his lord about his affairs, because Jesus
was infamous on turning on any one at any time for any reason. Since Jesus was prone to reacting rather than thinking
first, the focus and strength of his responses were most un-
predictable. Seraphim One thought it best to wait for Jesus

to reveal information at his leisure, if at all. His accidental eavesdropping did not make him privy to the lord's answer that day, but he thought Michael was insane for asking.

Whatever Michael and Jesus discussed that day and on others seemed to make Jesus a very happy man, sometimes to the point of granting his servants uncharacteristic reprieve from punishment for accidental missteps. As much as Seraphim One tried not to pry, he did wonder. To know what Jesus was thinking was bad, but not knowing was very bad and made for an extremely scary situation.

Chapter 49

New Earth was well on her way to becoming a utopia once more. The planet was cleaner and greener. Even major cities like New York, Tokyo, and Mexico City found balance with nature. Working alongside the natural elements—instead of trying to contain, conquer, or exploit them—had become a way of life. Environmental conservation was now the largest industry on the planet, and almost 50 percent of the NES was devoted to environmental issues. Whether enforcing laws against pollution of the air, water, or land, or protecting Earth's most valuable export, they worked day and night to ensure the continued wellbeing of the planet.

The rainforests were finally beginning to return to their previous unparalleled beauty, and life sprung up in them once again. Strict rules on tourism in those areas were put into place and strictly enforced. Oceans, lakes, and rivers also recovered nicely, and that would serve to ensure continued progress of nature's fight to heal itself.

As an unexpected byproduct of increased involvement with nature, people of all ages began to spend more time outdoors. They enjoyed the real, natural beauty of the world in which they lived, rather than seeing it all on monitors and television screens. Actually, going outdoors to touch a leaf or smell a flower was preferred over Googling it, and no longer did anyone vegetate in front of their gadgetry, falling into the time-wasting, mind-melting downward spiral of social media.

Although technology was still very much a part of everyone's life, a trend to enjoy simpler, more organic pleasures quickly evolved.

Along with environmental issues, preservation of the life forms fortunate enough to remain on New Earth became a priority. Due to the enforcement of Species Preservation Laws, over 500 plants and almost 400 animals regained enough momentum to be taken off the endangered species list. No longer were tigers killed so humans could maintain their erections. No more were sharks slaughtered en masse out of exaggerated, unreasonable, Hollywood-spun fear or because someone wanted to enjoy their fins in a bowl of soup. Justin was extremely proud of the progress that had been made since the inception of the New Earth United Council, but he was especially proud of his fellow Earthlings. Albeit reluctantly at first, they eventually came together, and they'd achieved much in a remarkably short amount of time. Without their help, none of it would have been possible, and that humbled and excited him.

Population control, however, remained a major issue. Laws aimed at limiting each family to two children attempted to ensure that the growth would slow a bit. Another aid in that situation was the colonization of two planets near Earth, Gaia and Terra. Almost 1.5 billion people had already moved off their home world, some to other planets in the Alliance but most to the new colonies. Those new worlds had one advantage over the healing planet Earth: the nature conservancy laws were a cornerstone of their beginning.

One unexpected side effect of the changes was the popularity of New Earth throughout the galaxy. Much of that could be credited to the export of the highly sought Longevity Factor, but tourism was also a quickly growing industry on the planet. Beings from 1,000 worlds came to vacation on the wholly wonderful planet, the source of their life-stretching Factor. Tours of the orchards and free samples from the Trees of Life were great attractions for the citizens of New Earth and visitors alike. To taste the fruit in its raw form was a completely amazing experience for everyone.

Chapter 50

After a particularly exhausting day of meetings and administrative duties that Justin still referred to as paperwork (even though there hadn't been an actual sheet of paper anywhere near him for years), Justin headed home. He hoped his family would help to break up the melancholy that had descended upon him during his daily waking dream.

When he walked through his front door, he was immediately attacked by two very small Alliance freedom fighters. He rolled and wrestled on the floor with his attackers for the next ten minutes, until Salome stepped in to try to gently separate her rambunctious ones from their father. Before she knew it, she was pulled into the middle of the fun, and they all tussled and laughed for quite some time, until Justin grabbed Salome and assaulted her with a hard kiss.

"Ew!" Jarod and Rachel chorused. Then, realizing their mother and father's nauseating romantic interlude might take a while, they ran from the room to seek another adventure.

Later that evening, with the gloom still lurking at the edge of his happiness, Justin grabbed his children under both arms and carried them to their room, then readied them for bed. As he tucked his little ones in, his son asked, "Daddy, can you tell us the story of Eden again?"

Justin smiled, patted the boy on the head, and went on to tell them, in the most vivid, colorful language he could muster, of the Tree of Life. He even included a few sound effects for good measure. He enlightened his offspring about their ancestors as well. "They lived for over 20,000 years," and he told them of the beautiful paradise world far away. Their eyes grew wide when his storytelling swerved toward the evil Empire that descended on Eden to greedily ravage the planet, and they were most interested in the great spaceships that carried their ancestors to Earth.

"Is anyone left on Eden, Daddy?" Jarod asked.

"Yes. Many of the old ones are still there, doing their best to survive under the rule of the evil hand of Jesus," Justin responded.

Rachel thought for a moment, then asked, "Why don't we go get them and bring them here or make that evil Jesus leave them alone?"

Justin offered his daughter a weak half-smile, sighed, and answered, "Honey, that would be nice, but it's just...not possible."

"Why, Daddy?" the girl pushed.

"Yeah, why, Daddy? If they're our antsisters, shouldn't we help them?" Jarod chimed in.

"Ancestors," Justin gently corrected, but as hard as he tried, Justin could not come up with a good answer to their question, and that really made him think. *Kids really do say the darndest things,* he pondered, *and maybe we adults should listen to them once in a while.* He then patted them both on the head and said, "It's time for you two to go to sleep. Daddy's got some thinking to do."

With his children safely tucked in and on their way to Dreamland for the night, Justin walked to his study. Rachel's question kept coming to mind: *"Why, Daddy?"* The more he thought about it, the greater his disappointment was that he couldn't come up with a reasonable answer. *After all, the Edenites are family, our ancestors, our blood. there must be some way to free them,* he thought, and he made a mental note that he needed to talk to Sandel as soon as possible.

The next day, he made arrangements for an impromptu vacation on Hell. Salome's father, Jarod, had a birthday coming up, the perfect excuse. In the meantime, he spent much time with the Illuminator, gaining all knowledge he could on Planet Eden and her surrounding space. Sadly, since Jesus' takeover of the planet, much of the intel about its history and the fate of his ancestors had been destroyed.

A week later, Justin was sitting in Sandel's office in the palace on Hell. Lucifer was there, along with Stolas and his ever-present protector, Jeqon. In all the years since Justin's kidnapping, Jeqon had remained by his side at every opportunity, just as he'd promised.

Once the room was secure, Sandel asked, "What is on your mind, my friend?"

Everyone listened intently for Justin's answer, fully aware that such a meeting would not have been called unless something major was bothering him.

Justin, certain that there was no need to try to justify his request, decided to just throw it out there. "I want to free Eden," he blurted.

The silence in the room became deafening, and none of them even dared to blink as they stared at him in seeming disbelief.

Justin looked at one and then the next, hoping they were just in deep thought and not under the assumption that he'd lost his mind. He explained that the notion came up during some pillow talk after a bedtime story with his children, and then he went on to say, "New Earth cannot possibly accomplish this alone. I hope a joint mission between the Free Will Alliance and Earth can be arranged."

Again, the silence intensified, and only Sandel dared to blink.

"The Edenites are my ancestors, my blood," Justin pleaded. "The thought of them suffering at the hand of that unholy asshole is..." he said, trailing off when he could not find ample words.

"Horrible, atrocious, sickening," Sandel offered.

"Yes, all of that and then some," Justin said, nodding.

Finally, Sandel smiled, and the others in the room seemed to resume their breathing and blinking. "My friend," Sandel said, "there is no need to justify yourself. Father and I know you come to no decisions without great thought and

243

contemplation. That is why you are so valuable to the New Earth United Council. In fact, we have been pondering this very action for some time. Perhaps now, the time has come."

Justin sat down, breathed a sigh of relief, and smiled, utterly grateful that no one considered him a fool or wanted to have him committed.

For the next five hours, they talked of possible scenarios. By the time the meeting ended, it had been decided that the mission was not only doable but critically important.

From the start, Justin had made it known that the New Earth security fleet, built with the help of the Alliance, would fight alongside the Alliance in the war against the Empire. Every member of the fleet was trained by the Alliance in all physical and tactical aspects. The humans proved to be worthy in every way; in fact, they were so skilled and trusted that the New Earth security fleet had already taken over about 70 percent of the responsibilities of protecting the star systems near Earth, including the New Earth colonies.

Over the next week, the most trusted advisers and generals worked with Sandel, Justin, and Lucifer to plan the mission to free Eden. Sandel and Justin glowed with the excitement of being in action again.

At dinner one night, while the men talked and laughed, Salome looked over at Lilith and asked, "What are we going to do with these children? First, they were drowning in self-pity, and now, they're so excited they are about to pee their pants."

"Hmm," Lilith said. "Well, I can't speak for yours, but as for mine, I'll expect him to put some of that excitement to use a little later on tonight."

"Oh, yeah!" Sandel said when he overheard it. He quickly jumped up from the table and performed a terribly clumsy happy dance. "Oh, gotta get some, baby... Oh, gonna get some, baby... Get some tonight," he sang, earning several eye-rolls and a few gagging sounds from the other dinner guests.

"Keep your day job, Sandel," Justin teased, "and quit looking up Earth lyrics on your Illuminator."

It was some time before they could control their laughter.

It was also evident in the smiles on their husbands' faces the next morning that the girls carried through with their promises.

By the time Justin and his family boarded their ship for Earth, the framework of the plan was in place. Sandel and his team, as always, would continue tweaking it and working through every aspect until it was as perfect and seamless as possible; it had to be to minimize loss of life and reduce the chance of failure. Too much was riding on it to leave any stone unturned.

Chapter 51

The Alliance had been keeping a close eye on Eden for many years. They had observed the space around the planet, and they were fully aware of the stronghold the Empire had there, in normal and deviant space. They'd placed some infiltrators and spies on the planet, so they also knew the strength of the Empire's ground forces. Every possible bit of information was collected and analyzed in preparation for their mission, and a date and time were set.

Such a large-scale operation had little chance of remaining a secret. Sooner than the Alliance would have liked, word of a possible attack reached Heaven, but the details were unclear. Alliance scout ships had been spotted near the border, so close to Heaven that it made the Empire more than a little anxious. In response to that, Heaven sent extra ships out to strengthen its force along that border. Two Alliance scouts raised red flags high when they flew so close to Heaven that they were barely able to escape back into Alliance space.

Once again, only the most trusted generals knew all the ins and outs of the plan as a whole. The Alliance fleet entered deviant space and headed in Heaven's direction. A signal was sent from an undisclosed ship among them, broadcasting a clear message: "Alliance fleet mobile, destination unknown, current direction in line with home world." General Sorath, now in command of the fleet, smiled, for all seemed to be going just as planned.

When they again entered normal space, they maneuvered into a completely different flight course. At that point, all signals were disrupted other than ship-to-ship communications. By the time anyone realized their destination, they would already be in Eden space.

The element of surprise was key to the mission. With every sensor on high and every weapon at the ready, the Alliance fleet entered normal space near Planet Eden. It became quickly apparent that the Empire was not so susceptible to surprise attacks. As if they were expecting an ambush, the Empire opened fire on the Alliance ships immediately upon their entry from deviant space. The more agile disciple fighters attacked the Alliance fighters as they poured from the battle cruisers. Three Alliance vessels were severely damaged, and two were destroyed. Just like that, the battle was on.

The darkness of space lit up like a randomly timed strobe. The crews of every ship, Alliance and Empire alike, clashed with trained reaction. All courageously remained at their posts, even as the walls of their ships ripped apart. They had been ordered to hold the line, and both sides aimed to do just that.

As before, the goal of the Alliance was to disable enemy weapons and engines. The Empire, on the other hand, shot to kill. Time slowed for everyone. As the battle raged on, it became evident that the Empire fleet was smaller than initially presumed. The Alliance breathed a collective sigh of relief, for it seemed that their ploy to misdirect the distribution of Heaven forces had succeeded; there were 100 more Empires ships than they hoped for, but it could have been a far, far greater onslaught.

Just when the Alliance felt victory was in sight, a second wave of fifty Empire ships arrived to defend their Eden. The battle intensified, but the 200 ships of the Alliance fleet and the 100 that arrived soon after Empire reinforcements appeared soon took control of the battle. Finally, victory was quickly realized. The Alliance lost seventeen ships and took heavy damage to twenty-eight others. All in all, their death toll stood at 170. As for the Empire, seventy-three ships retreated, nine were lost, and the rest were badly damaged or entirely disabled. Their loss of life was nearly 100. As the Alliance called for surrender, thirty–eight of the disabled disciple ships self-destructed; their captains believed exploding in space was a far better fate for them and their crewmembers than to face a pissed-off, all-powerful lord after their failure.

Sorath sat back in his chair on the bridge of the *Hellfire,* mentally drained from the firefight. After Commander Pruflas ordered the com-tech to open a channel to the fleet, he nodded, and that was Sorath's cue to speak. "Soldiers of the Free Will Alliance," he said, "you have fought bravely and with honor. This battle will be remembered proudly, just as were our victories in the Purgatorian War and the battle of New Earth. No victory comes without a cost though. Today, we lost many brave soldiers and friends, but rest assured that their names will be forever spoken with reverence and honor throughout the galaxy. This was merely one battle in an ongoing war, but we will win that war, and there will be free will for all in the galaxy. Thank you all."

After he signed off from that communication, Sorath thought for a moment. He then ordered Captain Rumel of the *Apollyon,* Captain Tarel of the *Legion,* and Captain Halphas of the *Valefar* to set up perimeter around Eden and along the new Alliance border. To Captain Barbas of the *Pithius,* he gave the assignment of searching for survivors among the wreckage, and he commanded Captain Agares of the *Eligos* to secure Eden itself. The level of resistance they would face on Eden was yet unknown to them, but with help from the agents who'd been on the planet for quite some time, most of the major problems were eliminated in quick order.

Once all the duties had been delegated, Sorath prepared to deliver the message he'd been eagerly waiting to announce. "Eden and the surrounding star systems are now under the protection of the Free Will Alliance. Any act of aggression against Eden or the ships that protect it will be met with extreme force. Refrain from any further aggression, and we will petition Eden to supply the Empire with the Longevity Factor at a fair and equitable price. The Longevity Factor is a thing to be shared, but only if it is the will of the people of Eden. It will not be taken by force. At all cost, the Alliance will protect

Eden's right to choose their future, whatever it may be." As he finished, Sorath couldn't help but smile, especially as he pictured the tempestuous Jesus hearing the news.

Chapter 52

Once again, Jesus took the news with restrained dignity. The council gave their lord a wide berth, hoping to escape his wrath and thanking God that there were more servants in the throne room than usual, more fodder for Jesus, more lives to devour before he descended upon them. As the servants tried to escape, the council members selfishly pushed them back and used them as shields. The rusty iron stench of blood permeated the room as the dead fell to the floor. Even a prized possession was not safe from his rage.

For the seventy years since Jesus had cruelly made an example of him by taking his tongue and his manhood, the speechless, bloated eunuch had been suspended in a cage above the throne room, a constant reminder to all of the power of Jesus' wrath. Many were surprised that the sickening ornament also turned out to be a signifier of the lord's love; in time, Jesus grew to adore the grotesque creature as something of a pet. He took delight in Jahoel's many failed attempts to communicate with unintelligible grunts, and he forced him to do humiliating tricks in exchange for table scraps. Now, in his blind rage, Jesus speared Jahoel in the chest.

Seraphim One watched his former enemy was about to die, and in that moment, he could have sworn he heard Jahoel utter the words, "Thank you," even without the aid of his tongue.

Michael, who was not normally present in the throne room, looked on with real amusement, truly enjoying the show. Seraphim One desperately wanted to beat the disturbing grin right off the archangel's face, but for the good of the Alliance, he could only look on with an expression of detached apathy.

As the show wound down, a panting, blood-covered Jesus sat back in his throne and simply said, "Seraphim One, see that this mess is cleaned up. Zabkiel, do not let Jahoel die." He then turned his gaze on Michael and ordered, "Meet me in my private chambers in one hour."

"Yes, my Lord," Michael said with a nod as Jesus stood, and left the throne room.

It wasn't so much that Seraphim One felt left out, he was just curious and more than a bit concerned about the secret meetings between them. He wondered what they were planning. Michael had not commanded the fleet of Heaven for a millennium, not since he was ordered to infiltrate Earth, so Seraphim One could only assume that an attack on the Alliance was not part of their agenda.

Seraphim One called for the healers. When they arrived, they immediately got to work on Jahoel. "Will he live?" Zabkiel asked.

"It was close, but he will pull through." They informed him.

"No, please no!" Jahoel pleaded, Zabkiel couldn't help feeling sorry for his old enemy. It would've been a mercy to let him die.

A couple of hours later, as Michael exited Jesus' private chambers, he looked back, and said, "Please be patient, my Lord. This will work, but it will take time, and all elements must be accomplished to perfection. Of course, you in your infinite wisdom, already know this to be true."

What a sycophant, Seraphim One thought when he heard it, but the answer to his question of what Michael was up to beyond flagrant flattery still eluded him.

Chapter 53

Justin wasn't sure to expect as he traveled through deviant space, on his way to Planet Eden. Regardless of the unknown, his excitement was almost more than he could stand. He imagined that in just a short time, he would be introduced to the oldest beings in the galaxy, perhaps his own flesh-and-blood ancient ancestors. Only one thought really struck him over and over again: *Damn, this is so cool!*

As the *Ronwe*, Justin's presidential ship, entered Eden space, his excitement was replaced with a bit of nervousness, coupled with a pang of unworthiness. Nevertheless, he knew he had to be the one; after all, the entire mission was his idea's, spawned by his own children after a bedtime story. Justin was the leading representative of Earth, and the Edenites were kin with him, whether they knew it or not.

He looked at the planet on the view screen as they approached. At once, he noticed that it appeared to be quite similar to Earth, with vast, blue oceans, green land masses, and swirling, white clouds. When he saw that, Justin felt a deep inner peace wash over him. Whether it was some sort of primal knowledge he was experiencing or something else, he wasn't sure, but he was suddenly very glad to be there, like a voyager returning home.

When Justin exited the ship, he was a little surprised that there was no one there to greet him other than a group of Alliance soldiers. Had one of the soldiers not explained that the Edenites did not find pomp and circumstance very appealing, he felt a little dejected. "They're just not much for ceremony, especially when there is work to be done," the soldier said. "They're all pretty busy trying to repair the damage caused by the heavenly occupation. It's an ongoing job."

Justin understood, because it was exactly what he'd been told about his primeval relatives. The Edenites had long since accepted their place as custodians of their world, and they chose to work hard and use technology sparingly and only when it did not interfere with Eden's natural processes.

While the soldiers escorted him to the village, Justin noticed workers everywhere, either planting trees, removing trash, or gardening. From what he could see, it would be many years before the world could live up to its name again. Heaven had destroyed much of Eden, and the people of that world were left to clean up the mess.

Finally, a representative of the Edenites came to him and said, "You will be our guest at our great hall this evening. The elders want to meet with you to discuss the future."

Several hours later, Justin was escorted into a large cavern and asked to be seated next to the so-called elders. He was in awe of who they were and what they represented. Also, while he wasn't sure why, he felt an instant connection with the Edenites. They must have felt it as well, because they welcomed him as a brother.

"I assure you that you are under no obligation to the Free Will Alliance," Justin announced, "but you are now protected from the Empire's grasp, since your world lies within Alliance space." He also told them of Earth and their many descendants who lived there, and he generously offered any assistance they required to help with the reconstruction of their world to its former glory.

He never left home without his handy, dandy Illuminator, so he used it to broaden their minds with the facts. He showed Earth to them, what it once was and what it had become. It was a quick whirlwind through a long history, with some details left out, but it was enough to show the Edenites the beautiful world he called home, and he sugarcoated nothing. He openly admitted, "I am afraid your descendants, we Earthlings, nearly decimated our own planet in the name of progress, but the Alliance has helped us find the path to a better way. We are New Earth now, and we are improving all the time." He also touched on Earth's struggle with the Empire and the historical deception they used to control the people.

As the images from the Illuminator faded, Justin noticed tears in the eyes of the elders. It was as if they were helpless parents witnessing the suffering of their children but unable to do anything to protect them. The elders were deeply saddened by the Empire's hold on Earth and its people, and that surprised Justin. The Edenites themselves had endured and survived a much greater struggle for much longer, but their concern was reserved for others. Earthlings had been oblivious until recently, yet the Edenites were openly oppressed for thousands of years. Somehow, after all the torment and destruction, they remained a people of great intellect, deep inner peace, and amazing compassion for others. They were content with themselves and their role as the guardians of their world.

Justin noticed the weariness in the faces of the elders and requested that they retire for the evening. "I don't know about all of you, but I've had a long day," he said, speaking more on their behalf than his own.

The elders somehow knew what was in his heart and thanked him for his kindness. Before they went their separate ways, they made sure to invite him to another meeting the next evening, at the very same time.

As they were all gathering their things to leave, an idea popped into Justin's head. "I would very much like to help with the work tomorrow before the meeting. Would that be all right with you?"

"One does not ever need to ask permission to help! We welcome you to our labor, with much gratitude," one of the elders said with a wrinkled smile on his face.

The next day, Justin was up early. He was thrilled that his entourage, along with several crewmembers from the *Ronwe*, wholeheartedly agreed to join the cleanup effort. He worked physically harder than he had in a long time, but he was more than happy to do it; it was the kind of work that made him feel good, inside and out. First, he helped a group of Edenites remove a monstrous pile of garbage and debris carelessly left behind by the Empire. Anything considered harmful to their world and all that could not be repurposed or recycled for use by the Edenites was collected for Justin to haul away. *Who'da thunk it? Justin Grant, Garbage Man of the Cosmos,* he jested in his head, though he was more than happy to volunteer for the task.

By the time he was to meet with the elders again that night, he was sore and tired but content. He was also excited and quite alert, for the Edenites had agreed to reveal to Justin a bit of their own history.

Using the Illuminator, Justin saw Eden as it was before the Empire invasion. It was indescribably beautiful. Then, he witnessed a much younger Lucifer, accompanied by Elohim, landing and greeting the Edenites. The deal was struck between them to supply the galaxy with the fruit of the Tree of Life. For some time, there was peaceful coexistence between Eden and the Empire, and God protected Eden from all harm. Then, like some terrible suspense movie where the happily-ever-after was shattered in a soul-crushing scene switch, he saw a time thousands of years later, when a not-so-happy invasion of the Empire burst in to tear their world apart, all at the command of Jesus, the son of the one who'd been so kind to them.

Justin watched as millions were forced to enter enormous space transports and evacuated from their world in an effort to reduce the threat of a civil uprising. As he stared at the happenings with a sick feeling in his gut, his heart tearing in two at the thought of so many being forced from their homes, it suddenly occurred to him that he could very well be witnessing the relocation of the people who eventually landed on Earth. He watched as merciless Empire forces ravaged the land like scavenging pirates, looting for anything of value. As the scene faded, he found himself crying silently, along with all the elders in the room. While they had all done their best to cope with it, the Empire had left deep scars on their spirits.

Justin remained on Eden for another month. He enjoyed working alongside his new friends and visiting their families, but he also missed his own. When he headed back to Earth, he promised, "I will return soon," and he meant it.

Chapter 54

Justin returned from Eden to a hero's welcome. The people of New Earth saw his new adventure as a positive step, a journey into their past to make for a better future. Everyone was eager to know everything about the Edenites. Justin did his best to convey to them how wonderful it was to actually shake hands with living, breathing pieces of history.

Justin did not feel much like a hero, but he felt good inside, and he was almost saddened by the fact that travel to Planet Eden would be strictly forbidden to others for the time being. There was good reason for it: Outsiders had to respect their way of life and their wishes. One exception was that teams of environmental workers would be sent to Eden to help with the restoration of the planet. Justin hoped that would pave the way for a future relationship between the two planets that had more in common than anyone had ever realized before.

When the Environmental Corps posted sign-up sheets for *Project Eden*, the response was overwhelming. The chance to spend two years or more in the home world of the ancestors was a coveted experience among the people of Earth. Essential personnel such as supervisors and environmental experts were automatically selected to go based on their experience and merit, but a lottery was held to choose others to go and help with the dirty work.

After six weeks of intense training and learning about the

culture and customs of their would-be host world, the first 1,000 volunteers left Earth to begin the adventure of their lives. Although they knew their days would be spent with hard work, they were more than excited to begin. Justin was beyond proud of the young members of the Corps, the first group headed to Eden.

Of course, Earth being what it was, not everyone on the planet still agreed on everything. Some felt quite different-ly about the Edenites or the Trees of Life they represented. Racism reared its ugly head once more, and hostile objectors to the growing alien presence on New Earth made it known that they wanted Earth to be pure. While their lives had been undeniably improved during the years following the move to the one-world government and the Longevity Factor given to all by the trees, they still raised their voices with bitter songs of intolerance.

Religion, too, was still part of New Earth culture and liberty guaranteed by the notion of free will. However, the anti-alien groups gladly took on archaic beliefs of intolerant religions of old. They held true to the King James Matthew 12:30 scripture, "He that is not with me is against me; and he that gathereth not with me scattereth abroad." Their message was as simple as it was simple-minded: "If you were not born on this Earth, then you are not welcome here."

Soon, Justin again felt the hand of Michael leading his flock against the New Earth government. The numbers were small but ever growing, not to be ignored. As before, they were destined to grow like an aggressive cancer if steps were not taken to eradicate them.

Offshoots of those groups took a more direct approach, attacking alien visitors and even trying to poison the source of the Longevity Factor, in the hope that ridding New Earth of the life-enhancing agriculture would ensure that the rest of the galaxy would lose interest and leave the planet alone. A few trees fell to their brand of terrorism, but the NES took prompt action to limit the amount and ferocity of the damage. Supply and demand being what it was, the Longevity Factor was as important to the Empire as it was to the people of New Earth, so it was not within their best interest to let anyone harm the Trees of Life. Therefore, since there was nowhere on New Earth to hide and Michael refused to protect them because they went against his orders, the appalling arboreal axmen were quickly rounded up. In a short time, they were no longer a threat.

All the while, the groups who were backed by the evil archangel grew in numbers. They protested everything, from the unwanted infestation of aliens on New Earth to a complete disregard for the word of God, the Trees of Life, and even the Free Will Alliance embassy. For the most part, their protests were peaceful, and they organized their outcries within the confines of the law to avoid arrest by the NES. Michael and Gabriel remained elusive as always, pulling the strings from a safe distance. They were always somewhere close to the action but wisely avoided being out in the open where they might be found.

Chapter 55

Another five years passed in relative peace, with New Earth moving ever closer to a sustainable ecological paradise. New Earth and Eden, linked together by their common purpose and their ancestral bond, worked in unison to realize their goals. Although Michael and his religious minions still made every attempt to subtly push their own agendas, they were no longer a real threat. Life on both worlds found a satisfying pace and peace as the Edenites and the Earthlings walked into the future hand in hand.

It was a very special day indeed; the day Chief Elder Lornash was scheduled to visit New Earth for the first time. His position on Eden mirrored Justin's role on Earth. It was thought that Lornash was the oldest living being in the galaxy, yet he looked like a healthy 50-something. Although space travel was not new to him, it had been over 15,000 years since he had ventured off his home planet, so it was an exciting experience for him to be sure.

Since travel to Eden had been restricted at the Edenites' request, a chance to see the leader of the mysterious, ancient world garnered much attention, attracting beings from every corner of the galaxy. Although Sandel could not attend due to pressing Alliance business, Lucifer and Lilith were there to serve as representatives of Hell.

Lornash landed near the New Earth United Council compound, which was almost adjacent to the former United Nations building in New York. The Big Apple was no longer the same city at all; it was more green than stone. While it was still home to more people per square mile than most places on New Earth, it shone as a truly modern city that adhered strictly to its environmental responsibility. Not only that, but no place on New Earth was more secure than the compound; Justin made sure of that, as he had no intention of taking any risks with the arrival of his VIP guest.

They entered the compound with as little pomp and circumstance as a restrained New Earth celebration would allow. Lornash managed a brief smile and a wave to the crowd. When Justin noticed the uncomfortable, overwhelmed look in the weathered elder's eyes, he quickly ushered him to a room where he was only surrounded by council members.

Justin began his introductions with Lucifer, and Lornash kindly cut in, "It is good to see you, old friend."

"It has been far too long, Lornash," Lucifer responded.

Although Justin was surprised that they still recognized one another, he managed to set his curiosity aside and call the meeting to order. They sat for some time around the enormous table, discussing the agenda for the day and for the remainder of Lornash's time on New Earth. His speech for the people of Earth was scheduled for 7:00 the next evening.

Until then, Lornash and Lilith agreed that they would stay at Justin's home. Lornash was excited to meet his family and seemed to get along easily with his New Earth friends, and he very much enjoyed the children and Justin's lovely wife.

Before dinner, Justin, Lornash and Lucifer were sitting in the living room enjoying some light conversation when a serious look suddenly washed over Lucifer's face. "Lornash, I am sorry I did not free your planet sooner. It just... Well, I just couldn't think of a scenario where I could be sure that the people of Eden would not be harmed."

Lornash shook his head and smiled. "On the contrary, old friend, you ultimately *did* save my planet. My people and I are grateful to you for that."

Lucifer responded with a headshake of his own, "No, not I. If not for the determination and planning of this young man…" He paused and gave a look of gratitude to Justin, then continued, "If not for him, you would still be under that evil bastard's thumb."

Justin, blushing a bit from the flattery, shrugged and smirked. "I can't take credit," he said. "After all, it was my children's idea!"

At that, they all had a laugh and lifted their drinks for a toast.

Lornash seemed particularly taken by Rachel and Jarod and spent as much time as he could with them. At bedtime, the elder regaled them with tales of happy days on Eden. His final goodnight story was about the day their hero of a father reached out to save his world. Before he left the room, he thanked the little ones for their role in the miraculous salvation of the Edenites.

Surprised, Justin's son and daughter looked at one another, but it was Rachel who spoke up. "We didn't do anything, Uncle Lornash," she sweetly said.

Lornash countered, "Oh, but you most certainly did. Your idea put everything in motion. Your daddy is not the only hero in this family!" With that, he gave Rachel a hug and Jarod a handshake, then made his way out of the room so they could go to sleep.

***

As time for Lornash's speech drew near, the naysayers went to great effort to spread nasty rumors. "An elder? Thousands of years old? Pssh! He's no older than 50, just an actor hired to dupe you!" They were the same kind of kind of people who, in the days of old earth, stubbornly refuted all evidence and spouted off about the moon landing being fake news, conspiracy theorists at best and fools at worst. The only difference between them and their ilk in times past was that they now had archangels from Heaven steering them in the wrong direction, and adding fuel to the fire of their vehement lies.

Thankfully, the majority seemed to believe the truth about Lornash. When the speech was broadcast around the world, it was well received, considered a great success. From the moment Lornash stepped up to the podium, the silence was palpable; literally, the audience heard a pen drop when one of the onlookers dropped it while he was taking notes. No one wanted to miss a single nuance of his words. With the help of Justin's Illuminator, he revealed the true, unadulterated, unmodified history of Eden and of the people who called the planet home. Earthlings bore witness the great spaceships, Arks, the vessels that more than likely carried their ancestors to Earth.

One particular remark in his speech seemed to stick out in everyone's mind: "I have brought with me samples of DNA from all the great families on Eden. With this genetic material, we may be able to confirm the ancestral history of our relatives on this world. We are excited at the prospect of meeting family we have never known."

The crowd released a collective gasp, and everyone held on to that promise with great anticipation. It was a magical idea that they might meet a long-lost relative from another world. For that reason, among many others, those who left the great hall that day were abuzz with excitement, as were all those at home who had listened to Lornash's encouraging discourse.

As uplifting as the elder's presentation was, they were also impressed by his demeanor. While he had a humble genuineness about him, he was also awe-inspiring. Even Michael, at 10,000, felt a tinge of jealousy and a taste of wonder, knowing that the being on the stage was truly his elder, somewhere in the neighborhood of 25,000 years old. His wonderment was short-lived, however, for he had other things to think about, a mission to accomplish for Jesus, and he didn't have much time to waste on idle admiration. *Anyway, he's just a lousy Edenite. I'm an archangel,* he consoled himself time and time again.

Chapter 56

Soon after the speech, Lucifer departed, and Lornash's visit was short and sweet as well. He did have a chance to meet some individuals Justin thought would give him a well-rounded taste of life on New Earth was like. His exodus was made with as much fanfare as his arrival, but he was less socially awkward and seemed better equipped to deal with the ordeal than before.

Lornash had one last thing to say before entering the ship: "Tell Jarod and Rachel that Uncle Lornash said good-bye, and that I will think of them often."

Lilith decided to stay on New Earth for another week, so she and Salome could enjoy some girl time, shopping and doing all the things women enjoyed. The two of them were as close as sisters. Unfortunately, even in that cleaned-up world, all good things eventually came to an end.

"I'm so sorry I must go," Lilith said, looking tearfully at her good friend, "but I am the first lady of Hell, and I have responsibilities there that extend well beyond just being the president's wife."

Of course, the same could be said for Salome, as she'd fallen behind in her obligations as well.

On their way to the spaceport, Justin was struck by a sudden uneasiness. "Are you sure you are okay to travel alone?" he asked Lilith. "I can easily send an escort with you to safely see you home. Stolas would jump at the chance."

Lilith smiled and waved a hand at him dismissively. "An escort? Nonsense!" she said. "I appreciate the offer, but I have my own ship with its own crew. My good friend Naamah is waiting there. I will be fine," she assured him.

Her parting was not such a mass-attended event as Lornash's. At the space port, Justin pulled her into a friendly hug, for she was like a sister to him as well. Then, after several more embraces and a few sniffles and sobs, as well as a short conversation with Salome, Lilith climbed into the shuttle that would carry her to her ship. Justin and Salome waved as the shuttle climbed into the air and watched it disappear from sight. Justin was happy that Sandel would be reunited with his lover soon, but he wouldn't feel comfortable until Lilith was back in her husband's arms once more.

When she reached the *Damien*, Lilith ordered Captain Purah Marax to prepare to leave immediately. Once things were underway for takeoff, she went to her room to look for Naamah, her personal aide. Oddly, her friend was not there, and she also noticed that many of the crewmembers were unfamiliar to her, and the regulars were not at their posts.

"Purah, have you seen Naamah?" Lilith asked when she returned to the bridge.

"No, ma'am, but I've been busy with pre-flight checks," he answered. "We will be leaving orbit soon." He answered.

She looked around the bridge. "Who are all these people, and where is my normal crew?"

"Many have fallen ill," the captain answered. "They've been quarantined in their quarters, and a few are in the infirmary for treatment. Please don't worry about it too much, ma'am."

"Ill, you say? Thank you, Purah. I will go to the infirmary, and consult the doctor for an update," Lilith said, more than a bit concerned.

"I don't think that's a good idea," Captain Marax replied. "Their sickness might be contagious. It's probably best for you to remain in your room until we reach our destination."

"No, I will be fine," she retorted with great resolve.

"Ma'am, please go to your room." The Captain raised his hand, and two guards instantly closed in on either side of her.

"I most certainly will not!" she shouted defiantly. "It is not within your right to order me around, Captain."

"Take her to her room, and make sure she stays there. We do not want any harm to befall her," Marax ordered.

After the squirming, cursing, flailing Lilith was hauled away, Captain Marax sent a message to New Earth: "We have Lilith, and we will be moving into deviant space shortly."

New Earth Security was relieved to pass the responsibility of her safety to the Alliance. Unfortunately, NES was not the only ones listening to the message. *Excellent*, Michael thought when it spat out over his communicator. *Most excellent indeed!*

The *Damien* moved into deviant space with every indication of taking a straight trip to Hell, but their final destination was quite the opposite. As thrilled and hopeful as Michael was, he would not dare to smile or relax until he heard that the ship had landed on Heaven.

Lilith frantically tried to think of a solution. Her only option was to try to send a message to Hell, a message she hoped they would receive on time. After she was locked in her room, and the guard was posted at her door, she quietly opened a secret panel and pressed a button that sent a distress signal in all directions. The electronic cry rocketed through to various locations just before they hit deviant space. As soon as Captain Marax detected the signal, guards were ordered to storm into her room and disable the device, but the damage was already done.

"You conniving bitch!" one very large guard yelled. He then backhanded poor Lilith so hard that she hit the floor.

"You're one to talk," Lilith muttered. When she tasted blood, she looked up at the guard and spat at him in defiance.

All attempts to reach the *Damien* went unanswered save one: "This ship is now the property of the disciple fleet, and will answer only to our lord God in the highest. Do not attempt to interfere, or we will destroy the *Damien* and everyone on board."

Chapter 57

Sandel was as white as a ghost when Lucifer entered the Alliance oval office. The whole place was in upheaval, a complete mess, and it was clear that Sandel had not taken the news of his beloved's kidnapping well. Glass crunched under Lucifer's shoes as he made his way to the desk where Sandel sat brooding.

"We need to attack Heaven...now," Sandel angrily said, in no uncertain terms.

"That, my son, is a bad idea. You know as well as I do that if we—" Lucifer started, only to be interrupted.

"No! I need her back, Father!" Sandel shouted, as furious as he was heartbroken.

"I know, but we must use our heads," Lucifer reasoned.

"I-I know, Father," Sandel said as his head fell into his hands. He sniffled and pleaded, "It's just... It hurts so bad!"

Lucifer walked around the desk and pulled Sandel into his arms. "We will get her back, my son. We will find a way." As strong as he tried to be, he soon joined Sandel in his crying, for he was no stranger to the grief and anger his son felt. He, too, had felt the bitter sting of losing a woman he loved; his first wife, Vepar, Sandel's mother, was killed in a battle at the beginning of the war, many years ago, and he'd never fully recovered from the pain of that.

"We have to save Lilith, Father, at all costs. We just have to. I know she is still alive. I feel it in my heart," Sandel said as salty tears ran down his face.

Lucifer responded in a gentle voice, his head hanging low, "I should have stayed, and brought her home to you," he said, somewhat shamefully. "Mark my words, Sandel. We will get her back. I will not rest until she is once again by your side."

As they settled into deep thought about the situation, silence took hold of the room. It was not until Nanael, Sandel's assistant, knocked on his door that either of them spoke.

"Yes?" Sandel said, trying to hide his sobs.

"Sir, you have received a communication."

"Whoever it is, please tell them I am unavailable. As a matter of fact, hold all my calls until further notice."

"Are you sure, sir? It is Justin Grant, from New Earth," Nanael clarified.

"Okay, put it through. Thank you, Nanael," Sandel said.

Nanael turned to walk out, then stopped and looked at him. "I'm quite sorry about Lilith, sir. If there's anything I can do..."

"Thank you, Nanael," Sandel said with a nod, gesturing his assistant out of the room.

"I'm so sorry, my friend," Justin said when Sandel picked up the communication. "I can't help feeling a bit guilty for not insisting more sternly for her to take an escort. I do not know what happened, but I should have been there for you and Lilith," he said, laboring through his words.

"Once again, you owe me no apologies," Sandel said, sounding worn out and frayed. "None of us had any way to know this would happen. As far as we can tell, Captain Marax is a Holy Ghost. He's been working deep undercover, just waiting for an opportunity to strike against the Alliance."

"Tell me what I can do, Sandel. All I have is at your disposal," Justin pleaded.

"Thank you, my friend. Until we can think of a feasible rescue plan, we can only wait," Sandel replied.

Justin spent the rest of the day in deep thought. He investigated all he could on Heaven and its surrounding star systems, but he saw no signs of weakness. By all reports, Heaven was the most well-guarded, well-protected place in the galaxy. Frustrated and feeling defeated, he decided his best course of action was to go home, to be with the people he loved and to try and clear his head.

"What's the matter, Daddy?" Rachel asked, sitting in his lap.

"Oh, I feel sad about Aunt Lilith, but I am happy to be with you," Justin said as he tickled her.

When she stopped laughing, she said something he'd never heard his child say before: "I feel crappy-happy too."

"Crappy-happy? What do you mean?" Justin inquired.

Rachel explained, "I miss Aunt Lilith, too, but I'm happy to have the best daddy in all the worlds. So, I feel crappy happy."

Out of the mouths of babes, Justin thought. He pulled her close and never wanted to let go.

Sometime during the wee hours, Justin was surprised by a call from Lornash, who had heard about the tragic events and wanted to offer his assistance. As they conversed, it occurred to Justin that over the many years of Heaven's domination of Eden, the Edenites might have discovered something he might use against them.

Lornash offered, "You cannot force your way into Heaven, Justin. You must be welcomed."

Maintaining his respect for the elder but feeling like Lornash was just stating the obvious, Justin said, "Your words are wise, my friend, but even if we were welcomed, we'd be taken prisoner immediately. It would not help us free Lilith if we found ourselves in the same position she's in."

"Then you must be welcomed without them knowing," Lornash said, and Justin could have sworn Lornash had woken something in his subconscious, but he wasn't sure of what it could be. "I hope that helps you in some way."

Justin wasn't sure what Lornash meant or how it could possibly prove beneficial, but he thanked the elder anyway and signed off. For several hours, he just sat in his chair with his eyes shut, thinking. *What am I not thinking of? What am I missing? What the hell did the old guy mean?*

Chapter 58

Jesus was in Heaven, both literally and figuratively. Finally, he had one thing he wanted more than anything in the galaxy, seconded only by galactic domination. Lilith was his at last. Whatever spell Sandel had cast upon her so many years ago no longer mattered; she was on Heaven, with him. So many nights, he'd dreamt of holding her in his arms, kissing her deeply, and taking her as only the lord God could. In his mind, there was no way his captive—or any woman, for that matter—could resist his charms. *I am the most powerful man in the galaxy,* he decided, but even as he thought it, he knew it was not quite right. *To call me a man is an understatement indeed!* "I am God, the ruler of the galaxy. Truly, I am that I am," he declared aloud, to anyone who dared to be within earshot at that hour.

Jesus knew she would resist at first, but he did not expect that to last long. He was certain that Lilith would soon be his queen. With that in mind, he readied himself, as excited as a teenager getting ready for a first date. He practiced what he would say and how he would say it, and he tried on several outfits to find just the right ensemble. As he dressed, he kept an eye on her on the video screen, and his yearning for her became even stronger as he watched her servants prepare her for the evening festivities. "I will show you a true leader, my love," he whispered, feeling empowered and every bit the God he knew himself to be. "You've missed out on so much all these years. Now, you shall have me!"

In the throne room, Seraphim One made sure everything was as his lord demanded. Servants busied themselves with cleaning and decorating. One unfortunate soul nervously dropped a bowl of fruit and cowered, waiting for her inevitable beating.

Much to her surprise and delight, Seraphim One just said, "Please clean it up quickly, before anyone notices." asked her to clean it up quickly before anyone noticed.

She looked at him with confusion, but there was great gratitude in her eyes as well. She was new, and knew nothing of his kindness. Nevertheless, she dared not speak, and instead made quick work of doing what she was told.

Seraphim One was well aware that the evening would have more than spilled fruit to worry about. He was certain things would not go as his lord had planned. While no one would speak it aloud, all knew that Jesus was ill equipped to please a lady of Lilith's qualities. Jesus had always had everything handed to him, and he only acted on impulses, and expected others to fully comply. He had not even the slightest hint of consequence. Seraphim One knew that Lilith would not be so tolerant of the stubborn child that he was.

"Zabkiel, you must instruct Lilith as to proper etiquette in my council chambers. It will not serve her well to embitter herself against me in front of the others," Jesus commanded.

Seraphim One was thankful for the command, for it would likely be his only chance to meet with Lilith privately. Rather than filling her in on Jesus' silly expectations and rules, he wanted to advise her of the grave situation she was in. The trouble was that even in her chambers, he feared he would be watched. For that reason, everything he said to her had to be measured and appear completely benign. It was not too far-fetched to believe Jesus himself would be watching, since she was one prize, he valued above almost all others.

"You must listen to what I'm about to tell you," Zabkiel quickly blurted. "Lilith, it is very important that you do not to react harshly to anything you see or hear. My lord does not take well to public humiliation or insubordination. You will witness many things here, but you mustn't cry out in opposition or defense. While it may disgust you, wear a smile. Your life and the lives of those around you depend on your strength. Good luck, milady."

"May I ask you one question?" Lilith said, arching her brow at him.

"You may," the seraphim answered.

"What happened to Naamah, my personal aide, and where is my original *Damien* crew?" She struggled to keep the quiver out of her voice, for even as she asked the question, she already knew the answer.

"I am sorry, milady, but Jesus ordered their deaths before you stepped foot on board," Seraphim One said, hanging his head. "I am truly, truly sorry."

She could barely fathom the evil that would spawn those heinous, unnecessary murders. She was about to brought before the most wretched, vilest person in the galaxy, yet the seraphim had told her to act as if anything and everything he said was not only acceptable but great. She understood the warning, but she wondered if she would be able to keep her composure. Jesus was not the same young man she remembered; the happy-go-lucky, fun-loving son of God had become a monster. Her thoughts were interrupted then by a knock at her door.

Lilith was taken from her room and led down a long corridor with white marble floors. As she approached the great doors of the throne room, they opened before her. The room was filled to capacity, but it was also divided into five distinct semicircular rings, obvious class separations. In the middle, looking as regal as one would expect God to look, sat Jesus, in all his glory. His gold-trimmed garments were so white that it almost stung her eyes to look upon him.

Jesus felt a shiver run through his body, and he feared he might wet himself with excitement. His Lilith was beautiful, in a gown of white, almost as pure white as his.

Seraphim One wanted to scream when he saw Michael there, decked out in his finest, stepping forward to escort Lilith to her throne beside Jesus. Watching Michael leading their prisoner along, wearing a smile almost as big as his overinflated head, Seraphim One suddenly realized that the capture of Lilith was what the archangel and Jesus had been planning for so long.

Jesus' children, Kadosh and Sophia, sat at a lower level in the middle ring. Magdalene was seated next to Dilyla, who had not aged well, a silent shell of her once beautiful presence; those two were confined to the far edge of the ring, at the lowest level. Magdalene was still lovely, but few would know it due to her constantly bowed head; since the day her indiscretion was revealed to all, she'd been ordered to never look upon her husband again. Not only that, but she was forced to wear a crude adornment around her neck, a chain that held the dried, shriveled penis Jesus had removed from her lover. Forever, she and all others would observe it as a remembrance of her evil deed. Magdalene had long since overcome the shame of her affair, but she still had to feign it in Jesus' presence. She was thankful for two things: First, she was able to do as she pleased most of the time, barring the occasional appearance at events that required her present; and second, the necklace had finally lost the stink of rotting flesh, though that small blessing seemed to take years.

As Lilith took her seat next to Jesus on the second-highest level, the room erupted with applause. The clapping went on for several moments, until their lord raised his hand, encouraging swift and complete silence.

Basking in the thought that Lilith could see and feel his power, Jesus said, "I want you all to welcome the next queen of Heaven and the Empire."

Again, the room erupted, for when Jesus was happy, all had to pretend to be happy. Then, once again, a raise of his hand shushed them immediately.

With a glance at Lilith, Jesus announced, "Let the feast and entertainment begin!"

It was then that Lilith noticed the large cage hanging from the ceiling. At first, she was at a loss as to what it contained, but she soon ascertained that it was a man. Part of the third ring was cleared, and a stage was erected there. The cage was lowered onto the stage, and the hunched man was prodded out for all to see. At the risk of severe punishment, the formerly regal Seraphim Two was forced to sing a tongueless, incoherent tune while he danced around the stage. He was a naked, dirty, bloated eunuch; a truly unsightly creature with a messy shock of greasy, gray hair atop his head.

Magdalene chanced a peak at her former lover, and barely recognized the man who had once satisfied her needs when her husband abandoned her. She had no tears to stifle on Jahoel's behalf, for the extent of her evil even outmatched that of Jesus. Only her servants knew the truth about her, and those in the know often said in whispered murmurs amongst themselves, "The Empire should be glad Jesus is in charge instead of her."

Lilith, on the other hand, felt pity for the poor soul who was forced to play the part of court jester for the delight of the crowd. She had the distinct feeling that their joy was the result of relief that they themselves were not tortured and placed on the stage. At one point, the filthy hunchback looked directly at her, and she saw deep sorrow in his cloudy, brown eyes.

Once the former second-in-command was violently goaded back into his cage, his cramped prison was again lifted above the stage, and the festivities continued. The dancers, singers, and comedians were careful with every move they made and every word they sang or spoke, as none wanted to offend their master. The diners complimented every dish, whether they liked the delicacies or not, always aiming their flattery at the lord who had chosen such a savory and delicious menu and giving little credit to the terrified cooks who had prepared it or the even more terrified servants who brought it to them.

After the dishes were cleared away, Jesus announced, "Now, for a truly special treat!"

At that moment, a man who looked slightly familiar to Lilith was led to the stage. She could not place him, for his hanging head was hardly recognizable, and he was so badly beaten that he was barely able to stand.

One of the men who held the broken man grabbed his hair and jerked it back to put his face on full display.

Lilith gasped when she realized where she'd seen him before, aboard the *Damien*, when he backhanded her across the face, called her a bitch, and drew blood from her lip. She recalled spitting on him, and she struggled to find a reason why one who seemed so loyal to Jesus was now standing before that crowd, looking as if he was about to knock on death's door.

"Let it be known throughout the galaxy that no one who touches my queen shall live to see another day!" Jesus boomed.

Immediately, the guard pulled the man's hair with more force, stretching his neck so the other guard could more easily slit his throat from ear to ear, sending a warm, crimson mist over those seated nearest the stage.

Jesus grinned sadistically, thrilled by his power and certain that his would-be lover felt it as well.

Lilith found it difficult to keep what little she had eaten from pushing its way back up, mixed with a bitter burst of bile. Fortunately for her, Jesus was too busy enjoying the show to notice the look of pure revulsion in her face. She also noticed that while everyone in the room stopped momentarily to watch the slashing of his throat, they instantly began cheering and laughing at the new act of entertainment. Even those who coated with the dead man's blood acted as if nothing had happened. *Can they really be that insensitive,* she wondered, *or are they just that frightened of their lord?*

When Jesus chanced a look at her, she could only afford him a weak, completely faux smile. It was all far too much violence and drama for one day, so after the mess was cleaned and the next act took to the stage, Lilith quietly asked Jesus, "Would it be all right for me to retire for the evening?"

After a brief look of disappointment, Jesus rose from his throne, once again causing a wash of silence to overtake the room. "My queen is weary. One can only handle the strain of so much joy in a day's time," he explained. "As she wishes, she will be excused."

At that, her attendants raced to help her back to her room. There, she immediately gave back all she had eaten. She also showered, trying in vain to wash it all away, but the ugliness and brutality could not be cleansed from her mind, and her body ached to be held by the loving, protecting arms of Sandel.

Chapter 59

Word spread quickly throughout the galaxy that Jesus aimed to take a new wife, and the official announcement would soon be made. Although only the worlds in Empire space received signals from heavenly broadcasts, the Alliance monitored the transmissions to stay informed.

For Sandel's part, he already knew, because Jesus cruelly rubbed it in with a personal message just for him: "Lilith is mine. You have kept her from me long enough. What you have made impure, I will make pure again. She will forever be at my side as queen of Heaven and the Empire. Any attempts to take her from me will result in her immediate death. Sandel, I have won. Lilith is mine."

Half a galaxy away, Sandel could hardly believe how pathetic and lovesick Jesus was. *Seriously? Their so-called God is still sore about losing a silly bet made some 5,000 years ago?* Nevertheless, he was certain Jesus was willing to carry out his threat to kill her if it came to that, because Jesus refused to be considered a loser of any contest. His sick, twisted boyhood friend had proven that he was capable of anything. Although Sandel and his advisers struggled for many sleepless nights to find a solution to the problem, they could not come up with any plan in which rescuing sweet Lilith alive was even remotely possible.

***

The next day, Jesus ordered Lilith brought to his chambers. After hospitably offering her a drink, he began, "My dear, you are even more beautiful than I remember. I waited until today to speak with you because I first wanted you to see how much my people love and respect me. I wanted you to see that I will defend your honor as I defend my own. Is it not an honor to be my queen?" He paused for her reaction, but when she gave him none, he continued, "Lilith, I know this is all new to you, and it will take some time to adjust. I am willing to grant you that, at least for a while."

Jesus smiled and went on, "As an incentive, I have in place those who will, at my command, take the lives of that troublesome human Mr. Grant, his half-breed wife, and their mutt children. What are their names? Jarod and Rachel? As an added incentive, my Holy Ghosts are prepared to take the life of my backstabbing friend Sandel and your children. I need only say the word, and it will be done."

She winced but still said nothing. Somehow, she managed to gulp back her tears.

"If you consent to be my queen, and sit at my side from this time forward, I will spare their lives. That, my love, will be my wedding gift to you." Jesus said.

Lilith's back was against the wall, and she was sure she had only one option. With tears burning in her eyes, she forced an answer past the lump in her throat: "Yes, I will be your queen, but you must promise never to harm Sandel and our children or Justin and his family."

"Good. I thought you would say as much," Jesus said, feeling victorious once more.

"And there is one other thing," she bravely managed.

"Which is?" Jesus asked, arching his brow at her in surprise. Few attempted to bargain with him, but he was slightly intrigued by her willingness to try.

"Please give me time to appreciate who you are, who you...have become," she said. "We have both changed since many years ago. Let us start with a proper courtship, the kind we both deserve."

Jesus smiled. "As you wish, my love."

Later that day, Seraphim One looked on while Jesus stood in his chambers, patting himself on the back.

"This is indeed a great victory against the Alliance," Jesus said, admiring himself in the mirror. "I have taken something he cannot replace. She is mine forevermore," he finished, aglow with self-satisfaction.

Seraphim One, a master at stroking his lord's ego, stated, "Lilith will soon realize the mistake she made so many years ago. Sandel is but a germ, while you are a God."

Jesus beamed at the analogy, as sappy and false as it was.

For many days, Seraphim One struggled to find a way to free Lilith, but all of his ideas proved unsuccessful. Since Justin's escape, a mere human slipping from Jesus' grasp, the lord had shored up security, and he would certainly take no chances when it came to Lilith. In fact, Jesus put her on house arrest, of sorts, fitting his bride-to-be not with an engagement ring but with a permanent necklace that monitored her every move and restricted her to visiting only certain places in the palace. She was a trophy, more valuable to Jesus than almost anything in the galaxy, and it would be over the lord's dead body that Lilith would ever see Hell again. Still, Seraphim One vowed that he would not rest until he could deliver her to Sandel's arms.

Chapter 60

Joseph and Susan Sanders, Leah's parents, joined Justin's mother and father for the celebration of New Earth Day. Justin was thankful to see them all so happy and healthy. It was also a great comfort to him that they had remained close friends for many years. Jarod had also come to see Salome and his grandchildren. They had a cookout and enjoyed a wonderful day together.

While sitting around the table enjoying their food that was slathered in barbecue sauce, Justin received the most wonderful news. Really?" he said, almost choking on his steak.

"Really. You're finally going to be a big brother," his mother said, "after all these years!"

"Congratulations, Mom and Dad." He paused, licked a glob of sauce from his lips, then feigned disgust. "Whoa! Wait a minute. You guys know what sex is? Ew! Gross!"

Everyone burst out in laughter except for little Jarod, whose face scrunched up in confusion and disapproval.

It was the happiest day Justin had experienced in a long time, but his joy was tarnished by the kidnapping of Lilith. As much as he wanted to fully enjoy the day, visions of his friend's wife in the hands of Jesus infiltrated his every thought.

That night, Justin's former in-laws told him they had plans to visit relatives in Indiana. "We'll probably leave in the morning," Leah's mother said.

He hated to see them go but understood that they had families of their own. "Well, I hope you have a safe trip and enjoy yourselves," he said.

On Monday morning, Justin, his father, and Jarod sat in his office, catching up on current events but mainly discussing the kidnapping.

"We've received official word from Heaven that Michael was behind her abduction," Jarod said.

"Anything else?" asked Justin.

"Our intel tells us she is still alive and well...for now."

"And how is Sandel?" Justin said, truly worried about his old friend.

Jarod looked at Justin's father, and both men shook their heads. When he turned his gaze back to Justin, he said, "Not so well, I'm afraid. He is not eating or sleeping much at all. I'm afraid the pain of losing the love of his life may be too much for him to bear."

"We must find a way to get her back," Justin said. "Lilith is more than just a friend. She's family."

"Well, as you might imagine, she is now the most protected person on Heaven next to Jesus. Since your escape, they've doubled security. We have yet to find a way for anyone to get in our out," Jarod explained.

Justin wasn't sure why, but it was at that moment that he took the opportunity to tell them about his conversation with Chief Elder Lornash. "It was pretty cryptic, what he said. I wasn't sure what to make of it. He said we cannot force our way onto Heaven, that we must be welcomed. Then, he informed me that we must be welcomed without them knowing." Justin raised his hands and rolled his eyes. "Does that make any sense to either of you? I feel like it means something, but I don't know what."

"He is right, you know," Justin's father said, after a moment of thought.

"What do you mean? About what?" Justin asked.

"About being welcomed without them knowing. It sounds to me like he is implying that we should send a gift, something like a Trojan horse."

Justin sat back in his chair and pondered it for a minute.

"What in the hell is a Trojan Horse?" Jarod asked. "I don't believe a horse will prove to be much of a challenge for Jesus."

The hilarious question jolted Justin back to the room. In tag-team style, he and his father explained the fall of Troy, and that started an all-out brainstorming session.

"Dad, you're a genius," Justin offered.

The next day, when the three met again in Justin's office for more brainstorming, they were interrupted by Justin's niece and personal assistant.

"Justin, I'm afraid I have some very bad news for you," Laura said, trembling from head to toe and with tears streaming down her cheeks. "Would you like to step into a private room, or..."

"No, Laura. Whatever you have to say, you can tell me here. What's wrong?" Justin hesitantly asked.

"Well, while visiting Indiana, Joseph and Susan Sanders were, uh...murdered," she sadly announced.

Everyone sat in stunned silence for a moment, until the woman spoke again.

"There is more, sir. Their bodies were found at your old home, along with a note."

"A note?" Justin inquired when he found his voice.

"Yes. Here." She reached out and handed a copy of it to him, even as her eyes welled with more tears.

Justin read it in silence, then passed it to Jarod as he hung his head.

Jarod read aloud, "This is just a start. I will not stop until everyone in your family is dead. As the blood of my daughter is on your hands, the blood of your family will be on mine."

Justin looked at Laura, while both men looked at him, as if searching for some clarification, some logic or reason in it.

Without realizing he was even speaking, Justin said robotically, "Thank you. That will be all for now, Laura. Please hold my calls."

Laura, who found herself standing behind her distraught grandfather, doing what she could to comfort him, suddenly realized Justin was talking to her. "Yes, Uncle J...uh...sir."

The Serpent's Gift

After she left, Justin filled his guests in about his history with Rebecca. It was not easy storytelling in the least, but he wanted to make sure they knew all the players and all the events that had led to that very moment.

As if Justin didn't have enough on his mind, now he had to tell Rachel and Jarod their Grandma and Grandpa Sanders were gone. The children had always felt special because they had three sets of grandparents, so he knew it would break their hearts. He could not help feeling sorry for himself either; they were his second mom and dad. Now, he had no living reminders of Leah or his little Joey, lost so long ago on that bloody night. Michael had made it personal by kidnapping Sandel's wife Lilith. Now, the bastard archangel had gone a step even further, and Justin vowed that Michael would pay for killing two of the most wonderfully kind and generous people he had ever known.

Chapter 61

No matter what went on in his personal life, Justin still had pressing responsibilities and obligations to the people of New Earth. Despite the dark cloud that hung over them, he and Laura had to review the export facts and figures for the Longevity Factor, in fresh fruit and processed form. Meeting the demand for the processed variety was not a problem, but when it came to the fresh fruit, there was definitely more demand than supply. As such, that luxury item fetched a premium price, one many in the galaxy were willing to pay.

No matter how much security NES put on the Trees of Life, some always seemed to slip through the cracks. One such area was what Justin referred to as the H Variance; even though Heaven was forbidden from purchasing the Longevity Factor from Earth, they somehow received a continuous, steady supply. They even found the method to smuggle it off the planet and into the hands of the Empire. Although they could have shut the H Variance down long ago, Justin thought it was a small price to pay for something that might prove useful at a future time.

As he pondered the H Variance, something his father said crossed his mind: *"It sounds to me like he is implying that we should send a gift, something like a Trojan horse."* He sat back and thought about that once more. *I think it could work. Yes, it just might...* He paused, bit his lip in thought, then said, with a bit more force than intended, "Hell, yeah, this could work!"

Laura jumped a little. "Excuse me, sir? What could work?"

Justin, still lost in thought, suddenly realized someone was speaking to him, and that he'd startled her by pounding a fist on his desk. "Oh! Uh, sorry, Laura. I was just thinking about something. Can we finish this tomorrow? There's something I need to think about."

"As you wish, sir," Laura said.

Justin frowned a little. "Are you ever going to quit calling me that? I'm your uncle, not a sir. After all, you *are* my niece."

She gave him a wicked little smile and replied, "Only when I'm not on the clock...sir." She then walked out the door, without another word.

Justin arranged a meeting with his old friend Stolas. "I need you here in my office in an hour," he said, and Stolas agreed.

Stolas was a high-ranking member of NES and had lived primarily on New Earth since they joined the Alliance. He and Lucy Beckman, formerly known as HellHathNoFury666, were married and were excitedly working on starting a family of their own. Justin had once tackled Stolas's ass in the Vietnamese district in Chicago, and the two had been the best of friends ever since.

When Stolas arrived, Justin poured him a drink and sealed the room. He looked at his friend and, once again, thought he looked very much like an American Indian, with his shoulder-length, black hair and dark complexion. "Thanks for coming," he said.

Stolas smiled and lifted his glass. "Sorry about your family, man."

"Thanks. It was a shock to us all," Justin replied. His somber tone was quickly replaced with excitement as he started right in. "Please sit and tell me everything you know about the Longevity Factor shipments making their way to Heaven."

For the next half-hour, Stolas briefed Justin about the methods and routes the smugglers used. "The fresh stuff originates in our Avon Park Groves in Florida. Once every two months, one of the nighttime shipping supervisors loads it up on two trucks. Needless to say, there are no bills of lading or any paper trail. From there, they travel to Kennedy Space Port. The cargo is transferred to a ship bound for the Leraje star system. Once they reach Leraje, the containers are loaded on another ship. That's where we lose track of their exact route. What we do know is that three days after the Longevity Factor leaves Earth, it ends up on Heaven."

Justin knew honesty was the best policy, so he said, "Stolas, my friend, I am not ready to tell you my reasons for asking you for this information, but I will soon call on you again. Please do me a favor and tell no one about what we discussed here today. Heaven must to continue believe they are smarter than us. They mustn't suspect we are on to them, not in any way. Also, remember that the only reason I talk to you at all is because of your beautiful wife. Tell Lucy I said hi." With that, Justin rose and shook Stolas's hand, and pulled him into a man hug.

As soon as Stolas walked out, Justin called Sandel and made arrangements to meet him in his office on Hell. He then instructed Laura to clear his schedule for the following week. "I'm taking the family on a little vacation," he fibbed. "We can use one after... Well, you know. We'll leave soon after the funeral."

A few moments later, the ever-efficient and capable Laura informed Justin that the *Ronwe* and his escort would be ready at a moment's notice.

Justin called home and advised Salome to pack enough things for a month and to tell her parents to do the same. He wanted his family to be safe, and the safest place he knew was, ironically enough from his previous thinking, Planet Hell.

Once they arrived on Hell and his family was safely situated at Jarod's house, Justin headed straight for Sandel's office. Sandel and Lucifer were engaged in a discussion as Justin entered the room, and he knew it was about Lilith.

He waited for Sandel to secure the room, then, as he did when he was excited about anything, blurted his ideas right out. "I believe I know a way to rescue Lilith," he said, wearing a broad grin. He let that hang in the air for a moment before he explained what Lornash had said and correlated it to the intel about the stolen shipments and the epic story of the Trojan horse.

"I believe we may be able to smuggle one or two people onto Heaven this way," he said. "Of course, our volunteers must have a working knowledge of that world. If they arrive safely, they can coordinate with forces there, get Lilith out of Jesus' grasp, and send her out the same way. Look, I know it's an incomplete plan and certainly not foolproof, but it's a start. What do you think?" Justin finished, looking uncertain.

"As you said, it lacks details, but it is a start," Sandel answered.

For some reason, Justin and Lucifer both felt there was a forthcoming but hanging in the air, and Sandel did not disappoint.

"But I refuse to go along with it unless one of those volunteers is me."

"What!? No, Sandel. No way!" Justin exclaimed

Lucifer was right behind him. "You cannot be serious. You are the leader of the Alliance. Your place is here."

For the next hour, Justin and Lucifer debated with Sandel about all the reasons he should not undertake the mission. They did everything but chain him to his desk, but nothing fazed his resolve.

Finally, Sandel rose from his chair and walked around to sit on the edge of the desk. "I forbid anyone to go in my place," he firmly said. "Lilith is *my* wife, and *I* will save her. If she does not return home, nor shall I. If I meet my death on Heaven, at least it will have been for true love, the worthiest of all causes. If I am captured, you should think of me as dead. I will no longer sit here doing nothing while my most cherished treasure suffers at the barbaric hands of that deranged deviant. Do not waste your breath, Father or Justin. There is no point in arguing with a mind you cannot change. Let us focus on tightening up a workable plan so I can save my beloved."

Chapter 62

For the next few days, they reviewed every possible scenario, with the help of spies who'd recently returned from assignments on Heaven. The Illuminator enabled them to see and feel Heaven through the spies' eyes, almost in real time. After many hours spent revisiting those memories, the three knew more about Heaven than most of the beings who lived there.

At Sandel's home, Justin said his goodbyes to his family. Although he would miss them dearly, he knew they would be safer there. As he hugged Salome and his children for the twentieth time, he noticed Lucifer setting an Illuminator on Sandel's head.

Soon, Sandel removed the device and Lucifer asked, "My son, do you understand?"

Sandel replied, "Yes, Father, I do. Thank you."

The two hugged for a long moment, then separated with tears running down their faces.

Lucifer had one more thing to say: "If it were your mother, I would go instead of you."

Sandel smiled at his father, and they hugged again.

At the shuttle, Sandel made a big show of sending Justin off. He then went back to his office, gathered his things, and, under the cloak of darkness, rose into the sky to rendezvous with the shuttle that was hovering high above Hell. They aimed to be very careful, and that super-secret takeoff was just one more precaution that was needed to ensure a successful mission.

As they entered the *Ronwe*, Justin asked the disguised Sandel, "What was that all about back there, with you, your father, and the Illuminator?"

"He just wanted to share something he's known about Heaven, since he was a boy," Sandel said. "He thought I should know about it, just in case." Then he stopped, and left it at that.

Just in case of what? Justin was left to wonder, but he decided to let it go. Instead, he gave Sandel an order: "Go to your room, and get some rest. Once we reach New Earth, there won't be much time for sleep."

Wanting to argue but knowing there was no use, Sandel just nodded, and pivoted on the balls of his feet to head straight to his room.

Justin's prediction turned out to be quite true: There was no time for dawdling or any R&R. When the *Ronwe* docked in the spaceport, they took the shuttle directly to the council compound in New York. In Justin's office there, Stolas and two NES agents were waiting for them.

"Welcome back, sir," Laura said with a bright smile.

"Thank you, Laura. Please hold all my calls again, and we'll have to postpone any upcoming meetings or appointments till further notice."

She nodded her understanding, and he closed the door and sealed the room.

One of the agents, whom Justin knew as Derek Hill, worked in the southern United States, including in the Avon Park area. Justin always thought he looked like a young Billy Dee Williams. The other agent, Michelle Swanson, was new to him, a very intense-looking blonde with striking, blue eyes. Her assignment for the last fifteen years had been central Florida, with an emphasis on Avon Park and Kennedy Space Port. Although she stood only five-four, Justin had no doubt she could make him cry like a baby in hand-to-hand combat.

"First of all," Stolas started, "let me say this is a very bad idea. Sandel, if I could talk you out of it, I would." He paused for a moment, then continued, "Now, with that out of the way, here is what we've got..."

For the next three hours, they went over every known detail of the Empire smuggling operation, from the point of the theft to the ships that left New Earth space. They already had the Alliance data, which detailed the rest of the journey to Heaven.

They all agreed that the hardest part would be finding a way to smuggle one or two people among the cargo without raising Empire suspicions. Luckily for Justin and his team, the containers that were used to smuggle the Longevity Factor were random, not barcoded or marked. The two most likely scenarios included adding a false bottom or creating a compartment in the lid. After much consideration, they elected the lid option. The cooling and ventilation equipment in the container lids could be repositioned to allow enough space for one passenger to last about four days in relative comfort.

"There will not be much room for movement, but of the two plans, I think this is our best chance for success," Solas said.

In a warehouse in Titusville, Florida, Sandel's Trojan horse was prepared. Two weeks later, the next shipment would be delivered. That meant they only had five days to design, implement, and test, as well as get the container back to Avon Park without raising any suspicion. It was a sure bet that the Empire had spies in both Avon Park and Kennedy Space Port, so every move had to be quick, concise, correct, and careful. There was absolutely no room for error, nor any time to waste.

Another reason why the lid was the best choice was because the interior of each container maintained a temperature of 3 to 7 degrees Celsius, with a relative humidity of 95 percent, while the lids remained a manageable 25 degrees. The lid could also be fitted with everything necessary to carry the uninvited into the heart of Heaven undetected. Cameras were even installed so Sandel could watch for external dangers.

"It will work, provided that all goes perfectly," Stolas said.

"It will. It has to," Sandel said. "I will jump out of our

Trojan horse, and reclaim my Helen, my Lilith!" he declared. "I cannot and will not fail."

Chapter 63

It was decided that Sandel would hole up with Stolas till the big day, as he would be safe there. Two days later, Agent Swanson called Stolas and said, "It is time. The pickup for the shipment to Heaven will occur within twenty-four hours."

Sandel climbed into the lid of the container, his snug-fitting home for the next few days. They bid him safe travels, then loaded the container, along with others, onto trucks bound for Avon Park. Once there, Sandel's container was placed on top of a pile of fifteen in the loading area. He spent the night settling in to his new place.

Once he was sure no one was around, thanks to the cameras they'd wisely installed, he opened the panel and lowered his body into the space below. He wasn't sure how long he would have to remain in the cramped secret compartment, so using the time to stretch out seemed like the right thing to do. All too soon, it would be time to lock himself in the lid once more.

The next evening, a truck entered the loading barn. A man, presumably one of the disciples, climbed out and made his way over to the nightshift supervisor's office. They talked for a few moments before they both walked to the loading floor. Hank, the night supervisor, instructed the forklift operator to pull down two containers to be filled with the Longevity Factor and loaded on the customer's semi. The forklift operator, an undercover NES agent, obediently selected two seemingly random containers.

The containers were placed on the loading platform and filled with raw fruit while the disciple watched. Once they were full, they were gently placed on the truck for transport.

So far, so good, thought Sandel, trying his best not to groan when his host container was jostled around.

Outside, the truck driver shook hands with Hank, then climbed into his vehicle. With a wave and not so much as a signature on so much as a scrap of paperwork or documentation, he took off.

It wasn't long before Sandel felt the semi slow, then stop. He looked at his forward camera and saw that they had arrived at Kennedy Space Port. They proceeded to the shuttle that would carry the precious cargo to the Leraje transport. As soon as he was loaded, the ship prepared to leave New Earth space. Sandel felt the acceleration, followed by the jerk of moving into deviant space.

Knowing he had some time to kill, Sandel set the Illuminator to put him into a kind of waking sleep; that would make it bearable to lie in that cramped area for a long period, yet he would still be aware of changes in his status quo, thus ensuring his best chance of survival.

Sandel dozed off for a while, only to be awakened by the scent of the Longevity Factor-laced fruits. *Who will ever know?* he asked himself. He opened the access panel to the cooling units, the door to his hiding place, emitting a squeal of metal against metal. He assumed the difference in temperatures between his hiding place and cargo area had caused a bit of friction in the hinges, so he didn't pay the noise much mind as he hung out of his hiding place to grab a snack.

Bang!

When the loud sound echoed from the cargo hold, Sandel quietly pulled himself back into his hole and checked the cameras. Much to his dismay, a guard was nearing, tapping each container he passed with a shock stick. *You just had to get a snack, you dumb ass. Always thinking with your stomach!* Sandel silently scolded himself.

He dared not move a muscle, as he could not take a

chance that the squeaky hinges would give him away. All he could do was watch in breathless horror as the guard moved ever closer.

Whap!

As the unsettling noise of the shock stick died down in Sandel's ears, he saw that the guard started to walk on, only to stop and turn around. The guard leaned in close to the container, as if listening for something, then tapped on it again. He darted his eyes to the front of the cargo hold, then to the back. A second later, Sandel could hear fingers working the latch, and the lid to the container slowly started to open.

Certain he was about to be caught, Sandel readied himself for a fight. *I've got to take him down, dispose of him, and hope no one misses him,* he thought. *Simple, right?* He could see the guard, and the guard would have caught sight of him if he had leaned down to look, but to Sandel's amazement, the nosy fool just reached in and grabbed a handful of fruits, stuffed them into his pocket, and quietly shut the lid.

Sandel watched the guard exit the cargo hold, banging every container as he walked by. Once he was confident he was alone again, he closed the sliding panel, but not before grabbing a handful of fruit for himself.

Sometime later, he felt the ship drop out of deviant space, and slow to a stop. Obviously, they'd reached the last transfer point before their arrival on Heaven. He watched as his container was loaded onto another vessel, but since the fruit could not survive a vacuum, he was unable to see the markings of the other ship. He spent the rest of the trip thinking of possible scenarios, and all of them ended with Lilith in his arms. *Of course, she may not even recognize me now,* he thought when he caught a glimpse of his reflection on the metal wall of his hiding place. He was a little worse for the wear, and the many sleepless, tearful nights during her absence had left him looking a bit emaciated and drained. Not only that, he'd let his beard grow out since his departure from Hell, as he could not afford being identified before his mission was complete.

Chapter 64

It had been almost two months since he had rescued Lilith from the fiery pits of Hell, and Jesus' miniscule patience was growing thin. He desperately wanted to take things to the next level, and he was tiring of her constant excuse: "Just a little more time, so you can have me freely." *Two more days, he decided, and not a moment longer. I have waited long enough. God should never, ever have to wait,* he raged to himself.

Jesus sent for Lilith to give her the wonderful news that the time was a hand. As always, before she was allowed to venture into his presence, she was carefully scrutinized and scanned, searched from head to toe, to alleviate any potential threat or harm to the master.

"Welcome, my love. You look exquisite, as always." Jesus complimented her, as she stood before him. "Please sit. I have wonderful news. In just two days, I will finally take you as my queen. You will be all mine, in mind as well as body."

"But, Jesus, I—"

"But nothing," he interrupted. "I have granted you more time than I would have given anyone else. We will move ahead as I say. Just think about it, my love. You must be thrilled to know that in just two days, you will know the ecstasy of pleasuring your king. You must realize by now, all the women in the galaxy, envy you."

She couldn't decide if she wanted to laugh or vomit. The

entire notion was hilariously wrong, yet she was sickened at the thought of actually touching the repulsive, self-aggrandizing being. He had always been physically attractive, even as the boy she first met, but the twisted, evil creature inside him made him repugnant beyond words. *How can I let him touch me when the mere sight of him makes me ill?* she thought. She did manage a smile at the thought of puking all over his so-called lordship. Lilith pushed the idea of suicide out of her mind, though she could not completely rule it out.

"You will join me for dinner, of course. Until then." With that, he turned away from her.

It was clear that the tyrant was done with her, so she rose to be escorted back to her chambers.

Two days! Two damn days, Lilith thought when she was alone once more. She was a strong woman, but she did not think even she could bear being intimate with such a beast. In a very short time, he expected her to become his bride in title as well as body. *Death might be my only escape,* she thought, as suicidal tendencies washed through her mind. As her thoughts grew darker, tears escaped her eyes like the first drops of an approaching storm. Soon, the downpour came, and she was lost in the dark, thunderous reality that rumbled through her mind, raining down on her very soul.

Just before midnight, Lilith fell into a fitful sleep. Her dreams carried her to visions of her children, Naberius and Deumos, chasing her beloved Sandel through their living room and falling onto the couch in laughter. Sandel tickled them both until they struggled to catch their breath. Then, her memories drifted to another day, when Sandel surprised her in the kitchen. He hugged her from behind, but just as she turned to kiss him, she awoke in a bed that was not her own. Instantly, she burst into uncontrollable crying. Gone was the joy of being with her family. She was still a captive in that awful heavenly palace, a half-galaxy away from the ones she loved.

Chapter 65

After landing at Paradise spaceport on Heaven, and passing through the standard security checks, the shipping container that had smuggled Sandel was loaded onto a transport. A short while later, he felt the container being offloaded to what he presumed was its final destination. He checked the camera and saw that he was now stashed just outside the food storage building, behind the palace grounds.

He quietly packed everything away in preparation to start the next phase of the plan. His main hope now, besides rescuing Lilith, was that no one on Hell suspected that he was gone. It was his daughter's birthday, which made for the perfect alibi; everyone was told he was spending a few days with her, since it was the first birthday the poor girl would have to spend without her mother.

Sandel remained completely silent as the workers carefully unloaded the fruit of life. Once the cargo was taken, the container was closed again. Now, all he could do was wait. Sometime after dark, he heard three taps and the sound of something scraping against the side of the container. *That's my cue to go,* he thought.

He quietly climbed out of his hiding place and mindfully replaced the panel, just in case the smuggling method might come in handy at a future date. He scraped the inside of the container and gave three taps on the wall. Just like that, the container was opened, and he was helped out.

When he climbed out of the shipping container, Sandel raised his arms high overhead, then bent his body as far
back as possible. After that glorious popping sound, he whispered, "Ah..." but he really wanted to scream his relief. He
had no idea until that moment just how badly he was in need
of a stretch.

Sandel was quickly ushered away to safety. A short while
later, they stopped at a building not far from the palace. Once
they were inside and the doors were locked, the lights came
on. When his rescuers removed their hoods, he recognized
them as three of the best undercover agents stationed on
Heaven: Mathim, Shanda, and Haures.

"Thank you so much for helping me," he said sincerely.
Then, with great hope in his voice, he asked, "Has there been
any progress in securing a plan to save Lilith?"

Mathim was the first to speak: "Sandel, try as we might,
we are no closer to finding a way to get her out safely. Since
the Earthling's escape and Lilith's arrival, Jesus has taken
every possible precaution to seal Heaven up tight. He's taken
extra measures to fortify security at the palace."

It was distressing news, but Sandel would never give
up entirely on his wife. "If we cannot figure anything out by
tonight, I might know of a way we can enter the palace unnoticed."

Everyone decided time was of the essence, so they got
right down to business.

"This is Lilith's room," Shanda said, pointing to a map,
"and here is Jesus' chamber."

Sandel pointed to a particular room and asked, "What's
in here?"

Shanda answered, "That is Magdalene's room. Why?"

"You will know soon enough, my friend," Sandel answered.

Interesting, Sandel thought. "We'll go in tomorrow. We'll
have to do it my way if we have no other options. Can you get
word to Zabkiel?" he asked.

"Yes. What message shall we give him?"

Sandel gave them the message, along with a stern warning: "Be sure to deliver it word for word."

Haures memorized the message and nodded. Word for word, he recited it back to Sandel, just to be sure.

Before Haures left, Sandel had just one more thing to say. "Tell Zabkiel we are coming in tomorrow."

They continued to struggle with worst-case scenarios late into the night. Finally, Sandel raised his hands high in the air for another stretch, followed by another satisfying pop. "Get some rest, my friends. We have a big day ahead of us."

The next evening at dusk, Sandel and Mathim headed out to find the secret entrance Lucifer had shown him with the Illuminator. He wasn't sure it would still be there, but he headed toward the right spot. Tall weeds had overtaken the area, preventing him from readily finding the entrance; it required five minutes of bushwhacking and crawling around in the dirt. While that was a bit annoying, Sandel was thankful that their passage was well out of view of any passersby.

They slid the stone aside and entered. It was pitch black inside once the stone was back in place, so they activated their enhanced night-vision glasses. A glance around told them they were in a space about three feet wide and six feet high. *Not again,* Sandel thought, having flashbacks of his claustrophobic journey inside the container. It had appeared much bigger with the illuminator, but he realized that was only because he'd envisioned it through his father's boyhood perspective. *Damn! It's hard to believe Father was ever that young,* he thought with a grin.

They quickly made their way through the narrow corridor. The thick layer of dust on the walls and floor made it evident that no one had been in there for a very long time. Thanks to the Illuminator, Sandel could almost make the trek with his eyes closed.

Ten minutes or so later, they reached the end of their journey when their walkway emptied into a ten-by-thirty room. On the other side of the far wall was Magdalene's room, though it used to have a different purpose; when it was a dormitory for female workers, curious and naughty little Elohim and Lucifer had lingered in the secret side to spy on the girls.

Sandel walked over to the far wall and slid the covers off the peepholes. He peered into the room beyond the wall and saw Magdalene enjoying a sponge bath by a male servant. As he watched something he was not supposed to see, he felt the same way he was sure his adolescent father felt so many years ago, a guilty pleasure. When his mind came back to him, he shut the peepholes and reached over to pop a still-watching Mathim in the arm.

Mathim shrugged, gave him a sheepish grin, and whispered, "She may be a royal bitch, but she's still pretty damn easy on the eyes."

They waited until Magdalene dressed and left her room, then waited five more minutes for safe measure. Once they were sure no one would hear, they pushed the spot on the wall that Sandel had seen with the Illuminator. The exit opened beneath an altar adorned with a bust of Jesus in the middle. Sandel was sure Magdalene hated that sort of décor, but he understood why she'd never complain or demand that it be removed.

As Sandel and Mathim stood to wipe the dust off their clothes, the room was suddenly illuminated. There, sitting with her legs crossed and smiling at them, was Magdalene. "I had the feeling someone was spying on me. Did you gentlemen like what you saw?"

Sandel and Mathim moved out of the shadows, both blushing a bit.

She glanced at the dry, shriveled penis on display on her shelf and thought of her ex-lover and the maniac who mutilated him. She then looked back at Sandel. "Well?" she said, with a gleam in her eye.

"I am—" Sandel started, but Magdalene interrupted.

"I know who you are and why you are here." She paused to study the intruders for a moment. "If that passage leads out of the palace and you promise to take me with you, I will help you rescue Lilith. If you kill him, I will do anything you ask. Remember, you must move to the statue of Elohim. That is the only place in the room where Jesus has no eyes. Also, lower your voices."

Sandel nodded in agreement with her demands, and he and Mathim did as they were told.

Suddenly, Magdalene rose from her seat and gestured,

and the room filled with fast-tempo music. She moved and gyrated her shapely figure in a combination of alluring exercise and dance. "He never watches my routine, she explained in a whisper, "but you should still be careful."

Sandel and Mathim said not a word, and at least one of them was fully entranced by the snakelike movements of her feminine figure.

After about five minutes, she continued dancing but asked, "Now, what is your plan, and how can I help?"

"We need to somehow safely spirit Lilith to this room so we can all leave the way we came in. Can that be done?" Sandel asked.

Magdalene thought for a moment, then answered, "It might be tricky, as her room is guarded day and night, but perhaps I can distract the guards until you take them down. If we do that, we might have a chance. Her room is down the hall and just around the corner. We must move quickly."

"Then let us go now," Sandel said.

Magdalene nodded and led her two unexpected guests to her door. There, she motioned for them to stay back for a minute. She opened the door and went into the hallway, then quickly returned and whispered, "Hurry!"

They entered the dark hallway, but as soon as they took two more footsteps, the corridor flooded with guards coming from all sides. Jesus' men quickly subdued Sandel and Mathim.

"Lilith!" was all Sandel had a chance to yell before he was taken down by the horrid sting of a shock stick. As he fell to his knees, he looked at the smiling Magdalene, and one thought crossed his mind: *You unholy bitch!*

Lilith, just beginning to doze off, thought she heard Sandel calling for her. She bolted upright in bed and listened intently, but there was only the cruel, lonely silence that had taunted her since her arrival. "Silly girl. It was only another dream," she muttered to herself as she lowered her head back onto her pillow. This time, she found sleep elusive. She so longed to be in her husband's loving embrace, and she again started to cry as she thought of her vile captor forcing himself on her. Finally, exhaustion carried her into an uneasy sleep, one plagued with nightmares she feared would become all too real.

Chapter 66

Jesus wanted to kill Sandel immediately, specifically in the presence of Lilith, but Seraphim One convinced him that it would make a far greater impact if he made a public spectacle of Sandel's demise. "My Lord, it must be something glorious for all of the galaxy to witness. Let everyone see the power of God," he coached.

In reality, Zabkiel was just stalling for time. He desperately wanted to save Sandel and Lilith, but he could not risk Jesus discovering his betrayal. He was prepared to kill Jesus himself, but that would require getting past his lordship's ever-present entourage of bodyguards, then shutting down his shield. As that was a nearly impossible feat, biding their time was the only option Seraphim One had. Fortunately, Jesus fell for it, hook, line, and sinker.

"What a wonderful idea! Imagine all eyes on me as I put him down like the animal the hellish scum is. Why, Lucifer will only be able to helplessly watch as I end his nasty offspring's life! Let's entertain the masses in the arena. His death will be the grand finale."

"My Lord, your intellect never ceases to amaze me," Zabkiel lied. "After you depose of the diseased animal, everyone in the galaxy will fear your power and know that no one is beyond your reach."

"My Lilith must not know of it till the day he dies in the arena. See that she is escorted to her room and sequestered there until then. Then, order the guards to bring Sandel to the arena, so I may show him where he will take his last breath."

"As you wish, my Lord," Zabkiel said, then bowed and backed away. His relief was overshadowed by fear; he'd managed to buy more time by playing on Jesus' ego, but he still had no workable plan in mind.

After a day of intense interrogation accompanied by much pain, Sandel was hauled by two guards to the arena. Jesus had ordered the construction of the facility, an exorbitant place meant to flaunt his bravado and affluence to all who beheld it. He'd fought many battles there himself, albeit never with any worthy opponents who had the slightest chance of besting him. To ensure that he was always the victor and that all applause was for his ears only, his competitors were always too weak, drugged, unarmed, or generally ill equipped. In case an adversary did happen to present a genuine challenge, Jesus made sure to take precautions: Scattered about the arena were those who were willing to intervene, as well as a surplus of weaponry or poisons that would give him an edge and helped him render everyone incapable. His enemies were also fitted with a neck restraint that would instantly incapacitate them if Jesus was in real danger. For this reason, he was undefeated, and it did not appear that his spotless record would be tarnished anytime soon.

"Sandel, my old friend, you will now enjoy a unique and rare privilege," the lord of Heaven said. "You are witnessing the place of your death. Soon, we will battle on this very ground, as Lilith looks on. She will finally see you for what you are, you weak, pathetic insect. You beguiled my beautiful Lilith many years ago. That is the only plausible explanation as to why she would choose you over the future one, true God. Soon, her eyes will behold the truth, and she will know you are not even worthy to walk where I walk or to breathe the air I breathe. I will have my revenge against your treachery. Once I show Lilith and the rest of the galaxy what you truly are, I will strike you down. As your blood spills out to stain the dirt where you now stand, and as you struggle to take in your final breath, you will know that I am taking

Lilith to my bed to show her how God makes love."

Furious beyond all control, Sandel lunged forward and spat at Jesus. "I will kill you, you bastard!"

A vicious backhand across the face was followed by an even more violent punch to the stomach before Jesus smiled and said, "Pick him up and take him away. Be sure to give him the heavenly greeting he deserves, but leave him un-marked." Then, Jesus simply turned and walked away.

For the next four hours, the guards made Sandel's time on Heaven a hell all its own. Their shock sticks sent ripples of energy tearing through is body, singeing every nerve like boiling-hot lava. Still, Sandel refused to scream. Once the welcome party was over, he was taken to his cell, fitted with a neck restraint, and thrown onto a filthy, uncomfortable bunk bed.

Where is Mathim? he wondered as he lay there, writh-ing in pain. He hoped for the best, but he knew his new-found friend's fate was grim. He then thought of Lilith, and his heart ached for her. *I hope she will at least know that I tried. Oh, Lilith, I so wanted to rescue you. I love you above all things.*

Sandel awoke the next day feeing completely drained. His body was sore all over from the punishment he'd endured, but he managed to sit up, stand, and stretch. When he sat back down on the bunk, he forced himself into a deep, medi-tative state; he hoped the relaxation methods he'd learned in his training on Hell would help to calm his aching nerves and to push the weariness and pain out of his body and mind. Af-ter a half-hour, he felt much better, though certainly not 100 percent restored.

Soon, the announcement was made that a special event would be held in the arena. It was proclaimed that Jesus would once again show his prowess as a fighter to all of the Empire. Jesus, who trained almost every day, was a master of hand-to-hand combat techniques, and his bloated self-con-fidence also made him completely fearless. Such shows usually consisted of Jesus publicly murdering his opponents in quick order. The adversaries were always those who'd been accused of committing terrible crimes against the Empire; their guilt or innocence was irrelevant, and most of the charges were trumped up. The prize for defeating Jesus was a full pardon, but the only freedom any opponents felt came as they took their last breaths before dying.

The guards left Sandel alone for most of the day, except when it was time to provide what they joyfully called his last meal. Then, an hour before he was to meet Jesus in the arena, he received a visit from Jesus and the guards who had taken such pleasure in welcoming him to Heaven. They held him down and gave him a shot, and a few moments later, his mind dimmed. One of the guards raised a hand to strike Sandel, but his reaction to protect himself was sluggish due to the drug.

Sandel struggled to state, "Our fathers were the best of friends, and I hoped the two of us could have followed suit. It was not to be though. Your jealousy over their friendship was all consuming. It defined your life. If Lilith had chosen you when we were young, you would have thrown her away like everything and everyone else in your life. You would have disposed of her just as you did to your father, your mother, your sense of right and wrong, and your duty to the people of the galaxy. You only want her now because she chose me. Your future is as unknown as mine, Jesus, but I hope you will one day look back and realize the damage you have cursed upon yourself and the Empire." Sandel blinked to clear his head, then continued, "M-Maybe you will see what could have been if you were a fraction of the leader your father was. The Empire loved him, rightfully so. That is more than I can say for you. Oh, you have worshippers, servants, and those who fear you, but no one in the galaxy calls you a f-friend."

Jesus allowed Sandel to speak his mind, and he smiled in the most heinous way when his old friend's words struggled to make their way through his trembling lips. After Sandel finished, Jesus calmly said, "Only God is worthy to befriend God. As I am the one and only God, I am the only friend I require. There was never any chance for friendship between you and me, for you are less than an insect. You have been a thorn in my side since the moment we met. Today, I will remove that thorn once and for all. Soon, everyone

in the galaxy will see the power of their God and his Empire.
As for your earthly friend, his time has also run its course. At
this very moment, Michael is making preparations to end the
lives of Justin Grant and his family." Jesus started to turn
and walk away, then stopped and turned to spit more venom:
"You are wrong, by the way. My parents do love me. In fact,
everyone does." Then, he walked away without another word.

Chapter 67

For many, it was the first opportunity to see their new queen, but most attended because they were curious about the promised special entertainment. Every video screen in Empire space had been announcing the once-in-a-lifetime event for several days, drumming up interest by divulging few details. It wasn't long before the arena was filled to capacity. A shield covered the field to protect Jesus from any potential harm from the crowd; he would be without a personal shield in the arena, and there was always the risk that a crazed individual with nothing to lose may try to seek publicity or revenge.

Jesus strutted onto the field to a chorus of ear-splitting cheers. He walked to the wall directly in front of Lilith, bowed a bit, and said, "For you, my Queen."

The first contestant was shoved onto the field, looking as scared as a man could look. The herald announced the charges against him, likely with no merit or proof whatsoever, and the one-sided fight began. Jesus nimbly danced around, toying with his prey. He punished him for a while before delivering the fatal blow. The crowd cheered him on, and Jesus perceived it as love, but most were crying out in adulation for the idea that it was not they who were about to die at their Lord's hand. Two other unfortunate, wrongly accused souls fell before the grand finale of the evening unfolded.

Typically, after each victim was toppled, Jesus raised his

arms high in the air to the seemingly excited crowd. He then sauntered arrogantly to where Lilith sat, smiled, and made great showmanship out of bowing. This time, however, was different. After the last man's blood was brutally spilled on the arena floor, Jesus called for silence and yelled, "My last opponent for the evening is very special to me. He has eluded the Empire for over 5,000 years. He beguiled the only woman I have ever truly loved, and took her away from me and Heaven. He had the audacity to hold her prisoner on his dreadful Planet Hell. Let us welcome to the field the leader of the so-called Free Will Alliance, Sandel Satanis."

The crowd booed as Sandel was led onto the field, though secretly, a great majority of them were rooting for the obvious underdog.

"Sandel!" Lilith screamed, hopping to her feet as warm tears filled her eyes. "My love, you're here!"

Jesus shook his head and looked at his audience as if he expected them to agree with his disapproval. "You see? My queen is still under this serpent's spell, but that spell will be broken before you tonight when I kill the vile beast. Do you have anything to say, beast?"

Sandel's mind was fuzzy from the beatings and the drug, and he did not seem to have any control of his faculties or movements, but he managed at a loud volume that all could hear, "I love you, Lilith."

Just as Jesus loved to do with all of his enemies, he toyed with Sandel, punching and kicking him to the ground with ease. Much to everyone's surprise, Sandel somehow ambled to his feet time and time again. He was bloodied, bruised, and off balance, and it seemed he was unable to defend against even the slightest attack. His mouth was filled with dirt and blood from falling to the arena floor face first, after each attack.

Finally, after what seemed like forever, Jesus stopped the assault and instructed his servants, "Give him some water!" It was a custom of his, a gesture meant to show his compassion even for a miserable wretch.

While the servants dribbled a few drops of water into Sandel's filthy, bloody mouth, Jesus strutted around the arena, raising his arms to cheers from almost everyone in attendance. It was meant to be his final act of mercy before he finished Sandel off.

Sandel drank as deeply as he could, and he tried to will himself to be stronger, but he was utterly exhausted. No matter how hard he tried, he could not react quickly enough to avoid the full force of Jesus' attacks. He wondered how long he would last, but even as every inch of his body ached and throbbed, and even as his mind cried out for the sweet mercy of death, thoughts of Lilith spun through his psyche. The deepest agony he felt, like a hot iron in his heart, was that he could not save her, and the loudest thought that echoed in his tortured mind was a desperate plea: *Please, Zabkiel. We cannot fail my love. Please, please find some way to save my Lilith.*

As he drank the stagnant water, Sandel began to feel a clearing in his head, and he seemed to regain some control of his body. He rose to his feet slowly. Jesus resumed pummeling and kicking him, but Sandel found that he was able to deflect some of the blows. With each onslaught, Sandel's muscles responded with greater quickness and strength, better at obeying the commands of his mind.

When Jesus came at him to knock him to the ground once more, Sandel blocked the battering and delivered a fist to the face of his unsuspecting former friend. Jesus tasted his own salty blood for the first time in a long time, and he heard the cheers turn to jeers and gasps of disbelief as the crowd witnessed a more dangerous Sandel. When Jesus turned to look at his challenger, he felt a new emotion, one he had been unfamiliar with for many, many years: fear. Although he had trained almost every day, no one ever bothered to use their full force against him; after all, to win meant death to opponents and their families, and most preferred to save their loved ones by sacrificing themselves, even in the rare even that they had a fighting chance. Sandel, though, looked as if he were not about to give up so easily, and that sent a frightening tremor through the master of Heaven.

Jesus then cast his gaze to Seraphim One, who only looked at him with great worry, shrugged, and mouthed, *"I-I don't know..."*

In a rage, Jesus charged at Sandel and caught him on the side of his face. Sandel was still suffering from the effects of whatever chemical they'd put into his body, but it was wearing off by the minute. All he could assume was that something in the water was working like an antidote, counteracting the drug that had disabled him.

Desperate to win and salvage his reputation, Jesus rushed to retrieve one of the weapons stashed strategically around the arena, only to find it missing. Angry and concerned, he threw dirt into his opponent's eyes, then tackled Sandel as he struggled to regain his sight. Jesus threw multiple wild punches, leaving Sandel to blindly anticipate his thwacks and block them. Finally, one of Sandel's eyes cleared, and he reclaimed enough vision to knock Jesus off of him with a slam into his face.

Jesus rolled away and quickly searched for another hidden weapon, but it, too, was missing. All he could find was a staff he'd used on the previous opponents. He swung it hard at Sandel and hit him in the side.

With a groan and a wince from the pain, Sandel felt a rib crack, but he weathered the hit, and remained on his feet.

Jesus was out of his comfort zone, as he'd never fought anyone who had the slightest bit of real hope or the true desire to win. "Get me out of here!" his lordship screamed, darting his eyes about for any means of escape. "Guards? Anyone! Shackle this Alliance scum, before I kill you all for this treachery!"

As his guards scrambled around, not sure of the protocol in such an unfamiliar situation, Jesus saw a glint and realized there was a knife still sticking out of the chest of his first victim. He ran to the corpse and pulled it out, then turned to brandish it at Sandel. He smiled, with his teeth outlined in his own red blood. The son of God advanced on the son of Lucifer, madly swinging the knife back and forth. He caught Sandel on the arm, drawing a gush of blood. When he swung the blade again, he clipped Sandel's cheek. Sandel was still reacting slower than usual, but he backed away from the knife just in time to avoid the worst of it.

Benjamin Oneal

As Jesus maneuvered for another attack, Sandel grabbed
his wrist and twisted it, then elbowed him in the chin. For
the first time, it was Jesus who collapsed to the dirt, and
the crowd let out a collective gasp, followed by whispers and
mumbling. Instantly, everyone was on their feet; it was a
grand finale indeed, a show they did not want to miss.

Jesus, still a bit stunned, looked at his hand and discovered that he was now unarmed. He had no idea where his
knife had gone, and he saw no sight of it anywhere nearby.
"Someone get in here and stop this beast! I command you
to put a halt to this right now! Raise the shield! Raise the
shield!" he screamed. Again, he looked toward Seraphim One,
who was frantically barking orders to anyone who would listen.

"My Lord, I cannot raise the shield," Seraphim One yelled
to his master. "There seems to be a malfunction with the
equipment. Just hold on for a moment longer, dear Lord.
Just a moment longer!"

Sandel, whose mind was now entirely clear, advanced
on Jesus. The prey had become the predator as he shouted, "There is no one to help you! We are all alone, just you
and me." Then, he punched him hard in the stomach and
followed with a vicious blow to the jaw, one that sent Jesus
down once more.

Real fear overtook Jesus for the first time in his life. With
tears running down his face, he whimpered, "Please do not
hurt me. Please! I beg of you, Sandel."

Sandel, with a look of rage in his eyes, delivered another
fist to the Jesus' midsection, so hard it knocked the air out of
him. "You took my wife, you asshole. For that, you must die."

After another brutal strike just beneath his left eye, Jesus crumpled to the ground once again. He began to sob like
the child he was.

Sandel felt no pity for the pathetic creature before him;
more than anything, he wanted to kill the miserable bastard.
He grabbed Jesus and jerked him to his feet, put his arm
around his neck, and began to squeeze.

With the shields still active over the arena, the door to
the right opened, and five guards rushed in, with a ner-

vous-looking Seraphim One in tow. Upon seeing them, Sandel ceased his strangulation and allowed Jesus' body to drop to the ground like a heap of garbage.

Slowly recovering and gasping for air, Jesus scrambled to his feet. In the croaking, raspy voice of a man nearly choked to death, he looked at Sandel and said, "Now you will see the power of God." He turned back to the guards and barked, "Kill him! Kill the bastard right now!"

"Guards, seize this man," Seraphim One ordered.

Jesus smiled at Seraphim One's loyalty, but that grin melted into a look of confusion as his guards walked right past Sandel and grabbed him. "What treachery is this? I am your God. I command you to release me. Now!" he screamed.

Ignoring his former master's rant, Seraphim One raised his hand to quiet the confused crowd. "People of the Empire, Jesus will be taken into custody to stand trial for his crimes against the citizens of the Empire. Until such time as a free and fair election can be executed, the council and I will speak for the Empire."

The crowd in the arena and those dispersed throughout Empire space cheered as they watched the guards lead Jesus away in chains, terrified and crying like a baby. "B-But I-I am your God," he blubbered, fluctuating between pouting and yelling. "I am your God! Release me now, or I will kill you all!" he shrieked, to no avail.

Among the onlookers, there was one who could not muster a cheer for Jesus' embarrassing demise. Magdalene quickly moved through the crowd, only to stop behind the chair that once belonged to her. She pulled out a knife and held it to Lilith's throat. "How dare you touch God? He is the Alpha and Omega. Let my Jesus go, or I will kill her!" she commanded.

"Madame," Seraphim One replied, "you, of all people, should rejoice at his removal. His vile treatment of you is well known throughout the Empire."

Sandel watched helplessly as his beloved was used as a bargaining chip. He was afraid to move, afraid to cry out, paralyzed by the terror that he might lose his sweet Lilith after all.

"He is God!" Magdalene declared, the shriveled penis bouncing against her chest with every word. "Jesus is the only one I have ever loved. I am his queen, not this harlot. Let my Jesus go, or I swear I will cut this God-stealing whore's throat."

Magdalene was so focused on Seraphim One and Sandel that she did not see the councilman who came up behind her, a councilman Sandel recognized as Shanda. He touched her with a shock stick and, in one fell swoop, grabbed her hand that held the knife. Magdalene went down, and the knife clattered to the floor.

Moments later, a trembling Lilith walked through the same door Seraphim One had used to enter earlier. She ran to Sandel, and the two held each other for a long moment.

With tears of joy still flowing from Sandel's eyes, he turned to Zabkiel and shook his hand. "Thank you, my friend! I will never, ever be able to repay you for what you have done here today."

"I am sorry I could not help sooner. I feared the water would not work quickly enough to save you. Although I removed all of his hidden arsenal, I was powerless to stop him from killing you. That, my friend, was all you. You, Sandel, are a warrior to be admired," Zabkiel said, in absolute awe.

"Nonsense! If not for you, I would have been the fourth dead in this arena today, and the only woman I have ever loved would have been doomed to live out her days with a sadistic brat."

"No, for I would have killed him the first time he put his greasy little hands on me," Lilith said. "I promise you that."

"I believe you, my dear," Sandel said with a laugh, though his chuckling was quickly replaced with winces from the pain. Suddenly, another thought occurred to him, and he turned to Seraphim One. "What of Mathim?" he asked. "Does he live?"

"He was in a very bad way by the time we got to him, but I believe that with proper care and time, he should make a full recovery," Zabkiel said with a smile. He then led them from the arena and ordered a ship to be readied for their return to Hell.

The Serpent's Gift

On the way to their escape vessel, Sandel caught his arm. "Zabkiel, it is very important that I get a message to New Earth. Can you help me with that?"

"Consider it done, my friend," the seraphim said with a smile, eager to please anyone other than his former lord.

Chapter 68

In his office, Justin, Salome, and Stolas watched in horror as Jesus spoke, then proceeded to murder two defenseless men in an arena that very much resembled those of ancient Rome. They direct-feed transmission came across the Alliance Intelligence Network, the AIN. Salome and Stolas had heard of Jesus' barbaric ways, and Justin had witnessed his cruelty firsthand, but seeing his glorification of needless mayhem was gut-wrenching.

After the third man died from a knife to the heart, Justin turned his head away and told Salome, "I will not watch another moment of this gory spectacle." He was on the way out the door when he heard Jesus announce Sandel's name.

Salome gasped and lifted her hand to her mouth, and Stolas stood and moved closer to the screen. Justin joined Stolas, and they all stared at the staggering Sandel.

"Those beasts must have drugged him," Stolas said. "It is not like him to be so...unsteady."

Unable to find his voice, Justin merely nodded, and Salome just openly wept.

The three watched as Jesus battered, taunted, and made a mockery of Sandel, beating and cutting him without much resistance as the mindless crowd cheered at every uncontested injury. Fifteen minutes into the travesty, Jesus allowed Sandel a drink of water while he strutted around and showboated, eliciting more cheers from the audience. When he returned to the fight, Jesus was even more brutal, but there was a nearly imperceptible difference: Sandel seemed to be a bit quicker on his feet and more capable than before, blocking some attacks and avoiding Jesus' knife thrusts. Finally, Sandel deftly blocked a blow from Jesus and landed a powerful one of his own.

From that point on, the three spectators were glued to the screen like super fans watching the last few minutes of a tied sporting event. They cheered as Sandel gained control and laughed as Jesus screamed in horror and frustration. The trio did not breathe for a long moment as Sandel raised his hand to deliver the death blow, but they released a collective exhale as he reached down to pick up the defeated supreme being. Sandel put his former friend in a headlock and began to squeeze, aiming to choke the life out of the self-proclaimed lord. Only when the side doors opened and royal guards rushed in did Sandel drop Jesus and await whatever fate was in store for him.

Justin, Salome, and Stolas stood frozen in place, hoping they would not witness the end of their Sandel. They all sighed in relief as the guards obeyed Seraphim One's command and grabbed Jesus instead of Sandel. When Jesus was hauled out of his own arena in changes, still pleading for someone to obey him, Stolas actually applauded, and Salome giggled and happily jumped up and down. Justin hugged Salome and clapped Stolas on the back, grinning from ear to ear. Just like that, the emotional rollercoaster ride was over, and they smiled at one another with tears of happiness in their eyes.

Suddenly, though, a wicked scream from inside the arena drew their attention back to the screen. The joy left them as they saw a crazed woman holding a knife to Lilith's throat.

Salome held her hand over her mouth to muffle a scream. "That's... Jesus' wife," she said, her eyes wide. "That's Magdalene."

They could only watch and hope as a man in robes made a stealthy approach from behind, grabbed the knife, and zapped her with the shock stick. This time, they all waited until they were sure the danger had passed before they em-

317

barked on a celebration.

After a toast to possibly the greatest day in galactic history, Justin made sure to tell Laura, "I am taking the next two days off, and I am not to be disturbed." Of course, Justin was on the top of all worlds, and he pulled Salome in close for a quick kiss before closing the door. They said their goodbyes to Stolas at his ride and walked home holding hands, like two young lovers caught in the blissful throes of a whirlwind romance.

They entered their home through the back door. Justin sat his communicator on the kitchen table and headed for his children's rooms. When he didn't find Rachel in hers, he assumed she was watching old movies with Jarod, something both kids enjoyed. He walked into Jarod's room expecting to see them huddled in front of the video screen but instead came face to face with someone he had no desire to see, especially not in his own home.

"Stop," Michael said, aiming a weapon at Justin's head. "Do not move, and do not speak."

Justin waited to take his last breath, but Michael just stood there, gawking at him for a painfully pregnant moment. *Why is it that villains always have to share a monologue before delivering the final blow?* Justin wondered.

"Jesus sent me to kill you because you embarrassed him before the council, but I am here for other reasons as well. You took my precious Rebecca. Did you think I would forget? For one moment, did you think I would allow the death of my beautiful daughter be left unavenged?" the archangel said as a bitter tear ran down his cheek.

"Michael, I—" Justin tried, only to be cut off.

"Shut up, you human pig!" Michael said with a growl in his voice.

Salome wrinkled up her brow in confusion when she heard a strange voice coming from her children's room. She was prepared for an evening of celebratory lovemaking, scantily clad in very sexy, white lingerie, but she wasn't sure what her lover was up to. "Hey, what are you doing, Justin?" she said outside Jarod's door. "Don't you know the children are staying with..." she questioned as she opened it, only to stop cold as she walked inside.

Michael looked at her and scoffed, "Ah, if it isn't the lovely half-breed. Nice! I may have to grant you the pleasure of sex with an archangel before I cut your pretty, little throat."

As the intruder forced them into the living room, Justin struggled to figure out a way to save Salome. Michael was not known for patience or mercy, so neither of them had a chance of survival unless he could stall for time or even out the playing field. The only solution he could come up with was to get under the archangel's skin by engaging him with a bit of trash talk. "Archangel, my ass!" he blurted. "You are no better than your master. You are both cowards who prefer chicken-shit ambushes to straight-up confrontation. You only face weak opponents who are at a disadvantage, when the fight is fixed, because you know you are lousy losers and you fear retaliation. Every time I have been with you, you've drugged me, chained me, or surrounded me with a convoy of your pathetic guards, you archangel pussy! Go ahead. Admit it. Tell my wife that you are afraid to face me unshielded, you sack of shit." Then, to push Michael over the edge, he added, "Oh, and by the way, Lucifer told me you were quite the crybaby during basic training."

As his face went from scrunched-up in anger to all-out, fiery red, unsuppressed rage, Michael walked to where Salome sat and greeted her with a backhand slapped that sent her reeling, left her seeing stars and lying sideways. He then disengaged his body shield, lowered his weapon, and dropped both on the table nearest him. "Is this what you want, you human excrement? Come on!" he screamed, standing before Justin with his hands outstretched. "Earth will soon be ours once more. Once again, your people will fear the wrath of God," Michael said with angered resolve.

A bit confused, Justin just stared at him. *Surely he knows about Jesus' downfall,* he thought, *or maybe not.*

Michael continued, "First, I will take you to the edge of death, and then, I will let you watch me kill your beautiful half-breed.

With that, Michael charged Justin, hitting him so hard that it nearly caused him to black out. Fortunately, Justin's training had given him the strength to work through the pain and continue to fend off his opponent. Justin rolled backward and got back on his feet. He blocked another punch, but he felt the crunch of Michael administering a heavy knee-blow to his stomach.

Damn. Only a minute into the fight, and I feel like I've been hit by a bus, Justin said.

When Michael came at him again, Justin managed to land a fist in the archangel's face.

The hit gave Michael pause, and he rubbed his jaw and smiled. "Good one, runt," he said. He did not charge again, for while his resolve was still strong, he was wise enough to make caution a factor.

Desperate to unnerve the angel further, Justin said, "Obviously, you haven't heard the latest, asshole," he said. "That prick Jesus does not rule the Empire anymore. An hour ago, Seraphim One had Jesus arrested and took control of Heaven and the Empire. You lose."

Michael laughed. "Liar," he said. "Seraphim One hasn't the power, brains, or balls to do anything of the sort. He is but a pawn in God's game of chess."

Justin offered a laugh of his own. "Turn on the video screen and see for yourself," he said. "Then, kill me if you want."

Michael nodded and gestured for Justin to turn on the device. He then watched in awe and disappointment as Jesus lost the battle with Sandel. He audibly moaned when he saw his master dragged away in chains.

Meanwhile, as the archangel was distracted, Justin used the opportunity to try to drum up some sort of defense mechanism, but he had little luck at devising a plan.

When the news report ended, Michael turned to the Earthling once more. "This changes nothing between you and me. I will kill you and every member of your family for my own pleasure. You owe me your lives for my Rebecca," he said before he grabbed Justin and threw him across the room like a sack of discarded potatoes.

Suddenly, Michael felt immense pain, something smacking against the small of his back with great force. The unexpected jab knocked him to his knees. His eyes widened in disgruntled surprise as he looked back and saw Salome rearing back with a Louisville Slugger, ready to deliver another homerun hit.

"No!" Michael screeched, then grabbed the bat just before it smacked him in the side of the head. With ease, he threw Salome, and she crashed against the table where Michael had left his weapon.

Thankful for the diversion and egged on by the desire to protect his wife, Justin took the opportunity to kick Michael square in the face. He then rolled into the broken table where the stunned Salome lay. He quickly moved to her, grabbed Michael's shield, and hooked it to her lacy panties. He switched it on and was immediately relieved that she would be safe. Ensuring his own safety would be the hard part.

At that moment, Michael grabbed Justin again and hurled him against the wall, so hard that it left a torso-sized hole. With Salome in the clear, Justin threw himself into the battle in earnest. Michael was around 9,000 years old but was kicking the living shit out of him. Even so, Justin was able to fight back with some success. Michael began to show symptoms of the punishment Justin delivered, and steady streams of blood ran down his face from his nose and mouth.

Whatever punishment Justin heaped upon Michael, the angel repaid two fold. At last, Michael knocked Justin to the floor and sat on his chest, pinning him down with his knees on his arms. Justin was nearly spent and too weak to move him.

Michael pulled a knife from somewhere, raised it over his head, and declared, "This is for my sweet Rebecca!"

As he brought the knife down toward Justin's unprotected heart, Michael suddenly stopped and shook violently. The weapon skidded across the floor, and Michael slowly stood, still shaking.

Behind him was Salome, holding a wireless shock gun. "Half-breed, my ass," she said with a growl of her own.

Michael reached for the darts now pinned to his shoulders. Through gritted teeth, he snarled, "I am g-going t-to k-kill you f-first, b-bitch." He wiped the shockers from his back and, still vibrating from the electricity, fought to regain his footing and moved toward Salome. He heard something behind him and turned just in time to see Justin's elbow smashing into his face. This time, he went down hard and found himself fighting to remain conscious.

"And this is for Leah's parents," Justin spat before kicking Michael with all the force his banged-up body could deliver, folding him over in the middle.

Suddenly, Stolas broke through the door with weapon in hand. He quickly crossed the room, followed by five NES agents. They grabbed Michael and applied restraints.

Salome rushed over to Justin, who had since fallen to the floor and looked tired. He was bruised and bleeding but smiling, happy to be rescued and happy that he and his wife were safe once more.

"Aw. The pretty boy isn't so pretty anymore," Salome observed.

She was quite right, for Michael was more disheveled than any of them had ever seen him before. Justin's kick had relieved him of one of his front teeth. A purple and red bruise was already forming on his back where Salome had hit him with the Louisville slugger, and the shiner on his left eye was a nice souvenir from Justin.

Justin looked into the face of the one he loved, then glanced at the bloodied bat lying near the table. "Hey, remind me to never, ever call you a half-breed," he said with a smile.

Chapter 69

After Jesus was taken into custody, Zabkiel entered Jesus's private room, that only Jesus had access to. It contained things Jesus had collected and kept secret for thousands of years. There were treasures from throughout the galaxy, all stolen, pilfered, and looted from planets the Empire controlled. Some were seemingly meaningless items with significance only known to Jesus.

The most prominent thing in the room was a large video screen. On it, Jesus could see into every room in the palace. Zabkiel was a bit disturbed when he took a look at his own room, and he realized how fortunate he was that he hadn't been found out by the prying eyes that always looked upon him.

Over the next week, Zabkiel learn many things that only Jesus had access to, and he discovered the power that came along with that knowledge. Much of the intel was obtained by the Holy Ghosts and reported directly to Jesus. He immediately alerted Hell, Earth, and other planets about the Holy Ghosts who were secretly stationed on their worlds. Once all had knowledge of who they were and where they were, the treacherous spies were taken into custody, if they didn't first die by their own hands to avoid capture by the Alliance they so hated.

On the fourth day, Zabkiel found a book entitled *The Land of Nod*. It told the story of a planet in a Limbus sector of the Empire, an area where inhabitable planets were few and far between. He remembered childhood tales about the land of Nod, a place where bad children were sent. As he recalled it, Nod was a prison planet, and none who went there ever returned.

As he continued to peruse the thick tome, he found loose paperwork that detailed small shipments of the Longevity Factor to Nod. It was not even enough to supply more than 1,000, and that puzzled Zabkiel greatly. He read on and discovered something that stirred him to great excitement. *This is big, very big,* the seraphim thought. *I have to know. I must.*

He desperately wanted to confirm the information, but he had difficulty trusting anyone with a mission of such great importance. After much thought, he contacted the one person he was sure he could rely on more than anyone in the galaxy, the devil himself.

Chapter 70

The people of Heaven had not seen or heard tell of a fair, just trial in thousands of years. In fact, it was still difficult for most to believe such a thing was actually going to occur. For so long, they had lived under the tyrannical reign of Jesus that they hardly remembered what justice or fearlessness was. Now, the bloody throne room had been converted into a great hall with the ultimate purpose of proper governing of the Empire, and the rings were a thing of the past.

The trial held in the great hall would be transmitted for all the Empire to see. After thousands of years of bowing to the adolescent sadist, they had a right to witness justice. The defenseless defendant sat in angry, pouting silence in a shielded area in front of the presiding council. Zabkiel occupied the head council seat in the middle of the nine members who would decide the fate of a truly disturbed individual.

Zabkiel brought the room to order by banging the stone of justice, an object that had not seen the light of day since the time of Jesus' father Elohim. "People of the Empire," he said, addressing the Empire and the galaxy, "we are here today to try Jesus El-Elyon for his crimes against our Empire. Since there is no way to ensure an unbiased jury, as no one on Heaven has been untouched by his crimes, in accordance with the laws set forth by the council under the reign of God Elohim, Jesus will be judged by a council of his peers. You will hear testimony from the accused and the accusers, and the council will decide his fate. We will now hear opening arguments."

The counsel in prosecution of Jesus rose and began, "Today, we are prepared to show the Empire a detailed account of Jesus' crimes against the people and against the Empire itself. Although most citizens have heard rumors of wanton acts of violence at the hands of this man, we are prepared to show proof of each and every crime he has committed since he seized control of Heaven and the galaxy. Thank you." He sat down, and everyone in the in the room sat silently, waiting to hear how the defense would respond.

Jesus, of course, had declined counsel, as he preferred to represent himself. His opening statement was brief and to the point: "I am God. I have no peers, and you have no right to judge me." With that and a dismissive wave of his hand, he took his seat once more.

The trial continued in that same vein. As the prosecution continued to build their case, Jesus sat in his shielded box, looking bored and apathetic to all the legal goings-on around him. He often interrupted to ask for petty things like a glass of wine or a servant to pleasure him while waited to go to his room.

With the help of an Illuminator, each and every person Jesus had murdered was put on full display before the court, though the actual murders were not shown, out of respect for the deceased and their loved ones. That portion of the trial took some time, as Jesus had personally taken over 1,000 lives during his reign of terror. To see the sheer number of the murdered and the level of violence of their unnecessary deaths was gruesome. This earned several gasps from the crowd, all while Jesus sat idly by, fiddling with his fingernails, and rolling his eyes. When Jesus was forced to view his crimes, he did so with detached amusement.

Other than that, Jesus only reacted to the trial when scenes were shared of Zabkiel saving thousands of lives, rescuing them from Jesus' kill orders. At that point, he became incensed, stood, and screamed at Zabkiel, "Seraphim One, you disobeyed my direct command! You are a traitor, and your disloyalty to your lord will cost you your life. Know that

I will make an example of you. You and all of your kin will
be destroyed while all in the galaxy bear witness. Everyone
must know the fate of those who disobey the lord God." Once
he was done with his tirade, he sat back down, smoothed out
his robes, and seemed to fade away.

Witness after witness took the stand to be questioned
about various crimes and murders. Even servants were
sworn in to testify, mainly about their lord's actions throughout the palace.

Once the prosecution concluded, it was time for Jesus to
offer his pro se defense. Rather than standing, he remained
in his seat and stated matter-of-factly, "I can no guiltier of a
crime than you pathetic beings are when you swat an annoying fly or step on a cockroach. That is all you are to me,
insects and nothing more. How dare you listen to lowly servants' accusations against me? They have no right to eval-
uate me, and you have neither the power nor the authority
to judge me. I am God, *your* God. Release me now, so I can
continue to rule my Empire."

Chapter 71

On the fifth and final day of the trial, just as Zabkiel was about to call the proceedings to order, someone unexpected walked into the courtroom. Everyone watched in awe as Lucifer came through the door, but it was not the ruler of Hell who caused all the commotion.

Even Jesus stood, and his mouth fell agape as he stared intently at the man next to Lucifer. "F-Father?" Jesus stuttered, incredulous.

Elohim looked at his son with disgust and continued to walk beside Lucifer toward their seats. Everyone in the courtroom and all throughout the galaxy stared at the proceedings in stunned silence. The common assumption was that he had died almost 5,000 years ago, but he was alive and looked every bit the man who had ruled the Empire with integrity and wisdom. Whispered conversations began slowly and built to a hushed roar, as even the council members joined in. It was clear that everyone wanted to know how he had come to join them, and it was even clearer that they wanted to hear what Elohim had to say.

When it became evident that order in the court would not be restored until their beloved, long-lost Lord God Elohim was allowed to speak, Zabkiel asked, "Sir, will you honor this court with your story?"

It was not why Elohim had come, and he did not really want to share all the details, but he knew the tale had to be told. He stepped up to the podium, and a hush fell over the courtroom as well as in every corner of every Empire and Alliance world where people were listening or watching.

"I will share this with you," Elohim began, "for the sake of all who have needlessly suffered at the cruel hand of Jesus. In particular, I am here on behalf of the people of Nod. If the council will allow me to use an Illuminator, I believe it will be beneficial in clarifying when my words are not enough. I want you to see both the beauty of Nod and the evil of this disease-minded child."

Zabkiel nodded. "Of course. The Illuminator is all yours."

Elohim thanked him with a smile and continued, "Before I was spirited away from Heaven, my thoughts were scattered. I was unable to realize who or what I was. Later, I discovered that I had been drugged and left to die, hidden away in the palace. Jesus was not content, though, with letting his father die, for he had a vested interest in keeping me alive, an interest known only to him at the time.

"My wicked son found a way to keep me alive and make me suffer, albeit far away from my beautiful Heaven. He sent me to Planet Nod, a lonely little star in the Limbus sector of space. It was discovered during the time when Jehovah, my father, was God. Much to my surprise, it was a gorgeous, uninhabited place, but because it was so isolated, so far away from any neighbors and trade routes, it was deemed undesirable for colonization.

"The drugs I'd been given filtered out of my system soon after I reached Nod, and I became fully aware once again. Jesus wanted it that way, for he hoped I would experience agony beyond belief. I found myself on a world where my only company were those who'd been exiled from all over the Empire, individuals and even entire families who'd found themselves in Jesus' disfavor for one reason or another. Although some blamed me for their fate, most learned to accept me, and many even trusted me enough to ask for my help in making their prison planet a better place. Initially, it was not my goal to lead the banished people, but I was able to contribute to their betterment. Together, we created a way of life that grew beyond survival, and we began to enjoy a rather pleasant existence..."

As he told his story, people across the galaxy watched in rapt attention as visions on their screens gave rise to his words. It was hard to believe that such a serene, majestic place as Nod was really a condemned planet for condemned people.

"Unlike the others there, I continued to receive the Longevity Factor, a luxury only granted to the guards. As the years waned on, I tired of watching my friends grow old. I could no longer bear seeing them die, and it was so painful to watch people I'd come to deeply care about wither away. At one point, I was so overcome with grief that I seriously considered taking my own life, but the thought in the back of my mind told me that was probably part of Jesus' cruel plan all along. He wanted me to agonize, to ache, and to ultimately give up, but I refused to let that diseased spawn defeat me.

"After a while, even surrounded by many wonderful people, loneliness threatened to consume me. I felt truly alone, and I suffered that severe, emotional loneliness that could only be cured by having someone to love. It was then, that I met Rachmiel, a woman who stole my heart. As our love grew, I realized I'd never really been in love before. Dilyla saw me as a means to an end, yet Rachmiel truly saw, and adored my heart and soul. Perhaps it was selfish, but I asked the guards to give me enough Longevity Factor for Rachmiel as well. I could not live through losing her. I was told that they had orders to administer it only to themselves and to me. While I'd gotten to know my jailers over the years and they seemed to like and respect me, their fear of my petulant brat of a son kept them from fulfilling my wishes.

"As the years passed, I helplessly watched time and age take a toll on my sweet Rachmiel, while I remained the same. She begged me not to feel sorry for her, even encouraged me to find someone younger and fairer to be with, but my love was unconditional and absolute. I remained by her side until she passed from this life."

At that moment, the only dry eyes in the room and all around the world belonged to Jesus. The site of Elohim openly weeping at his lover's bedside tore at the hearts of all in the

galaxy. Jesus, entirely unaffected, sat silently, with a mock-
ing, curious smile on his face.

After a few moments, Elohim regained his composure and
went on, "On the day of her death, I decided to stop taking
the Longevity Factor. All I wanted was to grow old and die,
but my son had other plans. Once a month, like clockwork,
his guards held me down and forced me to take it. Jesus
wanted me to live and suffer loss, which I did for over 5,000
years. I could only watch as countless friends who'd stepped
into my life were snatched out of it all too soon. Love became
a fickle thing that always, always ended in heartbreaking
loss.

"Although I did my best to deny my feelings, I grew close
to people many times. In each case, I had to watch my loved
ones, age and die. All of the women were fully aware of what
was to be, but I hold dear, cherished memories of each of
them in my heart to this day. Never was my love superficial.
It was always, always real...only doomed from the start.

"After I'd been on Nod for 3,156 years, I met Anael. I
knew what would become of us if I pursued her, but no
matter how hard I tried, I couldn't stay away. Finally, I was
able to convince one of the guards, the closest thing I had
to a friend among them, to give me enough of the Longevity
Factor for Anael. That gave me 500 precious years with her.
We moved every thirty years or so, so those around us would
not suspect anything odd about her perpetual youth. Thankfully, we were even able to hide her condition from the other
guards for all that time.

"In time, however, the sin of envy reared its ugly, green
head. Some who were close to us broke out in murmurs,
yearning for longevity of their own, and the guards were eventually informed. I don't know specifically who informed the
guards, but I really can't blame them. So many had to leave
their children and grandchildren early in life, while my sweet-
heart had been granted immortality. They loved their families
and didn't want to leave them, and they became jealous of
our longer lives together.

"During my 5,000 years on Nod, Jesus periodically visited. When he did, he made sure to tell me of all his conquests

and to brag about his awesome leadership, as if he expected me to be proud and to give him my blessing. The one thing he stressed above all else was that his people loved him. I believe he told me that so I would feel unwanted, unnecessary, and unremembered.

"On one of his visits, I barely had enough time to hide Anael I had barely enough time to . As usual, I was taken to his palace on Nod, and restrained in a chair next to his throne, except one level lower than he was. He seemed to enjoy the subtle displays of superiority. After the song-and-dance routine that was part of all of his visits, he had one more surprise in store. At his signal, his royal guards brought in a man who was so badly beaten that it took a moment for me to recognize him as the guard who had been supplying the Longevity Factor to me for my beloved."

While Elohim paused, everyone gasped. An ominous silence hung in the air for a moment as people in the courtroom and in front of their video screens across the galaxy involuntarily leaned forward, hanging on his every word but fearing the terrible truth they were about to hear.

"Jesus admonished his guard and asked, 'Did I not tell you that Elohim was the only one to be given the Longevity Factor besides you, my supposedly loyal guards?' The guard pleaded and promised that he would never disobey Jesus again, to which Jesus smiled in a sickening way I will never forget and said, 'Of that, I am sure.' He then gestured at his royal guards, and they closed in to kill the one who had helped me. That day, I lost another friend.

"After the murder, Jesus looked at me and had the audacity to ask, 'Do you see my power, Father? I possess control over life and death!'

"You are a monster," I said with a growl, but he stared at me and said, 'No, Father. I am...God!' Then, beaming a smile once more, he signaled his guards again, and my worst nightmare unfolded right before my eyes. The guards dragged in a struggling Anael and held her in front of us, and..." Elohim said, then trailed off because he'd begun to visibly sob.

All of the galaxy joined him in his crying but waited with bated breath and trepidation for what he would say next.

"I pleaded for Jesus to let her go. I screamed that it was not her fault, that it was my idea for her to be given the Longevity Factor, but he would hear nothing of it. 'Oh, Father,' he said, 'did you think I would not find out? I see everything, know everything.'

"When I saw him stand, and walk over to Anael, I struggled to free myself. I begged him, pleaded with him, but he killed my love with his own hands. Her last words to me, words that I still hear in my dreams, were, 'I'm sorry, my love.' I couldn't speak, couldn't think for the longest time. I couldn't believe how cruel my own offspring was. 'Damn you, Jesus,' I muttered weakly when I finally found my voice again.

"With her blood staining his robes, Jesus walked over to me and moved his face to within inches of mine. ''Twas not I who killed the woman. It was you,' he said. 'If you had not disobeyed me, she would have lived and died within a normal lifespan.'"

As the Illuminator ended its footage, Elohim said, "Yes, I wanted to kill Jesus for what he had done to my beautiful Anael, yet there was some truth in what he said. Nevertheless, her death almost killed me. I sank into a deep depression, and began to live like a hermit. I just... I couldn't face anyone. Years passed before I even spoke to anyone again. Even then, I was very guarded, and did not allow myself to become intimately close to anyone.

"After a time, I realized that I could not mentally survive without some contact and interaction with people. I forced myself to spend time with others on Nod, engrossed myself in helping them, in the hope that being involved would help me somehow cope. The downside was the all-too-familiar sting of losing friend after friend over the years.

"I knew, beyond a shadow of a doubt, that Jesus' aim was to send me into such emotional turmoil that I would desire to end my own life, but I simply would not do it. I would not give him the satisfaction. I held on to the hope that I might someday be free to once again walk among the stars. That dream became my new love, my new reason to live. Having seen the brutality of Jesus firsthand, I feared I had no loved ones left on Heaven, but I had to believe my dream of escaping the torturous situation would someday come true. That day came very recently.

"A few days ago, I felt as if I was hallucinating or going downright mad, because I saw my old friend Lucifer walking through the door of my home on Nod. The joy in my heart was overwhelming as I pulled him into a hug and realized he was truly there. I'd longed for so many years to be rescued, but with each passing day, my hope of ever seeing Heaven again had dimmed. My friends, I am here today because Zabkiel asked my friend Lucifer to find me, and bring me home.

"Now, I humbly stand before you to say one thing. I'm sorry. I'm sorry that I did not see the evil in Jesus, that I did not notice that he was becoming a monster. I'm sorry that I was unable to stop him. In spite of my own suffering on Planet Nod, I will never forgive myself for what Jesus has put you through. I will live the rest of my life trying to restore all that my son has willfully destroyed. Again, I'm sorry.

"One thing I ask of the new Empire and the Alliance is that you will make every effort to meet and include the people of Nod. Many were sent there unjustly, and over the generations, they have grown into a decent, honorable, civilized society. Give them the chance to join this galaxy. Let them show you that they are worthy, good people who deserve freedom."

With that, Elohim backed away from the podium and solemnly returned to his seat beside Lucifer, and all the worlds were in awe of what they'd heard.

***

Zabkiel and the council deliberated for two days. When court reconvened the following day, the room was crowded, with standing room only. In the end, Jesus was found guilty with overwhelming proof against him and no effort on his part to defend his actions, other than to refuse to do so because he claimed God owed no lower beings any sort of explanation.

Since the guilt of Jesus was never really in question, the time they spent in deliberations was used to come up with an appropriate punishment for his crimes. The decision of the council was shocking to most, as many expected a death sentence. Rather, with the permission of the Free Will Alliance, Jesus would spend life, without the possibility of parole, on the prison world of Naberus, located in the Purgatorian sector.

Initially, there was some public outcry and disagreement, but as the days went by and they had time to think it over, they saw the beauty and justice of the sentence. Much like the way he had forced his father to suffer centuries earlier, Jesus would be cast into an environment where he would have to work hard just to survive. Worst of all for him, though, was that he would be demoted to the position of a follower rather than a king. He would certainly not be among friends, as almost all convicts on Naberus were there because of him, and many had lost loved ones during his reign. On Naberus, all luxuries would be gone, no one would fear him any longer, and his life would be highly unpleasant and relatively short, as he would no longer have access to the fruit or the serum to maintain his longevity. Unlike his father, Jesus would face an expected end, and he would agonize through torment until that day came.

In the following months, more trials were held, and many others were found guilty of crimes against the Empire. Magdalene and her children, Sophia and Kadosh, were among the culprits. Complicit council members could not hide within their ranks and had to face the music for their roles in murders or acts against the Empire. Many of the Holy Ghosts also met justice, thanks to Jesus; in his paranoia and in an effort to control the powerful entities, he had secretly tagged them all to keep tabs on all of them so he could know where they were and where they had been. Zabkiel easily garnered that information from Jesus' records in his private chambers, along with details about the heavenly underground, and they made quick work of arresting as many as they could, on and off world.

Chapter 72

On New Earth, the NES quickly rounded up most of Michael's troops as well. Some were trying to hide in their underground network, but they were discovered and captured. Many fled New Earth as soon as they heard of Michael's capture. Reverend Gabe Brown, aka Gabriel, was nabbed while attempting to enter an escape shuttle a few days after Michael's arrest. Both archangels were set to stand trial for the mass murder of the millions who died in Macau, Amsterdam, Las Vegas, and Rio de Janeiro. Joanna Ariel Williams also had a debt to pay to society, but her assistance would be taken into consideration.

Justin recused himself from judging Michael and Gabriel, simply because there existed a conflict of interest. It was no secret that he wanted them both dead, and that he held a personal vendetta against them. Not only had they threatened his family, and kicked his ass just days before, but he was bitterly angry at them for the slaughter of millions, and also for taking the lives of Leah's parents. As was the case with Jesus' trial, it was nearly impossible to find unbiased people to judge them, so a nine-member council was established to hear the case, make the decision, and render any necessary punishment. Unlike the trial of their lord, though, Michael and Gabriel hired the best defense counsel they could find, as they were unwilling to go down without a fight.

Before New Earth government control, judges, attorneys,

and lawmakers had distorted justice and corrupted the law into something that primarily served the power structure of the time. The people were often left with table scraps, other than those who were willing to be blind followers. Most felt unease about their total lack of control of their government, but few were brave enough to voice those concerns for fear of retribution. What was supposed to be a government of the people, by the people, and for the people was instead a government of the rich and powerful, by the rich and powerful, and for the rich and powerful. Once New Earth government was established, no citizen held power over another due to the size of one's bank account or the title of one's rank or position. No one was above the law. Attorneys could no longer paint pictures of what could be; speculation was overruled, and they were required to present the facts for their clients. With the help of the Illuminator, the truth was just a thought away.

The archangels' trials were over in a week. Both Michael and Gabriel were found guilty of all charges against them. All that was left was to determine appropriate sentencing for their crimes. Joanna Ariel Williams was also found guilty for her crimes against New Earth, but she was acquitted of the murder charges. Due to her beneficial actions, which included testifying against her fellow archangels, and her help in rounding up the underground, she would serve a much lighter sentence.

A couple weeks after the trial, Justin visited a shackled Michael. He did not go to gloat; there was simply something the archangel needed to see. Through the thick Plexiglas wall between them, Justin saw a very different person than the maniac who'd tried to kill him and his wife just months before. Gone was the brash cockiness. Michael looked deflated, like a man defeated, both physically and mentally.

Justin sat a portable video screen on the counter in front of Michael and said, "I thought you might like to see this."

With the press of a button, a video began to play. Rebecca was the main focus. Her blonde hair was shoulder-length now, but there was no mistaking her beautiful features. She was happily waiting tables in a restaurant on Hell.

337

"Rebecca?" Michael muttered.

"Yes, Michael. She was interrogated for months on Hell before she finally gave up much information that proved useful to the Alliance. To pay for her crimes, she was given a choice. She could spend life in prison, or volunteer for mind reassignment. She chose the latter, is if and is happy in her new life, though she has no memory of you or her former self. I just thought you should know," Justin said, then pressed the button to stop the video.

"Thank you," the fallen angel whispered, not even taking his eyes off the video screen when it darkened.

Without another word, Justin stood, headed for the door, and never looked back.

Chapter 73

Everyone expected Lord God Elohim to assume the throne and once again lead Heaven and the Empire, but Elohim did not yet want the job. He had spent over 5,000 years on a prison planet, far away from the seat of the Empire, and he felt a bit unqualified to reclaim the reins of power. "Perhaps after some time I shall feel worthy again," he said, "but now is not the time."

When asked for his opinion on a better candidate, Elohim knew of only one person worthy of leading the Empire. "Zabkiel is the most logical choice, don't you think?" he said. Elohim reasoned, "He knows more about the Empire than anyone else."

Everyone agreed with Elohim's wise suggestion, for in the quarter-millennium during which Zabkiel had served Jesus as his chief counsel, he had dutifully and proficiently performed almost all of the day-to-day functions of running the galaxy. With little debate, it was decided that Zabkiel would lead the Empire until a proper election could be held.

The former Seraphim One's first act was to form a council to represent Heaven, and stand for its overall wellbeing. As such, he called a meeting with representatives from every sector in the Empire. He modeled his new Empire after the Free Will Alliance: All worlds would be required to adhere to basic ideals set forth in the new constitution to continue membership in the Empire and to keep all the benefits that entailed.

Once his government was organized and the key players were put in place, the next thing on Zabkiel's agenda was to conjure up a treaty with the Alliance. For the first time in over 5,000 years, the galaxy enjoyed peace. Of course, some sectors declined the offer to join the Empire or the Alliance, opting to remain independent. Nonetheless, even those worlds agreed to sign peace and trade agreements with the two major governments. Only a few let it be known that they wished to be left entirely alone, and the Empire and the Alliance honored those requests.

There were, of course, some disciples who were not ready to end the fight for the Empire. When peace was declared, those captains and their warships fled into the abyss. In all, 106 disciple vessels went AWOL. Although efforts were made to find them, no word of their whereabouts was forthcoming; they simply vanished into the vast blackness of space.

Precisely one year after Jesus' removal from office, elections were held on Heaven and throughout Empire space. Although there were a few contenders from some of the outer sectors, Zabkiel was the overwhelming choice to lead the Empire. One month after Zabkiel was elected as God, another major event ebbed toward coming to fruition.

The two most powerful men in the galaxy met on New Earth to sign the galactic treaty. Celebrations of the historic event were underway all throughout the galaxy. The very next day, both leaders signed agreements with New Earth to supply the Longevity Factor to all. That, in and of itself, ensured that New Earth was soon to become a very busy hub in the galaxy.

New Earth continued to improve and move toward becoming the paradise it was meant to be. The population was controlled, and the environment was cleaner, with plans in place to keep it that way. The two colonies, Gaia and Terra, progressed beautifully. New Earth and Eden formed a partnership: New Earth would provide security for Eden, thus protecting their joint venture to supply the Longevity Factor for all in the galaxy. Eden requested that travel to their planet remained restricted, as they preferred to be somewhat solitary. The Longevity Factor made New Earth and its partner, Eden, two of the most important planets in the galaxy.

The galaxy moved into a new age, one of peace and prosperity. Everyone in Alliance and Empire space enjoyed the benefits of free will, each individual and each world knowing that they, alone, had the power to choose their future and to live in freedom.

Long ago, a visitor from space landed on an obscure, little-known, blue and green planet that orbited a star, on a spiral arm at the edge of the Milky Way. No one—not even the one who found and aided that visitor—could have ever foreseen the effect that moment would have, but it had forever changed the galaxy for the better.

Chapter 74
Epilogue

Jesus found life on Naberus quite different than life as God on Heaven. People who had once trembled at his feet now saw him as not much more than the village idiot. The only skill he truly possessed was proficiency in being coddled and taken care of, and that certainly did not make survival on Naberus any easier.

Before it was mandated that he was not to be harmed, Jesus was beaten almost daily. During his reign as God, he had managed to ruin, maim, or kill someone close to almost every resident on Naberus. He had no friends or close acquaintances there, with the exception of Magdalene and his children, and even they didn't like him very much. Without the Longevity Factor, his health took a quick downturn. Unlike the other residents of Naberus, who accepted their fate, Jesus neglected his physical and mental wellbeing and preferred to wallow in self-pity. He walked around Bathim, his new hometown, in tattered clothing, ordering people who grudgingly resisted killing their former lord to do his bidding. When anyone gave in to the temptation to throw something at his uncrowned head, which was a daily occurrence, he called for his guards to have the offender eliminated.

Michael and Gabriel were taken to Vapula, a high-security prison planet also in the Purgatorian sector. They would spend the rest of their lives, a considerably shorter sentence now that they lacked the Longevity Factor, struggling to survive on a planet in an environment much harsher than the one Jesus had to contend with. There was no self-governing among the prisoners, movements were restricted, and interaction between prisoners were kept at a minimum.

Lucifer settled into his new life as chief adviser and man of leisure; preferring the latter to the former, he spent most days fishing and only advised when needed. He did willingly travel to Heaven to attend a ceremony in honor of his good friend Elohim. While he was there, he met with Zabkiel daily to discuss the future of the Empire, and he agreed to advise him for as long as needed. Mostly, he relaxed on Heaven and enticed Elohim to cast a line with him in the heavenly pools.

The one thing the two friends enjoyed more than fishing was settling disputes in the Alliance. Lucifer, wearing a cherished pentagon stone over his heart, Elohim, and a group of their old buddies from days gone by, traveled to all points of space to settle border disagreements, chase and apprehend pirates, and keep the peace by whatever means necessary. Whatever they did, they had the time of their lives, as long as they did it together.

Sandel ruled the Alliance just as his father had, with the great respect and trust of his council and his government and, most importantly of all, the love of the people on Hell and throughout the Alliance. He stopped complaining as much about the responsibilities of leadership and all the work that was involved because he was happy at his core. He had Lilith by his side, and she served as a council member and the education minister for Hell. He figured that was more than any man could want or deserve.

Sandel made sure to travel to New Earth two or three times a year, so he and his wife could spend time with their good friends, Justin and Salome. He often thought of the fateful day when he fell to Earth. Whenever it came to mind, he still winced in remembrance of the pain, but he smiled to think of what had happened since.

Justin found that he also had great leadership talents, especially when it came to running New Earth and the newly formed Long Life Cooperative, which consisted of New Earth, Eden, Gaia, and Terra. Three newly colonized planets were also included: Paradisus, Haven, and Aurora. Salome had taken on the role of environmental secretary, which placed her in charge of all things environmental on all the planets of the Long Life Cooperative. With her stewardship, seven world environmental mandates were implemented, based on the laws that were responsible for the ecological *renaissance of New Earth.* Keeping the cooperative running smoothly was a full-time job, but they enjoyed the work.

Justin and Salome also found time to vacation on Hell. He and Sandel remained as close as brothers. The one thing the two of them enjoyed most of all was to join Lucifer and Elohim on Alliance peacekeeping missions. They both knew it was not the wisest thing to do, but they agreed that it beat sitting behind a desk. When the men went on their so-called fishing trips, Salome and Lilith just shook their heads and smiled; they both knew the danger of two of the most important men in the galaxy gallivanting around Alliance space to fight crime, but they also knew their men would always be boys at heart.

As the two galactic powers settled into a much-welcomed peace, everyone set their eyes on exploration. Empire and Alliance space combined only involved around 40 percent of the entire galaxy. Both governments set sail into the unknown in an attempt to make it known. It was exciting to think of the wonders and dangers that might be waiting for them beyond their borders.

Perhaps, somewhere out there in the abyss, there is another garden that is home to another miracle. Maybe the Tree of Knowledge of Good and Evil is waiting for us. I wonder what its fruit tastes like? Justin thought. He could hardly imagine the possibility of using 100 percent of his brain, of taking his awareness to its limits. *There's still 60 percent of the galaxy out there. What will we discover?* he wondered, feeling fortunate that he lived in a time when the formerly impossible now seemed possible and there were plenty of unknowns to keep life interesting.

As he sat at home, Justin put his head in Salome's lap and put his feet up on the arm of the couch. Salome, busy with reading her environmental reports, stroked his hair. He fell into a sleepy state, dreaming of new worlds and all the discoveries they might hold.

Just a few years prior in galactic time, he was once a professor of religious studies. He was a man of blind faith. Now, he counted God and Lucifer among his closest friends. They were not the supreme beings he'd been taught to believe they were; they were merely living, breathing, mortal individuals who stood for free will for all, not blind obedience.

Justin opened his eyes again, crossed his arms, and donned a huge, shit-eating grin.

"What are you up to?" Salome asked, looking down at him curiously.

"Oh, just being the luckiest man in the galaxy," he said as he thought of his Salome, his children, his good friends, and possibly 10,000 years to enjoy them.

Made in the USA
Middletown, DE
23 October 2022

13310616R00208